LO *REFUGE*

Instinctively, Diana ran searching hands over Garrett's back. Beneath her touch, the muscles rippled as he lifted her for another demanding kiss. With a sigh, her lips parted beneath his.

Warmth, heat, a burning tension gathered and weakened her until she leaned against him, unable to support herself. His caresses swept over her, drowning her in sensation, enclosing them in a safe haven where only they existed. Gasping, she stretched upward and kissed his lips, chin, throat—anywhere she could reach. Her lashes drooped closed as he returned her kisses with searing passion . . .

St. Martin's Press Mass Market Titles by Sarah Edwards

CRYSTAL RAPTURE
(an *Americans Abroad* Romance)

FIRE AND SAND

FIRE AND SAND

SARAH EDWARDS

ST. MARTIN'S PRESS/NEW YORK

FIRE AND SAND

Copyright © 1989 by Sharon and Robert Bills.

ISBN: 0-312-91656-6   Can. ISBN: 0-312-91657-4

Printed in the United States of America

First St. Martin's Press mass market edition/ September 1989

10 9 8 7 6 5 4 3 2 1

To Vi, for her gallant fight; to Ivan, for putting up with her; and to Jo, for her help in making the details of the Catalonian section accurate.

Author's Note

A reliable (?) source from last century reported the incidents in chapters 3 and 4 as factual. They were too wonderfully outrageous to pass up. See the Note to Readers, at the end of the book, for more details.

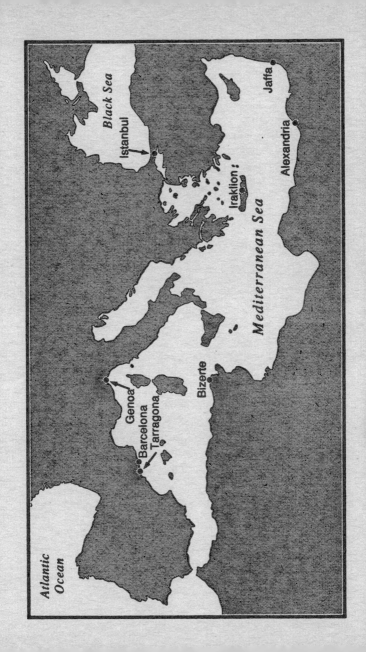

CHAPTER I

"IT'S TOO DAMN' DANGEROUS." THE CAPTAIN'S DEEP voice echoed above the creak of the ship's rigging and the noise of sailors and dockhands loading cargo.

Diana Graham shoved a strand of wind-whipped silver-blond hair beneath her hood. They'd been over this *so* many times. And he still acted as if she were a child.

"Captain Andrews," Diana said patiently, ignoring his slip into profanity, "didn't you find the most reliable guide in Bizerte?"

His grizzled face flushed with the effort of restraining his language. "It's still too dangerous. Just a native guide to prevent pirates or who knows what from . . . attacking." The flush deepened with the search for words to describe his fears.

A soft smile curved Diana's full lips. Just like her grandmother. Gran always warned of improbable, impossible, dire consequences of the simplest acts. Turning guileless blue eyes up to his face and seeing the determination there, she swiftly lowered dark gold lashes to hide her own. "I doubt I'm in much danger from pirates in the city.

"That's not what I meant, and you know it." His full cheeks puffed out with swallowed exasperation. "Come with me to Egypt, Miss Graham. In a month or so I can escort you to your parents in Jerusalem." Beaming, he waited for his reasoning to sway her this time.

"In a month or so, I'd miss their expedition to Masada." Marshaling her arguments, Diana's pale blue eyes grew thoughtful. "You said the captain of the *Redstart* would take good care of me when we sail to Jaffa next week."

Chill wind lifted locks of silvered hair as Captain Andrews nodded. "He's a good man, but—"

"And the lady who runs the boardinghouse in Bizerte will chaperon me like a daughter," Diana interrupted the time-worn array of arguments.

"She's a Christian lady despite living in this heathen land. But—"

"Then all I have to do is stay close to the boardinghouse." Carefully avoiding a promise to keep away from the markets, she neatly sidestepped the captain's real goal. "And if this is fall in North Africa, it'll be easy to stay inside." Diana shivered as another chill gust found its way beneath her hood.

Above, clouds scudded, low and menacing, toward the foothills of the Atlas Mountains, giving force to the implied promise. In Boston, Diana would have predicted a storm within hours. In Bizerte, she couldn't foretell even that much, adding spice to her adventure.

The captain shifted uncertainly. "The boardinghouse isn't in the best part of town."

Peering surreptitiously around his shoulder, Diana didn't answer. Her luggage was finally being carried down the gangway. She smiled dazzlingly up at him, a solitary dimple deepening in her softly curved cheek. Both the smile and the dimple banished the air of childlike innocence that triggered the captain's protective response.

"Captain Andrews!" she exclaimed, her tone a teasing invitation to acknowledge the humor of the situation.

"You've done everything possible to ensure my safety." He nodded reluctantly. "So there's nothing left to worry about."

"I still don't like it."

Her smile widened. "I promise to be careful, Captain Andrews, really I do."

"Well"—his experienced eye swept over the activities of various sailors and cargo handlers—"there's no time left for argument. If I'm to finish loading in time to catch the tide, I can't take you to Madame Ferije. But you'll go straight there, understand?"

"You needn't worry, Captain." Gathering her skirt along with the billowing cloak, Diana stepped onto the gangway. "Thank you for all the care you've taken of me during the voyage. You couldn't have done more if I'd been your daughter."

She leaned forward, hands resting briefly on the captain's heavy chest, and placed a light kiss on his cheek. In a sudden lull, her cloak hung perversely still. "Good-bye."

Turning, she skipped lightly down the gangway. Free! Free, at last, of Gran's foolish restrictions. And the captain's gloomy predictions. Only she wasn't free. The gangway swayed as the captain followed.

Reaching the dock, she demurely waited for him. For a man of his bulk, he moved lightly on the narrow gangway. Then, arm in arm, they crossed to the patiently waiting Arab.

"This is Abdullah ibn Hassan," Captain Andrews introduced the swarthy, narrow-faced Arab, the foreign syllables harsh on his lips.

"How do you do, Abdullah," Diana said.

He responded in an incomprehensible flood. Startled, she glanced at the captain, who shifted into French marked with a solid New England twang. "Mademoiselle Graham speaks French, Abdullah." Andrews turned to her, adding in English, "His accent's odd but easy to understand."

Diana smiled at the Arab and switched to French. "I appreciate your taking me to Madame Ferije's, Abdullah."

With eyes unblinkingly fixed on her face, Abdullah half bowed. "The *sitt* has only to command."

Her smile faltered under his intense stare, and she turned to the captain in relief. "Thank you again. It's been a delightful voyage."

"You're sure you won't stay on board till Jaffa?" Worry crept back into his face. "It's no trouble to take you to your parents."

"I'll arrive weeks earlier if I follow my original plan. And with winter coming, the Mediterranean won't be an easy sea to sail."

"Well"—he patted her hand—"please take care of yourself, Miss Graham. And write me when you arrive. The Boston office always knows where to find me."

Diana stretched on tiptoe and brushed another kiss on his weather-beaten cheek. Then, hands neatly clasped before her and reticule swinging from one wrist, she watched him climb the gangway before turning to Abdullah, who appraised her calculatingly.

"What is it, Abdullah?" she asked, her tone sharper than intended.

"Does the *sitt* desire to go directly to Madame Ferije's?" The landlady's name had a strange, lilting accent when he said it.

"I'd prefer to visit the market. But what about my luggage?"

Abdullah shrugged gracefully, a shrug that absolved him of all responsibility and passed it onto other shoulders. "The captain has said it will be sent on, and it has been done."

A mischievous, secret smile lit Diana's face. Looking back, she waved a final farewell, disappointed that the captain's back was turned. Slowly, she turned to the guide. Eagerness to explore the exotic life of Bizerte replaced disappointment.

Most of the men—no women were visible—wore drab colors ranging from off-white, oddly wrapped cloaks like

Abdullah's to sand-beige and dull black. They seemed oblivious to the brisk wind blowing off the sea as they carted large bales and chests filled with gold, precious stones, pearls, fine silks, and brocades. She didn't need to see inside. In detailed, affectionate letters, Mama had described the wonders of the markets, and now they were here before her.

"*Sitt,*" Abdullah interrupted, "are you ready?"

Diana nodded eagerly. "Lead the way."

Inclining his head, he plunged down a street opening on the docks, cloak flapping briskly at his sandaled heels. Diana followed, her eyes sparkling with suppressed excitement. She was actually here. Well, maybe not in Palestine, but certainly closer than Boston. She'd dreamed of this moment since her parents left for the Holy Land when she was barely fifteen. Her stomach filling with flutters of excitement, she hurried to catch the guide.

"Stay close to me, *sitt,*" Abdullah ordered, dropping back.

She tried, but he knew every nook of the crooked street. As she hurried after him, men leading donkeys burdened with large loads or hauling heavily laden carts stopped and stared. Disturbed, Diana caught up with the guide. Why did they stare so oddly?

"You are unveiled, *sitt,*" Abdullah explained. "No Arab demoiselle would be permitted outside with face uncovered. That is why you must stay close. They do not realize Western ways are different. But you are safe with me." He gave a toothy smile and gestured in the direction they were going. "The largest market is through here."

Diving between a burdened donkey and a high-nosed camel, he again left her to follow as best she could. Only the drab white cloak standing out against the occasional faded blue door kept him in sight. In minutes, they were free of the maze of crooked, narrow streets and into a large square where noise drowned the sound of the wind. Stalls overflowing with merchandise covered every inch the crowd didn't require. Diana forgot the guide in her enchantment.

The market was everything she'd ever dreamed it would be. Her gaze strayed hungrily to the astonishing assortment of pastries and colorful fruit arranged on one particular stall's counters. Between the excitement of leaving the ship and packing, she hadn't breakfasted. Pointing to a pastry crusted with sugar and filled with nuts and cinnamon, she asked slowly in French, hoping the man behind the counter would understand, "How much is this?"

He didn't. In a high-pitched singsong, he extolled his wares' virtues, picking up delicacy after delicacy and holding it for an instant before going on to the next. The fruit glistened with honey, the fancifully shaped pastries looked intriguing, but she'd already made her decision. She repeated the question, indicating the cinnamon-and-nut confection. The vendor repeated his entire performance. This could go on forever.

Diana spotted Abdullah only a few feet away gesturing earnestly to a man in black. They both turned to stare strangely at her before the second man disappeared into the crowd. Ignoring a tinge of disquiet, she called Abdullah over to translate. He shook his head, then, lifting his hands in a gesture of exasperated resignation, complied. The price sounded exorbitant.

"No, *sitt*. Sugar, nuts, and cinnamon are too expensive for any but a sultan." The stall holder said something Abdullah translated. "The harem ordered the pastries, but the bey refused to pay."

"But this man already made them," Diana protested.

Abdullah shrugged elaborately. "The bey's word is law."

"Then I shall buy one. They look delicious, and besides" —her smile flashed again—"I'm hungry."

"Very well, *sitt*," Abdullah agreed, rolling his eyes heavenward in a plea to be spared the follies of women. "The merchant will be delighted." He completed the transaction. "Now, do not stray so far again."

Nibbling the rich pastry, Diana strolled behind him as he wove through the crowd. Stalls along their path displayed gauzy silk scarves, brass and silver, jewelry, and finely worked embroidery that made her itch to stop. However, Abdullah had a special treat in store. Yet when they reached the promised shop, she barely swallowed disappointment. The counters were filled with drab bolts of coarse fabric.

"No, *sitt,*" Abdullah answered her expression. "This is for the *canaille.*" Proudly, he produced the derogatory French term for the lower classes. "Inside are fabrics such that you have never seen."

Hesitantly, she stepped into the gloomy shop. Waiting for her eyes to adjust, she flinched as he brushed past, calling out softly in sibilant Arabic. A higher-pitched voice answered, and a lamp flared. Blinking, Diana gasped.

It was all the fairy tales she'd ever read combined into one. Shelves lining the back of the stall held bolt after bolt of silk and brocade in a dazzling bouquet of colors. The edges, elaborately embroidered in gold and silver, glittered in the lamplight. Her lips parted, Diana drew the hood back and slowly stepped forward. Her silver-blond hair gleamed as richly as the embroidery in the lantern light.

"Abdullah!" she exclaimed softly. "Ask him to take down the rose silk with the silver, please."

A frown drew the heavy slash of black eyebrows together above Abdullah's opaque brown eyes. "Do not show eagerness, *sitt.* It will raise the price."

"Oh, of course."

Half laughing at herself, Diana assumed a disinterested expression and casually approached the counter where the stall owner laid the rose silk. He took down a bolt of matching brocade, shot with silver thread. While his thin, heavy-jointed fingers caressed the silk, his eyes narrowed assessingly. Ignoring the merchant's sales talk, she stroked the brocade. This was a color she'd always wanted. And Gran always refused to let her wear.

"*Sitt,* he says you will look the fairest of flowers for your lord in a gown of such glorious color. It casts the glow of sunrise on your porcelain-petaled face." Abdullah added dryly, "He means skin, *sitt.*"

Torn between amusement at the effusions and annoyance at the assumption she had a lord, Diana just shook her head. "How much for both bolts?"

The conversation between Abdullah and the merchant lasted forever. She wandered away to look for more fabrics. While the men haggled, a subtly rich indigo, laced with silver, and a delicate untrimmed moss green caught her eye. Taking both bolts down, she brought them back to the counter.

"Well, Abdullah?"

"He asks too much, *sitt.*" Abdullah named an amount that seemed tiny when converted into American dollars.

Frowning, Diana asked, "That's too much?"

Her frown deepened. Mama said the stall owners in the *suqs* loved to bargain. Offering a fifth that amount should be a good starting point. Less couldn't be acceptable. Abdullah half bowed.

The offer brought an explosion of protests from the silk seller. Gesticulating fiercely, he prayed for preservation from infidels before loosing a torrent of explanation. She didn't need a translation.

"Tell him," she interrupted, "I have no intention of beggaring him or sending his children to the poorhouse or whatever's the local equivalent. I'll give him half his original price, but only if he includes the other two bolts." Diana hesitated, then asked in a softer voice, "Is that fair?"

Abdullah bowed respectfully. "More than fair, *sitt.*"

The silk seller countered, but Diana held firm. "That's my final offer."

The merchant protested, but Abdullah gestured toward Diana. Eyeing her resolute expression, the merchant's face changed slowly from dourness to smiles that transformed him into a brown-skinned cherub. A fat chuckle filled the stall, and he bowed to Abdullah, then to her.

The guide returned the bow and faced Diana. "I have

arranged that he send the fabric to Madame Ferije's. You would not wish me to be burdened while you explore the rest of the market."

The merchant's smug expression made it clear Diana paid too much—though four bolts of cloth cost less than four pastries. She shook her head in disbelief. This certainly wasn't Boston.

"The money, if you please, *sitt.*" Abdullah accepted the gold coins and passed them to the merchant. "He offers Allah's blessing on you and your lord." Glancing out of the darkening doorway, Abdullah added, "Now, we must hurry before the storm arrives."

Outside, a ragged urchin, no older than nine, ran up and tugged Abdullah's long sleeve. The pair exchanged rapid-fire conversation, and the guide smiled.

"Ah, *sitt,* I am happy to report that my cousin Ahmed tells of a merchant who has just received the most wondrous jewelry to complement these glorious fabrics with which you will bedazzle your future husband. Ahmed describes the most exquisite sapphires, emeralds, and rubies, all in the most perfect silver and gold settings. They will become most elegantly your bewitching face and perfect fair skin."

Cocking her eyebrow ironically, Diana turned to smile at the thin boy. "Would you care for a pastry?"

"Naturally my unworthy cousin would enjoy any gift from the too generous *sitt.*" Slyly, Abdullah's gaze flicked down to her reticule. He smiled blandly until she offered the money directly to Ahmed.

His eyes rounding, the boy started to grab before he caught himself. Tucking his hand behind his back, he bowed low and took the coins only at her smile. Grinning cheekily, he made them disappear in his voluminous robe and said something Abdullah cut off with a harsh order. It sent the boy running into the thinning crowd.

"I have sent my most insignificant cousin ahead to warn this special jeweler of our coming," Abdullah told her, irritation tightening his mouth, "so only his finest, rarest gems are ready for your inspection."

He took off through a market where the gray, cloud-heavy sky had slowed business at the stalls. Fewer people milled about tasting food, haggling over brasses and bridles, or dictating letters to scribes huddled against the walls to escape the wind's blast. Overriding the scent of exotic foods came the smell of the sea and the promise of rain mingled with the cool briskness of autumn.

"Hurry, *sitt*. Soon it must break, and we will be drenched," he called over his shoulder.

Head bowed against tearing gusts that grew stronger with each step, she entered the darker, quieter protection of a narrow street leading from the square. The market faded from view almost at once. Even with the approaching storm, it had been filled with cheerful noise. The contrast with this narrow, too quiet street filled only with the wind's whine made her uneasy. And the guide plunged ahead as usual without waiting. Diana frowned with annoyance.

"Abdullah."

He turned, frowning. "Yes, *sitt*?"

"We're going to the boardinghouse." She looked up at the sky. "This storm is approaching too rapidly."

Sketching a bow, he acquiesced. "As you wish. It is still this direction."

Annoyance radiated from him as he swung abruptly around and darted down the street. Displeased, Diana hurried after. Even with his light robe, she quickly lost him in the shadows.

She squinted against the tearing wind. There he was, turning into a narrow, mean alley where a preternatural silence descended. Combined with the filtered, shadowed darkness, it made the boisterous market seem even farther away. Recalling Captain Andrews's disparagement of Madame Ferije's neighborhood, Diana felt a moment of foolish fear. And it was foolish, she told herself defiantly. Gathering her cloak more tightly about her, she extended her stride until she was almost running.

"Abdullah, wait!"

If anything, he hurried faster. She almost tripped on the uneven cobblestones. Blank buildings lined the alley, and low clouds added to shadows hovering and dipping from the few doorways. As the sky darkened even further, it grew difficult to see. The alley seemed empty. Only an occasional bundle, or bale, or large jar huddled against the walls, mere shadows in the darker shadows of the storm-darkened alley. Ahead, Diana caught a glimpse of a wider street with lighter buildings. Perhaps there she'd catch Abdullah. Hurrying, she passed the shadowed mouth of a doorway.

A black-robed arm shot out, and a point of pain blossomed at the back of her head to cut off her call for help.

The air was warm and stuffy in her bedroom. Twisted covers imprisoned her arms, her entire body. And the bed moved. Not the way it had on board ship, though. The dull ache radiating from the back of her head made her feel worse than during those first hours of seasickness. Then she remembered the black-robed arm.

Moaning softly, she twisted feebly and regretted it. Even with her eyes closed, everything spun dizzily while her entire body kept moving in a rhythm—a rhythm of footsteps. Opening her eyes, she tried to focus, but there wasn't enough light. She had to think. Abdullah wasn't going to help. So much for trustworthiness. Moving gingerly, she explored the stiff fabric wrapped around her. The rough backing felt like a . . . like a rug. She sniffed. It smelled like a rug, too.

A sudden change in direction left her giddy. She tried to wriggle free, but the rug held her securely bound. They stopped, and a man called. She'd know what they intended soon. The rug's warmth couldn't stop the chill of uncertainty.

A gate creaked open and another voice invited entrance.

The voices engaged in a quick-spirited discussion, like the haggling over the bolts of fabric.

Twisting again, she tried to free herself, but she cried out with pain when the man carrying the rug dumped his burden heavily on the ground. Hands groped along her body; then a jerk yanked the rug and spun her out. Head throbbing with sickening fierceness, she rolled over and over until a boot halted her tumble. Her eyes focusing blearily, she looked up. A man loomed over her, tall, silent. And smiling cruelly.

Free of the rug's cocoon, the wind ripped through the thin primrose yellow muslin of her dress. She darted glances around the cobblestone courtyard. Smooth high walls, broken only by a closed gate, rose in every direction. Abdullah and a black-robed man slouched at the edge of her vision. Scrambling to her feet, she started toward them, fists clenched.

The tall man who'd so arrogantly inspected her blocked her way. Diana sidestepped, intent on Abdullah, but the tall man pinned her against the cold wall, a smile broadening his thin mouth. The heavy black beard and mustache shadowed it ominously. Fear returned, and it wasn't foolish.

She tried to scream, but he forced her mouth open and casually examined her teeth as though buying a horse. Jerking futilely, she fought against his brutal grip until he released her and stepped back to continue his contemptuous inspection.

After the long silence in the courtyard, his voice was a shock. "The teeth are good, although she's old," he observed disdainfully in French so she'd understand. "Too bad you couldn't find one who speaks Arabic. I doubt she's bright enough to learn."

Her blue eyes darkening with fury, Diana kicked. Despite soft kid boots, the blow landed hard on his shin. A stinging slap sent her reeling back to the cold wall, where she slumped for an instant before straightening. She took a step toward him when his icy voice stopped her.

"Know your place, woman. To survive in the harem, you must learn obedience."

Harem! Ignoring her burning cheek and throbbing head, Diana swung to face Abdullah, all idea of retribution gone. "I'll pay double his offer if you take me to Madame Ferije's now."

Greed lit the opaque brown eyes, but he bowed regretfully. "Unfortunately, *sitt,* it is not possible. Lord Karim is our bey's younger brother."

"Three times!"

Abdullah spread his hands in an elaborate gesture of apology. "Alas, the bey controls Bizerte in the name of the Sultan himself." After a glance at the man behind her, he grimaced. "He also has the ability to make Bizerte unhealthy should I accept your obliging offer. And we are in *his* palace, surrounded by *his* men, with the gates *closed.*"

Karim's grating voice cut across their conversation. "Enough foolishness. Hold her while I finish the examination."

Diana tried to run, but the black-robed man grabbed her. Biting wind cut through the thin muslin of her gown, leaving her cold, frightened, helpless. Until Karim casually massaged her breasts. Glaring, she shifted to kick again but stopped at his amused expression.

"Very wise. Take the female over to the portico. I have seen enough." Inspecting Diana again, he added, "These Western women are too thin, but my brother enjoys them."

The last of this rain squall spat against the warehouse walls. Garrett Hamilton shoved the burnoose hood back and ran a hand through thick black hair. A stubborn lock fell back over his wide forehead and brushed the thick, inky strokes his brows made against heavily tanned skin. Indifferent to the man who stealthily followed, Garrett opened the warehouse door and entered.

"Yusuf," he called, his sherry-colored eyes sparkling with anticipation.

The door closed to leave him in sweet-smelling shadow. Without waiting for his eyes to adjust, he strode toward the dim light haloing stacked bales at the back of the warehouse. Crates towered toward the high ceiling, carving straight, narrow aisles.

"Yusuf, where are the men?" he demanded in fluent Arabic, rounding the corner to the cubbyhole the warehouseman used as an office.

A thin, nervous man with gray hair sticking out in tufts sat behind the desk. Yusuf looked up from the books as Garrett strode in, filling the small space. "Making the latest delivery." A worried frown drew Yusuf's sparse brows together, deepening the lines furrowing his forehead. "What's wrong?"

Shrugging easily, Garrett pulled up an empty crate and settled comfortably. Leaning against a bale smelling faintly of sandalwood, he met Yusuf's harassed, questioning gaze with a reckless grin.

"All good things must come to an end. Anyway, this caper was becoming too much like work." Garrett took a half-full bottle of Scotch from Yusuf's desk and wiped it fastidiously with a handkerchief bearing an intricate monogram in one corner. Lifting the bottle, he took a long swig. "Ah. I wish you people didn't insist on doing your drinking in private. It makes for dry conversation."

"What's wrong?" Yusuf repeated.

"You worry too much. It'll ruin your digestion if you're not careful." Teasing laughter lit his eyes at the deepening concern on Yusuf's face. "Our little business is finished"— Garrett shrugged—"though I don't like the way it's ended. Partners shouldn't separate with a stab in the back."

"Bey Haroun plans treachery?" Yusuf's thin, brown fingers curled around the quill used to keep the books. He waited grimly for the answer.

"Haroun's decided to make his move," Garrett agreed, setting the bottle back on the desk. Crossing his arms over his chest, a smile still lurked at the edges of his sharply-etched mouth. It widened at Yusuf's nervous swallow. "Put your faith in Allah and have a drink."

The quill broke between Yusuf's fingers. "When?"

"Tomorrow." Garrett shrugged. "We've plenty of time. I'm trusting you to get the men to safety as arranged, and" —he glanced about the shadowed warehouse, gaze halting briefly on one particular section—"remove the goods."

Yusuf did a quick mental calculation. "It'll be close, but most of it can be gone by then if the men work through the night." Looking back at Garrett, he asked, "Are you absolutely sure?"

Garrett laughed, the single unruly lock of black hair slipping farther over his deeply tanned forehead at his nod. "I'm to be executed as a salutary lesson to other ne'er-do-well infidels and proof to the Sultan that our bey is keeping the faith. Besides, he's worried I'd reveal his part in smuggling liquor." Garrett reached for the bottle, took another drink, and grinned widely. "Such duplicity requires a *personal* revenge."

Swallowing, Yusuf grimaced. "Let's just clear out. We've made more than enough—"

"No." The word hung clear and cold between them; the amusement turned hard in Garrett's expression. "Haroun is betraying me for a miserable piaster per bottle. I'm too dangerous to live long enough even for the usual rigged trial. Little brother Karim will do the dirty work for him."

"Karim's not one to cross," Yusuf warned, his complexion paling further in the harsh lamplight.

"His older brother doesn't hold him in the same high regard. What a pity Karim's never met me." Garrett dismissed the bey's younger brother with a wave of his hand. "You've never discovered the joy of living, Yusuf. Besides, it's only my neck."

In terse sentences that made Yusuf's eyes grow wider and wider, Garret ended, "Save what you can, but be gone by morning." A grin slowly spread across his face. "I'll take care of our bey."

"You'll never get away with it," Yusuf whispered.

Chuckling softly, Garrett raised the bottle to salute the bey with Scotch. "It seems suitable to end our partnership by taking one last dirty little task off his hands." At Yusuf's awe, Garrett passed the bottle. "A last toast, old friend. 'Dishonor before Death!' "

CHAPTER II

"THREE GUARDS SEEM EXCESSIVE FOR ONE LONE FE-male." Diana tried Italian since French had failed when they entered the tiny bare room. "Especially with your companions littering the walls outside."

Hands on their sword hilts, they regarded her impassively, although she was certain one understood. Flickers of comprehension on the plump, short man's face revealed that. But he said nothing.

"If you help me escape," Diana offered with calculated softness, staring directly into his eyes, "I'll reward you with . . ."—she named a sum more than four times the amount Karim paid for her—". . . and," she added hastily at the contempt in the guard's face, "my parents will give ten times that when I arrive safely in Jerusalem. They're extremely wealthy."

Straightening from the support of the cold stone wall, she watched the deliberation in his round face. If he agreed, if he could talk the others into it, they'd have to hurry. Mentally she retraced the ground covered since leaving Karim. Escape routes hadn't been obvious, but they marched here so quickly there was no chance to note anything beyond the guards on the walls.

These men would know the best way to escape the bey's palace undetected. If only the plump man could be bribed quickly. Every second he took to decide—Karim sent her to this bare little room for a reason. There wasn't time to dawdle.

Arms clasped about her waist to conceal her overpowering tension, Diana watched her quarry glance speculatively at the man on either side. The deliberation in his eyes faded, and he shook his head slightly. Blandly, he leaned against the door and said something in Arabic that set his companions chuckling.

"I'll double the amount," Diana offered. Her fingers dug into her waist beneath the shelter of her arms. "For each of you."

Again the infinitesimal, implacable shake of the head.

Color drained from her face, and she held herself erect only by force of will. The guards must fear Bey Haroun greatly. Or Karim. But she couldn't allow that to matter. She'd find another way to escape. If Madame Ferije hadn't alerted the authorities to her disappearance already.

"What is this?"

A tiny woman, muffled in a thick dark veil and concealing black wrap, swept into the room through a different door. The woman's quick, comprehensive glance took in Diana's paleness and the suddenly uncomfortable posture of the guards across the room. Her warm brown eyes, barely visible above the veil, hardened abruptly. Taking a pair of flowing steps over to Diana, she slowly lifted the torn frill that had gaily decorated the neck of Diana's primrose yellow muslin gown. It drooped dejectedly now against her bodice.

The woman swung about, her stature growing as the guards shrank in on themselves. Pointing, she demanded something in Arabic, the tone uncannily harsh after the gentleness when she entered the room. Swallowing hard, the guards all answered at the same time. They gesticulated toward Diana then beyond the door on their side.

Though she couldn't understand the language, Diana caught the same words repeated over and over in their explanation. Clearly the small woman held power. Their explanation had to satisfy her, or they'd suffer.

Apparently it did. Several times Diana heard Karim's name. After the final repetition, the little woman nodded and turned back to Diana. As she covered the short distance across the room, she switched back to French as rapid as her Arabic.

"It's dreadful you've had to wait in this nasty little room. I must see about making it more comfortable." Before Diana could respond, the woman patted her arm. "Don't worry, everything will be all right. I'll take care of it."

Glancing angrily back at the guards, the woman gestured and issued an order. Docilely, all three men bowed jerkily and backed from the room. After the door closed, the tiny woman tested it and faced Diana. A heavy veil obscured everything but her eyes. Ring-laden fingers appeared from underneath the cloak, and she lowered the veil and pushed off the black hood. Middle-aged, her hair was silver-threaded black. An aristocratic nose, and friendly, bow-shaped lips surprised Diana before the woman engulfed her in a warm, motherly embrace.

"Poor child, you're chilled. We must do something about it immediately."

She stepped back, looked up into Diana's face, and nodded approvingly. Chatting softly, the woman guided Diana toward a door. But not the one the guards had used.

Inside, cool silence welcomed them. A dim corridor stretched into the distance, single and double elaborately carved doors opening off it. A straight strip of lime green carpet with darker green geometrical figures covered the center of the marble floor. It absorbed their footsteps so they moved soundlessly. On the walls hung pale draperies blocking the November chill oozing into the hall.

The woman smiled and guided Diana into a cross corridor paved with more marble but different carpet. As they entered it, the woman continued her ceaseless chatter.

"You'll soon become accustomed to the ways of the harem. Each corridor is carpeted in a different color, making it easy to find your way. We'll do all we can to make you comfortable. Diana, isn't it?" The woman glanced up.

"Yes, I'm Diana Gra——"

"I'm Leila," the tiny woman continued heedlessly, "Bey Haroun's first wife. I have already given him several heirs so there need be no jealousy between us. You'll be in my charge during your training period to become my lord's newest concubine."

"You don't understand. I've been kidnapped. My parents will pay a fortune for my release."

"Now you'll want a hot bath. And something warm to wear. The weather is terrible this time of year. What happened to your dress? Was it Karim and not those guards?" She surveyed the bedraggled primrose yellow muslin critically. "Not that it's a good color for you."

"I kicked him," Diana answered. Her feet carried her automatically down the long cool hall at Leila's gentle prodding. "I'm boarding the *Redstart* next week to join my parents in Jerusalem. They're scholars, studying antiquities. And they are really very wealthy," she finished.

"Oui, petite." Opening a door between two beautifully ornate Oriental carpets hanging on the stone walls, Leila waved Diana in. "Here are the baths. They're my favorite rooms in both summer and winter. In the summer, the heat is so enervating."

Casting a sidelong look at Diana's stubborn expression, Leila sighed, then stepped past and clapped her hands once. Several plump girls in simple sleeveless dresses entered and bowed. Leila issued rapid, lengthy instructions, and the girls scattered. Frowning thoughtfully, she glided back to her charge.

Diana stood near the door, watching. *There's still Madame Ferije,* she told herself firmly. The landlady would make public Diana's disappearance, and the bey would be forced to release her. He'd remember the American marines at Tripoli some years ago. She couldn't recall details, but Muslim pirates had been punished for their raids against American ships. The same thing would happen once America learned of her kidnapping.

But she wasn't going to depend on an unknown landlady alerting some American consul to rescue her. She'd need a way to escape if Madame Ferije failed. Or took too long. Until then, she'd take the warm bath. Anything to drive out the chill.

Diana walked slowly to the middle of the large square chamber. Steamy mist rose from three pools lined with marble. Marble benches surrounded them, and charcoal-filled braziers burned in each corner, with another in the center of the room. The humid warmth of the pools along with the drier heat radiating from the braziers drained a little of the bone-deep chill clutching her.

"Now," Leila said—Diana realized the little harem mistress had been standing beside her for some time—"you'll need to take those things off. I find the central bath is best. Its warmth is so relaxing, warm but not too hot."

Stepping behind Diana, Leila started to unhook the despised muslin dress. Diana protested, "Would you please leave?"

"Petite"— Leila smiled charmingly—"I must tell you of the training period and what you must know before you meet your sisters. They are delightful girls, although older than you. You will enjoy meeting them."

"I'm twenty-one," Diana answered the unspoken question, "and not terribly *petite.*"

"I thought you younger." Leila's black brows, unmarked by the silver in her hair, arched. "Couldn't your parents afford a husband?" she asked sympathetically. "No girl should remain unwed at such an advanced age. It is most unseemly."

Diana stared at the harem mistress in stunned disbelief.

With the competence of a fine lady's maid, Leila peeled off the dress and unfastened the tapes and hooks holding the petticoat, chemise, and the minimal corset Gran insisted on, fashion or no fashion.

"It is a woman's business to be married as soon as she's of proper age," Leila continued firmly. She gathered up the muslin gown from the floor and considered it. "Although I can understand a lack of suitors if you wear such abominable dresses. You have the eyes which take color from what you wear, almost the hue of lapis lazuli. Jewel tones will bring out the exquisite tone of your hair, too. You should never wear yellow." Leila shook her head disapprovingly. "Why didn't your parents get you married?"

"They're in Jerusalem."

Leila murmured consolation for her misfortune as Diana's clothes were carried off by a servant. A frustrating sense of helplessness threatened before she realized she'd be better off with things that didn't mark her as a Westerner —at least until she could board a ship sailing from Bizerte. She'd steal one of those all-enveloping cloaks for her escape. Hugging her bare torso, Diana shivered despite the room's humid warmth.

Standing stiffly under Leila's intent inspection, Diana fought embarrassment as she went down marble steps into the heated pool. For an instant, she thought the harem mistress intended to join her, but Leila threaded between the benches and stopped at the pool's edge.

"Yes, you will do. My lord enjoys fair Europeans, and you will be to his taste." She tilted her head to the side consideringly. "Although perhaps you're too tall." Diana's head came around, her tangled hair floating in streamers about her shoulders. "My lord prefers his harem to be only—" Leila indicated a point an inch or so above her own head. "No taller. But"—she hastened to reassure Diana—"you'll be to his taste."

Grateful for the soothing, caressing warmth of the water and the small shield it provided, Diana shook off the remnants of shock. Whatever the harem mistress thought, she wasn't going to suit the bey's tastes.

Leila removed her black wool cloak and tossed it onto the bench. Beneath it, she wore a scarlet velvet robe richly embroidered in gold at hem and front closing. Full sleeves billowed gracefully with her hands' every movement, while a gold sash clasped by a diamond-encrusted brooch finished the outfit. From under the robe's hem, tiny feet clad in red-and-gold slippers peeped.

Leila arranged her clothing before continuing. "That is why there is so much immorality in your lands," she stated firmly. "A maiden cannot be trusted to choose her lord."

The pool's warmth seeping into Diana's body made it possible to ignore that ridiculous sentiment. She ducked under the water so Leila couldn't see her face. Escape had to be possible. She didn't know how or when. But she'd escape. Taking the jar of shampoo from a bath attendant, Diana soaped her hair.

Fresh hot water was such a luxury. After weeks of only having sea water for bathing on the voyage from Boston, her hair felt faintly stiff and sticky. Now, leaning back into the water to rinse, she savored its silken smoothness beneath her fingers. Eyes half closed, she let the water's warmth work its wonders. Her long hair, a delicate fawn beige, moved gently on the wavelets of the pool surface. Finally, sweeping it back from her face, Diana sat up, her headache only a dull memory. Leila had said something, something that might be important.

"The bey is careful," Leila repeated proudly. "At great expense, he has bought eunuchs to guard us. Despite being slaves, our lord rewards them well. Thus, they are impervious to all forms of bribery." Leila paused delicately for the expected response, but at Diana's blank stare continued. "Eunuchs are gelded."

Astonished, Diana stared open-mouthed at Leila. Why would anybody allow the bey to do that to them? And why should she care? Then it struck her. Leila was warning her not to seduce the guards. A vision of herself as The Great Seductress wavered before her. In spite of her predicament —or perhaps because of it—her remaining tension dissolved in a fit of giggles. And Leila's amazement only made it worse.

Despite the rain, this corridor smelled of dust and feathers. Bey Haroun rubbed his itching nose, careful not to disturb the perfectly trimmed mustache, and approached the falcon mews. The servants had searched everywhere else and not found Karim. But none dared enter here.

Opening the door, a bit of down floated past Haroun's nose. He stifled a sneeze with one finger. Waving the down away with the air of a martyr, he closed the door behind him with a distinct click.

"Yes, my precious." Karim gently stroked the young falcon on his wrist. "Soon we will soar high after game." After a glance in the direction of the door, he ignored the bey.

"This obsession with birds is ridiculous, brother," Haroun snapped. Rubbing his itching nose again, he crossed the mews, ruby velvet caftan stirring the faint film of dust and feathers on the floor. "You should let the servants clean this place." His irritated tone ruffled the falcon's feathers, stopping Haroun several feet away. "Put that bird down. You should be checking details instead of playing where the servants can't find you." He stepped back hastily when the young falcon hissed and mantled her wings.

Karim shrugged powerful shoulders casually beneath a pale sand wool robe. "All that can be done has been done."

Soothing the falcon, he went to a perch, his stride fluid, powerful, yet oddly gentle—like his voice. While the bird contentedly ate a bit of meat, Karim returned soundlessly. Aware that his greater height annoyed Haroun, he draped an arm about his brother's shoulders and started toward the door. A half smile lifted his thin lips when Haroun put several feet between them. Well away from the falcon's perch, Karim leaned negligently against the wall and crossed his arms over his chest. He watched Haroun fussily resettle his caftan on his shoulders.

"Well, brother?" he asked when Haroun finished brushing the ruby velvet free of bits of down. "What's so important you disturb me here?"

"The men are in place for tomorrow?"

Haroun tugged absently at his sleek beard before smoothing it back in place. He was proud of it. Despite advancing middle age, no silver marred the perfect blackness.

"If you're that concerned, we can move tonight." Karim's eyes crinkled at the instant refusal.

Haroun's vehement head shake dislodged several strands of glossy black hair over his broad forehead. Still he smiled beatifically. The smile deepened the lines surrounding his golden brown eyes. "Tonight is too special a treat. Our friend Hamilton is having dinner with me *tonight.*" His voice caressed the word. "He thinks I intend to expand our little business."

A soft chuckle echoed wispily in the room. The falcon shifted on her perch, then returned to grooming already pristine feathers while fitful wind gusted against shutters set high in the stuccoed wall. Chill drafts creeping through them stirred the dust and down on the floor, but Haroun didn't notice.

Rubbing his hands in anticipation, he paced three steps forward, three back, between empty perches. "What a surprise tomorrow when he learns of my little plan."

Pleasure lit his face at the prospect, yet Haroun looked sharply at his brother. Forgetting the disparity in heights, he stepped closer. "You *are* certain you can arrest all his followers at one time? Hamilton pays high wages." The harsh lines about his eyes deepened. "That kind of loyalty doesn't last long."

"Perhaps, dearest brother," Karim agreed dryly. "Although none showed susceptibility to a bribe." He paused deliberately. "Of the amount I was able to offer." Irony laced his tone.

"You didn't let them know the source?" Haroun resumed pacing, absently rubbing his nose again.

"Naturally not." Eyes half closed, he watched the bey fastidiously pluck a small, downy feather missed earlier from the gold embroidery binding the edge of his sleeve. Karim chuckled softly. "Any more than I let the Italian know your intentions for next year."

The bey's wide smile disturbed the symmetry of beard and mustache; he didn't care. "A perfect plan. I save a piaster a bottle, and he trains new people. He won't make Hamilton's mistake of paying too high salaries, either. Then, I dispose of the Italian and give the underlings a choice of serving me or rowing in my galleys."

This time, his laughter was louder, filling the room and disturbing the young falcon. Wings flapping, she tried to rise from the perch, but the short tether prevented her from flying.

An impatient frown drew Karim's black brows together. Casting an annoyed glance at his brother, he hurried to the bird's perch before she hurt herself. His voice, soothing as honey, calmed her, while Haroun fumed and sneezed at the opposite end of the mews. Carefully, Karim placed a hood over the falcon's head.

"You know better than to make loud noises in the presence of a half-trained falcon." Karim strode impatiently but soundlessly back. "She's not used to people. She can't understand your lack of self-control. Come." Karim held the door open commandingly. Outside, he continued, deliberately defusing the explosion that was building in Haroun. "I have a treat for you."

"What?" Eagerness diverted Haroun easily.

"An addition to your harem." Karim's smile widened. "A young American with hair like spun gold and eyes you will lose your soul in." His deep brown eyes, glinting with malicious amusement, measured Haroun's diminutive height.

* * *

The small calico kitten rose on his back legs and batted at the wide leather belt dangling from the pile of clothes Garrett carried. His claws caught and dragged it free, toppling a shirt to the floor. With a muted rumble of a purr, he pounced and sent the shirt spinning across the dusty floor of Garrett's small, hidden warehouse room.

"Prinny!" His voice echoed from the white stucco walls. "It's bad enough leaving half my wardrobe behind without you using the remainder as a mop." He saved the shirt just before Prinny pounced again.

Shaking it, he folded and replaced it on the pile waiting on the narrow bed thrust against one wall. Instantly the kitten sprang at the bed. Claws catching in the blanket, he scrambled the rest of the way up and investigated. After a delicate sniff at the clean shirts proved they were no longer interesting, he took a swipe with one paw, claws sheathed, at Garrett's hand.

"You're as bad as your namesake. Maybe worse. Even he wouldn't attack the hand that petted him. Or maybe he would." Garrett scratched the kitten behind an ear.

He opened a valise and took shirts from the pile. With difficulty, he prevented Prinny from climbing in with them. The kitten rolled over on his back and grappled with Garrett's hand, purring ferociously.

"No! Here, go play." Lifting Prinny off the bed, Garrett rolled a small wooden ball across the uneven floor. "I've got to get this down to the *Medea* before dinner."

Prinny raced after the ball and batted experimentally with one paw. When it simply clunked against the wall and stayed there, he plopped down on his haunches, splotched tail wrapped about his paws, and stared at it in disgust. The tip of his tail twitched rhythmically until a drawer closed. Scrambling back up on the bed, he purred mightily, the sound shaking his round little body.

Absently fending off Prinny's attempts to explore the interior of the valise, Garrett put the last of the clothes inside.

Taking a leather bag from beneath the bed, he checked the bottle of Scotch and put it carefully aside. Then he loaded the double-barreled pistol, gleaming dully against the dark green blanket.

"You know, Prinny," he said when the kitten tried to capture the pistol with his front paws, "I'm not sure which of these is more important tonight. I'm not even sure which of us is crazier." Grinning, Garrett answered himself. "Probably me. But *tonight* will be fun."

Laughing again, he picked up Prinny and scratched him under the chin to the encouragement of raucous purrs. The kitten's golden eyes narrowed to slits and he sank his claws into Garrett's white shirt, kneading in time with the scratching.

"Ouch!" Garrett freed the claws from the linen shirt gently and held the kitten away. With Prinny's indignant eyes open again, he warned, "That's enough of that," and dropped him back on the bed. He stroked the kitten's sleek fur. "What am I going to do with you?"

Unconcerned once Garrett resumed his attentions, Prinny stretched beneath the long, firm fingers and angled his head to offer first the hollow behind one ear, then the other. At a slight interruption, he cast a reproachful glance up but resumed purring when Garrett dropped the pistol in the small leather bag and stroked him along his spine. With each stroke, he arched more contentedly. Concern filled Garrett's sherry-colored eyes as he rubbed the kitten's ears.

"Karim won't stop with just searching my rooms at the inn. He'll find this hole, and when he finds it empty—" Garrett shook his head. "We'll have to get you out of here." With Prinny trying to pounce on the shiny toes of Garrett's boots, he strode to the door and scooped the kitten up in his arms.

"Yusuf," Garrett called from the doorway into the dark interior of the warehouse.

Small scuffles of someone sliding something heavy along the floor came from one direction, while from another a low-voiced murmur reached them. Prinny's ears pricked with interest, and he tried to twist free of Garrett's restraining hold. Only when Yusuf hurried into the circle of light thrown by the lantern from the room behind Garrett did Prinny's struggles cease. Thrusting his head toward the warehouseman, he waited for a chin rub.

"We're just about through," Yusuf said after he'd greeted the kitten. "Is something wrong?"

"We can't leave Prinny to Karim's tender mercy. Besides, the *Medea* probably needs a ship's cat. Have the man who's delivering my baggage take him, too."

Yusuf bowed, the first smile since Garrett arrived widening his mouth. "It will be my personal honor to take the most noble Prince Regent to the ship. And I shall not forget his leather mouse."

Diana jerked when a drop of water from the tree branch hit her nose. Her full, soft mouth firming, she wiped it away and stepped back on the path of the small garden provided for the harem's use. Its tiny crushed shells dug into the soft leather slippers Leila had given her once she'd finished bathing. How did the harem's inmates manage to walk here without hurting their feet? She reached the stone-paved colonnade before turning back for one last look.

Leila's tour of the harem's environs had ended in this garden. Though few flowers bloomed, she'd smiled sympathetically at Diana's request to walk there alone.

During the past hours, Diana had paced along the silent, colonnaded promenades, noticing, comparing, watching the guards make their rounds. Fewer patrolled the walls here than outside the harem compound. Diana, Leila had offered, could sit on the roof and watch the traffic going to the market. So only one wall separated them from the outside.

The walls were well patrolled, Diana conceded. That was the real reason Leila had left her alone—to discover there was no escape. But there was. For a few minutes every hour, one part of the wall seemed unobserved. A corner with a tall palm arcing gracefully near it as an accent. A palm tree that looked simple to climb.

With proper clothes—Diana glanced down at her sapphire wool caftan worn over soft cotton loosely gathered trousers and knee-length tunic—she could climb that tree and disappear over the wall. All she needed was rope, one of those odd, veiling cloaks, and the right moment. She had until the completion of her training to find it. And that would take longer than the few weeks Leila confidently predicted.

Shivering with the increasing chill as dusk drew in, Diana turned back toward the inner rooms where the women gathered in the evenings. Leaving the colonnade, she winced as tiny shells dug into her feet again. Rounding a curve in the path, she paused fractionally, then resumed her unhurried pace. If only Leila hadn't seen her scrutiny of that section of wall.

"Good evening," Diana said when the older woman joined her.

"Petite, your room is ready." Leila sedately turned and fell into step with her. "And your luggage has arrived from Madame Ferije's."

Paling, Diana didn't notice Leila's difficulty in keeping up with her longer stride. "What explanation did they give to Madame Ferije?" she asked, struggling to keep her tone calm and only mildly curious. No marines would sail to the rescue.

Leila shrugged, the movement beneath an evening caftan of aquamarine velvet elegant despite the effort to keep pace. "That's not important. You'll be pleased they paid her for several days' lodging as compensation." She looked up at Diana with a bright, yet sympathetic smile curving her tinted lips.

"Quite pleased," Diana agreed hollowly.

Never would the harem mistress have a slower student in the training program. And before Leila declared her ready to grace the bey's bed, she'd be over the wall. With her own clothing! And money to buy passage to safety.

"They've delivered everything?"

"Oh, yes." Leila's eyes met Diana's with understanding. "I've confiscated the money in your trunk, though."

"I was afraid you'd think of that." Diana shrugged, her gaze fixed unhappily before her.

"Come, *petite,* you will soon grow accustomed to our ways. And it's a good life." Touching her arm, Leila pointed to a door off the main corridor. "Here is the room I have selected for you."

Although filled with small luxuries, it looked alien. Heavy brocade draperies shielded the one window looking out toward the garden they'd just left. A thick, muted gold carpet protected her feet from the chill rising from the marble floor, and gold and green silk draped the alcove containing the bed. Each detail, down to the gleam of the brass brazier warming the room, spoke of care and attention. Leila'd made every effort to make her feel at home—and failed.

"It's lovely, Leila," Diana said absently. "Such lovely brocade and perfect silks. Thank you. But I don't see my luggage." Tonight she'd have to begin sorting her clothes for the escape. Finding one of those cloaks could wait a day or two.

"Already unpacked—" Leila began.

Before she could finish, a light scratch on the door interrupted her. A small slave girl, silver bands holding wool trousers tightly against her ankles, entered. The two talked animatedly in Arabic for several minutes, while Leila grew increasingly agitated.

Diana knew something had happened. The harem mistress's naturally olive skin paled at the message. Taking the slave girl by the shoulders, Leila asked a question, and the girl nodded.

Repeating her message calmly, the girl's eyes wandered past Leila to inspect Diana curiously. Finishing, she listened gravely to the harem mistress's instructions, smiled at Diana, and skipped lightly from the room. For several seconds, Leila paced, sending troubled glances at Diana, and wringing her hands.

"What is it?" Diana asked, no longer able to bear the suspense. Whatever had happened, it concerned her.

"The bey," Leila began, and came over to take Diana's hands in hers, "has called for you to grace his couch this very night."

CHAPTER III

LEATHER BAG TIGHT AGAINST HIS THIGH, GARRETT waited to be announced into the bey's presence. Black lashes veiled the excitement in his eyes. As expected, Bey Haroun had chosen the small room off the audience chamber. Solid blue doors carved like rows of organ pipes capped with gracefully curved, pointed arches would separate them from the rest of the palace. A slow smile tugged at Garrett's lips.

A pair of brass braziers heated the room from opposite corners, while the bey sprawled on a low couch near one. Rising at the servant's announcement, he straightened the swathed amethyst turban covering his black hair and extended his right hand in Western fashion. He didn't bother to hide the broad victory smile lighting his face.

Garrett stepped forward, inclining his head in a gesture midway between a bow and a nod to hide his amusement. The bey's hand was faintly damp in the brief second they touched.

"Hamilton, your presence brings honor to my miserable home." Haroun's gaze dropped to the leather bag, and his smile grew gleeful. "After dinner we will have our . . . discussion."

Haroun motioned toward the couches. Garrett wasn't as tall as Karim, but the infidel's extra inches disturbed Haroun nearly as much. Especially with laughter always lurking in Garrett's eyes.

In flawless French, Garrett imitated Haroun's normal flowery eloquence. "Bey of beys, your most munificent hospitality is even more welcome than usual. Crass commercial considerations have prevented my supping. The rare, exquisite, and most sumptuous banquets, for which you are so justly famous, will render me even more in your debt."

There, Garrett laughed quietly, *let Haroun top that.* Stopping before the low divan opposite the bey, he threw off the barely ankle-length wool robe the fitful rain outside dictated. Haroun enjoyed warmer rooms than he did.

The bey laughed, then smoothed his beard. "Hamilton, my dearest friend, I fear you've enjoyed our humble Arab hospitality too long. Even I am incapable of such flawless phrasing. Perhaps tonight we should declare you the winner and speak in the more direct, less courtly English style. You're becoming too good with Arabic expressions. What a pity you don't speak the language."

Tapping a small gong, he waited impatiently for the servant. Garrett studiously feigned ignorance of the bey's fluid Arabic orders. Serving was to begin immediately. "My cook," Haroun said, turning to his guest, "has outdone himself tonight. As I ordered." At Garrett's questioning expression, he continued. "Our little plan deserves a celebration, don't you agree?"

Garrett patted the small bag he'd put on the couch beside him. "I've found something out of the ordinary. It should complement your chef's delicacies."

The bey's tongue passed over his full lips. "Ah, yes," he murmured. A servant entered the room bearing a heavily laden tray. "But more about that later. First the couscous."

Steam gently rose from the pot. Perfect miniature vegetables glistened with honey atop the semolina. Lamb and poultry stews, each on its own platter, surrounded it. Only one, the sweetened chicken with tomatoes and almonds, was expected. It was the bey's favorite.

And the chef had fixed *tchermila,* trout marinated in a combination of sweet and hot peppers, garlic and onions, then baked until barely done. Its highly seasoned flavor appealed to Garrett more than the honey-glazed dishes the bey preferred.

Everything was perfect in every detail. Except for one thing. The couscous shouldn't have been on the table yet. Normally, stews were served before it was brought in. Garrett observed the deviation from courteous Muslim behavior with interest. And anticipation.

When the servant retreated, Haroun dipped into the couscous using only the thumb and first two fingers of the right hand. "Try it," he commanded. "A delightful recipe. I value your opinion."

"Would you like something with it?" Garrett asked, touching the leather bag to whet the bey's appetite.

A low, wispy chuckle startled the servant backing out of the room. "Wait until after dinner, my dear Hamilton. Each delight should be savored in its own time."

Garrett shot a glance at the bey and politely dipped the appropriate fingers into the grain dish. Haroun was gleefully impatient, looking forward to something. Had he decided to move tonight instead of waiting? That singularly unpleasant smile on his face boded ill. A moment's uneasiness gripped Garrett before he shook it off. He'd just have to make his own move first.

Fastidiously, he tried the grain and a baby carrot. The honey glaze cloyed, but he nodded and smiled. "Delicious." Taking a quick sip of mint tea to clear his palate, he followed it with a slice of trout. The spicy burn finished the tea's work.

With a quick bounce at odds with his usual studied, languid grace, Haroun scooped up a slice of eggplant and took a healthy bite. "You should find a house befitting your station, Hamilton," he said around it. "You could savor delights like this . . . every night of your life."

"I prefer to avoid the expense." Unspoken lay the certainty that Haroun would also prefer to avoid it. Unfortunately, the bey's position demanded it. "Besides, a bachelor household is tiresome."

"Ah"—Haroun waggled a finger—"that's the thing which makes the expense of a household worthwhile. Evenings one may relax in the harem after the pressures of the day. It makes it all—" The bey broke off, sighing beatifically and smiling at the ceiling as though remembering uncounted delights.

Suppressing a choke of laughter, Garrett scooped up another slice of fish and swallowed it quickly. "I'm sure," he commented dryly when his mouth was empty, "what you say is true. However, women bring a pack of trouble along with their other attributes."

In his excitement, the bey was eating sketchily and already showing signs of sending for the servant to remove the tray, although that didn't prevent him from licking his fingers with every mouthful. Not a drop of honey escaped his searching tongue. Garrett ate several slices of fish and more of the semolina. He needed to be finished before the food was sent away.

Stomach comfortably full, he watched, narrow-eyed, as Haroun absently reached for more couscous. Garrett measured how little of it and the chicken with tomatoes and almonds was gone.

"Compliment your chef." He settled against the low back of the divan. "Dinner was delicious."

"Would you care for more?" Haroun asked, suddenly the anxious host. He licked a dribble of honey running down one knuckle.

Garrett patted his stomach. "I'd be too full to savor our little treat."

An arrested expression arched the bey's brows. "We must save room for that."

Dipping his fingers in a finger bowl, he dried them on a napkin, then struck the gong. A servant scurried through the door. Haroun issued a series of instructions and waited while the low table between the two men was cleared. Rubbing his hands along the skirt of his amethyst brocade caftan, he leaned forward eagerly.

"I've ordered that we're not to be disturbed."

With a bland smile, Garrett ceremoniously opened the bag and drew out a bottle of aged Scotch. Handing it to the bey, he sat back and watched appreciatively. Though Haroun knew no English, he inspected the label closely, his lips moving in the pretense of reading.

"This is different than what you've brought before." The bey looked over for confirmation.

"It isn't easy to get."

Taking the bottle, Garrett removed the cork and poured some into a pair of glasses taken from the leather bag. "I hope you enjoy it," he said, handing the bey a glass fuller than his own.

Haroun lifted the glass in a sketchy toast and downed it in a swallow. His eyes widened in astonishment. Breath escaping gustily, he struck his chest several times with one fist below the thick gold chain draped over his shoulders.

"What was that?" he asked hoarsely after another second.

"The best Scotch from Britain." Garrett raised his glass in a toast and took a sip. "More?"

Lifting the bottle suggestively, he watched the bey. He'd stopped thumping just below the breastbone and was rubbing his stomach gently. Extending his glass, Haroun smiled.

"It warms you, this Scotch, doesn't it?"

"That's its purpose. Remember, we live in a chilly climate." Garrett filled the glass fuller than last time.

"Barbaric." Haroun shuddered. Drinking half the whiskey, he gestured, and Scotch nearly slopped onto his hand. "How do you English stand it? No wonder you all flock down here where the sun shines." Rain spat at the closed window set high in the wall above his head. "Most of the time."

"That's one reason I came to Tunisia," Garrett said. He took another small sip and shrugged suggestively. "But just one of the reasons."

Haroun laughed and emptied his glass. 'I like this Scotch. I couldn't pronounce the name. Is it English?" He held out the glass when Garrett raised the bottle.

Garrett gave a Scots Gaelic name and took another sip. When the bey tipped his head back to drain his glass, Garrett tipped the bottle over his own. As the bey lowered his head and gazed blearily across the table, Garrett seemed to be topping off his drink.

Wetting his lips with the Scotch, Garrett frowned consideringly "I hate to be the bearer of bad news," he began, watching the bey through thick lashes, "but there are rumors."

Haroun waggled his fingers for the bottle. "There are always rumors." Garrett refilled the glass.

"Your brother, they say, plots to replace you."

Haroun stared, bewildered, then howled with laughter. "Of course he's planning a coup. He's my brother! Don' worry about Karim. I . . ."—he pounded his chest and belched—". . . I can handle him." The bey savored a small swallow of Scotch. "That's good," he said, downing the rest of it. "But, Allah, 's potent."

"I'm glad you like it." Trying to hide his smile, Garrett put the bottle down in the middle of the table. "Help yourself."

"Got a s'prise for you, too."

"What?"

"Can't tell. Wouldn' be a surprise."

The bey lifted the glass in a salute; the Scotch nearly overflowed. He steadied it with both hands and brought it to his mouth. Greedily, he licked up a drop hanging from the rim before draining it. Then he poured more Scotch with extreme care.

Almost laughing aloud at the bey's eagerness, Garrett watched Haroun drink. He'd only given the bey heavily watered whiskey before. The most he'd had before he met Garrett was bad Italian wine. Every time they met, he'd been maudlin after just a little watered scotch. Another glass of the straight stuff would put him under the table, unconscious.

It took little more than that before the bey sprawled on his divan snoring stertorously. Smiling in anticipation, Garrett rose stealthily and locked the door. Returning, he put the small leather bag on the table and opened it.

"My lady." The small servant girl bowed before Leila. "Lord Karim is in the antechamber."

"Karim?" Leila repeated, puzzled. "Where's my lord?"

The child shrugged insouciantly. "I know not, my lady. Lord Karim awaits your pleasure in the antechamber."

Frowning, Leila nodded brusquely. "Very well, Rabi. Inform Karim I will join him. What about a eunuch?"

"There is one there, my lady." At Leila's nod, Rabi ran off in the direction of the antechamber.

Black brows drawn together in a frown, Leila pulled on a veil and the enveloping robe worn by women of the harem when in view of men other than Haroun. She hurried into the corridor, turning in the direction Rabi had taken. Leila preferred to be with Diana, helping her prepare. But she'd sent out one last appeal in hopes of a delay. Karim's presence in the antechamber argued against it.

"Yes, Karim," Leila said, stepping through the door.

Although Karim bowed courteously, the impression he gave was of unbending height, making the silent eunuch at his side almost invisible. "I hope I see you well, Lady."

"I was expecting my lord."

Karim smiled thinly. "It grieves me to be the bearer of bad news, but that will not be possible. My brother has given the strictest orders he is not to be disturbed. The infidel, Hamilton, is with him." Something even colder flickered in his remote brown eyes for an instant. "A reckoning will take place tomorrow, and Haroun is enjoying the anticipation. To be disturbed will make him most unhappy."

"It can't be that important," Leila protested. Frowning beneath the veil, she considered alternatives. "Have the servants taken in dinner?"

Nodding, Karim smiled. "And removed the remains. It was but a brief meal."

Leila caught the hidden meaning. Haroun was drinking again this evening. Perhaps it wouldn't be so bad for Diana after all. After each of Hamilton's visits, Haroun grew slightly less interested in the harem. Her husband's illicit love of the infidel's alcohol just might give Diana one more night.

"My lord won't wish to be bothered with an untrained concubine," Leila suggested smoothly.

"Ah, but she will be a welcome relief after the tensions of the past days." Karim's smile turned spiteful. "I told him all about her."

"Everything?" Leila allowed a delicate trace of irony to color her tone.

Karim gestured negligently. "Everything of importance. All that concerns my brother is her beauty."

"What should concern my husband is the number of shocks she's been subjected to in just a few hours."

"Other females survive worse." Karim moved as though something—one of his shins?—hurt. "Besides, the girl has too high an opinion of herself to be disturbed by a little thing like this."

So Diana *had* landed a blow on Karim's precious hide. Leila smiled beneath her veil. Then it faded. "She knows nothing of pleasing a man. It's as if you took a falcon hunting without training." The appeal was useless, but she had to try.

"My lady, I regret the necessity of refusing you with all my heart, but—" Karim shrugged elaborately, his eyes glittering with malicious laughter. "I must obey my lord bey's commands—as we all must—and he has ordered that *no one* may disturb him."

Another protest hovered on her lips but went unvoiced. Pleading would only amuse Karim. "As my lord and Allah will it," Leila answered, her lips tight beneath the veil. She summarily dismissed the security chief. "You may go."

Annoyance flashed in Karim's face before he regained control. Without another word, he bowed and left the ante-chamber, the eunuch trailing behind. Leila caught the eunuch's sympathetic glance but didn't acknowledge it. Karim was petty enough to take revenge. She didn't want two victims of his vengeance to succor tomorrow.

Keeping one eye on the locked door, Garrett worked up a lather. Perching on the edge of the low table, he stripped the bey of the brilliant amethyst brocade robe and the shirt beneath. Watermarks might give him away. Already the gold chain and amethyst turban lay in a glittering pile in the center of the table. With the robes and shirt on the other divan, he lathered the bey's face lavishly.

A half smile hovered on his lips as Garrett carefully stretched the bey's cheek. The razor left a swath through the glossy black beard. Pale olive skin gleamed beneath it. Fortunately, he didn't have a heavy tan. With dim light, no one would notice the difference. Thanks to Haroun's parsimony, Karim would think nothing of it if half the lamps were out when he arrived.

Garrett chuckled softly, wiped the razor, and continued removing the beard. Even the mustache had to go. How long, he wondered idly, wiping lather on the towel from the leather bag, would it take for Haroun to grow it back? A month? Two? Possibly longer. It was so glossy and perfect, yet not as heavy as expected. Haroun must have struggled for years to get it this far. Garrett wished he could stay in Bizerte one more day to savor the aftereffects of the shave.

But he couldn't. He flicked the last bit of beard from the bey's chin.

Carefully removing all traces of soap from Haroun's face and neck, he turned the bey's head from side to side and chuckled softly again. The bey hadn't gone without a beard in many years, probably not since he was old enough to grow one. The chin beneath was all the explanation Garrett needed for the carefully tended beard. It was weak, receding into his neck.

Dropping the dirtied towels behind the divan in a corner where they wouldn't be discovered until morning, Garrett fetched his robe. Grunting, he heaved the bey upright and fought to dress him. With a few more tugs, Garrett pulled the robe down over the legs. It wasn't neat; it shouldn't be. With the Scotch from his glass and the dregs of the bottle, he sprinkled the bey until he smelled like a tavern.

Stepping back, Garrett gleefully inspected the scene. The stage manager for the great actor Edmund Kean couldn't have done better. They bey sprawled across the divan with drunken abandon, exuding Scotch with his snores. Karim wouldn't recognize his brother even if he sat up and issued orders.

Now for himself. Garrett pasted on the false beard from the bag, checking in the tiny hand mirror he'd brought. Too bad there hadn't been more room, but he didn't want to risk the bey's curiosity. Cat-footed, he slipped about the room and extinguished lamps.

The bey's amethyst brocade robe was tight across the shoulders, but not so tight he couldn't handle a pistol. Draping the chain around his neck and tipping the turban forward to shadow the upper part of his face, he surveyed the carefully staged scene again. Quickly, he arranged the empty Scotch bottle beside the somnolent form.

Dropping the bag behind the divan, Garrett settled in the darkest corner. He concealed the gun beneath the skirt of the robe and covered the doorway with it. Picking up the gong's small mallet, he checked one final time. Yes, quite convincing. Smiling with reckless gaiety, he struck the gong.

Diana started when the door to her small room opened without warning. It was Leila. Poppy red clothes, some filmy silk, some rich, warm velvet, hung over her arm. The slave girl who had brought the bey's order followed her. Frowning studiously, the girl carried a full tray balanced on one arm and a large pot of tea in her free hand. Leila directed her to put the tray of pastries on a low table surrounded by cushions.

Turning to Diana, Leila smiled, her eyes tired. "Come, *petite,* I must talk to you."

After the young slave girl ran happily from the room, Leila sank wearily onto a plump cushion beside the low table and tossed the clothes onto another of the cushions. She poured a scented stream of liquid into a glass and put it at the place beside Diana before pouring her own.

"Come," Leila repeated, an edge of impatience in her tone at Diana's frozen silence. "Pardon." She sighed and patted the cushion. "I am upset with Karim." She sighed again. "We have much to discuss and little time to do it." Reluctantly, Diana crossed the room and knelt on the moss green cushion. "Don't worry, *petite,* I shall help you all I can." Preoccupied, she patted Diana's arm before reaching for the tray of pastries. "Rabi tells me you ate none of your dinner. That will not help you at all tonight."

Diana flashed Leila an ironic look. "Will anything help?"

"Yes." Closing her eyes, she took a long swallow of the steaming mint tea. Revived, Leila straightened and watched Diana closely as she spoke. "If you approach tonight with an open mind, it could be quite pleasant. Our bodies were made for love, but to make love for the first time in the wrong mood"—her grimace was graphic—"you will betray yourself. Wallowing in self-pity can be quite painful."

A flush staining her cheeks, Diana took a pastry. "It's not self-pity."

The pastry was rich with honey, nuts, sugar, and cinnamon. The kind she'd eaten only this morning. Diana swallowed convulsively, a nut scratching her throat as it slid down. Coughing huskily, she sipped at the sweet mint tea.

"What then?"

"Pure, unadulterated rage," Diana admitted, "and a little fear."

"Petite, you are of my family now, and I wish to help. Cleanse your mind of rage. Not for my lord, but for yourself."

Leila inspected her and frowned. Faint freckles dusted across Diana's nose stood out against her pale skin, and her hands, free now of the sticky pastry, lay tightly clasped in her lap. Leila placed a comforting hand over Diana's chilly fingers.

"It will happen. If not tonight, then soon. I wish to see you happy." She pried Diana's pale, tense fingers apart and handed her the tea. "Please, *petite,* as a favor to me, do not harm yourself."

Warmth from Leila's hand struck through the ice holding her tightly in its grip. Slowly, Diana raised her head to meet Leila's concerned brown eyes. The harem mistress's expression melted the ice, and Diana leaned forward to hug Leila.

"Will you help me escape?"

"Petite, there is no escape from the harem!" The little woman's jaw firming, she shook her head. "This is what comes from missing dinner."

Diane felt an insane desire to giggle. Leila was serious. She might even be right. Her hand hovering for an instant over the tray of sugar-coated pastries, Diana looked back up at the harem mistress. "Do you have anything a little less sweet?"

Leila regarded her with approval. "I am glad you are being sensible. Has your mother prepared you for your wedding night?"

Licking her fingers one by one, Diana looked wryly at

Leila. "My mother left for the Holy Land when I was fifteen."

"*Mon Dieu!* Is it possible for a girl to reach fifteen without instruction in the ways of pleasing her lord? This is what is wrong with your culture. You fight nature. Never do that. It's uncomfortable." Leila settled more thoroughly into her cushions and arranged the warm velvet robe about her. "Come, we will get you something beyond these fripperies to eat, then I shall take you to the baths for a warm, relaxing soak before a deep massage with aromatic oils." She nodded triumphantly. "Yes, that will turn the trick. You shall be so relaxed and warm you'll have no choice but to enjoy tonight." Nodding importantly again, she struck a gong on the table. "I promise it."

A small, unbelieving smile tugged at Diana's lips. "You promise it?"

Leila nodded impressively. "But only if you obey the dictates of your body."

Rabi skipped back into the room, and Leila broke off to give the girl instructions.

"There, everything is arranged. While we wait, I shall describe exactly what you may expect so you will no longer be afraid."

Diana doubted her assurances but listened disbelievingly to the harem mistress's description of physical love. It sounded ridiculous, comical, even on a full stomach. Conscientiously, she ate the meal brought within minutes of the order while listening. Leila was right about one thing at least. She felt better with hot food in her.

"You will feel strong, pleasant, even overpowering sensations and urges," Leila finished. "Go with them; do not fight them. I tell you as a mother should tell her daughter. If you fight your body, there is only pain and misery." She shrugged. "And it will still happen." Leila straightened her spine to its full extent. Pinning Diana's faintly disbelieving gaze with one of formidable warning, she continued.

"Promise me, *petite,* that you will accept what is to happen. It is for your sake that I ask."

At the very real concern in Leila's face, Diana blushed. "I promise to follow your advice, obey the dictates of my body, and accept what is to come."

"We must hurry," Leila said, smiling with relief, "to get you fully relaxed, for our time is short." She surged to her feet and held a hand out to Diana. "Come, *petite.*"

Diana slowly followed the harem mistress out into the hall. She'd keep her promise to Leila. But she added a silent vow. Later, when she could do it with a fair chance to escape, she'd kill this man who took her virginity.

"I'm pleased to see you so ready to assist me," Garrett said, his voice low and slurred.

Karim bowed, the depth just short of what courtesy required. "You have but to command, brother."

His hand tightened on the butt of the gun. Karim was looking too closely at him in the dim light. Garrett gestured toward the bey's somnolent form. Karim's eyes followed automatically. "Do you see the infidel?" Haroun snored raucously to punctuate the question.

"How could I avoid it?" Contempt on his face, Karim dismissed the body sprawled on the divan.

"Eject him," Garrett ordered tersely. He wanted—no, needed—to get Karim out of here with the bey as quickly as possible. The room's warmth was making him sweat. He wasn't sure how well the glue would hold the false beard.

Karim's brows rose higher. "Brother, leave us kill him now," he suggested with chilling sweetness, "and save time tomorrow. We can then concentrate on netting his followers."

"No!"

The word echoed harshly, vehemently, in the small room. Wind blasted against the wall, rattling the shutters protecting the window. At the sound, the bey grunted and shifted before resuming snoring with a snort. Karim gave the drunken figure another glance. Starting to gesture again, Garrett caught himself. The tiniest hint of gun metal in the dim light would warn Karim.

"I won't have my plans changed," Garrett continued after a fractional pause, his voice under control again. Karim's expression grew mutinous. Garrett had to satisfy him. And get rid of him. Otherwise, everything would miscarry.

"However," Garrett added, "you have permission to express your, uh, displeasure with the infidel's drunkenness. I doubt he'll notice your gentle attentions. Until the morning."

Satisfaction replaced Karim's displeasure. "Then when he returns to the palace to protest, he dies?" A hard-edged laugh reverberated against the plaster walls. "I underestimated you, brother." Eyes narrowed, he whispered, "I definitely underestimated you."

Prying himself from the supporting door, Karim strolled negligently over to the divan and yanked the inert form upright. Garrett's hand tensed around the gun butt again. If Karim looked closely into the "infidel's" face and recognized his elder brother— But if Karim didn't recognize him now, he wouldn't later.

Karim hauled the inert form over his shoulder and staggered to the door. "The infidel carries too much weight," he complained.

"He will feel your tender ministrations all the more. I leave him to your pleasures." He waited until Karim reached for the handle. "And Karim, send my newest concubine here. Allow no one to disturb us."

CHAPTER IV

IF ONLY THERE'D BEEN TIME. THE RED SILKS HADN'T suited Diana. Now she'd grace her lord's couch without proper training, without proper clothing. And without time to recover from all the day's shocks. A frown creased Leila's smooth forehead. Diana had listened to reason, promised to obey. Still, how would she react tonight?

If only there'd been time. But Karim had made sure there wasn't. Karim and Haroun. Haroun was drinking with the infidel again. Otherwise, Leila could appeal to him. Instead, all she could do to help Diana was to make her as relaxed as possible.

Holding up a rose brocade caftan, Leila carefully considered, then rejected it, even though it wasn't as ridiculously short as the poppy red silks. Next, she picked up a shimmering green velvet caftan laced with delicate silver embroidery and matching embroidered silk blouse and trousers. Yes, Diana would look a naiad rising from the sea. And, best of all, it was long enough.

Leila hurried from the storeroom. When the search began, she hadn't hoped to find anything attractive, just clothing that might fit. Normally, the seamstress would design something especially for Diana's wedding night.

"My lady." Hopping on one foot, Rabi pulled her slipper back over her heel and grinned at the harem mistress.

"Yes, child?"

"Oh, that's lovely," Rabi crooned while she stroked the sea green silk longingly.

Patting Rabi's shoulder, Leila drew her along toward Diana's room. "Was there a message?" Leila prompted gently.

"The new lady, Dji—Diana, is summoned to the antechamber off the audience room at once." Rabi looked up quizzically. "When is Dji—Diana to have a proper name?"

"When the astrologer has time to cast her horoscope," Leila answered absently. "Diana is to come to the antechamber?"

Rabi nodded. "Where our lord meets the infidel. The room always smells peculiar afterward, Hakim says. If infidels smell that way, why doesn't Diana?" The child's yawn smothered Leila's short choke of laughter.

"Because she doesn't. Now off to bed with you, and don't dawdle on the way." Leila shook her head firmly at Rabi's protest. "You heard me. Now, off with you."

With a last unconvincing protest, Rabi obeyed. Leila waited until she turned the corner to the servants' quarters before starting forward again, this time more slowly. Why the antechamber? And why so early? Haroun always sat with the infidel until much later. Puzzled, she entered Diana's room.

"Ah, *madame,* we are ready for you."

The soft voice of the masseuse, so at odds with her rippling muscles, distracted Leila. Beneath the masseuse's strong brown hands, Diana's back glowed palely. A linen towel covered her buttocks, while her long legs stretched limply the length of the table, her toes dangling over the end. She might have been asleep for all the attention she paid to the conversation. Good. Even better, there would be no long wait for the summons, allowing tension to rebuild.

"Thank you, Yasmin." Putting the clothes down, Leila switched to French. *"Petite,* it is time."

She repeated the quiet reminder before Diana levered herself up to half sit, half lay on the table. Leila's eyes narrowed in pleased assessment. Warm baths and a massage with aromatic oils had erased the worst effects of the day's shocks. Even better, Diana was limp with relaxation.

She swayed before dropping her legs over the edge to dangle above the floor. When she pushed off, Yasmin's strong, gentle hands caught and held Diana until her muscles gained the strength to stand.

Yasmin had done well. Some token of appreciation would have to be found for her when this was all over. Signing for the masseuse to leave, Leila waited for the door to close before speaking again.

"Here, *petite.*" Leila shook out the filmy silk trousers, blouse, and concealing velvet caftan. "These are for you."

"They're lovely!" Diana exclaimed softly.

Holding each garment up in turn, she delighted in the light's play on the silver embroidery, the mysterious shadows cast by the gauzy silk. They flowed over her fair skin like foam on a restless green sea in the sunlight. Her single dimple flashing with delight, Diana held the silk against her cheek like a bouquet of flowers, fresh rose petals against her skin.

And she wasn't even conscious of her nudity. Leila's smile widened, remembering Diana's discomfort in the baths. Without tension, nature would take its course.

"Come," Leila said, trying not to jar Diana. "I will help you dress." Diana didn't move. *"Petite"*— Leila touched her shoulder gently—"much time has passed."

Diana docilely obeyed her and stepped into the clothes at her direction, giggling at strange fastenings that were so different from her own dresses. The blouse wrapped about her narrow waist and fastened in the back with a single knot, while the trousers tied both front and back. As the delicate fabric whispered over skin made exquisitely sensitive by the massage, she sighed with pleasure.

Even the silver embroidery wasn't stiff and scratchy. A

delicious sensation rippled through her. Then the thickly brocaded caftan enfolded her, and the gleaming weight of her hair was tugged free to hang straight down her back.

As she looked at Leila through sleepy eyes, the harem mistress patted her hand. "Your eyes glow like turquoise, and your hair gleams like gold. The color is perfect for you. Tomorrow, I shall set the seamstresses to work on other things. Now, I must arrange your hair and veils."

"Veils?" Diana asked lazily. The gentle touch of the silks maintained the deliciously detached feeling.

"You must be veiled so no other man can look upon you. Also"—she studied the caftan molding the slender lines of Diana's body, frowning consideringly—"you must wear a djellabah as well as the mandeel."

Slowly stepping around the harem mistress, Diana gazed into the mirror with its silver-gilt border. A stranger stood there; exotic, foreign. Even the clothing was odd, however lovely. The stranger's eyes glowed turquoise beneath drowsing lids, and a delicate flush tinted cheeks and lips. Below, soft velvet clung lovingly to full breasts, and the silver sash holding the robe closed accented a tiny waist. Diana stretched indolently, and the image followed every move.

Reaching up, Leila pressed the girl down onto a small ottoman before the mirror and took a brush from the dressing table. Swift, practiced strokes reduced the tangles into gleaming order. Taking jewel-studded ribbons that matched the sea green caftan, the harem mistress bound Diana's hair simply to pour down her back.

As the harem mistress worked, Leila's running commentary flowed over Diana. The things they'd do tomorrow, the clothes and jewelry, seemed impossibly distant and unimportant. Nothing seemed to matter. Her eyelids drooped lower with each brushstroke.

They were as mesmerizing as the masseuse's hands. Then the first silken veil brushed her face, followed by another, and a warm woolen robe that enveloped her from shoulders to the pair of her own slippers that encased her feet.

Obedient to the gentle tug of Leila's hands, Diana moved slowly to the door, barely aware of the pause when the harem mistress assumed her own djellabah and mandeel. In the corridor, a pair of guards materialized and matched their steps to Leila's gliding, sedate pace.

Lamps glowed at intervals down the dim, silent corridor lighting their path. Eventually, they stopped before a blue door set into the wall of a cavernous room. It was silent, remote, dreamy, and unreal as everything else. Leila rapped gently on the door panel, then opened it. Liquid Arabic containing Diana's name flowed.

The man's voice— Diana took an involuntary step forward. It was rich, deep, attractive, yet strangely slurred. After the high-pitched voices of women all afternoon, it soothed and attracted.

Leila bowed, glanced with satisfaction at Diana, and prodded her forward. "Go in, *petite.*"

The door closed and Diana was alone with the man lounging on cushions in the shadows across the small room. A room that smelled like— Diana sniffed through the veils covering her nose. A distillery. A tiny choke of laughter escaped. It stilled in her throat at his first movement.

The shadowy figure opposite rose and stepped into the pool of light cast by the lamps. Bey Haroun wasn't anything like she'd expected. Eyes widening, she surveyed his lithe figure while silence stretched.

He was taller than expected from Leila's comments reassuring Diana about her height. Instead of a paunch rolling over a sash, his stomach was flat, muscular, and his shoulders broad, his movements graceful. From the open neck of the silk shirt, his throat gleamed golden bronze. A neatly trimmed black beard and mustache hid the jaw, but his cheeks and forehead were the same golden bronze as his throat with the accent of inky brows stroked above his eyes.

More striking than anything else, though, were the eyes that held her. They glowed a rich brown, the color of sherry wine. Drawn, Diana took a step nearer.

* * *

Stepping from behind giant sealed jars outside the oil merchant's gate, the boys approached the inert figure the soldiers had dumped there. Rain dripping from the overhanging roofs occasionally hit the man full on the face. He didn't move despite snorts and snores and mutters.

"Should we?" one boy whispered to the other.

After the faintest hesitation, the older one nodded. "He's an infidel," he answered, his voice growing stronger with each word. He looked nervously down the curving alley toward the palace. They'd never visited this part of town during their nightly forays before. "The soldiers are gone, anyway."

Swallowing hard, the younger boy wiped damp hands on a damper djellabah and edged cautiously forward. "Why did they dump him here?" he whispered.

"Didn't you listen?" The older boy took the lead. "The bey said to throw him outside the palace. Come on," he ordered. Dodging underneath the roof's overhang, he approached the man from the far side.

With experienced hands, he searched the pockets of the strange suit. Nothing valuable was there that he could find. With disgust, he fumbled at the foreign fastenings, then tried to turn the man over. The lax, soft flesh weighed more than expected.

"Help me," the boy commanded. "He weighs more than our mothers combined. Come on, don't be scared."

Hesitating, the younger boy sidled nearer until he stood on the opposite side of the man. Studying him, he frowned. "He looks familiar."

The older boy flicked an exasperated glance up at his companion. "Of course. We've seen him along the docks. I recognize this suit."

"It won't bring much," the younger boy complained.

"He always carries a bag of gold. I've seen it!"

At the mention of gold, the younger boy forgot his fears. Puffing and straining, they flopped the man over. His inert figure sprawled on his belly in a puddle, the oddly naked face propped against one hand.

Silently, the older boy stripped and searched with efficient hands. Sitting back on his heels, he looked at his companion. "The soldiers must've stolen it." He pushed himself up with both hands and wiped them on his patched djellabah before wadding the infidel's clothes into a bundle he stuffed under one arm. "We should've stuck to the docks," he grumbled. "The pickings are richer down there."

No one fell in love at first sight—outside fairy tales. Of course, it'd happened to Mama, but she was a hopeless romantic. Diana was a hardheaded realist, impetuous but hardheaded.

Yet she was hopelessly in love with a man she'd met two hours ago. She didn't understand it. He was her enemy. But so damnably attractive. Her fingers resumed repetitive tracing of the silver scrollwork edging her caftan. Feelings new, novel, powerful, interwove with wonderful relaxation to leave her almost . . . intoxicated. Everything was perfect. Almost. He was her enemy. But his resonant voice and handsome face, the way he moved, and, most of all, his courtesy and sensitivity were what she'd dreamed of.

". . . your parents in Jerusalem," he finished.

"Papa's studying ancient languages. He's corresponding with Champollion about the Rosetta Stone, and—" Her voice faded at the amusement in his eyes. "That wasn't what you asked."

One corner of his finely cut mouth twitching, he poured a thin stream of mint tea into tiny handleless cups. "More tea?" Deliberately, his fingers brushed hers.

The brief touch still vibrated along the back of her hand when he withdrew his and raised a cup in a silent toast. Lifting the other in return, she contemplated him over the rim. He knew her mind had wandered but made it seem natural.

Putting down his cup and smiling slowly, sensually, he

leaned toward her. Time stretched, and she could no longer meet his eyes. Fingers clenching about the cup, she waited with a racing heart that subsided disconsolately when he lightly brushed a tendril of hair off her temple and stroked the curve of her cheek.

Wind rattling the shutter above their heads intensified the silence. Taking a hasty sip of tea, Diana put the cup down and leaned back in the cushions to put extra inches between them. Her cheek still felt his caress. Yet he was her enemy. She couldn't forget it. More than anything, she needed to break the silence, the air of unreality. Soft light glittering off the gold chain draped about his neck drew her attention.

"That's lovely," she murmured huskily, touching it. And jerked her hand back as if it'd been burned.

His smile widening, the bey lifted it over his head. A single lock of black hair fell forward, an inky stroke across his forehead. "It's the official badge of office for the beys of Bizerte that traditionally goes from father to eldest son." Weighing it in one hand, mischief lit his sherry-colored eyes. "Unless, of course, he flagrantly abuses the tenets of the Holy Koran."

He tossed it carelessly on the divan, chuckled softly, and bent, extending one hand toward her. Breath catching in her throat, she moved, but he caught her gently and murmured assurances. She darted a watchful look through the screen of her lashes, intensely conscious of his every movement. The gentle play of his fingers intensified burning awareness.

"Now, about this Rosetta Stone."

"Papa . . ."—she started precipitately, hesitated, and resumed—". . . Papa believes it's the key to—"

The words faded at the delicate tracery of fingers along her slender neck. They came to rest in the hollow at the base of her throat. Swallowing hard, she shivered.

"Yes?" he prompted, and drew one teasing finger in a

feather-light trail along her collarbone. His brows drew together at her tense response.

Taking a deep, shuddering breath, she continued. "The hieroglyphics. Champollion's research in the ruined—"

Her breathing quickened and quickened again at his narrowing gaze. When his hand slipped inside the neck of her caftan and silk blouse to knead her nape strongly, her eyes closed and she arched against the rhythmic pressure. It felt so delicious, the tension in her muscles started to ease. How easy to capitulate. She caught herself guiltily. It'd be disastrous.

Her teeth biting into her lower lip, Diana caught and held his wrist. Concern darkening his eyes, he carefully unwound and placed a kiss on the tip of each of her fingers, then her palm. He resumed the gentle, sensual massage. In spite of herself, she moved in time to the renewed rhythmic pressure of his hand.

Tensing, she grabbed his wrist again, as something flared in his eyes. Unconsciously, she touched her upper lip with the tip of her tongue. He chuckled softly and swooped to feather a kiss across parted lips. Air rushed out in a small, soft breath. Light-headed, Diana lifted dazed eyes, her promise to Leila haunting her.

But that was before she fell in love. If she gave in, she'd never escape. If she escaped, she'd never see him again. It wasn't fair!

"Go on," he urged quietly.

"The ruined temple—" She gasped as he touched the vulnerable inner flesh of her wrist with his tongue.

"What temple?"

Beard and mustache grazed sensitive skin of the inside of her forearm. Her throat tightened unbearably. "King Solomon's—" she whispered.

Laughter sparkling in his eyes, he laid a finger across her mouth. "You talk too much."

The motion of his lips held her mesmerized; the timbre of his voice stroked her nerves like velvet. Somehow everything would work out. She felt like singing. Dear, sweet, romantic Mama was right. Had she felt like this when she fell in love with Papa? Wonderfully bemused, Diana watched the bey reach up to her hair.

He tugged once, and the heavy weight fell in a soft cloud about her shoulders and neck. As she pushed it back from her face, he tossed the restraining jeweled hair ribbons away. Sailing in a fluttering arc, they landed beside chain and turban and glittered in the soft flare of dying lamplight, mere diamond splinters against sea green.

Lifting the glowing curtain of silver-gilt hair, he let it sift through his fingers, until it tumbled free of his hand, over her shoulders, and spilled on to the cushions behind. Scooting a few inches back, Diana tucked her hair out of the way and tried to think. There had to be a way out.

Trembling, she hastened on, wanting but unable to give in. "The temple was razed by the Romans."

The distance wasn't enough. Stretching easily, he traced the edge of her lips, the dusting of freckles on nose and cheeks, the shallow dimple, with a single finger. He smiled with curious gentleness.

Diana shifted restlessly. Retreating farther was impossible. She sat at the end of the divan, and beyond that was the wall. Besides, there was no place to run to, and he made running seem futile.

Not thinking, she stroked his cheek and down the strong column of his neck. The silken crispness of the hair curling from his chest was another delicious shock. Involuntarily, she shivered and pulled her hand back. This was what she must guard against—herself. She was dangerously close to forgetting.

And the bey wasn't helping. In one enticing sweep of his hand, he molded the sea-green caftan to her body. Even through the velvet, his touch left a burning trail along her skin. More than ever, she wanted to surrender. But she couldn't.

Exhilarating sensation nearly overwhelmed her when his

hand fleetingly brushed the side of her breast. Small tremors rippled over her skin, yet she was so warm. Loosening the caftan's neck in search of cooler air, she took a shuddering breath.

Dimly, the sound of cold, fitful rain and gusty wind hitting the shutters high above registered. That was outside. Inside was delightfully, enticingly warm, almost too warm.

Loosening the silver sash binding her narrow waist, he negligently cast it aside. It tumbled through the air to drape over the beaten-brass tea tray, gathering wan light from every part of the room.

Taking a deep breath, Diana dragged her gaze from the gleaming brass-and-silver tableau as he leaned forward, looming over her. "M-my-" she began, and never finished.

He explored the exposed hollow beneath her ear while kneading the soft flesh just beneath her breasts. With a deep-throated purr, her lashes drifted closed as she kneaded the silk of his shirt. With deliberation, he brought their lips together.

Sensuality submerged her—sensuality that centered first on sensitized lips, then fueled an ache building deep within. A small sound escaping her throat, she strained upward, striving to press full length against him and end the sensual torture. The rise and fall of his chest brushing her swollen breasts tantalized unbearably through the silk.

It was no barrier. Feverishly, Diana plucked at his shoulders, arms, chest, before winding her hands in his hair and holding his face tightly against her. Long seconds passed as his lips caressed, seconds that increased the aching throb. Desolation struck when he leaned back to remove his shirt, desolation that cleared her head. Gathering strength, Diana pushed away, holding him at arm's length. If she didn't now, she never would.

"M-my lord, please stop," she said, and swallowed. Karim had warned of the consequences, but she had to chance it.

"Why, *petite?*"

The bey's concubines were well-trained beauties who knew how to please a man. They were eager and pliant. Yet, Diana— He stroked the side of her neck, desire building at the satin smoothness.

He frowned when she tensed and pushed harder against his chest. She'd been enjoying herself, yet there was tension and fear in her face. He wouldn't have an unwilling woman sharing his bed, no matter how much he wanted her.

Her fingers tensed on his chest as she spoke. "I was kidnapped, my lord, and sold into your harem. My parents will pay a large ransom for me if I'm returned . . ."—a soft flush climbed her cheeks, and she drew the caftan closed about her—". . . unharmed."

Straightening away from her, Garrett's eyes narrowed. Absently, he scratched his cheek. Her expression stopped him.

With one hand holding the front of the caftan closed, she reached up. In a quick jerk, she pulled the fake beard off and held it, dangling between them. Her eyes still on his face, her own went white.

"You aren't the bey."

CHAPTER V

SCRAMBLING OFF THE DIVAN, DIANA DEMANDED, "WHO
are you?"

Rising, he moved casually between her and the door and
swept an elegant bow despite tousled hair and half-open
shirt. "Garrett Hamilton at your service, Miss—"

"Graham." She tossed the beard beside the chain and
retrieved her silver sash. "Diana Graham, Mr. Hamilton."

"Delighted to make your acquaintance. You're American,
aren't you?"

"From Boston, Massachusetts." Turning away, she tied
the caftan closed and held it shut with one trembling hand
at her throat. Facing him, she asked, "What are you doing
in the bey's palace?" Diana pushed tumbled hair behind her
ear.

With a grin that was supremely confident, he lounged at
ease in the dim light, arms crossed over his chest. "Just
cutting a lark." He looked at her and sighed. "Why did it
have to be you, Diana? The day was going so well."

Shocked, Diana stared at him. "You're mad." She'd fallen
in love with a madman.

"That's the consensus of my family," he agreed. His grin
widened. "And I think we know each other well enough for
you to call me Garrett, Diana."

A slow blush crept up her cheeks, and she tightened her hold on the robe. "I hope you've thought of how to get out of here."

Garrett shrugged negligently. "My men are gone from Bizerte by now, and there's a ship waiting for me."

A soft sigh of relief escaped Diana. "How long do we have?"

"We?" He paused in the act of picking up a cushion. "This escape"—he settled on the divan—"was planned for one."

Diana stared in shock. He didn't feel for her what she did for him. Worse, she still loved him. Fingers stiff on the velvet caftan where she clutched it, she straightened. "This escape is about to be replanned."

"There's no way I can take Haroun's concubine with me." He tossed the cushion onto the floor.

"I am *not* Haroun's concubine, I am *not* your concubine, and I'm *not* staying here!" Diana gestured emphatically with each statement. He tossed two more cushions off the divan and stuffed another beneath his head.

"Sorry, Diana," he answered abstractedly, "it's not possible." He shoved at the low table beside the divan with one foot.

"Listen, Garrett, either we both go or—"

Focusing on her for the first time since lounging back, his grin widened engagingly. "Haroun would be furious!"

Garrett threw his head back with a soft shout of laughter that echoed faintly around the small room. Arms crossed and fingers tapping, Diana waited for him to finish.

Wiping tears from his eyes, he said in a half-strangled voice, "It's too good to pass up."

"What is?" she asked, not trusting the devilry lurking in his face. Chuckling, he wiped his eyes again and tossed another handful of cushions onto the floor to give him more room. Diana repeated the question.

The dangerous glint increasing, he snagged her wrist abruptly and pulled her down. "You're coming," he whispered, his lips delicately brushing her temple. Already his hands created seductive magic that rekindled the fires.

Despite the demands of her senses, Diana desperately pushed away. "We've got to hurry."

An amused rumble deep in his throat greeted her warning. "I never hurry." With gentle force, he brought her down for a luxuriant kiss.

"That's not what I meant." She gasped when he finally released her lips. "We've got to escape before Karim discovers us."

"If we leave now"—Garrett stretched up and feathered a kiss across her parted lips—"Karim will," he explained, punctuating each word with another kiss, "be suspicious."

"Garrett, no." Putting her fingers over his mouth, she shoved against his chest with her other hand. He yielded a few inches, his eyes dancing with merriment and sensuality. She sighed. "If we leave quietly, he'll never know."

His voice slightly muffled by her fingers, he corrected her, "If we leave, the guards will report it to their captain." He squeezed her shoulder reassuringly when she tensed. "Jamil won't dare not wake Karim and tell him the bey and his newest concubine left without escort at a highly unusual time."

"We'll be long gone by then on the ship."

"Not in the middle of this dark a night. We might as well put up a sign telling them we're breaking the law. They'd stop us before we could cast off. We'll have plenty of time to leave with the tide in the morning."

"But we're still in the palace," she protested.

"What better place to hide? I'm always up early." Smiling sensuously, he pulled her toward him, one hand compelling on the back of her neck. "Don't worry so much. We have better ways to pass the time."

Without the beard, his mouth felt like velvet. And his hands worked magic again. With a supreme effort, she stiffened, refusing to respond.

Finally, he freed her lips and propped himself on one

elbow. "No?" he asked, eyes heavy-lidded and face flushed with desire.

Mutely, she shook her head.

"Then I suppose we should go to sleep." With one hand still resting on her stomach, Garrett stretched for a blanket and started to cover them. "Although it's not going to be easy."

"I'm not sleeping with you."

One inky brow arched in wry comprehension. "What do you suggest? There's only one blanket." He held it up, then nodded toward the small brass brazier in the corner. "That's going to die. When it does, it'll get chilly in here. And I'm not calling the servants for more coal," he finished, with a significant glance at the door with its fluted curves that reminded her of the men guarding it.

"But I won't sleep with you."

"It's your choice"—Garrett stole a quick kiss—"but it's my blanket."

A gleam of humor flared in her eyes, and she rolled free of the hand still resting lightly on her. Taking the smallest cushions, she arranged them in a row down the center. With the last one tucked beneath her head, she smiled at Garrett as she pulled the cover over her.

"The bundling board is an old New England custom. Winters in Massachusetts are long, cold, and most houses have few rooms. A courting couple goes to the girl's bedroom for privacy." Garrett's expression nearly disrupted the calm facade held carefully in place. "To stay warm, they climb into bed fully clothed and put a board between them." Smiling sweetly, she finished, "It's very innocent. Good night." Turning away, she closed her eyes.

Silence descended, punctuated by the intermittent rattle of wind on the shutters. Holding still, Diana lay on her side, eyes closed, but listening. Nothing happened, but she could feel his gaze on her. And he was still sitting up, watching, waiting. The shutters rattled four, then five, times before he finally moved.

The divan bounced as he stretched full length. A disgruntled sound made her lips twitch. Turning twice, he finally settled with the blanket pulled taut.

The wind beating against the shutters slowly died. The room cooled, the lamps dimmed, and tension drained gradually from her. Until Garrett turned.

Cold air flowed in to bathe Diana. She grabbed the blanket, tucked it firmly beneath her, and waited for a response. None came. Slowly relaxing, her breathing evened, and she slept restlessly.

His hand drifting over her hip nearly shot her out of bed some time later. Heart racing, Diana shoved it over the pillow barrier and stared at him in the dim light. He was sleeping; at least he seemed to be. She drifted off again into an uneasy doze. One of the lamps burned out with a small hiss, and Diana shivered, pulling the blanket more tightly about her shoulders. The night went on forever.

She awoke, warm, comfortable, with light in her eyes. Something prickly tickled cheek and palm through silk, and she was warm, so very nice and warm. Sighing, she snuggled closer, fingers tracing a tiny pattern. She felt so safe, so . . . contented until slowly contentment mounted into awareness. Tipping her head back, she met Garrett's eyes. They glowed, gold lighting the rich sherry color, and held her prisoner. Slowly, giving her time to pull back, he moved, his lips closing on hers.

"Garrett—" she began, not sure what to say, and stopped when he stiffened.

He sat up, gaze on the shuttered window. "What time is it?" Sunlight pried through a thousand cracks to illuminate the room.

Diana pushed herself up as he scrambled off the bed. "Are we late?"

"Very," he answered with a grimace. "That was *not* a good night's sleep. Hurry. Although," he said, eyeing her, "I wish we had longer."

Ready color ran up under her fair skin as she looked

down at herself. Somehow during the night—with Garrett's aid?—the sash had come off and the caftan hung open. Sea-green silk shimmered across pale skin but hid nothing. If anything, it emphasized. Her nipples tautened at his almost tactile gaze before she pulled the caftan closed.

"But it can't be helped. Dress as you did last night, and the guards won't suspect anything." He winked at her. "Trust me."

A studied expression drew Garrett's brows together and replaced the wink. He weighed the gold necklace in one hand before draping it around his neck over the amethyst brocade caftan. Bending again, he pulled a djellabah of sand beige wool from behind the divan.

Shoving the blankets away, she searched for the slippers kicked off sometime during the previous evening. Finally, she spotted them beneath the low table, bent to retrieve them, and straightened with a gasp. She knocked away the hand fondling her rear. "Behave yourself." She stretched for the slippers again, the caftan taut around her shoulders.

"Can you ride in that?"

"Of course I can. Oh!" An unwelcome thought drew her brows together. "No sidesaddle."

"Have you ever ridden astride?"

"I'll manage." Diana tightened the sash about her slender waist.

"I believe you will." His smile held a measure of respect. "Now quit fooling around and hurry."

Sending him an annoyed look, she dropped the sheer wool mandeel on the divan and grabbed the veils. The fine cords holding the silk veil tangled insistently with her tousled hair. It seemed so simple when Leila fastened them for her. Muttering, she smoothed her hair and tried again. And again. Nothing worked, not even knotting it in front and twisting the veil around her head. Frustrated, she glanced at Garrett.

He was inspecting his beard and mustache. Satisfied, he dropped the small bag with the mirror and jar of glue behind the divan. Thrusting a pistol into the caftan's sash around his lean waist, he concealed it beneath his djellabah.

"Ready?"

She shook her head and extended the veils. "Can you tie these?"

Crossing the small room in a pair of easy strides, he tipped her chin up. "Your wish is my command."

The gold in his eyes glistened, and Diana knew she should step back. Nothing kept her from moving. His grip was no barrier, yet she couldn't move. Slowly, he lowered his head and covered her lips with his.

Diana stiffened, but only for an instant. Insidious warmth arrowed through her, renewing the delicious ache she'd slept with all night. Without volition, her hands went about his neck to pull him closer, her lips softening beneath his. She felt him tremble, and his hands moved searchingly on her back.

Shaken, Garrett pulled away. "Control yourself. We haven't time to fool around."

Keeping silent with an effort, Diana let him tie her veils and pull the hood of her djellabah up over the shining, pale swathe of hair. She was a hardheaded realist, she reminded herself, and he was her only means of escape. Fuming inwardly, she followed him out the door, a proper step and a half behind. The *only* means.

Jamil ibn Fazi blinked at the figure striding across the courtyard silhouetted against the brilliance of the rising sun. It was the bey, though it couldn't be. Behind the bey, another figure scurried, a harem concubine.

Jamil raced forward to greet Haroun. What was he doing here this early in the morning? For that matter, why was he here at all? He never came near the stable and barracks. If he wanted a horse or guards, he sent a message, and Jamil dispatched them to the courtyard outside the audience chamber doors.

"Captain." The bey's icy voice halted him ten feet away. "The men are a disgrace."

"My lord? But—"

Darting a nervous glance around the courtyard, Jamil snapped to attention and locked his heels. Things were in the usual early morning disarray, and the stableboys were still mucking out the stalls. Yet the horses had all been groomed, and the guards not on duty were preparing for drill. Jamil's gaze returned to the bey's frown and promptly dropped to the cobblestones beneath his feet. A wisp of dung-spattered straw lay there. Before he could step on it, the bey saw it, and his voice grew even icier.

"I am disgraced by such slovenliness among the soldiers sworn to preserve our city. Have the men turn out for a full dress inspection, one fit for the Sultan. And have a pair of horses saddled instantly. My concubine and I will ride while you rectify your errors."

"Yes, my lord." Jamil bowed low and backed a step away. "I shall—"

"Don't bother with an escort." The bey's cold voice cut him off. "I wish to inspect all the men when I return. Now, where are those horses?"

Blinking in the bright sunlight, Jamil kept his eyes fixed on the cobblestones. From one darted glance he'd recognized the fury in the bey. Jamil swallowed hard and hurried to obey. He had never yet decorated the bey's infrequently used whipping post, and wished to keep the record intact.

Garrett watched him scurry across the courtyard with pleasure. Rudeness carried such a convincing air of verisimilitude. Jamil had no more than glanced at his face once he was close enough for recognition. And Diana had remembered her role. She hadn't spoken since they left the antechamber.

"Garrett!" The urgent whisper reached his ears as she tugged on his sleeve. Frowning, he motioned her to hush. Ignoring the gesture, she tugged again and whispered, "Karim's coming! Do we have time to wait for the horses?"

From the barracks compound next to the stable came Karim's voice riding over other early morning noises. Listening intently, Garrett translated in a voiceless whisper. "Karim's telling off a servant. We still have a few minutes."

Brows drawn together, Diana darted a look toward the stable. From inside, the guard captain's shouted commands provided a counterpoint to Karim's tirade. A horse neighed and kicked at the wooden sides of its stall.

Squeezing her arm in reassurance, Garrett scanned the courtyard. Nothing unusual yet. Now, to escape before Karim arrived. Fortunately, the horses were being led from the stables by a pair of worried guards, with Jamil hurrying them along like a shepherd with recalcitrant sheep.

Diana broke free of his grip and ran over to the smaller horse, a cream-colored mare. Garrett followed quickly. "You call this grooming?" he demanded, indicating the gleaming saddle leathers. "I will not have my newest concubine see such disgraceful sloppiness."

"Yes, my lord—" Jamil bowed deeply again and didn't rise.

"Braid satin ribbons in the manes and tails of all the horses. And see that they are properly caparisoned."

Jamil jerked, starting to straighten, until he took in Garrett's uncompromising posture. Bobbing in a series of dips, he responded obsequiously, "As you say, my lord."

As he spoke, Garrett shot a glance at Diana to see if she'd mounted. She'd managed to get her left foot into the stirrup and had the reins properly gathered in one hand. Balancing on the ball of the other foot, she tried to swing up into the saddle but failed. The cream-colored horse stood rock-steady. A soft word brought a quick grin to Garrett's face. Her next attempt was successful, if not graceful. Once mounted, she sat in the saddle with djellabah and caftan hiked up about her knees.

Shooting Diana a look of pure recklessness, he resumed. "While we're gone, see the men and their mounts wear matching ribbons." As he spoke, Garrett swept the courtyard with a comprehensive gaze; the guards had faded away from the presence of the irate bey.

"But my lord—"

"Enough! To your duties."

As Jamil scurried off, Garrett swung up into the saddle and urged the sorrel to a trot as soon as the outer gate opened. Diana's horse kept up easily. Garrett flashed a smile at her once they were out into the square, then looked up at the sky and swore softly. From the angle of the sun, the tide had turned. They were late.

"Hurry up!" he yelled over his shoulder.

At the touch of a spur, his horse leapt ahead into the crowd filling the street leading out of the square. Diana leaned forward and eased her grip on the reins. The small Arabian mare stretched into an easy gallop that took her breath away. The brisk wind of their passage pushed the veils into her face, but that didn't bother her. Not even riding astride kept exhilaration down. She was free of the palace. Excitement flared in her. If the ship was still in the harbor, she was completely free. Except that she never could be again. And she gloried at the thought of Garrett at her side. When they finally escaped. But, unless she wanted to be left behind, she needed to keep up with him now.

Intent on the flying pennon of the sorrel's pale gold tail, she almost didn't see the pack of youngsters dart from beneath the hooves. Her hands tightened on the reins. Misinterpreting the signal, the mare gathered herself to hop over the mound of spilled baskets the youngsters had left behind. Nearly falling on the mare's neck, Diana clutched wildly at the saddle, the mane, anything to keep from falling. But she didn't drop the reins.

"Garrett!" she shouted. "Not so fast!" She clung desperately to the saddle, thighs aching from the unfamiliar riding style.

Slowing, he yelled back, "Keep your heels down and hold on with your knees! Now hurry up!"

He spurred his horse back into a gallop. Mouth dry, she

followed, heels down and knees gripping tightly. She still kept one hand on the saddle.

Shrieks of terror and anguish met their headlong pace. She kept the mare behind the pale gold tail of Garrett's horse. He seemed intent on creating as much chaos as possible. But he cleared a path for them.

Jerking hard on the reins, she swerved to keep from running down a panicked woman. Diana's heart settled permanently in her throat. A basket tumbled as someone scurried to safety against the terra-cotta wall. Fortunately, the well-trained mare didn't rear.

Her mouth thinned grimly beneath the veil as she brought her horse's nose back in line with Garrett's. Behind, the wails and shrieks faded beneath noise ahead. Tightening her grip, Diana leaned forward and urged her horse on.

A water drop hit his cheek and rolled off his nose. Haroun slapped at it, then groaned. Every muscle in his body ached like evil jinns had made merry. He shifted, his hand splashing in water. He was soaking wet. Another drop hit, this time on his temple, sending a stab of pain through his head.

Allah, Hamilton's liquor was potent. He ached from head to toe. But why was he wet and chilled? Haroun struggled to a sitting position. Groaning, he pressed both hands to his temples and waited for his head to stop spinning. Moving slowly, he looked around. This wasn't his palace.

Giant oil jars huddled near a flimsy wooden gate across the alley. A light breeze gusted, sending a shower of water drops off the overhanging roof and onto the bey's bare back. Haroun started to rise, and sank back with a groan. By the beard of the Prophet, he had the grandfather of all headaches. Why had he imbibed so freely from the infidel's pestilential bottle of whiskey?

And where were his clothes? Splotches of mud covered his body from shoulder to toe. And beneath were developing bruises, some already gaudily purple and blue, others barely green.

Bracing himself against the wall, he staggered to his feet, moaning and grumbling softly under his breath. Hamilton's death would be slow for urging him to drink this whiskey. Questions must be answered, punishments meted out; but first he must find something to wear. A flash of colored fabric through the rickety gate across the way caught his eye.

Gingerly, he started across the alley, wincing at every stone cutting into his soft feet, every stab of pain through his head, and every shiver that aggravated the ache in his muscles. At least the giant oil jars protected him from the sting of the breeze. And the stick wedging the gate shut was easy to reach through the wide cracks.

Squeezing through the opening, Haroun stepped into the silent, empty yard. A dull red caftan hung on a railed stairway leading up to the warehouse's double doors across the courtyard. Pace quickening, the bey winced across to the stairway and yanked the caftan down.

By the time he reached the square before the palace, the coarse red wool was torturing his skin. The sweat pouring off him at the smallest exertion only made his discomfort worse. Squinting in the brilliant sun, Haroun hunched his shoulders against the prickly fabric. The main gate was open, though it shouldn't be, and the street across from the alley was in turmoil. A babble of noise that made him flinch poured from it.

Holding his head stiffly against the fireball behind his eyes, he strode across the square. A few feet short of the open gate, a guard ordered him to halt. Haroun smiled grimly, lifted his pounding head for the guard to see his face, and strode on.

"Halt, dog!"

Haroun winced at the shout in his ear and turned. A sword hovered inches from his belly. "How dare you? Give me your name and rank—"

"Shut up, scum. How dare *you* enter our bey's palace!"

The soldier prodded Haroun's belly lightly with the tip of the sword.

"I am your bey." Haroun knocked the sword away.

Disdain gave way to sympathy in the young guard's face. "Allah has blessed you by taking your reason." Stepping back, his sword dropped to his side. "I will not call the captain of the guard, but you must leave."

"I am the bey, you son of a dog." Icy rage edged Haroun's voice.

"Our bey has a beard and mustache. And he wouldn't wear that caftan." The guard patted Haroun's shoulder consolingly. "You must leave before Lord Karim comes. He is not very understanding."

Haroun clapped both hands on his chin and found bare skin and the prickle of a single night's whiskers. Fury routed his headache. Haroun pointed at the guard captain, Jamil, who'd arrived to investigate.

"You. Find my brother, Karim. And if you value your skin, don't come back without him." Not waiting to see if Jamil left, the bey turned back to the young guard. "I don't know your name, but you will clean the stables from now until next Ramadan."

Shifting, the younger guard swallowed and looked to Jamil for guidance. The guard captain leaned forward to peer at Haroun's face. Remembering recent odd events, Jamil spoke uneasily. "He . . . he could be the bey."

"But that caftan!" the younger guardsman protested. "And—"

"Jamil, find Karim. Don't make me tell you again."

Jamil hesitated, then turned to the guardsman. "Keep an eye on him until I return with Lord Karim."

Jamil dashed toward Karim's private courtyard. Haroun's lips tightened with grim satisfaction. Soon this farrago would be over, and he'd soothe his aching body with a warm bath and soft clothing. And contemplate the pleasure of Hamilton's slow death. The bey moved his shoulders against the prickly discomfort of the caftan and ignored the agitated young guardsman standing beside him, his sword tip dragging against the cobblestones now.

Karim strode at a leisurely pace toward them a few minutes later. Annoyance joined the discomfort, frustration, and anger inside Haroun. His brother would soon realize whom he kept waiting at the gate.

"Karim!" the bey called, his deep voice booming against the high stone walls. "Get over here."

His brother's even stride hesitated before he continued at the same unhurried pace. Arriving, he bowed with ironic grace. Peering down at the beardless face in the dimmer light, Karim stroked his own luxuriant beard.

"Is this the madman—" Karim cleared his throat "—the blessed of Allah who claims to be our bey?"

"Brother!" Karim's cool insolence as much as his beard further incensed Haroun. "Tell these fools who I am."

"Who are you?"

"Your brother. The one you failed to protect so that I awoke in an alley this morning." Haroun tugged at the collar of his caftan where the wool particularly abraded his skin.

"My Lord Karim, the bey left already this morning with his latest concubine," Jamil blurted. He looked stricken, then moved hastily back, worried over his temerity.

"Is this true, brother?" Forgetting the difference in their height, the bey closed the distance between them.

Karim took a hasty step back, a grimace of distaste twisting his thin mouth at the smell of stale whiskey. Waving his hand before his face, he nodded. "You must be Haroun. No other true believer would—" He stopped at the bey's ferocious glare.

"Is it true that a man masquerading as me has left with my latest concubine?" the bey asked with deadly softness. "You fail to protect me and allow infidels to raid my harem!"

Certainty narrowed Karim's eyes, and he turned to Jamil. "Which direction did Hamilton and the girl take?"

"They went through there, my lord." Jamil pointed toward the street Haroun had noticed as he entered the square. People milled about, picking up goods and brushing dirt from their clothing. "On horseback, my lord. The concubine rode her own horse."

Gulping at the displeasure in Karim's face, Jamil followed the security chief's gaze. A blue ribbon dangled from his hand. A flush climbing his thin cheeks, he yanked it behind his back. Karim's smile promised retribution.

"So she can ride." Karim's eyes narrowed. "We shall have to work that into her punishment. You gave them horses, Jamil. What else have you done?"

Jamil swallowed and licked his lips again. "The b-bey ordered a full dress inspection. Including," he finished in a rush, "ribbons for the horses' tails and in the guards' beards."

He shrank in on himself, waiting for the explosion.

"What!" Pressing his fingers to his temples for a moment, Haroun shook his head slightly. "Karim, find them! They'll head for the docks." He plucked at the irritatingly coarse fabric covering his belly. "Have them back here within the hour."

How Diana's thighs hurt. Ahead, Garrett yelled and waved his left arm wildly. A man dove for the side of the street. And a small, overburdened camel kicked free of his master and joined the mad procession behind Diana. She kept the mare behind the sorrel and held on. Grinning behind her veils, she yelled wildly, too. The whole episode was mad, crazy, but incredibly exhilarating.

A half-unloaded donkey, the straps binding his baskets hanging to the ground, took exception to their noisy passage. Braying, he broke free and ran, bucking, straight for her. A small basket flew free of the last remaining strap and sailed over her head, while a streak of brightly colored fabric streamed behind him.

Enjoying a rare gallop, the mare was determined to catch

the sorrel, and no donkey was going to stop her. Without guidance from Diana, she swerved. Neighing shrilly, the horse gathered herself and leapt lightly over several rolled rugs stacked to the right of their path. Instinctively, Diana balanced on the balls of her feet in the stirrups and leaned forward over the horse's mane. And when the mare landed on the other side with the donkey balked by the rug barrier, Diana settled back into the saddle.

Taking a deep breath, her grin widened. Riding astride was easy. Intoxicated with exuberance, she urged the mare on. Garrett had gained several lengths on her, and he wasn't slowing for anything. Not even for the knot of people gathered before a vendor's stall.

With a louder roar than any before, he drove toward them. Screaming, some dived on the stall counter. It collapsed with slow grace, carrying them and the vendor down in a tangle of blankets and his lunch. Others scattered in the opposite direction, where they safely mingled with the throng huddled to one side. But one youngster tried to outrun Garrett's horse.

The breath caught in Diana's throat as the pounding hooves came closer and closer to the boy. In the confusion ahead, there was nowhere for him to escape. Her hands tightened on saddle and reins, and her voice rose over the cries of the crowd.

Whether Garrett heard or not, she couldn't tell. But he guided his mount a hair to the side, and with one arm swept the child up and carried him a few strides. Barely slowing at a stall displaying mounds of cushions, Garrett dropped the boy onto a soft pile, where he began crying. Straightening in the saddle, Garrett roared another warning and charged on.

With a fleet stride, the mare wove through the chaos down the path Garrett had cleared until she hovered once again behind the sorrel's tail. Diana shouted in glee and let the mare choose her own way behind him.

The color and clamor surrounding them were fabulous. As they swept past, people clambered out of their way, heeding Garrett's bellowed warnings. Then he plunged abruptly to the left.

Her heart quickened painfully as she hauled on the reins. Tossing her head, the mare ignored Diana and soared over a pile of fabric and poles that had been a vendor's stall. With a dextrous twist, the mare skirted the dense throng that Garrett had avoided and was back behind the sorrel in another few strides.

Heart pounding, Diana grabbed the saddle with one hand again. Maybe she didn't have quite the hang of riding astride yet. They swept around the congested heart of the market toward a wide street leading out of it. Both the mare and the sorrel stretched into a fast gallop, and Garrett's bellows sent some stragglers diving against the wall among the scribes.

A stall that looked familiar flashed past, and Diana twisted in the saddle. And as quickly faced forward to keep her balance. But she'd seen enough. That was the stall where she'd bought all that glorious cloth—the rose brocade and silk, the silver-trimmed indigo, and the moss green. She was going to miss those dresses.

The last few stalls disappeared, and they thundered into the relatively less crowded street leading down to the docks. Flashing past the last of the blue doors, the last stretch of drab sand-colored walls, they plunged onto the open docks. Garrett pulled his rearing mount up. A pair of cargo ships and a galley were tied up at the docks. The fishing fleet was gone in search of the day's catch.

"Which is it?" Diana asked when the mare finished dancing in protest against the tight rein.

Garrett smiled ironically and pointed.

Turning her head, she saw a brig slowly making its way out of the harbor.

CHAPTER VI

KARIM SWEPT OUT OF HIS QUARTERS, SCIMITAR SWINGING at his side and an elaborately inlaid rifle slung over his shoulder. He ran down the stairs to the last step overlooking the barracks courtyard. Stopping, his mouth twisted with disgust. Damned infidel. A very few men were properly dressed, but even their weapons showed signs of hasty polishing. Brightly colored ribbons dangled from a few horsetails, fluttering in the light breeze.

Hamilton would pay dearly.

"Jamil," Karim bellowed, moving down the last step.

Horses reared or nipped each other, reflecting the soldiers' tension. Rumors had flown the moment Haroun appeared at the gate, ragged and beardless. Who spread them, Karim didn't know. He'd find out, though. His riding whip tapped a relentless tattoo on his riding boot. And his face didn't relax when the guard captain ran up and saluted.

"Sir!"

"Send a squad of men to the city gates. Have them mount a search and let no strangers out of the city. It could be a ruse. Hamilton and the girl may not have fled to the harbor."

"Yes, my lord."

"And, Jamil," he added with icy softness, "since the men are so fond of dressing up, see they're prepared for a particularly rigorous inspection when we return." The whip stilled against the riding boot. "Without those damned ribbons."

Jamil swallowed and took a deep breath. "Yes, my lord."

Karim swung up onto a silvery gray mare held by a nervous stableboy. Kamillah, the perfect one, was the color of his favorite falcon, and just as sensitive. Running a soothing hand down her arched neck, he waited until the guard captain was in the saddle before giving the signal to ride.

In seconds they were through the palace gate and galloping across the square. From the uproar in the street, Hamilton and the girl were only a short distance ahead.

Racing along the stone dock, Diana clung grimly to the saddle. They'd hurried before, but now, without obstacles impeding them, they raced full out. Yet, where were they going? High walls bristled with guns above the harbor. There was no escape that way.

Hugging the mare's neck, her eyes teared in the wind blasting her face. Then they were away from the docks and on the sandy beach, where the tide ebbed strongly. As they stopped near some ramshackle houses, Garrett swung down from the sweating sorrel, and she scrambled off her mare. He thrust the reins at Diana and pointed to the cluster of low buildings.

"Hide them up there. Hurry." He started toward a beached European longboat.

Remembering his reluctance to take her along, Diana caught his arm. "You won't leave without me?"

A reckless grin on his face, he feathered a brief kiss across her lips. "Trust me."

Then he was gone, running toward the boat and a fisherman repairing a net. Dazed, she watched him go. The sorrel pulling restively at the reins released her frozen legs. Stumbling and slipping in the loose sand, she towed the horses behind her.

Panting, she stopped when scraggly grass and stony ground replaced loose sand. A straggling row of terra-cotta and sandy beige houses stretched along the shore. Dark red and blue shutters blocked the breeze angling in off the bay; the front steps and yards were deserted. Even the gates leading into walled passages and courtyards presented a silent, forbidding appearance.

Except one. A few houses away a gate stood open. Forcing her exhausted legs to move, she towed the horses inside the yard. There was barely room for them, but scrubby grass grew in the pavement cracks, and a chipped basin was full of yesterday's rainwater. Crooning soft apologies for not walking them after their wild run, she tethered them within reach of grass and water and closed the gate.

Her ears straining for the sound of hoofbeats, Diana ran across the sand. As she raced up, Garrett was throwing the half-repaired net out of the boat into which he'd already tossed his caftan and djellabah. The fisherman gestured wildly toward the small damaged mast and babbled in Arabic.

Diana didn't need a translation. This boat wasn't going to sail today. But there were three sets of oarlocks.

His silk shirt billowing in the light breeze, Garrett snarled something that made the fisherman jump from the boat onto the sand. With both of them shoving on the bow, it moved a few inches, then stuck. The fisherman straightened, opened his hands, and shrugged.

Tucking up her sleeves, Diana joined them. "Tell him to push harder."

The ice in Garrett's voice galvanized the man into furious action. Along with Garrett and Diana, he leaned against the boat. It finally, with nerve-stretching slowness, began to move again.

Inch by inch it crept toward the retreating waterline until the stern began to float. In spasms, the boat slid into the water, alternately floating and then grounding in sand. Cold water lapped about their toes, their ankles, then their calves. Shoving harder when it lifted on the next wave, they took a long step forward and plunged unexpectedly into water up to their waists. The skirts of her caftan and djellabah drifted about her, tangling, but Diana didn't care. Over the waves' slap, she thought she heard the sound of horses' hooves. But the docks were still innocent of abnormal activity.

While the fisherman held the boat steady, Garrett scrambled in, Diana after him a second later. While she wrung out dripping skirts, he grabbed the fisherman and hauled him into the boat before he could retreat to the shore. The little man hunkered down in the stern, darting resentful glances at them.

Dropping the wadded skirt, Diana asked quietly, "What's wrong with him?" They hefted oars into the oarlocks while the fisherman watched uncomprehendingly.

"He's scared he's done something wrong." Garrett nodded at the fisherman who started at the sound of their voices. "Even though he believes I'm the bey, he's afraid the boat's owner won't like it."

"He's probably right." She seated herself toward the bow and grasped the oars.

The bent, wizened man scrambled over to the rudder at a brusque order. Garrett pointed at the ship drawing near the mouth of the harbor and the open sea. Although the light breeze barely filled the sails, the ebb tide carried her relentlessly away. "Row," he added briefly in English.

Their goal seemed impossibly far, but Diana leaned into the oars in time with Garrett's strokes. The weather-beaten wood bit into the soft skin of her palms. These oars weren't like the ones she'd used on the Charles River.

Nor was the boat; it was too long. At first, it responded sluggishly. Then they slipped free of the shallows, and the boat slid through the water faster, aided by the tide. Garrett's oars moved in a regular rhythm she worked hard to match. If she didn't, they'd interfere with each other and lose time.

With each dip of the oars, they pulled farther from shore, farther from Karim and recapture. They'd made good their escape. Diana smiled joyously. She was *free*. And the day promised to be glorious. Gulls soared against the sun-washed pale blue sky, their cries in raucous counterpoint to the rhythmic creak of the oars in their locks. Even the befuddled little man at the rudder finally seemed to accept his fate.

In spite of the light, cool breeze, Garrett was sweating, and his white silk shirt clung in patches. Beneath it, muscles tensed and relaxed in a fascinating rhythm. Spellbound, she kept her oars moving in time with his and savored the rippling of powerful muscles.

Breathing quickly, Diana laughed aloud. "Isn't it wonderful?"

"What?" Garrett asked absently. Though his strokes didn't falter, his attention remained fixed on the docks.

"We've escaped. They can't catch us now."

He nodded toward shore. "We're still in musket range."

"Clear the way," Karim roared and spurred his mare forward.

The men swept out of the street behind him, their horses at a canter. Still yelling, Karim's eyes narrowed grimly. From the destruction, it was obvious the infidels had passed this way. Karim lifted his mare, Kamillah, over a pile of baskets. She landed lightly on the far side of the jumble and dodged a chest lying with contents scattered across the roadway.

Unwanted respect filled him. The infidel had left chaos in his wake, chaos that slowed his pursuers. Only Allah's blessing would keep several horses from breaking legs. Patting Kamillah's neck, he urged her on. She wouldn't fail him. Karim roared at a man running with a clumsy bundle of clothes to get out of the way.

As he sailed over a collapsed stall, women's screams rent

the cool morning air, but he didn't turn. They must have tried to cross before Jamil and his men thundered through.

Karim pounded around a stall leaning drunkenly out into the path and yelled at a bent, elderly woman stiffly lifting a basket onto a shelf. He wouldn't risk Kamillah. Rising in the stirrups, he reined the mare to one side and swore violently when her hooves slipped in an oil patch on the cobblestones. Kamillah brushed the woman, but Karim didn't have time to look back to learn her fate.

She wasn't the last of the obstacles. Ahead, a toddler ambled down the row between stalls sagging against their poles. Keeping the mare at a collected canter, Karim signaled her to jump. She soared over as the child squatted down to touch a bit of colored glass.

As the mare landed lightly, raucous confusion erupted behind Karim that drowned the market's uproar. Slewing around in the saddle, he glimpsed a horse down and thrashing in the remains of a vendor's stall. The guard's body lay sprawled motionless nearby. That damned oil. Nails digging into his palms, Karim swore viciously. If that horse was injured, Hamilton's death would be even slower.

Karim swiveled back just in time to miss a rain of brass bottles and basins bouncing and clattering across the pavement. In panicked flight, a terrified passerby had upset a brass vendor's wares. Karim leaned over the mare's neck, soothing her softly as she shied at the bright, flashing, noisy jumble beneath her hooves. Prancing through the clutter, Kamillah steadied with his calming voice and lengthened her stride once free of the obstacles.

A few yards more and they reached the street leading to the docks. Relaxing his grip on the reins, Karim carefully let the mare extend her stride even further. But she no longer held the lead.

A bay shot ahead of them out of control. Although the guard sawed on the reins, the horse raced down the narrow, crooked street, barely keeping its feet. Caroming around a curve, it collided with a camel. Karim raced past as the camel attacked, and he saw no more. If that horse was damaged as well—

Stomach tightening with anticipation, he could almost taste retribution. Just around this next curve were the docks. Past the last blue door, Karim and his mare plunged to a halt.

Despite the tight rein, Kamillah pulled at the bit, but he wouldn't let her move. He scanned the harbor area while the men straggled up—even the guard mounted on the bay. Beyond patches of heavy sweat staining the horse's hide, the bay had taken no apparent injury from the camel. Karim dismissed it from his mind.

The two cargo ships loading along the wharf were owned by loyal Muslims who'd never aid an infidel no matter what profit was offered. Especially one absconding with the bey's concubine. And there was no movement on the galley. The only other ship visible had sailed too long ago for Hamilton to be on it.

But a small boat bobbed on the waves in the middle of the harbor, a man and woman at the oars, while another man sat at the rudder. Raising an arm in signal to his men, Karim released the restive Kamillah and sent her racing along the docks and onto the soft sand.

"I, Lord Karim, command you to return!" he bellowed once he was as close as he could get.

The small man at the rudder turned toward him and stared. But the others kept rowing. Karim shouted again, and the man at the rudder turned back to the other two, gesticulating as he talked.

The gleam of sunlight on metal from beside Karim distracted him from the drama in the fishing boat. "Don't shoot. I want them alive."

"I am your bey." Reaching for the pistol stuck in his sash, Garrett quietly reminded the frightened fisherman. "Lord Karim is merely my brother."

The boat slid through the water at a slower rate without

his strength at the oars. The sound of Diana's heavy breathing drew his approval. She was still rowing.

"But— Your brother may have an important message for you." His eyes bulging, the fisherman saw only the pistol in Garrett's hand.

"It will wait," Garrett assured him soothingly. "Don't worry. I'll see you face no punishment upon your return."

Holding his arm up, he tightened his finger on the front trigger. The sharp crack echoed against high walls and hills surrounding the harbor, and a cloud of smoke drifted on the breeze back toward the open sea. The fisherman's frightened gaze darted from the double-barreled pistol to Garrett's face.

"Karim will know you have no choice." The little man nodded sharply once. "And this is for your trouble."

Stuffing the pistol into his sash, Garrett tossed a gold coin in a low arc to the fisherman. It started to disappear into the fish-scented djellabah when he paused and stared at it suspiciously. Keeping it close to his body so no one onshore could see, he brought it to his mouth and bit hard with stained yellow teeth. Satisfied, he stuffed it inside his robe, grinned amiably, and resumed control of the rudder.

With Garrett joining Diana once again in rowing, the old longboat jumped toward their goal. "Can they stop us?" she asked.

"No," Garrett answered, but picked up the pace at the oars. "Those ships aren't fast enough."

"That isn't what I mean, and you know it," she said more sharply than intended.

Her breath came harshly as she matched Garrett's pace at the oars. But the shore was the focus of her attention. Karim and his men quickly dismounted, one man leading the horses away from the water's edge. Puffs of smoke bloomed there. The concerted crack of muskets echoed from walls, water, and buildings until the sound came from all sides. As punctuation to the echoes, small plumes of water rose nearby.

She licked her lips. "That's what I meant."

Instead of answering, Garret yelled something at the little man. When the musket balls had hit the water, he'd looked wildly about, then dived into the bottom of the boat. He was still huddled there. Garrett's frigid order brought him back to the rudder, but hunched down as far as he could get.

In a ragged line along the shore, Karim's troop fumbled with ramrods and powder horns, elbows flying. Behind them, the horses reared and sidled at the noise. But soon, too soon, the men lifted their guns to fire again.

"You worry too much," Garrett assured Diana once he was certain the fisherman would remain on duty. "The bey's guards have beautiful muskets, but we're out of accurate musket range now."

Another round of cracks, more ragged this time, punctuated his reassurance. Tiny geysers spurted into the air in a scattered array farther from the boat. Relieved, Diana matched his pace and watched the pantomime being played out onshore. The guard troop struggled frantically with ramrods and powder horns once again. With each second, though, the boat was a few feet nearer the ship, a few feet farther from accurate range. As well, the men lacked precision and skill when they raised their arms for another volley. All but one.

A sharp crack followed by a ragged series erupted. This time the echo didn't quite surround them. Diana waited for the plumes of water marking where the musket balls hit. Instead, splinters erupted near Garrett's oarlock, and the little man subsided even further into the bottom of the boat, although his hand stayed on the rudder. Garrett's oath cut her gasp short as a trickle of blood ran down the side of his hand. She tried twice before she could speak.

"Garrett?"

"I'm all right."

"Was that a fluke?" she asked.

"A lucky shot." Garrett tossed an apologetic grin over his

shoulder. "And I forgot about Karim's rifle. We're almost out of even his range."

"I'm delighted to hear it."

Another flurry of cracks erupted from the shore. The shots landed even farther from the boat. Karim gestured toward the horses. Mounting swiftly, they rode away.

"Where are they going?" Diana demanded.

"He's remembered the cannons."

Karim took a last look as he gained the street leading up to the walls on this side of the harbor. Damn Hamilton! But he wouldn't make it out of the harbor alive. Walls cut off Karim's view in the next second.

The puddled street leading up to the fortress was deserted. Everyone was at the market or out fishing. With a terse command, Karim gave Kamillah her head. They led the men up the winding, narrow passage at a gallop, the clatter of hooves echoing against the high stone walls. Within minutes, they were through the open gate and calling for gunners.

Karim rode to the wall and looked down at the entrance to the harbor. Hamilton and the girl were nearing the ship. But they weren't near enough. Before they could get aboard, they'd be sunk. A thin smile crossed Karim's face. Hamilton wouldn't escape death, just slow death.

"Sink that ship," Karim ordered, turning to the gunnery captain who'd rushed to his side.

Saluting briskly, the captain shouted orders to the cannoneers who commanded the entrance to the harbor. Already, men were rolling out kegs of powder and stacking merkins and ramrods beside buckets of water. Balls stood ready next to each cannon. With silent, deadly efficiency, each gun crew opened its keg and prepared to load.

"Captain, look!" one of the nearest gunners called, pointing at the back of the cannon.

The captain behind him, Karim dashed over. "What is it?" he snapped.

"The gun's been spiked," the captain answered unhappily. Unable to meet the security chief's eyes, he kept his gaze on the cannon, tiny beads of sweat rimming his forehead despite the cool morning breeze. A tightly wedged wooden spike extended fractionally above the touchhole.

"All of them?" Karim's riding whip tapped his boot in a tense rhythm.

With Karim at his side, the captain raced from one cannon to the next. All were spiked. Saluting, the captain stood at attention as he reported, his nervous gaze meeting Karim's. A trail of sweat ran down one temple into his beard.

"My lord, we cannot fire."

"How long before you can?" The tattoo of whip against boot increased in speed.

"The spikes are only wood, but, still, at least an hour, my lord." The captain's voice was strained as he answered, and he shifted his weight from one leg to the other as though he'd stood at attention for hours.

Leaning over the rampart, Karim squinted at the harbor entrance. The diamond-edged sparkle of sunlight on blue water made it hard to see, but the boat was alongside the ship.

Hamilton had won this round.

No matter. He wouldn't win another.

Karim gestured to a guard. "Find out what ship that is and where she's bound." Turning back to the gunnery captain, he smiled without humor but said pleasantly, "Condescend to explain to me how cannon in your charge came to be spiked."

While the fisherman secured the line, a rope ladder tumbled down. It slapped and swung against the ship in time with the sway of the swells. The top of it seemed a thousand feet away.

"You'll have to climb," Garrett told Diana tersely. "We don't have time to rig a sling."

Lurching to her feet in the rocking boat, Diana grabbed the ladder. Thick hemp rope bit into now tender palms. "I'll make it."

"Good girl." He moved closer to help.

Kicking the wet weight of caftan and djellabah away from her ankles, she thrust a foot at the first rung of the ladder. Perversely, it swung the other way. Stepping closer, Garrett caught and steadied the twisting, bobbing ladder. Judging its swing, Diana tried again and succeeded.

The ladder swung like the pendulum of a clock with her weight on it. Each rung jerked away in response to her movements, and partway up, her foot slipped as she reached for the next handhold. Her breath caught as she dangled for an instant. Then Garrett's large hand closed on her rump. She shot up toward the deck, where a hand caught her wrist and hauled her the last few feet. Garrett scrambled on board scant seconds later, caftan and djellabah in hand.

"Nikos," Garret called in Greek from beside her, "we've got to hurry. Raise more sail."

The gentle breeze barely filled the sails that were unfurled. Diana watched the ship's captain casually saunter across the deck to greet them. Behind, a sailor leisurely rolled the rope ladder for storage.

Nikos chuckled easily and clapped Garrett on the shoulder. "If you wish, my friend."

He called orders to sailors standing on the deck. They obeyed without a great flurry of activity. More sail caught the light breeze, yet the *Medea* continued on at a leisurely pace. It wasn't enough. Each crenel in the wall's embrasures stood clearly etched against the brilliant blue sky. They were close, too close.

"Can't we go faster?" Garrett asked Nikos. "Karim's about to blow us out of the water."

Nikos shrugged philosophically. "With this breeze, we can't make more headway. I hope it doesn't stay like this. Time is money for a ship." With an ostentatious air of nonchalance, he studied the sky, as though expecting a change in the weather.

Suspicious, Garrett stared at him. "You're taking this very calmly."

"Me?" Nikos touched his chest in exaggerated surprise.

"What's more, you love this tub too much to risk her," Garrett continued as though Nikos hadn't spoken. "What'd you do?"

"Found out why you English say someone's drunk as an artilleryman."

Garrett's glance flicked from Nikos to the silent walls above the harbor. Slowly the *Medea* gained the open sea. "And after you learned that little tidbit?"

"We spiked the guns."

"You—"

A yell from the fisherman below interrupted them. Garrett strode to the railing, Diana close behind. Leaning over, they peered into the upturned face of the little man. He demanded something, and Garrett answered briefly. Sourly, the fisherman cast off, went to the rudder, and sat back, arms crossed over his chest. As the ship pulled away, he emphatically spat and made a rude gesture.

"What'll happen to him?" Diana asked.

"Nothing." Stepping back from the rail, Garrett looked down at her. "Karim saw me shoot my pistol."

"He won't be able to row back against the tide."

"The tide'll turn. Then he'll make it back in. The worst he'll suffer is missing lunch." Garrett squeezed her hand. "That reminds me, I'm hungry." As he spoke, he draped an arm about her shoulders and gave her a casual hug. Raising his head, he gauged the light breeze. Anticipation lit his eyes when he looked back at Diana. "I hope the wind picks up. I've got business in Crete."

"Crete?" Surprise filled Diana. Since yesterday morning, all she'd thought about was escaping from Bizerte. And now it turned out she was escaping to Crete. "I want to go to Jerusalem."

"You'll like Crete." Garrett kissed her lightly on the nose, his grin widening at her expression. "There's ruins and stuff there."

His arm still comforting her, he swung around. "Nikos, how long before we make Crete?"

"Seven or eight days. Maybe nine. It depends on the winds." The answer was absent.

The captain's attention was on Garrett's arm draped about Diana's shoulders. Color rising in her cheeks, she stepped free, not seeing Garrett's brief frown. The wet skirts of her djellabah and caftan swayed with the movement, and a weight pounced and clung. Startled, Diana looked down. Clinging to the skirt was a calico kitten ferociously wrestling it into submission. Exclaiming softly, she knelt and picked him up. Reluctantly releasing his claws, he curled contentedly in her arms when she rubbed behind his ears.

Looking up to ask the kitten's name, Diana felt the eyes of every man on her. The breeze blew coolly against exposed flesh. Her leg, lightly veiled in sea-green silk, peeked through the open front of caftan and djellabah. Snatching them closed, she scrambled to her feet. She needed to change. . . . She couldn't.

She didn't have any clothes.

CHAPTER VII

FREEDOM, EVEN WITHOUT CLOTHES, WAS SOMETHING TO savor. Replete with breakfast and safety and freedom, Diana leaned back in her chair. The ship's gentle creak, the steady sense of motion *away* from Bizerte, was something else to savor. She took a sip of coffee and smiled across the cozy cabin at the captain's wife, seated in the flood of light coming through a porthole, her husband lounging beside her with an unlit pipe in one hand. With tiny stitches, Ariadne was darning a hole in a thick woolen sock.

Looking up from the stitchery, she returned Diana's smile. "Now that you are fed, perhaps Garrett won't mind if we discuss clothing."

"I never objected in the first place," Garrett said around a mouthful of bread and cheese. He washed it down with a draft of ale and continued. "I just thought we could discuss it while we ate."

"You're through eating now," Diana said with suspicious sweetness. "I need more than one outfit for the voyage." She pointed to his amethyst brocade caftan thrown carelessly across a chair. "Remaking that will give me a change."

"Two outfits aren't enough," Ariadne interrupted. "You'll need more."

Diana grimaced. "I suppose I could sew a wool dress from a djellabah."

"That beige is not for you." Ariadne shook her head decidedly. "Please accept some of my clothes until we reach Crete."

Looking up in surprise, Garrett compared Diana's fair coloring with Ariadne's pale olive complexion and intensely black hair. Ariadne was also three inches shorter and plump. Although he kept silent, his expression showed skepticism.

Taking the pipe from his mouth, Nikos joined the discussion for the first time. "Ariadne may lend clothing to Miss Graham, but not to be altered." He gestured gracefully and smiled, his plain face becoming engaging with animation. "Now, if there were compensation—" He let the thought trail off.

Ariadne dropped the sock to her lap. "Nikos, for what you'd ask, Diana could buy a complete wardrobe."

"Where will she buy these clothes?" He waved his pipe in dismissal of the objection.

An instant's silence filled the small cabin. "Have you any fabric on board?" Diana asked, tracing the silver embroidery scrolled down the front of her caftan.

"None. And don't forget the cost of your passage."

"I don't have any money," Diana admitted. Her fingers halted at the end of one fanciful scroll just below her throat.

"I'll pay." Garrett broke into the silence that greeted this revelation. Annoyance drawing his brows into a single inky stroke across his forehead, he glared at Nikos.

Smiling her thanks, Diana refused. "My parents will pay for my passage and clothing, plus a substantial reward when I get to Jerusalem."

The name of the city affected Nikos strongly. "No, Miss Graham. The Holy Land isn't possible." He loosened the neck of his shirt. "The climate is bad for my health."

"I think your head would look good in a noose, Nikos."

Relaxing again in his chair, Garrett turned a speculative gaze on Diana.

Reluctantly, she faced him. "I'll pay you back, Garrett, when I reach Jerusalem."

Lowering the velvet caftan with the half-ripped seam to her lap, Diana stared out the single porthole in her cabin. The sea stretched to the horizon, gray as the cold drizzle falling from the gray sky. Yet inside it was warm; the lanterns swaying with the gentle swells bathed her in a golden glow. She was heading to Jerusalem with just a minor halt to her journey in Crete. Yet something was wrong, something missing. She felt empty.

"Why the frown?" Ariadne closed the door behind her. Not giving Diana time to answer, she continued. "This will cheer you."

She dropped a bundle of dresses and nightgowns on the sea chest beside Diana and held up a violet gown of fine wool. In the golden light suffusing the cabin, it was the warm color of the sky before dusk gave way to night.

"Oh, how can you bear to give it up?" Diana asked, rising. Head nearly touching the rafters, she held the dress against her and giggled. The color was perfect; the length wasn't.

"In my situation, it's simple." Ariadne gestured philosophically and settled onto the tiny rug before the bed to clip the threads holding the hem. Glancing up, she caught Diana's puzzled expression. "I'm pregnant again, although Nikos doesn't know it yet. In another month or two, I won't be able to wear that dress. Now, let's drop that hem."

Congratulating her, Diana removed the uncomfortably short robe Ariadne had loaned her and tried on a corset from the pile of clothing. Both women collapsed in laughter. Laced tightly, it drooped from Diana's shoulders and dangled about her waist.

"That," Ariadne said after she caught her breath, "was my smallest." She smoothed the chemise along Diana's sides. "You're too thin. Men prefer ladies with something to hold on to." She cast a speculative look at Diana's face.

When Diana failed to respond, Ariadne continued cheerfully. "Not that Garrett has ever shown a preference one way or another. Let's pin this up and use it as a pattern." After Diana slipped out of the corset, Ariadne extended the violet wool and took up a paper of pins.

She fitted the loose dress competently, while offering a running commentary on men's vagaries. It rolled over Diana until the captain's wife mentioned Garrett again. Diana's legs felt stiff and clumsy when instructed to turn. But she obeyed gladly; her face would be hidden from Ariadne's inspection.

"A good man," Ariadne said when Diana finished the quarter turn, "but he needs a woman to steady him. Any little thing sends him off on some harebrained start." She made a fondly disgusted noise. "When I tell you—" Leaning back, she surveyed the skirt, motioning Diana to revolve slowly. "Yes, that'll do. Put on the caftan and we'll pin it up."

Pulling the violet wool over her head, Diana slipped on Garrett's amethyst caftan. It hung where her caftan had been tight. The sleeves brushed the ends of her fingers, and the hem pooled on the floor. Stepping back in the space available, Ariadne surveyed her and nodded.

"A good color," she observed, speculation still in her face. "When we finish with this and the wool, we'll have two patterns. I'll take this in, while you let the other out."

Diana half listened to Ariadne's directions, revolving with infinitesimal pauses when bidden. How to lead Ariadne back to finish her revelations about Garrett?

At last Ariadne held up the pinned hem. "There's more than enough left to make a flounce for another dress, along with matching trim for the neck and sleeves. This, I think." She held the white one up. "I wasn't happy when I chose it, but with the amethyst brocade trimming, Garret won't be able to keep his eyes off you."

Diana put the robe back on and subsided into the chair with the amethyst brocade draped across her lap and onto the floor. She smoothed the fabric with longing fingers.

Ariadne's sturdy body was comfortably supported by the wall at the head of the narrow bed, the violet wool in her lap. She continued. "Garrett has a good heart. Well, he rescued that boy from the slave merchant in Egypt."

From the corner of her eye, Diana saw Ariadne dart a look at her profile. Diana bent further over the amethyst brocade, pinning pleats into the shoulders. They staggered unevenly across the bodice. They'd have to be taken out again, but when Ariadne wasn't here.

"Garrett and I haven't known each other long." Less than twenty-four hours. "He probably felt sorry for the boy." He hadn't rescued her for that good a reason, but merely to cut a lark. And even then he'd been reluctant.

"That wasn't his only reason. He did it—" Ariadne lifted her head from the sewing and met Diana's gaze with an impressive look "—for the fun of it."

Slowly Diana nodded. That fitted his actions last night. But hadn't there been something warmer than humor or . . . or gallantry afterward?

"A good man," Ariadne repeated. "And he has fine instincts in business, when one considers his family."

With a tiny pair of embroidery scissors Diana cut through a stubborn thread holding a band onto the neckline. Expectant silence filled the cabin. "What about his family?"

"English gentry. I realize," she said, holding up a seam to the light and picking at a loose thread, "that even for such a man, it's difficult for a woman to give up her freedom."

Diana stared.

No unmarried lady willingly roamed about the Mediterranean with a man. But Ariadne obviously followed a different school of behavior.

"What you could make of such a man," Ariadne continued, a small, secret smile hovering over her mouth. "My Nikos was such a one before our betrothal."

"What—" Diana broke off, not precisely sure what to say.

Ariadne smiled with perfect reasonableness. "A girl should have fun when she's young. But when you meet a man such as Garrett"—she waved one finger admonitorily —"marry him."

Ariadne's advice chanted in Diana's head when Garrett bent, smiling, over her hand as though she were his hostess. His presence filled the tiny cabin even when she wasn't looking at him. Rising from an automatic curtsy, Diana raised her eyes slowly. A flush deepened the color in her cheeks at the amusement she saw in his face.

"Where are Ariadne and Nikos?" she asked.

Offering his arm to lead her to the table, Garrett explained easily, too easily, "Something's happened to delay Nikos, and Ariadne prefers to eat dinner with her husband."

He waited for the reaction she wasn't going to give. Diana took the chair Garrett held and spread a napkin over her lap. She didn't believe him, but he wouldn't learn it from her.

"Soup?" He lifted the lid of a tureen. Inside, golden chicken broth, slices of lemon floating on top, swayed gently with the ship's motion.

"What is it?" Diana asked, unwilling to let him know how uncomfortable she felt at eating alone with a man.

"Avgolemono." Garrett ladled some into small bowls. "Lemon-and-egg soup made with chicken broth."

Tasting it cautiously, Diana nodded and took another spoonful. "What were you doing in the palace pretending to be the bey?"

A muscle twitching beside his mouth, he met her questioning gaze. Briefly recounting the story, he chuckled over Karim's ejection of the beardless bey. "And the rest you know."

Setting aside the empty bowl, the lemon's acid churning

in her stomach, Diana buried her hands beneath her napkin. Ariadne was right. Garrett took too many chances, cut things too finely. He *needed* someone to take care of him.

"Won't they pursue us?"

"The bey is too much a nip-farthing to do it right. He'll use the merchantman heading to the eastern end of the Mediterranean. But it stops once before Crete."

"Karim will be several days behind us then?" Diana's hands relaxed on the crumpled napkin. "What's a nip-farthing?"

"A miser," Garrett answered, and put his empty soup bowl aside, "and you know Haroun's one, or you wouldn't have tried to bribe him—me—last night."

Taking a plate from the pair stacked at his elbow, Garrett removed the lids from the covered platters. "Fruit-stuffed lamb breast and baby vegetables. Ariadne thought you'd enjoy Greek cuisine this evening." He smiled warmly. "Good food, good friends, and a little fun are all that make life worth living."

"Thank you." Diana took the plate and set it down, her hands going back to her lap. "What will we do in Crete?"

"There's Knossos." He ate a sliver of lamb and apricot and shrugged. "And clothes shopping." For some obscure reason, his tone sharpened and didn't invite questioning, although it wasn't forbidding.

Flicking a glance at his face, Diana lowered her gaze back to her plate immediately. His expression warmed rapidly and increased her uncertainty of all but one thing. The intentions reflected there had to be changed.

"What were you doing in Bizerte?"

She gestured with her fork at his impeccable English evening clothes. Without the ship's creaking, they might have been guests at a dinner party, although the amethyst brocade evening dress spoiled the illusion. It was too grand for an ordinary dinner. Her hair hanging straight and fine, down her back, bound only with a simple band made from a scrap of brocade left over from the caftan, was wrong as well. Considering they were alone together, they were more like honeymooners. Diana flushed.

"You must"—she rushed on before he could read the thoughts in her face—"have felt out of place. You'd look more at home in a ballroom."

"You sound like Aunt Sophy. Only my parents understood why I sold out after Waterloo. The social round was so predictable: The season in the spring, hunting in the fall, and house parties winter and summer."

"Your Aunt Sophy sounds like Gran." Grimacing, she explained, "That's why I left Boston."

Realizing she held a full fork in one hand, she took a small bite of the fruit-stuffed lamb. It tasted odd, but Diana decided she liked it and took another mouthful.

"What are you doing in the Mediterranean?"

"Fleeing to my parents." She swallowed and nodded vigorously. "They're in Jerusalem."

Amusement laced his tone. "You mentioned that last night." Cocking his head, he looked at her suspiciously. "Does your grandmother know where you are?"

Diana flicked a glance from her plate to his face and back again at the tone of his voice. "Of course . . . well, she's probably guessed by now." The fork heading to his mouth stopped in mid-flight. "But I only promised to stay in Boston until my twenty-first birthday."

"You ran away?" Awe edged his voice.

"Not precisely," Diana answered carefully. She'd gone over the explanation often enough in her mind. In Jerusalem, she'd need it. "Mama and Papa promised if I finished school, made my debut, and didn't find a husband, I could join them."

"So you just took a ship for the Holy Land?"

She took a mouthful of lamb and nodded as a kaleidoscope of emotions crossed his face. The last one to take possession was admiration with a tinge of amusement.

"You're lucky you were only kidnapped."

Shrugging, Diana said, "I escaped," and discovered the

plate was empty. Her stomach felt comfortably full for the first time since her last shipboard dinner. "With your help," she added. "Anyway, in Crete, I'll find some way to reach Jerusalem."

Neatly laying her cutlery across the plate, she raised her eyes to his. Dazed, Garrett shook his head slowly. Was he about to lecture her? As she'd done so often with Captain Andrews, she distracted him with a question.

An hour later, Diana was absolutely convinced Ariadne was right. Garrett took too many risks and not just in Bizerte. Although he joked about his adventures, his escapes had been too narrow, and she told him so.

"But what would I do at home? The life my parents lead would bore me within a month. Even thinking about it—" He shuddered. "That's why I'm here."

Head cocked to one side, Diana considered. "There must be some way of keeping you amused."

"Such as?"

She pushed back from the table and put the napkin beside her empty plate. "I'm sure you could think of something, if you tried. Now, I must—"

"Come up on deck with me," he interrupted.

"Is it drizzling still?"

Picking up the shawl, he draped it tenderly about her shoulders. Immediately, butterflies she was determined to ignore took up residence in her stomach. "Let's go see. There's a protected area where we can watch the stars." His hands remained on her until she took a step away.

"What if no stars are out?" Diana asked.

His answer was silence as he watched her. Recklessness danced in his expression. Offering his arm, he waited without urging for her decision.

Not intending to, she placed her hand on it, the fine broadcloth masking hard muscles with its texture. Allowing him to lead, she went up the companionway and on deck. Even an extra hour in his company was welcome. All too soon, she'd go to her lonely cabin and plan how to protect Garrett from his reckless urges.

"Beautiful, isn't it?" he asked softly.

Diana took a step toward the rail and pulled the shawl tighter about her. The panorama was everything he said and more. In the distance a dim glow outlined a headland projecting out to sea. An encampment was spending the night there, their fires keeping the dark of night at bay.

The gentle stirring of the chill breeze made her shiver. Wind creaked through the rigging high above, the sound as cold as the diamond points of light sprinkled across the night sky and reflecting on black water. It was beautiful but inhuman. Only the fires haloing the headland in the distance promised warmth and companionship. Diana shivered again.

"You're chilled," Garrett said softly behind her. His breath stirring her hair left her anything but chilled. But before she could protest, he drew her into his sheltering warmth. "I didn't tell you earlier how well that brocade suits you."

His arms about her felt so right. "You think so?"

One of the hands resting at her waist lifted and touched her chin. The faint roughness of his callused hand sent a shiver through her. "It turns your eyes violet."

Although she couldn't see his face, a new timbre in his voice warned her. Before she could speak, step away from his sheltering arms, it was too late. Garrett's lips were firm, seeking, on hers. They tasted of the wine they'd shared, and his taste, his touch, intoxicated her.

Relaxing, Diana molded her body to the beckoning warmth. Freeing her hands from beneath her shawl, she buried her fingers in the silken thickness of his hair and murmured, "Garrett," when he freed her lips. The wind chilling the backs of her hands increased the contrast with his warmth, made it more enticing.

Responding to the summons of her voice, he ran his hands down her spine with a demanding caress that ignited tremors. His arms felt like home. Fingers tightening in his hair, she tugged his head lower. Trailing kisses along the line of his jaw, the faint roughness of new beard delighted her.

Instinctively, she released his head and ran searching hands over his back. Beneath her touch, the muscles rippled as he lifted her for another demanding kiss. With a sigh, her lips parted beneath his.

Warmth, heat, a burning tension gathered and weakened her until she leaned against him, unable to support herself. His caresses swept over her, drowning her in sensation, enclosing them in a safe haven where only they existed. Then he brushed her breast with a gentle palm. Gasping, she stretched upward and kissed his lips, chin, throat— anywhere she could reach. Her lashes drooped closed when he returned her kisses with searing passion, and his hand over her breast tightened.

He wasn't the bey, wasn't her enemy. The realization was a delight. She was free to—

But she wasn't.

"Garrett," she gasped. Pushing with all her strength against the hard wall of his chest, she repeated his name strongly and forced her body to go rigid.

His fingers dug into her rib cage for an excruciating second then slowly relaxed. Opening her eyes fully, she watched him shake his head and take a half step back. "Still no?" he asked, cradling her around the waist.

She shook her head and pulled the shawl tight. Without his body, she felt chilled and lost.

"Allow me to escort you to your cabin?" Half bowing, he offered his arm. "Before I forget myself."

"It took you long enough," the bey snapped after the servant bowed out of the private audience chamber. The combined scent of hot foods wafted from the covered dishes spread over a low table near him, but Haroun ignored it. He pushed his chair from the table to see his brother better. "Which ship?"

Remaining silent for an instant longer than absolutely necessary, Karim stifled a grin. His brother looked irresistible wrapped in an elaborate ruby velvet robe with splotchy day-old stubble on cheeks and weak chin. Karim fingered his own sleek beard, and annoyed Haroun even more. But a breach of security cast shame on Karim also. Even so, he could almost applaud Hamilton's audacity.

"Captain Hassan offered the *Kalila* tomorrow," Karim answered. "Your"—he paused, his voice underlining the word —*"persuasions* were adequate."

"If Hassan wants to sail his ship into Bizerte again, they're adequate. Who spiked the cannons?" the bey demanded grumpily.

"Sailors from the *Medea.* Hamilton paid them, of course. He had this well planned. Even his henchman, Yusuf, is no longer in the city."

His hands gripping the armrests of the chair, Haroun half rose. Subsiding with a wince, he pressed his fingers against throbbing temples. "You let him escape, too?" he asked harshly.

"The men will search, while I chase the infidel and the girl. They're headed for Iraklion in Crete, unless Nikos Kalogeropoulos lied to the port officials. There will be no difficulty finding them." Taking the elaborately chased rifle off his shoulder, Karim leaned it against the wall. He took a seat on the opposite side of the low table.

"Kalogeropoulos wouldn't dare lie. Besides, Pasha Selim owes me money." Haroun waved away the suggestion while shooting his brother a glance of intense dislike. "This wouldn't be necessary, if you'd done your work properly."

"I did not invite Hamilton into the palace, into a private chamber for dinner and—" Deliberately, Karim broke off.

Haroun's sudden movement ended in a wince and groan. With a disgruntled look at Karim, the bey shifted carefully forward and lifted lid after lid. His lips curled in distaste.

His favorite foods, the ones he'd eaten last night, filled the dishes. "Who ordered this?"

"Leila undoubtedly wished to remind you of your folly, brother." Karim chose a morsel with an elaborate display and licked his finger even more elaborately when a dribble of honey ran down it. The taste cloyed, but his actions annoyed Haroun. "Eat. You'll feel better."

Unwilling to open himself to further ridicule from his younger brother, Haroun ate a morsel with distaste. "Hamilton didn't steal just the girl. He's taken the badge of office."

Karim's head jerked up. Then he leaned back and sipped his tea delicately. It ran soothingly down, spreading warmth as it went. Haroun was helpless without the badge of the bey of Bizerte.

"Well?"

Thoughtfully flicking the tip of his beard with the back of his fingers, Karim's thin lips curved in a cold smile. How auspicious. When he captured the infidel, he captured the office.

"All we need to do, brother, is follow my plans." Karim shrugged negligently. "Hassan requires no additional explanation. I told him," he reassured Haroun, "only that a dangerous infidel, under threat of death for dealing in liquor, has fled the city. Hassan knows you don't make threats lightly. If he wishes to continue trading in Bizerte, he'll take my troop—"

"A troop is too expensive." Watching the chicken rapidly disappear from the platter into Karim's mouth, Haroun decided, "Two men will be sufficient. I'll not have a whole troop eating their heads off, touring the empire, and accomplishing nothing."

"Two men? You flatter me."

"You're my brother, aren't you?" Haroun looked thoughtful. "Hamilton and the girl must be alive and able to pay, however, you may enjoy yourself with her. She's ruined goods." Smiling maliciously, he waved away consideration of Diana. "Leaving tomorrow, you'll be just a day behind, and with Pasha Selim's help, it will be easy. Who will you take?"

"Mustafa and Umar. They speak only Arabic, so the girl can't suborn them. I'll see Hamilton doesn't have a chance."

"Why not a eunuch if you're worried about the girl?" Haroun asked, the malice in his expression increasing.

Distaste rose in Karim's mouth, distaste he rinsed away with another cup of mint tea. Eunuchs bothered him. Besides, they were loyal to Haroun, not him.

"If they manage to flee Crete, I intend to follow," Karim warned, ignoring Haroun's jibe.

"To the ends of the earth," his brother agreed instantly. "But—" Haroun pointed warningly. Tea slopped onto his hand, burning. Dropping the cup, he wiped his hand on the velvet robe. "Be careful how you spend my money."

"If Hamilton leaves Crete before I arrive, it will take time. And," Karim added, "money."

Taking a purse from his sash, Haroun tossed it to him. "Spend it wisely. I expect an accounting of every piaster. I refuse to pay for a luxury excursion. And keep me informed."

"You will know all as soon as possible." The lie rolled smoothly off Karim's tongue before his voice caressed the last words. "You needn't worry. Hamilton and the girl will be returned quickly for a long lingering death."

CHAPTER VIII

"No, PRINNY." DIANA DELICATELY PRIED THE KITTEN'S claws out of her skirt and cuddled him beneath her chin. "I only have a few clothes, and I can't let you snag them."

He purred and rubbed his head against her face, then twisted to be let down. Sighing, she set him on the patch-work quilt covering her bed and gave him a scrap of fabric.

"I'm not like this ordinarily." The kitten raised his head, mangled amethyst brocade dangling from his mouth. "I don't believe in love at first sight. Yet here I am mooning over Garrett Hamilton."

While Prinny went back to the serious business of mauling the fabric, Diana stretched for the hooks marching down the back of the dress she'd made from Garrett's caftan. Even worse than falling in love at first sight was the error of obviously responding to him. Garrett was aware how she reacted to his touch, although not how she felt.

"Although," she assured Prinny, bending down to tickle his belly, "I said no again this evening." Prinny batted at the bodice of the dress hanging loosely from her shoulders.

Pulling it over her head, coolness touched her bare arms. She folded the dress lovingly and hurried to put on Garrett's dressing gown. Silk-lined ruby velvet clung tantalizingly, and instead of a chill, it held a faint warmth. Eyes half closed, Diana buried her face in the collar. It was as though his arms were around her, his body pressed close to hers. Dreamily, she sank onto the bed.

It was strange how free she felt. Free not because of escaping Bizerte, Karim, and the shadowy bey, but because she'd never dined alone with a man, never gone a day without a corset, never—she blushed—loved a man. Tucking her bare feet under her and arranging the dressing gown comfortably, Diana stroked Prinny down the arching curve of his back.

"You're not paying attention, Prinny. This is important. Ariadne says I should marry him." Picking Prinny up, she held the kitten before her face and looked at him sternly. "Maybe she's right." Wriggling fiercely, he mewed in annoyance. "All right." She let him go. "Now behave yourself."

Reaching for Garrett's comb, she removed the last of the tangles, then began braiding her hair for sleep. Parted down the middle and brought forward over her shoulders, the silver gilt swathe gleamed against the ruby velvet. Diana's fingers moved nimbly but absently as she bound one side.

"What should I do?" she burst out suddenly, startling the kitten. "I can't set my cap at him. It's not decent. Yet he needs someone." When she made the point with her index finger on the quilt, Prinny came off his haunches. "Look at all the risks he runs." Another finger came down; the kitten was just two squares away. "Somebody's going to kill Garrett if he keeps this up." Prinny gathered himself to leap, but Diana's sweeping gesture tumbled him over.

"I'm sorry, sweetheart. It's just that I'm so confused." Holding the purring kitten against her, Diana stroked the velvety soft ears with delicate fingers while shaking her head mournfully. "I'll never laugh at other girls again. Love's awful. Especially when it's Garrett." She lifted Prinny to look in his sleepily blinking eyes. "He thinks I'll come running if he just crooks his finger."

Cradling the kitten against her chest again, she smiled tenderly as his eyes closed, and his purr lowered a notch. "Yes, I know. You're not interested."

Stroking his deliciously soft fur, Diana leaned her head against the wall. After a long pause, she roused herself from dreamy contemplation. "I've more important things to do than make a cake of myself over Mr. Garrett Hamilton."

She put the sleeping kitten down in the protected corner between pillow and wall, fingers gently trailing over fur. "For instance, what will I do once we reach Crete?" Straightening abruptly, she frowned. "Crete," she repeated in a different tone.

Falling silent, Diana dropped onto the pillow beside Prinny and contemplated patchy water stains on the low ceiling. How long would it take to find a trustworthy captain to take her to the Holy Land? How would she pay for board and lodging? Not to mention a new wardrobe.

Stroking the rich skirt of the dressing gown, the velvet beneath her palms felt like his cheek, rough, seductive. Garrett would want this back, too. Nor would he stay in Iraklion for very long. He wouldn't abandon her. But—she frowned and drew the fringed silk sash coolly and enticingly along her throat and chin—how long would he stay?

He might just hire a chaperon. Panic fluttered in her stomach before slowly fading. Garrett wouldn't do that. Not to her. Still, Diana wished they'd discussed plans during dinner. She'd gone into the cabin where they'd eaten intending to discuss it. And every practical thought fled at the sight of him.

She wouldn't let that happen again.

And never again would she go through the embarrassment she'd faced that morning over breakfast. If she had to ask for a loan, she'd do it without witnesses. And that way she could offer Garrett recompense. It would be just a business deal. He deserved interest on the money, payment for the time and risks he took.

There was nothing improper about speaking to him in

private. It was purely business. Even if it was conducted in his cabin. Garrett was no danger. She'd proven tonight that she could say no to his blandishments, his attractions.

With determination, Diana slid off the bed and smoothed the dressing gown's skirt. Perhaps she should change before going, but the only gown finished was the one she'd worn for dinner and was singularly inappropriate for a business meeting. She took the single step separating her from the door into the corridor.

"But, Nikos, she's right for Garrett." Drawing a finger down his arm, Ariadne pouted prettily up at her husband. "They should marry, don't you agree?" From beneath dark lashes, she threw a flirtatious glance at him and made an even more outrageous suggestion. "Marry them before we reach Crete."

Shaking his head, Nikos's brows arched comically. "I'm not a priest, love."

"You're a ship's captain, aren't you?" Ariadne demanded. "And this is the high seas."

She giggled as he traced the plunging neckline of her dress. Catching his hand, she held it away, then kissed him lightly on the nose in compensation.

"What," he asked, unbuttoning the row of tiny buttons fastening her tight sleeves between wrist and elbow, "makes you sure Garrett wants to marry her?"

"Oh, he doesn't." Lowering her lashes, she giggled softly at the look in Nikos's eyes. "But Diana's so in love with him, and he hovers over her like a—"

"That, my love, is lust. He won't marry her."

"That's where you're wrong, husband."

Instead of pulling her into his lap as he'd intended, Nikos leaned back in the chair. "In all the years I've known Garrett Hamilton, he's never once been seriously interested."

"The sort of woman he meets in the places he goes—" Ariadne waved her free hand airily in dismissal. "Diana's different. For one thing—" she held up a finger and jerked it back when Nikos grabbed at it. "For one thing," she repeated, "she's a lady of his own class. And an heiress. And of greater importance," she concluded, holding up a third triumphant finger, "Diana's transparently honest."

"You're a romantic." Nikos shook his head, chuckling.

"Not so much as you think." Letting him capture her free hand and draw her onto his lap, she smiled lovingly at him. "Garrett's more than halfway in love with Diana, of course, but even that wouldn't make the difference if it weren't for one thing." Laughing, she kissed his drolly wrinkled forehead.

"And that is—" Under Nikos's tone was an absent, husky growl. He fumbled with the hooks holding her burnt orange dress closed.

"His principles." Ariadne gasped and melted against him when he freed the last hook and peeled the dress off her shoulders.

"What have principles to do with it?" The question sounded more absent than any before.

"He's a gentleman." The words escaped her throat in staccato gasps.

"You're still a hopeless romantic." Face flushed with desire, he raised his head and looked at her lovingly. "Now, leave Garrett and Diana to their own devices."

"This is delightful." Garrett welcomed Diana with a sweeping bow. A white silk shirt collar peeped from the neck of a silk dressing gown in rich blue. "I was lonely."

In the low light of the single lamp swaying in the passageway, the ruby velvet molded Diana's figure in alternating shimmer and shadow. The rolled-up sleeves showed it wasn't hers. Studying her closely, he recognized the other difference: On him, it ended midway down the calf. On her, only bare feet and ankles extended below the hem.

Flushing at his intent study, she brushed a wisp of hair off her temple and stepped inside the tiny cabin. "I'm here on business." Her tone was light, reserved, and her features calm.

Amused, Garrett closed the door and waved at the bed filling more than half the cabin. "Chairs aren't part of the accoutrements down here in steerage. But make yourself comfortable."

Intensely conscious of him looming bare inches away, Diana looked past him surreptitiously. There *was* nowhere else to sit. Other than the few square feet of deck where they stood, the wide bed occupied the cabin, with a pair of round-topped trunks completing the inventory. Irresistibly, her attention drifted back to the bed.

Seated, her feet wouldn't reach the deck. Yet the only alternative was to make a fool of herself. She was here on business, after all, however unbusinesslike the setting. They would discuss this calmly, reasonably.

Head high, she stepped around him, the dressing gown dragging across his legs. It caught and clung on the silk of his, parting it in front and revealing a glimpse of white linen chemise with its single chaste ruffle around the hem. Flushing delicately, Diana drew the gown closed and settled herself primly on the bed. Hands folded in her lap, she arranged the dressing-gown skirt over tucked-up feet.

She looked up, waiting.

For some time, he didn't move. The flickering light of the oil lamp accented the amused, beckoning sherry-gold eyes, intensified the shimmering blue of the silk dressing gown. Diana swallowed hard when he joined her on the bed. This was absolutely ridiculous. It shouldn't be this difficult.

"You came here to discuss business," he prompted gently.

Diana nodded, the unbraided half of her hair clinging to the velvet dressing gown. "What will happen when we reach Crete?"

"We'll get you to the Holy Land." He watched her intently, the amused expression arrested on his face.

"And between leaving the *Medea* and embarking on another ship?" Diana twisted the end of her braid around first one finger, then another.

"We'll stay at an inn—Nikos recommended one—and replenish your wardrobe." Settling back in the corner formed by the wall and the head of the bed, Garrett regarded her quizzically, puzzled but still amused. "Don't worry. Karim is at *least* a week behind us."

"I haven't any money."

Touching a dry upper lip with her tongue, Diana raised her head fleetingly, then looked down uncomfortably at the hair entwining her fingers. The swaying lamplight, glinting first on his black hair then his eyes, formed an indelible picture superimposed over the sash.

"I wish to borrow enough to pay for passage to the Holy Land, clothes, and room and board." She hurried on. "Purely a business arrangement."

Garrett remained silent.

Swallowing hard, Diana stole a glimpse through her lashes. He still lounged half turned in the corner of the wall at the head of the bed, one leg drawn casually up under the other. The posture was deceptive; a muscle twitched angrily in one cheek.

"Go on."

Hearing the edge to his voice, she untangled her fingers from the silver-gilt braid and twisted them in the fringed sash. Inexplicably, she'd annoyed him. "Once I join my parents, I'll repay you. Plus, of course, interest."

"I'm not a damned cent-percent." Straightening into rigidity, his voice became frigid.

"What's a cent-percent?" She blinked in confusion. Only the ship's creaking marred the silence lengthening between them.

"Moneylender," he snapped eventually. Consciously relaxing his fists, he repeated the word in a lower tone. "Moneylender, a person who preys on his friends. A man who is not a gentleman." Each word lay between them hard and stony.

"I didn't mean—" Color ran high along her cheekbones.

"In Boston, a man can be both a gentleman and a businessman. Besides, I wasn't sure you could afford—"

, "I can afford it."

Taking a deep breath, Diana twisted onto her knees and took his hand in hers. It lay there, warm, strong. Stroking it soothingly, she swallowed, searching for a way to explain, to allay this anger.

"I didn't mean to insult you." The pattern her fingers traced on the back of his hand changed. Words died in her throat as his gaze caught hers. Her fingers stilled on his hand. "In America," she repeated in the charged silence, "it's possible for—"

"A man to be both a businessman and a gentleman," he finished. "You said that." His tone gentled, his expression softened. Dangerously.

Responsive tremors rippled through her, while their eyes met again and clung for stretched seconds. "What's wrong with business?"

Diana didn't recognize her own voice. The tremors increased when his thumb started a steady, teasing stroke on the back of her hand. Taking a shuddering breath, she waited for the reply.

"There's nothing wrong with business. But it's wrong to profit from a friend. Besides, I can afford it." He hesitated, his hand squeezing hers. "That's the least of my worries."

Something different in his voice puzzled Diana. Looking up from their linked hands, she saw a hint of amusement crinkling the corners of his eyes. Men were inexplicable. Why had he ever felt insulted?

"It's not proper for me to be in debt to you."

"It's proper to run away from Boston, get kidnapped, wind up in a harem, and insult a gentleman in his rooms," he said in a voice choked with laughter, "but not to take money from a friend?"

"It wasn't my fault. Nor is it improper to meet a man on a matter of business. But it is improper for me to remain in debt to you. You must see that."

The crinkling around his eyes grew more pronounced. "I'm still not a moneylender."

Freeing her imprisoned hand, Diana lifted both in exasperation. "Can't you see—" She stopped in mid-sentence and looked hard at him. "You knew I wasn't accusing you of being a moneylender." She shook her head in vexation. "You also know it's improper for me to be in debt to you." Settling back against the wall, feet tucked beneath her again, she crossed her arms over her chest.

Cocking his head to one side and smiling, Garrett used a lurch of the ship to shift closer. In an instant, the tiny cabin contracted about them until it centered on him. "Forgive me?"

Diana shot a sideways glance at him, then refocused on the round-topped trunk. That mischievously innocent look was dangerous. Almost as dangerous as the increasing certainty she couldn't say no at will.

Moving even closer, he stroked the curve of her cheek, then raised her face to his. "Friends?" he whispered.

The gentle puff of the word brushed her lips. Fighting down a rising longing, her eyes dropped.

"If you accept repayment. Otherwise"—she wished the flutters would stop—"I can't accept a loan." His hand drifted down the long column of her throat and rested there, increasing the warmth gathering inside.

"If you want to when the time comes." Tenderly, Garrett raised her chin again, forcing her to look into his eyes. "You can."

"I need to repay you." Breath catching in her throat, she twisted the sash about her free hand. "Even though you're . . . a friend."

His eyes were that fascinating shade of sherry, and the vagrant lock of hair swooped rebelliously over his forehead, an inky stroke accentuating the golden bronze of his skin. His eyes drew her toward him, until, catching herself with a surprised start, she jerked back. She folded and refolded the edge of the dressing gown.

"I'm your friend. Although, I won't be if you keep torturing that robe," he said. "It's my favorite."

The stroke of gentle fingers along her cheek was incredibly seductive, and her breathing quickened. For stretched seconds, it held her immobile, mesmerized. She loved him so much.

Swallowing, she forced herself to say the dreaded words. "I'd better return to my cabin."

His eyes remained on her, but lower, on her shoulder. Shifting uncertainly, Diana rose, then subsided back on the bed when his hard, restraining hand closed gently on her shoulder.

A quizzical smile curving his lips, he gathered the swathe of silver-gilt hair, parting it into three unequal sections. "If," he said, dropping one when he tried to pass it under another, "you visit a friend on business, you should match both sides of your hair."

Diana stared in astonishment at the unkempt clumps of hair flopping over her shoulder and breast. They clung with tenacious life to the velvet nap, defying Garrett's efforts to smooth them into a braid. His hands—his strong hands incessantly brushed her shoulder.

Velvet and silk should have been a barrier. But they weren't. Her breath caught, and her heart raced a beat faster with each brush of his hands. Braiding lower and lower, he fleetingly caressed first her shoulder, then her breast. The fabric grew thinner and thinner, and the caresses lasted longer and longer.

Looking into his face, she expected a glint of wicked amusement, a teasing delight. Neither was there. Instead, the expression was serious, with an ever-deepening intensity. His hands stilled. "You represent a delightful problem."

He dropped the braid onto her breast. A wash of flame shot through Diana as though it were an extension of him. Another shot through her when he cupped her chin in one hand and tilted her face up. Her eyes slowly climbed from the blue silk of his dressing gown to his face. It was only inches away. She hadn't felt him move, yet his closeness drew and enfolded. A soft tremor shook her. Instinctively, lovingly, she brushed his silk dressing gown, the cool material a delicious contrast to the warmth beneath.

Garrett's lips closed over hers. Her hands slipped upward along the silk dressing gown. They shaped the silk to his shoulders in conscious delight. Pressing against him, her breasts tautened, longing for his touch to soothe the swelling ache. Ecstatic sensations swamped her with the masterful sweep of hands over the curve of her buttocks. Heavy, throbbing need gathered low inside, building at each touch, each caress.

Whispering, "Garrett," she trailed kisses over the strong line of his jaw. Nibbling at an earlobe enticingly, her hands slid down. His robe and shirt were in the way. Softly murmuring, she pushed them aside and twined fingers through a dusting of silken black hair covering his chest. A soft moan penetrated the delightful haze of unreality, of sensuality surrounding her. Diana's eyes rose.

Sooty lashes partially masked the golden glitter of sherry-colored eyes, but not the brooding hunger lurking there. Sliding one hand along her thigh and under her knees, Garrett lifted her across the bed until she lay half on, half off, him. Silk and velvet robes clung and whispered as they moved.

Diana nestled closer, savoring the hard strength of his long, lean body, and met his gaze. Approval and tenderness warred with nearly uncontrollable desire in his expression. As he held her eyes prisoner, awareness of every point of contact blazed into being. His powerful thighs moved against her legs, nudging them slightly apart. The wool trousers provided a delightful abrasion even through the skirt of her chemise. Whispering his name on a soundless breath, she stretched to place a fleeting kiss on the point of his chin.

Hands splayed over his chest, Diana stretched again,

nestling closer. Everything was right, everything about him perfect. Exhilaration filling her, she tried to return the excitement, the love. But too many clothes separated them.

She writhed, trying to remain in his embrace, yet shed the chemise that divided them. Glorying in the shudder that shook him, she abandoned the effort and pushed Garrett's shirt away. Then, in one easy movement, he took the initiative and swung her onto the quilt.

Looming above, he was poised, waiting, one hand curved at her narrow waist, the other possessively supporting her head. Diana pulled him down, anxious to assuage the aching hunger. His hands restlessly explored first her breast then grazed the gentle curve of her stomach. Eyes closing under the surge of emotion, her head snuggled into the cradle formed by his hand. Then, nibbling down her throat to the edge of her chemise, his lips resumed the exploration.

Unable to remain still, she stroked his back, his ribs, the taut muscles of his stomach. The skin, the hard muscles rippling beneath, was more silken than their robes. She savored the sensations.

Suddenly, Diana was alone and bereft.

From beneath weighted lashes, she watched Garrett lever himself off the bed. The light cast mystical shadows over the cabin, over Garrett. For a stretched second, he stood looking down, flaring pleasure illuminating his face. He reached for the small lamp above the bed and lowered the flame.

In the dimmed light, his eyes glowed. They touched her almost tangibly—first her bare arms, then the curve of her breast above the ruffled neckline of the chemise; even one long, slender leg, where the hem lay rucked over her thigh. Shivering, Diana extended her arms in welcome. He delayed only to unfasten belt and waistband before he was back beside her.

As he bent to brush a kiss across her nose, she murmured his name again. Wanting only him, his gentle caresses, his touch on her stomach, her breasts, her legs, she stirred, stroking the smooth skin of his back, the hair-roughened skin of his thigh. Everything was perfect. Suspended in time, Diana's hands moved restlessly. The burning need for him mounted; yet, when Garrett shifted she protested incoherently.

Coolness flowed where he'd been. Then they were side by side, his weight an oddly familiar warmth. Through the fine linen chemise, his hand burned and stroked from breast to hip, while his lips traced the fine lines of her throat and shoulder. Each velvet brush on bare skin was a powerful summons that increased her shivers. Delighting in the incredible need to show her love for him, only him, Diana nibbled kisses over his shoulders and arms, over a masculine nipple, evoking a shuddering moan.

His lips lightly grazed her shoulder and the upper curve of her breast above the delicate ruffle edging the neckline of her chemise. Touching a tiny mole nestled beside the ruffle with the tip of his tongue, he murmured encouragement at her soft moan. Then faintly trembling fingers tugged at the drawstring bow holding the neckline. Tenderly, he folded back the open bodice and trailed a path of kisses over Diana's taut breasts until he reached the the delicate pink crest. A low sigh escaping, she arched upward as his tongue circled first one nipple, then the other.

Her responsive tremor found an echo in him. As deepening color ran up her throat and over her cheeks, his fingers drew a fiery pattern that followed the persuasive trail of kisses. Shafts of desire shot through her, leaving her shivering even more strongly than before.

Coolness bathed her when he drew the chemise over her head. Trembling, she waited, unsure, yet eager. With delicate caresses, he fed the burning fires until she moved ceaselessly. Lower he searched with lips and fingers, circling the faint curve of navel and stomach down to the nest of pale curls at the apex of her thighs. Her legs parting instinctively, she caught at his shoulders, urging him on. Touching deep inside, a paroxysm of pleasure shook her.

For the first time since their lips met, she heard his voice, dark, husky, filled with hunger. It was the voice, the one that had drawn her from the beginning. "Gently, sweetheart."

"Please, Garrett."

"Hush," he whispered and kissed her.

Lips still on hers, his weight was poised between her legs. Then his mouth moved upward, kissing her closed eyelids. Diana arched upward, seeking, her hands dancing down his back to his buttocks.

Finally, his control broke, his lips fastened on hers, and he thrust powerfully. A soft, ripping pain disrupted the delicious sensations holding her. She tensed, but only for an instant. With soft, reassuring murmurs, his gentle touch returned the smoldering world of love and desire. Diana moved instinctively beneath him. Time stood still in a delicious haze, the certainty of love the only reality.

Each movement brought them closer together, made them one, until a soft cry escaped. Tremors shook her, and as she collapsed, Garrett gave a final, inarticulate cry. They belonged to each other. Her arms closed, holding his head against her breast. Sifting the damp curls and brushing a kiss on his forehead, she whispered her love inaudibly.

Time resumed, yet had no reality. It drifted aimlessly in the shelter of Garrett's arms. His was a beloved weight across her body, bringing a slow smile to her lips. Stirring, he tenderly kissed her before drawing a blanket over them. But always, Garrett kept one hand possessively on her, and when he settled, he fitted her into the curve of his body, sheltering her. Belonging to the man she loved was heaven.

Curling willingly into him, Diana smiled, her lashes drifting closed with contentment. Mama was right.

CHAPTER IX

Iraklion, Crete—November, 1819

THE FACE IN THE MIRROR WAS THE SAME. NOTHING HAD changed, yet everything had. And once disembarked, she'd be alone with Garrett. The prospect delighted yet terrified her. In all the days and all the nights after that night, she'd faced the truth that she couldn't trust her instincts. Or her desires.

Diana swung a pelisse over her dress, made from the sea-green velvet caftan, and took a last look back. Returned to their former size, Ariadne's clothes were folded and stacked on the end of the bed. All the make-work tasks were done; nothing remained to delay her. This small cabin where she'd played with Prinny was no longer sanctuary.

"Diana," Ariadne called when she arrived on deck, "isn't it a glorious day?"

With one hand, she swept an exuberant gesture that encompassed the harbor, with its forest of masts, and the sun, already high in the sky, glittering off the water and pouring over terra-cotta buildings so like Bizerte.

The fleet was already back in port with the day's catch. The small fishing boats huddled where stone docks dwindled to shingle beach, while merchant ships, large and small, rode at anchor at the other end of the harbor, waiting for cargoes and the tide.

Ariadne was right. The day was glorious despite the crisp breeze. Iraklion reminded Diana of Bizerte, but there were subtle differences that made the day even more glorious. A church spire in the distance, and women without veils shrouding their faces, made it clear that danger from the bey no longer existed. She was free. Yet sadness mixed with exhilaration.

Turning to Ariadne, Diana extended a hand. "I wish you didn't have to leave for Greece so soon."

"I'll miss you, too." Ariadne patted the hand in consolation. "But we have to go. Our new cargo is perishable. Don't worry. Garrett will take care of you." Looking past Diana, she smiled.

"Good morning, ladies."

Though he spoke to both, Garrett's arm casually encircled Diana's waist. His breath brushed her ear and sent a quickly controlled shiver through her. His arm tightened in response.

Sherry-brown eyes gleamed with humor above her. "I feel the same way." His voice was pitched too low for Ariadne to hear.

A flush rising in her cheeks, Diana turned. The comprehension on Ariadne's face heightened the flush. She didn't understand. Life with Garrett would be impossible no matter how much Diana loved him. She'd always worry whether he'd survive his next escapade. Then, one day he wouldn't.

Parting from him was intolerable. Yet, to be his widow in a year, perhaps two, sickened her. He'd never change. She couldn't fool herself that he would.

"Would you fetch Nikos for me?" Ariadne asked Garrett.

"My pleasure."

When his arm left her shoulders, Diana felt bereft, yet relieved. She cast a wistful glance after his departing figure under the pretext of tucking a strand of silver-blond hair into a braid. In a few days she'd become accustomed to being alone.

"Garrett prefers your hair with that tousled look that so becomes you." Ariadne suggested, "When you're married—"

"That's fantasy. We don't suit."

Ariadne chuckled softly, knowingly. "I've never seen two people more made for each other. Think of what I've said. Adventure's all very well, but take my advice and marry him."

"He has to ask first." Face unconsciously shadowed, Diana shifted uneasily under Ariadne's gaze.

"Any woman can make her man propose. I, Ariadne Kalogeropoulos, know this for a fact." She nodded impressively and continued in a louder voice. "Thank you, Garrett."

"Nikos has a small emergency with the cargo. He begs to be excused, and sends his love." Smiling, Garrett handed Ariadne the small bundle he'd brought up for her. "Don't worry, he has Prinny helping him." He winked outrageously. "Close your eyes, Ariadne. I wouldn't want you to see Nikos's gift."

Hands closing on Diana's waist, he drew her against him. She went willingly. One last chance to luxuriate in his kiss, his touch. A wash of heat struck as his lips closed over hers. Her arms went up instinctively around his neck.

His lips were everything she remembered, but he could never be hers. Bittersweet thoughts mingled with memories of that night. She pressed into him, unable to stop, to let him go. Disappointment surged when he reluctantly lifted his head. The hands on her waist tightened, then dropped.

Stepping away, he whispered, "Behave yourself."

Hot color stained her cheeks. An amused twinkle in Ariadne's eyes said she recalled Diana's protest that they "wouldn't suit." Then Ariadne took pity on her and held out the bundle Garrett had brought.

"For you. I want you to happily remember your time aboard the *Medea*."

With inexplicably stiff fingers, Diana fumbled at the cord binding the brown-paper-wrapped parcel. In a rustle of paper, the cord parted. A lacy white wool shawl was inside. One that would go well with any dress. Looking from the shawl to Ariadne's animated face, tears started in Diana's eyes.

"Thank you," she whispered, and hugged the smaller woman. "I— Thank you."

Ariadne's lips brushed Diana's cheek before murmuring in her ear, "Marry him."

Tear-choked laughter rose in Diana's throat. "Thank you, again."

"Garrett, take good care of her." Ariadne's eyes were damp, too.

Another flurry of tearful good-byes left Diana drained, and she allowed Garrett to guide her down the swaying gangway, up the street, and into the market near the docks. One last time, she waved good-bye to Ariadne before obeying the comforting touch of Garrett's hand at her waist.

"Where to?" she asked when the *Medea* was no longer in sight.

"First, a room at an inn. Then"—he inspected her, taking in the demure pelisse and the tightly held bundle—"find you some clothes. A dressing gown, nightgowns, underthings"—he touched the velvet of her sleeve briefly—"if you need them."

"I need them," she said with equally forced casualness. "I'm looking forward to clothes that actually fit."

Not waiting for an answer, she hurried forward, putting a small distance between them and making herself concentrate on her surroundings. They were easier to think about than Garrett and the coming separation.

The market was like, yet strangely unlike, the one in Bizerte, and the difference was the people. Leaning against barrels or bales near their stalls, old men fingered beads and

smoked pipes in the brilliant autumn sunshine. Their
spouses, dressed in unrelieved black with shawls drawn
over silvered hair, tended stalls or created lace with nimble,
gnarled fingers. Others watched livestock for sale or the
swarms of children playing. A cautious matron examined a
goat.

The market was just like the *suq* in Bizerte in other re-
spects. Stalls filled the small square to the detriment of easy
movement. Everything from scarves and baskets to jewelry
and food stocked the counters or dangled from corners
above and below. Yet she wasn't enthralled as she'd been in
Bizerte; the joy of shopping paled.

"Diana."

Garrett's tone made her turn in a swirl of skirts. "Yes?"
He looked annoyed.

"Haven't you learned yet not to wander off by yourself?"
Garrett closed the few yards separating them in a pair of
long strides and glowered down at her.

Blinking, Diana slowly shook her head. "This isn't Bizerte."

"Crete," he said, speaking as though she were a particularly dull child, "is part of the Ottoman Empire."

Gesturing at the steady trickle of people passing on either
side, she objected, "But the women aren't veiled."

"True. And I doubt the pasha has any burning interest in
blonds. His problems are more with politics than harems.
But women don't travel around the Mediterranean alone. At
least not twice." Drawing a finger along her cheek, Garrett's
face softened. "As a favor to me, be careful and don't trust
Cretan men." Turning through an archway that led into a
courtyard, he held open a door for her.

"All right," Diana answered absently, stepping into the
shaded darkness of the inn's interior.

After the pure, golden sunlight outside, the low room,
with its white walls and heavy, dark wooden beams, seemed
dim. As her eyes adjusted, the fuzzy things hanging from the
ceiling and exuding spicy, pungent odors resolved into

bunches of herbs drying. Everything—from the bare wooden floor to settles drawn up before the small beehive fireplace to stairs rising along one wall—was spotlessly clean. Gran would have approved. A slow smile widened Diana's generous mouth at the thought of her aristocratic grandmother in a common inn.

A door leading to the back terrace opened, and a plump woman, wiping her hands on a towel, swept in. She bustled across the room with a pleased exclamation welcoming them.

Thanking her gravely, Garrett said, "We'd like a room for the next few days, please."

The landlady offered her largest room for the young couple. Before he could agree, Diana broke in, "Two rooms!"

"You speak Greek." The landlady smiled widely and hurried over to a tall bureau secretary near the stairs. "You're wise to have your own room. We women need our privacy."

The landlady inspected Garrett thoroughly before giving Diana a nod of approval, accompanied by a conspiratorial wink. Startled, Diana winked back. Amazing. These Greek women seemed unshockable. Anywhere else, traveling with a man who was neither husband nor brother would make her the object of scandal and snubbing, but not with Ariadne. And clearly not with this woman.

While she and Garrett signed the register, the woman chattered on. Although the accent was unusual and a few of the words strange, Diana gathered she thought they were a runaway couple. The landlady assured them she wouldn't reveal their presence, no matter what the bribe.

"Thank you," Garrett said, straightening. "If a very tall Arab with a black beard asks for us, we're not here." Taking money from his pocket, he smiled. "Could we have a *mezze* when we return?"

"Of course. With the weather so lovely, would you like it on the terrace?" The landlady tucked the coin carefully into a small purse. "Or, perhaps, the balcony off your rooms?"

"The terrace—" A soft flush colored Diana's cheeks when Garrett's voice overrode hers.

"The balcony off our rooms." Smiling down at the landlady, he took Diana's package and handed it to her. "Please place this in her room, and when my luggage arrives from the *Medea,* put it in mine."

Nodding farewell, he guided Diana into the street and headed back the way they'd come. A small frown wrinkled her forehead. "Garrett, are we still in danger from Karim?"

"No. Haroun is the greatest nip-farthing I've ever met. Karim'll have to forgo a direct ship. He'll arrive days after we leave."

A flock of children in ragged, patched, but clean clothes swirled past. Their cheerful young voices echoed against the beige stucco walls lining the street. A smile smoothed Diana's frown away.

Laughter gleaming in the sherry-colored eyes, Garrett waited until the exuberant shouts died before continuing. "He'd better. I have plans."

"What plans?" Diana asked, eyeing him suspiciously.

"Karim will arrive in Iraklion in about a week." Garrett drew her hand back through his arm and ignored the question. "When he does, he'll find we've gone to Portugal. A merchantman's heading there, and it'll be easy to lay a false trail."

Hand at Diana's waist, Garrett guided her past a fabric merchant's stall. A small dress shop was set into the wall behind it.

Grinning widely, he asked, "Wouldn't you love to see Haroun's face when he receives the bill for Karim's chase? And all for naught."

"That's a pleasure I can forgo." She stepped into the modiste's shop.

"Good morning. We're looking for a new wardrobe for this young lady," Garrett said to a stern-faced woman in black bombazine.

Surveying Diana, the proprietress came forward slowly.

"It will take weeks for one. But"—she hesitated, then smiled ingratiatingly—"if you're willing to consider an order another customer refused—"

"If the price is right," Diana agreed.

"Mais, naturellement, madame," the proprietress said in an accent that mangled the French. Clapping her hands sharply, she called to her assistant, Callista, to bring the dresses made for Madame Harlow. "The wife of an English merchant, *madame,"* the proprietress explained, her hands folded disapprovingly before her. "A most capricious lady."

Murmuring commiseration, Diana watched as a girl nearly buried beneath the clothing she carried pushed through the curtained doorway and dropped it on the single chair the shop possessed. Shooing Callista away, the proprietress surged over to the pile and held up the first garment.

"Is not this lovely?" she asked. It was acid green and covered with knots of ribbon and ruffles.

"That's not quite what I'm looking for, Madame—"

"Madame Elise." She tossed the green gown to Callista and picked up a rose one. "This will look beautiful on *madame."*

Involuntarily, Diana smiled. It was the shade of fabric left behind in Bizerte. Madame Elise described its manifold charms in praise sprinkled with fractured French.

"It's the wrong color," Garrett said in English.

"Blonds can wear rose," Diana objected.

"Not you."

He pulled an intense sapphire from the pile on the chair. Holding it against her cheek flirtatiously, he nodded approval. Then, at the heightened color in her face, he molded the dress lovingly to her figure. Madame Elise smirked with sharp calculation.

"This will suit you much better." His finely cut mouth quirked at one corner. "Once," he added, flicking disparagingly at the overload of decorations, "you cut off those."

"Mrs. Harlow certainly liked ruffles. But she's close to my height." Diana kicked out the skirt with one foot.

"I don't mind your ankles showing." Deliberately, Garrett shifted into English again.

Diana's brows arched as she turned. "This will do nicely, Madame Elise."

For the next hour, they went through the clothing, discarding most of it. Several times, Garrett rejected one she considered possible, and to her chagrin, she rarely protested. In fact, she invariably bought the dresses he liked. Finished with the frilly rejects, Garrett called for fashion sketches. Madame Elise triumphantly produced a year-old *Ackermann's Repository* and sent Callista for another chair for *monsieur*.

Thumbing through the pages, he shook his head. "What do you have in the way of nightwear?"

"Ah. *Les négligées,*" the modiste exclaimed in a tortured accent. "*Monsieur* will like this." From behind a counter, she drew out a diaphanous nightgown and robe of white silk gauze trimmed with peach satin. "It will show *madame's* excellent figure to the best advantage."

Garrett sat up straighter and smiled.

"Th-thank you, *madame,* but I don't think so." Diana quickly cut off his response. Laughter vied with embarrassment in her voice, and the laughter won, her solitary dimple flashing. "Have you anything warmer?" Fortunately, Garrett stayed quiet beyond a disappointed murmur meant only for her ears.

Wild hawks soared above low cliffs, late sunlight warming the brown of their wings to bronze. Smiling softly, Karim watched, his hands curling about the railing when one swooped. A splash of intense white showed on the blue water before the hawk climbed back to the sky, a fish flopping in its talons.

That was the way he'd swoop when he caught up with Hamilton and the girl in Crete. He wasn't far behind now, no more than a day. In Iraklion it wouldn't take long to find and arrest them. His smile fading, Karim considered the one possible hitch.

The pasha, Selim, who governed Crete, was renowned for avoiding responsibility. Yet, somehow, he balanced his official position against the menace of the Greek pirates who truly governed Crete and the threat from Bey Mehmed Ali of Egypt.

How long would Egypt's bey remain loyal to the Sultan this time? Even more, how long would Egypt's bey remain at home? Those questions had to occupy Selim's mind. Since the massacre of the Mameluks, Mehmed Ali's power had spread insidiously through this part of the Mediterranean, until Egypt did little more than give the Sultan lip service. Balancing the Sultan and Mehmed Ali against each other, and both against the pirates, took up most of Selim's time. Still, he retained power and, in reality, reported to no one. The bey of Bizerte's problems would come low on the list of things he found important.

Except—Karim fingered his chin and smoothed his beard, smiling as he watched the hawks soar and soar again —Selim owed Haroun a sizable amount of money. How much that would influence the pasha, Karim didn't know. But it should be useful. Another hawk swooped into a dive.

"My lord."

Karim swung about, fists clenching at his sides with the interruption. "Yes?"

"My lord." Umar shifted uneasily, then snapped to attention at Karim's glare. "The captain wishes me to inform you that dinner awaits your attendance."

"Tell the captain I'm not hungry."

"But, my lord—" Umar broke off at Karim's sharp gesture.

"Tell the captain I'm not hungry," he repeated with precise enunciation, pausing between each word.

"Yes, my lord." Saluting, Umar faded into the shadow blanketing that side of the ship.

Karim swung back to the rail, searching for the hawks.

They were mere specks above the cliffs in the distance now, the chance of seeing one dive from the sky and return with its catch gone. He slowly forced himself to relax. There would be other hawks, other days.

As evening approached, the wind freshened. Already, they were leaving these insignificant islands with their nesting hawks behind. Crete and victory were little more than a day away. Karim smiled triumphantly. Along with Hamilton, he'd get the badge of Bizerte.

And the means to power.

"What's ouzo?"

Diana looked at the teapot and a stone pitcher on the balcony table. Two cups flanked the teapot; two tiny glasses, the pitcher. A platter of small appetizers occupied the rest of the iron table. Holding a chair, Garrett seated her, his hand deliberately trailing along her shoulder and cupping the nape of her neck briefly, affectionately.

"A liqueur with anise." Grinning, he settled in the chair he'd pulled intimately close. "You'll have to try it."

"I'm more interested in how we're going to get out of Iraklion before Karim arrives. Did you find a ship?" Reluctance to learn about anything that would take her away from him edged her voice.

Laughter sparkled in his eyes, and for a moment it seemed he intended to make the nightly seduction attempt early. Instead, Garrett held out a teacup.

"We're going to make a fortune."

"But I don't need another fortune."

Tea slopped over the rim and onto her thumb as her cup rattled in its saucer. Diana put it down barely on the edge of the table and stared at Garrett in amazement. She'd thought he couldn't surprise her anymore. She was wrong.

Garrett dismissed the objection with a wave of his hand. "Nor I. But this is irresistible. Here's what we'll do," he explained, leaning forward, the excitement in him barely leashed. Describing assorted Machiavellian arrangements for secret passage to Greece and various bizarre schemes, he swept his hands wide to the imminent peril of the stone pitcher, finishing, "And we'll trade for ancient statues."

Stunned, Diana blinked and barely saved the pitcher. Picking up her cup, she took a sip. "What," she asked slowly, "are we going to do with these ancient statues?"

"Ever since the Elgin marbles hit London, the *ton* have been mad for antiquities. There's a huge market there. And the Greek rebels need guns to free themselves from the Ottomans. So," he gestured exuberantly, his grin widening even further, "we run guns to the Greeks, take payment in antique statuary, sell it at a huge profit, and tweak the noses of the Turks all at the same time."

Diana stared at him. Around them the breeze strengthened as the sun gradually set, rustling the last leaves clinging to the grapevines in the garden below. The light wind freed a tendril of hair from loosely bound braids to tickle her cheek. Pushing it behind her ear, she absorbed the sense of unreality settling over her.

Everything else was *normal,* just as she'd always imagined Greece from her mother's letters. It was Garrett who was mad. Even worse, she was tempted. They'd be together.

A cloud passed over his face. "It'll serve them right if the Greeks win with our guns. One lousy piaster a bottle." Shaking his head, natural ebullience reasserted itself. "We'll have a fabulous time."

A faint tremor shaking her hand, Diana lowered her tea cup, nearly knocking it off the edge of the small table. He really was serious. Completely serious. Tea dripping back into the saucer, she raised the cup for a long sip. Over the rim, she watched his face closely.

He thrust back a black lock of hair fallen over his forehead. "I don't know why I didn't think of this sooner. Smuggling liquor was getting to be a bore."

She'd save Garrett from himself. He wouldn't admit it, but they almost hadn't escaped from Bizerte. Eventually the Turks would kill him—if someone else didn't first. Maybe they weren't meant for each other, but she'd save the man she loved from himself.

"Garrett." She carefully moved the stone pitcher out of danger before plunging on. "Come with me to Jerusalem. You can trade in antiquities there. My father . . ." Her voice died away at the decisive shake of his head.

"I can't." Absently, he reached for one of the vine leaves stuffed with meat on the *mezze* tray and finished it in two bites. "I'm persona non grata in Jerusalem."

"Why?" Her mouth was dry despite all the tea.

"Remember that little *contretemps* in the Holy Land Nikos mentioned?" One brow wryly arched up to the lock of inky hair that had fallen on his brow again.

"Don't tell me." Diana sighed and shook her head in resignation. "You were involved."

"Don't worry. I lead a charmed life." He spread his hands palms up in lighthearted apology. "They'll never catch me."

Shivering, Diana hugged her arms tightly to her. The breeze increasing with the lowering sun had cooled the air sharply in the last few minutes. "In Greece, you're still in the Ottoman Empire. What happens if the bey asks for your extradition?"

Humor danced in his expression. "Haroun doesn't dare complain. He'd be the laughingstock of the empire. Greece is safe."

"With that argument, you're just as safe in Jerusalem." Diana shivered again.

"Are you cold?" Garrett asked, concerned.

"A little." More than the slight lowering of temperature as day ended bothered her. A lot more.

He rose and extended a hand. "Let's go in."

At the compelling tug, Diana rose. She let her hand rest in his after gaining her feet. Intent on hiding her tension, she withdrew it reluctantly. She'd have to do it. There wasn't any other way.

"The Mediterranean's too dangerous for me to travel alone," she said quietly.

"Well, yes," Garrett admitted, his face shadowy in the gathering dusk.

Peering up at him, she made no move toward the French door he held open. "I want you to come with me, Garrett."

Coming to her, his hands settled on her shoulders and began a seductive massage. "Sweetheart, I would if I could, but—"

Swallowing, she stepped free. "If you don't, I'll report your plans to the Turks."

His expression closed, but not before she saw a flicker of disappointment. Or hurt?

"Blackmail isn't pretty."

As he took a step closer, she backed away until the ornate iron railing pressed into her thighs. Licking dry lips, she slowly shook her head. "Blackmail's too harsh a word." Flexing her fingers, she barely stopped herself from reaching out to him. "Garrett," she said quietly, "I'm doing it for your own good."

Eyes narrowed, he closed the distance between them and loomed over her. After a fractional pause, he smiled winningly and resumed the steady, gentle manipulation of the muscles in neck and shoulders.

"If you go to the authorities," Garrett said, pulling her a few inches nearer, his voice tangible against her face as he spoke softly, "you'll wind up in Haroun's harem again."

"Have you ever heard of a letter."

CHAPTER X

"MY LORD." HER VOICE SOOTHING, LEILA SHUT THE door quietly. With the tray balanced carefully, she came to Haroun's side and put it on a small table beside him. "It's honey sorbet made from the first snows on the mountains." She knelt on the cushion at his feet.

His hand jerking to his beard, he touched his receding chin, and his face settled into petulant lines. "Who paid for the horseman to go to the Atlas Mountains?"

"I did, my lord, from my slipper money." Leila smiled persuasively. "As a special treat for you."

"It's too chilly," he grumbled, barely hiding reluctant pleasure. The pale honey ice floated on a plate of shimmering intense green. Haroun tugged the neck of his robe closed and savored a mouthful.

"I'll put coal on the brazier to warm you."

Rising gracefully from the cushion, Leila crossed to the intricately pierced brass brazier and knelt there. Placing another coal on the fire, she closed the top, then drew the drapes to close out the insistent sound of dripping rain.

Ever since Karim left in pursuit, the rain had persisted. Each day was chill with damp creeping throughout the palace. Not even in the baths was it truly warm. Nothing was more likely to upset Haroun. He loved the sun and warmth of summer, although he tolerated autumn and winter for the sorbets they brought to feed an insatiable sweet tooth. The persistent rain incessantly reminded him of the day he lost his prized beard.

"Are you comfortable, my lord?" she asked, returning to his side.

Haroun dropped the empty plate on the tray with a clatter. "How can I be comfortable when this beard itches like the very fiends of hell were scratching their way out?"

"My lord"—Leila seated herself with boneless grace on the cushion—"have you considered why gardeners prune bushes in the early spring?" She took his hand between hers and squeezed consolingly.

"Gardeners!" Disarranging his maroon silk robe, Haroun twitched in his chair, but his hand remained in hers. "What do gardeners have to do with anything, woman?"

Leila cast a glance at Haroun's face. He stared moodily at the drapes moving in the small drafts that found their way through the walls and windows.

"If my lord would cast his mind on such an insignificant puzzle"—she ignored the skeptical snort—"think what happens to bushes after they are pruned." Deliberately, she paused. Only after Haroun shifted in the chair, interest showing in his face, did she continue. "The bush grows much fuller and thicker for the shearing. But without clipping, it grows spindly and thin."

Haroun's hand rose to the scraggly patches. Smiling for the first time in days, he settled in his chair. Without remembering to wince, he poured two cups of mint tea in the traditional long streaming arc and handed one to Leila. She received it in both hands with an elegant bow.

"That girl!" He touched the stubble-covered chin again.

To hide her dismay, Leila bent over the teacup cradled in her hands. "I should not speak ill of your brother, but mustn't Karim bear the burden of guilt, husband?"

Haroun raised his brows and sipped his tea. "He is still

my brother, though of a different mother. What has he to do with the girl?"

Putting her cup down carefully, Leila took his hand between both of hers again. "My lord, did not Karim suggest you send for Diana that night?"

The bey nodded reluctantly. "He did."

"Lord, did Karim tell you she was ready to grace your couch?"

His small mouth pursed thoughtfully, Haroun nodded.

"We received her only that day." Pausing, she let the statement sink in. "And she was American. Those girls are raised with peculiar notions." Shaking her head in perplexity, she added, "Diana showed signs of being more difficult than usual to train."

"Karim knew this?"

Leila nodded. "He bought her. And suffered a kicked shin for examining her." Stroking Haroun's hand, she watched his face without appearing to as she continued. "He dreamed of your discomfiture when Diana fought like a wildcat."

"Maybe he thought I'd enjoy subduing her."

"My lord, why should your brother wish you enjoyment?" She smiled when the bey's face settled into stern lines at Karim's duplicity. "He forgot me, however."

Haroun sat up straighter in his chair, and his hand returned her gentle caresses absently.

"My dearest lord, before allowing an untrained maiden to grace your bed, I made sure she was compliant, however inexperienced." Rising on her knees to sit more erect, Leila folded her hands demurely in her lap. "Diana promised not to fight, plus"—the small smile on her lips urged him to join her amusement—"Yasmin gave her a deep-muscle massage."

His lips twitching, Haroun fought laughter. But eventually, he gave in. The deep, rich laugh filled the luxurious bedchamber and delighted Leila. Finishing, Haroun leaned toward her, still smiling. "Could she stand when Yasmin was through?"

"Barely, my lord."

The smile slowly faded. "Still, she did escape." His free hand beating a slow rhythm on the arm of the chair, he settled back, face thoughtful. "When Karim brings her back, she must be punished."

"But consider, lord, how frightened she was, how untrained."

He shrugged off the protest.

"And Karim?" Leila asked quietly.

Another irritable shrug dismissed the security chief. "There's the costs of buying her and sending men to catch her. I'm not going to be out that amount of money." Staring into the distance, a thin smile slowly curved his small mouth. "After all, it's Karim's fault she's damaged goods. He'll have to buy her as the start of his harem." The smile grew wider. "For double my expenses."

Straightening, Leila started to protest, but the wave of his hand stopped her.

"I'm being lenient. She deserves to be executed."

Leila studied her husband. Nothing would change his mind. Diana must escape from the men he sent after her. Despite her foolish resistance to the life of the harem, somehow, some way, Leila would save her.

A stab of guilt shook her resolution, but only for a moment. Even a week as Karim's bride would kill a gently reared girl. Haroun would have to be thwarted. Just this once Leila would circumvent her husband.

Diana dropped the cinnamon muslin on the white candlewick bedspread and turned reluctantly to the other dress. She trailed gentle fingers down the indigo silk skirt of the gown lying across the bed. Too formal for dinner at an inn, it was the same color as the fabric left behind in Bizerte, and with the furbelows removed, it had made up almost as well as that fabric should have. Not that she'd had a special design in mind when she chose it, but she would have chosen something like this.

But it *was* too formal for dinner here. Stroking it again, Garrett's face when he held it against her danced in her mind. And then the way he'd looked when they left the balcony to change. He hadn't taken the—she closed her eyes and forced herself to face the word—blackmail well, and she felt guilty over it. How could she insist on Jerusalem if she was trying to save him? He'd already gotten into trouble there once. It was a dilemma—a dilemma she'd solve over dinner, but only if she talked him into a better mood.

Picking up the dress, Diana held it in front of her and stooped down to look in the small mirror. The pale, changeable blue of her eyes picked up the indigo, giving them a dark, mysterious cast. She stooped for an instant longer, undecided, then pulled off her robe. Looking her best would improve his mood. She'd wear it for him.

After a brief struggle, she hooked the indigo dress over chemise and corset and perched on a low stool before the mirror. A branch of candles on either side bathed her in golden light that put warm highlights into her hair. Brushing the heavy length, she braided it. With a few strategic pins in place, it formed a coronet. What a difference to be able to wear her hair up, unlike on board the ship.

How would Garrett react to seeing her properly attired, her hair properly coiffed? A slow, sensual smile curved the mirror image's mouth as she patted the last stray wisp into place. Satisfied, she went to the door of her small room and let herself out.

"Diana," Garrett called softly.

She turned, the heavy silk skirt flowing about her ankles. At the opposite end of the hall, a dim and mysterious figure stood in the faint glow of small lamps. Skirting the railing protecting the unwary from tumbling down the stairwell, he came toward her.

"Good evening, Garrett." She felt tongue-tied, uncertain after their confrontation earlier.

"Good evening, Diana." He returned the greeting with no trace of his usual mockery. "You look"—he paused consideringly—"elegant and"—pausing again, he joined her—"lovely."

Diana touched the swathed bodice of the dress with one hand. "It's too formal for tonight. But I couldn't resist."

"You should never resist your instincts." He offered his arm to lead her downstairs.

"I probably should have worn muslin, or"—a draft struck them as the door opened into the foyer two steps below—"wool to keep warm."

"Nothing in wool suited you half so well."

Shaking her head, Diana laughed and stopped. "I almost feel like Gran will be downstairs to lecture me about being escorted to dinner by a man who's not a Bostonian." Peering into his face, she balanced on the narrow step. "Worse, you're English."

Garrett gave her a questioning look.

"She'd blame you for our family's shipping losses during the war."

"Your grandmother and my Aunt Sophy would probably get along—if they ignored nationality, of course. But they'd probably spend their days sparring."

"Or, worse, combine their talents against us." Diana shuddered delicately. "If your Aunt Sophy is as formidable as Gran at matchmaking."

Garrett scowled. "Aunt Sophy constantly pushed insipid girls merely because they possessed birth, breeding, and, of course, a large fortune." Looking at Diana, his expression softened, and he stroked her cheek with a gentle finger. "Let's make a pact and find a more pleasant topic of conversation."

Agreeing, Diana started down the stairs again. In the darkness accompanying evening, a branch of candles on the tall bureau secretary and a low fire suffused the room in soft golden light. The herbs drying overhead smelled spicier in the eddying drafts, while cheerful noise poured through a door hidden by the curve of the fireplace. Garrett led the way and stepped aside for her to enter first.

The noise and confusion of the dining room enfolded her from the moment she stepped inside. More people than the inn could possibly hold filled the room; the sounds of conversation, orders, utensils scraping on plates echoed off dark beams supporting the low whitewashed ceiling. Through the dodging waiters and crowds, Diana saw only one small table empty.

She edged around the first set of tables, some of the noise subsiding. Short glances right and left confirmed the diners were staring at her. She swallowed and held her head a little higher. The other women were dark-haired and soberly clad in serviceable wools and linen. Diana indicated them with a barely perceptible nod as Garrett seated her.

"See. This isn't the dress for tonight."

His hand rested on the back of her chair. Looking around, he squeezed her shoulder in reassurance, then rounded the table to his own chair. Signaling the harried waiter, he smiled at her.

"If they were half as lovely, they'd wear nicer dresses." He gave their orders to the waiter, who, after one appreciative glance, ignored Diana. "Of course," Garrett added after he left, "their escorts wouldn't appreciate it."

Diana nodded at the waiter's retreating back. "Why did he act like I wasn't here?"

"You're with me, and therefore not for his eyes."

A flush climbing her cheeks, Diana straightened at the intimate expression on his face. "You're joking."

Laughter glinted in the depths of his eyes. "This is still part of the Ottoman Empire," he reminded her softly. "Women are kept hidden here."

"That's barbaric."

"Don't look so superior. In London or Boston, I couldn't

escort you to a hotel for dinner without a chaperon. For that matter, I couldn't speak to you in private."

The palace was as floridly overdecorated as the bey's was spare. Feet sinking into the deep, silencing carpet, Karim followed the lavishly dressed servant. Haroun wouldn't purchase brocades that lush for himself. Nor would he display wealth where anyone might see it.

"In here, my lord." Pushing the door open, the servant bowed to an insulting depth, then departed, leaving Karim to announce himself.

"Lord Karim." Pasha Selim waved at the circle of divans ranged about a low table laden with delicacies. "Join me. Have my useless servants made you comfortable? Accept my humble excuse for not greeting you when you arrived, but the bandits in the hills become ever more of a nuisance."

Looking at the pasha's paunch, Karim doubted he ever left the luxuries of palace and harem. Selim's chins wobbled beneath a small goatee as he scooped up a tidbit and popped it whole into his mouth.

"Your servants treated us as envoys from the Sultan's Sublime Porte itself," Karim answered with mechanical civility. Sitting on the divan opposite, he stared, revolted, at the lavish array of foods.

"How is my brother ruler, Haroun? Something important must have happened to bring you here." Dabbling fingers in a small bowl of water at his elbow, Selim wiped them on a tiny napkin and tossed it on a pile in the corner. "Help yourself. I hope my cook found some means in his inadequate power to please you. It's merely local cuisine, but what else can a poor man do?"

"How could I not enjoy such a munificent offering and such gracious hospitality?"

Taking the smallest morsel of an unidentifiable meat fastidiously between two fingers, Karim bit into it with a polite smile. He swallowed rapidly and wiped his fingers clean.

"Too bad my brother was unable to join me," Karim said

colorlessly and poured a cup of tea to cleanse his palate. After a quick sip, he chose a mushroom dripping with a marinade and held it between his fingers.

"I'm sure you didn't come all this way to sample the delicacies of my humble home. Tell me your troubles, and I will solve them to the best of my meager abilities." Selim scooped up another delicacy and popped it into his mouth.

Karim put the mushroom down and fastidiously wiped his fingers again. "I'm tracking down two infidels to return them to Bizerte."

"They must be exceptionally dangerous felons to merit such an important man to be sent after them." Not even the folds of flesh surrounding his eyes could disguise the sharpness there.

"One is an infidel who smuggled liquor into Bizerte."

"How embarrassing for dear Haroun. It is widely known how vigilant he is in maintaining the purity of the Holy Koran." Selim patted his lips with another silk napkin and prompted, "The other?" He sipped a glass of rosewater sherbet and waited. The rose water shimmered palely pink through the crystal.

"A concubine from Haroun's harem. My men were still investigating how she escaped when I left. She fled on the same ship as the infidel."

"What a pity." A snort of mirth from Selim was quickly masked as a cough. "You've traced them here?"

"To Iraklion," Karim agreed, intent on using as few words as possible.

"What nationality are these dangerous and heretical felons." In a gesture irritatingly similar to one of Haroun's, Selim stroked his tiny beard.

"The infidel is English by birth, the girl American."

Selim's brows shot up. "Hmm. That presents some little difficulty. Didn't the Americans create a fuss about a small matter of piracy at Tripoli a few years back?"

Karim nodded.

"And the English behave most unreasonably about the

Sultan's governors in Greece." Selim picked up another sweetmeat and studied it before biting a sizable chunk off. "But you don't eat. If there is something else you would prefer"—he picked up the hammer for the small silver gong at his side—"I will summon my cook."

"That's not necessary," Karim assured him. With more haste than elegance, he stuffed some rice in his mouth. "I haven't regained my appetite since returning to land."

"Try these mushrooms. Charcoal-grilled with the lightest touch of lemon. And sherbet is always prescribed by the very best doctors when the stomach rebels." He patted the rolling paunch above his sash and handed Karim a small glass of revolting green liquid.

Repelled, Karim shook his head. "Your generosity exceeds even your reputation, but I shall be all right if I eat slowly." He selected a pastry and bit into it. At least this time, the flavors weren't overpowering. "We were discussing my mission in Iraklion."

"Ah, yes. Do the American girl and the Englishman intend to remain on Crete for long?" Finishing one tidbit, Selim reached for a pickled walnut.

Karim stiffened, watching the pasha narrowly. "Not more than a few days."

"Pity." Licking a dribble from the back of his hand, the pasha shook his head. "It takes a minimum of two weeks to receive word from the government at the Sublime Porte in Istanbul—if the winds are right. I could not"—he nibbled delicately on the walnut between words—"arrest anyone of those nationalities without the august direction of the Sultan himself."

"Then you refuse to aid the bey of Bizerte in his lawful pursuit of these felons?"

"I will send my fastest ship to Istanbul. Once instructions come, I shall arrest them and turn them over to you immediately." Spreading his hands widely, he tossed another napkin into the corner, his smile clearly adding "if they're still here."

"I'm forced to remind you of your debt to my brother!"

Karim cursed silently. The reminder should have been phrased more diplomatically, but the fat, pompous oaf had gotten under his skin.

"I'm sure," he continued when he'd regained control, "that Haroun would rush to your aid in similar circumstances."

"He is further from the Sublime Porte," Selim drawled. "And from Mehmed Ali in Egypt. I, on the other hand, must never forget these facts."

Crumpling the small silk napkin between his fingers, Karim indulged himself with the imagined pleasure of having Selim a member of his guards in Bizerte. But only for a fraction of a second.

"Egypt's bey plans expansion—not only on Crete, but westward." Selim smiled when Karim's head jerked up. "Including Bizerte."

"He has large eyes."

"If I suggest"—Selim emphasized the word lightly—"not that I would, mind you, to Mehmed Ali that I would support him, I feel sure he would speak to your brother about canceling my debt."

The phrasing was no longer as polite, as courteous as custom dictated. "If you thought you could get away with it, you'd have done it before this," Karim growled.

"Mehmed Ali grows too powerful," Selim admitted with an airy wave of one hand. Noticing a sticky spot on his cuff, he dipped a fresh napkin in his finger bowl and dabbed at it. "One places oneself in the jaws of the lion when other choices are worse." The deprecating gesture with napkin dangling from his fingers left Karim in little doubt of Selim's enjoyment. "Or when compromise isn't possible."

What little he'd eaten weighed heavily in Karim's stomach. It was blackmail, pure and simple. "Does not the Holy Koran speak of the need for cooperation against infidels?"

"Does not the Holy Koran speak against usury?" the pasha asked slowly. "Can the Holy Book not be used to justify all actions?" His fingers trailed through the water and rose petals in the shallow bowl before him. "Haroun shall forgive half the interest on my debt." Without drying his fingers, he gestured, sending water drops flying. "And there will be no need for the disappearance of a pair of infidels to come to my attention."

Haroun would scream at the number of piasters this "aid" would cost. A thin smile touched Karim's lips. Haroun *would* scream. It served him right for allowing Karim only two men for this search.

"The ways of the pasha of Crete are hard but acceptable," he assured Selim. "How many men can you loan me for the search?"

"To my infinite sorrow, none. The Sultan has many spies among my men." Selim laughed sorrowfully. "As does Mehmed Ali. You must rely on no assistance from me unless we wait for permission from the Sublime Porte."

"You were right, the baklava reminds me of the pastries in Bizerte."

Diana shifted, uncomfortable with the intensity of Garrett's expression. They were nearly alone now. The dining room had quieted with the slow drift of people, one after another, out of it. From the veranda, the sound of an unidentifiable instrument, the stomping of feet, and the clapping of hands revealed where they had gone. Garrett glanced in the music's direction and smiled.

"Would you care to see Greek dancing?"

"Wait," she interrupted as he started to rise. Readily, he subsided back into the chair. "If it's dangerous for you in Jerusalem, then take me to Genoa instead."

"Genoa?"

"The merchant who supplies my parents, Giovanni di Benedetto, has headquarters there. He will arrange my passage on a safe ship."

The trip to Genoa was longer than the one to Jerusalem. She'd have him that much longer.

Something unreadable flickered in his eyes, and he leaned back in the chair. "Would you like to watch the dancing?"

Accepting the change of subject, Diana rose. Warm and strong, his hand rested at her waist as he escorted her out of the dining room to the veranda.

Lanterns, hung on grape trellises edging the garden, cast golden light over the few leaves clinging to vines stretching out into the darkness. The breeze gently moved the leaves' shadows in random patterns that provided a counterpoint to the laughing male dancers, clapping in time to the music. The light bathed first one bearded face, then another, as they swayed. Here and there, men stamped to the music's rhythm and shouted.

Their enthusiasm was infectious. Even settled on a bench a discreet distance from them, it was difficult to keep her feet quiet. Laughter sparkling in her eyes, Diana tipped her head back to look at Garrett. With her arms hugging her waist, he hovered just behind her, a solid warmth protecting her against the brisk air.

Yet he noticed her arms cradling her body. "Would you like a shawl?"

"I can go for one."

"No." His hand closed briefly on her shoulder holding her in place. "I'll send a waiter."

In the next instant, he was gone. Grateful for the shadow cloaking the bench, Diana curled into a corner and waited. Without his body blocking the slight breeze filtering into the garden, she felt the chill more. But even without the promised shawl, she wouldn't have missed this sight.

The men who had been stamping their feet to the music's rhythm slowly drifted to the center of the circle. Diana couldn't see clearly. But glimpses caught through the clapping, shifting figures blocking her view fascinated her. The dance seemed to consist of leaps and kicks with hands clasped among the dancers.

Her foot tapping to the infectious rhythm, she shivered

with the sharpening breeze. She'd have a better view of the dancers a little nearer. And be out of the wind. Rising, she took a pair of steps toward the leaping figures. Concentrating on them, she forgot everything else.

When her new cashmere shawl settled about her shoulders, Diana jumped. Garrett stood behind her, two glasses of wine held in one hand. He gave one to her and raised his own in a toast.

"You never learn, do you?"

"What?" she asked. The sweet wine tasted good despite the admonishment.

He nodded toward the increasingly boisterous dancers. "Not to go wandering."

Staring at him in disbelief, she glanced at the men. Not one paid the least attention to this quiet, shadowed corner of the veranda. Nor could she imagine any of them disturbing her. They knew she was here with Garrett.

"All I did was watch the dancing."

Shaking his head, he extended a hand. "Come on. We'll watch it together. At least I'll know you're safe if you're with me."

The coronet of braids surmounting her head brushed against his chest when he moved her in front of him for a better view, and his arms slipped about her waist. Contented in his shelter, she watched the men whirl and kick in time to the music.

"Why aren't there women here?" she asked.

"I've never seen women dancing in Greece. Always it's been like this." Garrett nodded toward the laughing, perspiring men as they circled nearer. "Probably women have their own dances, perhaps at weddings. Certainly not at the taverns."

The dancers came for Garrett to join them. He raised his brows in a question.

"Go ahead. I'll be all right here."

In an instant, he was kicking and dipping with the rest. Despite black evening coat and pearl gray trousers that contrasted oddly with their colorful costumes, he moved in perfect time with them.

Diana smiled and tapped one foot. Catching Garrett's eye, she laughed in response to an exaggerated wink. He whirled and leapt, kicked and circled, until, finally, the music ended on a dramatic chord, and the men halted in their places. Arms dropping from one another's shoulders, they clapped each other on the back.

He might have been born among them except for his height and the way he moved. She lifted her glass in a tiny toast, sipped, and shivered as another cool breeze found its way through her shawl.

"Cold?" Garrett asked, joining her.

"A little," she whispered. The flush of exertion made his cheekbones more prominent, and his hair waved over his forehead in disarray.

"Shall we go?" He offered an arm, his chest rising and falling with quickened breathing.

She gestured with the glasses. "What do we do with these?"

"Drink them." Taking his glass, he drained it while she sipped. "Don't you want yours?"

"Not really, thank you." Chuckling softly, she watched him turn her glass to drink from precisely the same place her lips had rested on the rim.

Both glasses in one hand, he swept her a bow and offered his arm again. "Applause is always gratefully received, Miss Graham." Putting the glasses on the table in the dining room, he led her through the foyer and up the stairs. In the hall before her door, he turned her to face him.

"Thank you for a lovely evening, Diana." Eyes fiercely bright and expression serious, he kissed her gently.

Dazed, Diana blinked in the dim light. Everything had changed so quickly. She brushed his cheek with the back of her fingers. The familiar harsh velvet skin sent a ripple of awareness through her.

"Why do you have to be so—" he whispered, drawing

her into his arms and bending to claim her lips with his. Fire spread; it licked and fed on the passionate roving of his hands over her back. Pulling her fully against him, she felt the waiting heaviness.

Stretching to return his kisses, she leaned into his strength, delighting in it while memory flooded her. She loved this man so much.

Sliding her hands beneath his jacket, savoring the rippling strength of the muscles ridging his back, she kissed his neck, caught the lobe of his ear between her teeth. He held her away after an impassioned moment, a question implicit between them.

"Diana?"

Hearing the heavy tread of someone mounting the stairs, she stepped sharply back from Garrett, the moment past. Smiling shyly, she squeezed his hands, then hurried to her lonely room.

CHAPTER XI

"REMEMBER WHAT I SAID," GARRETT REPEATED sternly. Feet planted well apart with hands on his hips, he stood between her and the street leading down to the port. "Stay in this section of the market." He gestured at the gaily decorated stalls with their fabrics, flowers, and small household items. A group of urchins played boisterously in and out among the stalls. "I'll check on a ship for us."

"Yes, Garrett. Whatever you say, Garrett."

Dipping a curtsy of fake submission, Diana's smile flashed her solitary dimple engagingly. She was well aware of admiring looks from the men manning the stalls. And that their admiration annoyed Garrett. Mostly, they stared at her hair in its intricate coronet of braids. Madame Elise's selection of hats hadn't included any simple enough to wear. An uncovered head and pale hair was enough to make any Cretan stare, yet every man she'd met had been polite. Garrett worried unnecessarily.

"I won't stray. Besides, I can probably find something to occupy me for the entire half hour or so you'll be gone," she said, fluttering her lashes as demurely yet outrageously as she could.

"Baggage." Shaking his head and laughing, Garrett

turned to go. "Just don't forget your promise," he called over his shoulder.

Before returning to the middle-aged man who owned the stall, Diana watched Garrett stride down the street. Everything about him was so right. If only they could overcome the minor problems that confronted them. Until Garrett decided to behave like a responsible adult, she'd take steps to protect him from himself.

Sighing, she watched him fade out of sight around a wagon unloading in the street. Last night was necessary. Blackmailing him had been hard enough, but any advantage gained would have been lost if she hadn't refused him later on. Thank goodness they'd been interrupted. The one night they made love, everything had seemed right, yet it wasn't. Once alone again, she'd realized it.

Regret plagued her. About everything. She wouldn't mention the regret to him. She'd made mistakes, but not that one. Nor would she repeat the error of making love with him again. Even though that decision promised more restless nights.

Garrett appeared from behind the wagon and—she had to squint to pick his figure out in the distance—headed for the corner that would take him down the hill to the docks. With a last glimpse of him disappearing, the glittering sea dancing blue beyond, Diana reluctantly turned back to the task of shopping. She needed to choose a few dress lengths to make up herself, ones that wouldn't require removal of Madame Elise-style frills and ruffles.

The stall keeper had a selection of bolts ready when she turned. Not one was pastel. Stroking the rich jewel tones in wool, velvet, silk, and linen, she smiled down at him. He returned the smile, his engaging face creased with the width of it.

"These are perfect. Thank you."

The stall keeper flourished a bow. "Don't thank me, *kyria,* I cannot take the credit. Your admirable husband suggested these when he stopped at my stall last evening. It is rare for a man to take so much interest in his wife's wardrobe, but now I see why he does." He looked admiringly at her. "Your parents did well in choosing a husband for you."

"Thank you." Explaining that Garrett wasn't her husband, could never be her husband, would do no good. "I'll take these."

She indicated fine wools in turquoise and garnet. While he measured off dress lengths and wrapped them, she examined the rest of the fabrics. Pointing to a bolt at the back of the stall, she asked to see it. It looked interesting, but since the sun failed to penetrate into the depths of the stall, she wasn't sure.

It was moss green in wool and silk barege with a silky, foamy texture. "Oh, yes," she whispered, stroking it. What a pelisse it would make, perhaps trimmed with velvet and lined with heavy silk.

"Perhaps the *kyria* would like these as well." Without waiting, he dragged several more bolts of wool, barege, and silk in varying weights and colors. "Many of my foreign customers have chosen these for walking dresses, carriage dresses, and ball dresses, even"—he held up a slate gray merino—"riding dresses."

Fingering the merino, Diana hesitated. She'd love a riding habit to explore Crete on horseback. But it was a waste of Garrett's money. Even though he'd tell her to buy it, it was foolish to think about. Regretfully, she shook her head.

"These four will do for the time being. Thank you, though."

Smiling, she shook her head when he tried to sell her more. While he wrapped the final purchase, Diana wandered over to another stall within the circumscribed area where she'd promised to stay. A bank of delicate silk flowers covered the front, making it impossible to see inside. Every sort of bloom had been copied in silk, from full-blown roses to delicate violets and branches of dogwood.

With dew on them, they might have been picked from the woods only that morning. Reaching over, she stroked a lovely silk dogwood petal, a smile on her full lips. The proprietor, a handsome man in his mid-twenties, hurried out.

"They're beautiful," Diana told him softly. His bold smile and flourishing bow made her smile widen even further.

"Perhaps the *kyria* would accept a gift from my humble self?"

A delicate blush stole up her cheeks. Plucking a small bunch of violets from the mass of flowers covering the stall, he extended them. They were exquisite, but she regretfully shook her head.

"But, *kyria,* at least look. Are they not perfect? Yet their beauty pales beside yours." Rarely had she seen a more soulful look.

She lifted them to her face. They looked real enough to have the fresh scent of violets, although they didn't. Yet the brush of silk against her cheek reminded her of fresh-picked flowers. As she lifted her head, the playing urchins bumped her accidentally in their excited game and ran off to another stall.

"Are you hurt?" At the shake of her head, he gestured toward the bank of flowers cascading colorfully down the front of his stall. "Please. Choose some of my poor flowers. Your exquisite beauty will only enhance them."

The flush in her cheeks deepening, she shook her head. Such elaborate effusions made her feel tongue-tied—and brought home how far she was from Boston. "Your flowers, *kyrios,* are as exquisite as your manners."

With the violets in one hand, she looked at the others. Among the tumbled colors and shapes, a bunch of fragile, pink-tinged white flowers, two to a stem, provided an oasis of restrained beauty. With their simple petals, these would trim perfectly the slashes in the puff sleeves on the garnet. Turning to the young man, she asked how much they were.

"You would honor my stall by accepting them as my gift, *kyria,* as well as the violets."

"Oh, but I couldn't," Diana protested swiftly until she

realized she'd hurt him. *"Kyrios* Hamilton would . . ." She lowered her eyes and let her voice trail away as the young man brightened.

"I understand, *kyria.* But would the gift of these few violets disturb him unduly?" He pointed to the bunch in her hand.

"No, I don't think it would."

A small smile touched her lips as she paid for the branch of pink-tipped flowers without haggling and thanked the young man again. Garrett would neither mind the gift nor believe the courtesy everyone displayed. Looking about the remaining stalls, could she find a gift for him? Something to recall their adventure together. Perhaps an antiquarian gift would remind Garrett of her. Soon they'd be aboard a ship with the end of their adventure in sight.

The thought was depressing. She wanted to see her parents at Christmas—although it was now too late for the trip to Masada—yet she didn't want the journey to end. She went to the next stall with an air of determination, while still keeping an eye on the street he'd return by.

Why was he displeased. The captain of the *Artemis* was reliable and had two cabins for the trip to Jaffa. He'd even asked a reasonable price for passage. Garrett would surprise Diana by getting her to the Holy Land in time for Christmas. And he'd be back in Iraklion in time to get a shipment of guns to the mainland before the holidays.

So why didn't he feel more cheerful?

The whole thing was idiotic. Shrugging irritably, he strode up the street at a brisk pace. The chit had gotten to be a habit, and rescuing her even more of a habit. Trouble found her too easily, and she never realized how she'd gotten into it in the first place.

From what he'd heard, her father wouldn't be much better at keeping her safe. She needed a keeper. Or, at least, something to get her out of a scrape once she got into it.

A pistol was what she needed. He'd ask around in the

day they had left in Iraklion to find a gun dealer. If he was lucky, he'd find something with attractive carving on the grip.

Frowning, he moved his shoulders irritably again and glanced around. There was an eerie feeling someone was following him. But there wasn't any reason. He'd never done anything in Iraklion, at least nothing he could recall. Still—Garrett turned sharply about.

No, there wasn't anybody behind him. Small clumps of people filled the streets talking or going about their business. Nor did he recognize anyone. Besides, he knew of no one in Iraklion who held a grudge against him. Yet the prickly sensation of someone watching remained.

Listening for the sound of footsteps closing in behind him, Garrett continued up the street. All he heard were the usual sounds of haggling and laden donkeys clopping over the cobblestones, goods being unloaded and people walking. Nothing unusual at all.

He was being foolish, as foolish as Diana was about continuing their affair. The successful blackmail attempt irked him, although the certainty he could've stopped it irked even more.

What if he simply put her aboard the *Artemis* tomorrow morning and let her sail to Jaffa alone? The captain was trustworthy, the journey short. She didn't *need* his protection. That knowledge rankled. Almost as much as the sensation of someone watching him.

It could be one of the smugglers he'd contacted yesterday, but he doubted it. With the *bona fides* Nikos provided, they had no reason to mistrust each other. It couldn't be Karim. With the way Haroun husbanded his money, the security chief was still four or five days from Crete.

Garrett cast a quick glance behind anyway. The same people hovered outside shops. The same people went about their business, berating stubborn donkeys and unloading goods. The same people walked up and down the street. None looked familiar.

Would he even recognize Karim after one brief meeting? He didn't have to concern himself with Karim, he told himself one more time. Yet he hurried up the hill, intent on finding Diana. She might be the target, not him. The whole notion was ridiculous, of course, though he couldn't rid himself of it.

When he found her—and she'd better still be in the area where he'd left her—he'd keep her close for the rest of the day. Perhaps, he smiled, all night, too.

Garrett dodged a man rolling a barrel across the paving and toward wide doors into a warehouse. For a brief moment, the sense of being watched left. He covered another fifteen or twenty feet before it returned.

Swinging about, he surveyed the street. The man rolling the barrel was disappearing into the warehouse. Beyond the flow of people tending to daily concerns, there was still nothing that stood out. Several men walked along the street behind him. Nothing suspicious in that. He was going to the market; so were they.

Yet, why this constant sense of danger? Turning, he extended his stride. Reaching Diana quickly took on a sudden importance. His instincts for danger were too good; they'd saved him more than once. First find Diana, then a bolt-hole. After that, he'd worry about what was wrong. It was illogical, but logic could go hang.

Holding the framed bit of fresco, Diana glanced upward to check the angle of the sun instead. Surely it'd been almost an hour since Garrett left for the docks. Maybe it had taken longer than expected, but, somehow, she doubted it. With a final look at the fresco, she put it down, smiled, and shook her head at the disappointed stall keeper.

His wares somehow weren't right, weren't special enough for Garrett. Besides, they didn't have a sense of antiquity to them. Mama said antiquarian fakes were a major problem, and Diana couldn't be too careful. She'd find something else.

Somewhere else, too. She'd visited all the stalls in the small area she'd agreed to stay in, and she was determined not to break her word, not even inadvertently. Sighing because she couldn't find anything special enough for Garrett, Diana wandered back to the first stall where she could see down the street better.

A man rolled a barrel across the street toward a pair of doors opening on the yawning darkness of a warehouse. Beyond, she caught the flash of a tall, black-haired man striding purposefully toward her. She waited impatiently for Garrett. Starting forward, she caught herself. No, she'd promised she'd wait here.

Besides, she loved watching the way he moved. The fluid strength to his stride, the way he carried his head, his hair lifting in the breeze—all gave her pleasure. She watched him stop suddenly to look behind. Diana followed the direction of his gaze.

A number of people walked behind him, yet one in particular caught her attention. Squinting, she studied a trio of men, the color draining slowly from her face. She'd never forget *that* arrogant stride, nor the even more arrogant way he held his head.

It was Karim.

Fingers clenching the drawstrings of her reticule, she started forward to warn Garrett. They'd go to the authorities. Diana hesitated. Karim was "the authorities," even in Crete. No one could help them except themselves.

Flinging a haunted look about the market, she'd find a way to handle Karim. But how? No matter how much the Greeks hated their Muslim oppressors, explanations would take too long. Karim and his men were closing in on Garrett. She had to do something now.

And she knew what. The pack of urchins who'd played near the stalls all morning streamed out of the shadows toward her. Decision made, she called out to their leader, a boy who stood half a head taller than the others.

"Yes, *kyria.*" He swept an elegant bow at odds with trousers patched at knee and seat.

"Would you and your companions care to earn some money?" The question came out faintly breathless, and Diana caught her lower lip between her teeth.

The dark eyes glittered. "What does the *kyria* wish?"

Diana pointed at Garrett. "See that man?"

"The one who was with you earlier?"

"Yes." Pointing at Karim and his men, she said, "They're going to kidnap him."

"Should we fetch the guards?"

"No!" Diana looked at Garrett and Karim again. The distance between them looked smaller. "That'd take time we don't have. Here's what I want you to do." Rapidly, she outlined a sketchy plan. "Do you understand?"

"Yes, *kyria.*" Grinning, the boy rubbed his hands together. "How much?" he asked shrewdly.

Diana fumbled in her reticule. There was a silver piece and two copper ones. Shifting them into her other palm, she plunged in again. Another silver piece, and she thought she'd felt the shape of one more in the soft folds of the knitted bottom.

Watching the hurried search, the boy announced, "Three silver pieces."

Diana looked up quickly. He knew she didn't have time to bargain. "I've only got"—she hauled the last coin from the recesses of her reticule—"two silver pieces and three coppers."

"Done."

With the single word, the boy scooped them from her palm and, signaling his companions, scampered around the nearest stall. As they disappeared, a cold sensation gripped her. What if they didn't keep their promise? What if they merely absconded with the money? It didn't matter. If they did, she'd find some other way to rescue Garrett.

Tugging the reticule closed, she strode down the street, intent on doing what she could. As she passed the last stall, the stream of urchins ran past. Their leader sent her a small sign of reassurance. A rush of relief tempered the tension holding her.

Running and playing their infinite game of tag, the boys inserted themselves between Garrett and his pursuers. While she watched, they swarmed around Karim, holding out hands for money. The press of their bodies halted the trio. Without slowing, Diana grinned. As expected, Karim refused the beggars—they did look like beggars in their patched, dusty clothes.

When the boys wouldn't move, Karim pushed a small one out of the way. The youngster lay on the street, shouting, "The nasty man broke my arm!" Clutching it, he yelled for his mother. The uproar drew the attention of half the street. The other boys joined in the shouting, while the older ones threw rocks at Karim and his companions.

The stall keepers joined the attack, too. Instead of being orphaned flotsam of the streets, it seemed the boys were the sons of market vendors. Karim and his men were strange Turks who'd injured one of their children. That was all the women pouring from homes and stalls knew. The noise spiraled to new heights, and Diana could barely see Karim and his men for the bodies surrounding them.

"Why didn't you wait at the market?" Garrett demanded from beside her. "And what's going on?"

Diana pointed at the swirling mass of humanity behind him. "Karim's following you. Where can we hide?"

Garrett didn't answer. Quickly surveying the crowd swirling around Karim, he grabbed her hand. "We're leaving. It'd be too easy to find us if we hide." He plunged toward a narrow opening between crowd and wall and rushed sideways past a small girl with a doll dangling from beneath her arm.

A thin woman dressed in black, the mother of the boy claiming a broken arm, planted herself in front of Karim. With raised fist, she berated him in a screech that soared over the roar of the others.

"Hurry up," Garrett whispered in Diana's ear. "We haven't time to watch the show."

Holding the skirt of her aquamarine dress away from the dusty wall, she dodged a paper-and-string-wrapped package abandoned on the cobblestones. Ahead, the crowd thinned, and Garrett pulled her faster toward the docks.

In seconds they were past the bottleneck of the crowd in the narrow street and walking rapidly down the hill. Without asking, Diana knew Garrett was intent on not calling attention to them. Otherwise—her breath came quickly at the rapid pace—they'd be running.

Concentrating on keeping her footing on the uneven cobblestones, she didn't notice the change in the noise ahead until almost too late. The steady tramp of feet marching in quick time finally penetrated, and she looked up. A squad of guards wearing Turkish uniforms hurried to put down the incipient riot. The stragglers from the crowd near the market drifted away before the guards reached them.

"In here," Garrett said with undue harshness.

His hand still holding hers, he hurried toward the yawning darkness of open warehouse doors. Quiet shadow scented with the heady odor of hops swallowed them safely. Diana caught a shuddering breath. Soon the soldiers would free Karim and his men. But how soon? She watched the small squad quick-march past and started out almost before they'd cleared the door.

"Wait," Garrett hissed. He edged forward and checked both directions, careful not to show himself. He caught her hand again. "It's safe. Let's go."

Diana didn't waste time looking behind. However long it took to free Karim from the irate parents—and she hoped it took forever—it wouldn't be long enough. All they could do was hurry and, on her part, hope Garrett had a plan. There wasn't time to ask. Besides, the brief respite in the warehouse hadn't been long enough to catch her breath.

Catching her around the waist, Garrett swung her out of the way of a man running toward the noise. He had the look of a guard although unarmed. Garrett hurried faster. Purposely, he kept himself between her and the curious. Then they turned the corner and were on the docks.

A large merchantman slipping her moorings and heading for the open sea provided the only movement around the harbor. The other merchantmen loaded and unloaded cargo, while beached at this end of the harbor near a huddle of small homes was the fishing fleet back with the day's catch. The scene was oddly peaceful. None of the uproar from the market had penetrated.

Approaching the shingle beach from the stone docks, Garrett reined in their pace to hide their fugitive status. It was all Diana could do to keep from looking behind constantly. The stitch in her side easing, she allowed herself one glance over her shoulder.

No one paid any attention to them, and the fishermen worked calmly about their boats. As they worked, they called to one another and to an old man sitting on a boulder near the shore whittling. Garrett headed for him.

Halting next to the whittling man, Garrett's call brought the fishermen scrambling out of their feluccas. Waiting tensely at his side, Diana hoped he knew what he was doing. She'd saved him. Now it was his turn.

"How would you like to earn two pieces of silver?" Garrett asked when the men were gathered around them. An enthusiastic cheer went up. "I'm English and want to depart your lovely city in style. So I'm sponsoring a race to reach that point." He indicated a small spit of land extending far out into the harbor. "All can race except you." He selected the man from the fastest-looking felucca. "You, *kyrios,* will take us to that ship, for an equal sum."

Silence greeted the offer. Looking at one another, they shifted uneasily. Hands clasped tensely before her, Diana glanced back at the docks. No pursuit yet. How long would the children and their parents hold Karim captive now that the guards had arrived? She turned back, willing the fishermen to speak, to agree.

"Who'll reward the winner if you're gone?" a young man finally asked. The knot of fishermen, grubby from the day's work, shuffled their feet and nodded agreement.

Garrett smiled and indicated the old man seated on the boulder. "This kind gentleman will hold the stakes and declare the winner."

A raspy chuckle issued from him. Putting the small figurehead he was carving down on the shingle beach, he tilted his head back to look up at Garrett and Diana and waved a finger at them. "And if I don't choose to?" A tiny splinter of wood sticking from one corner of his mouth waggled with each word.

"A piece of silver for holding the stakes and judging the winner," Garrett suggested.

"I choose to." The man grinned toothlessly and turned his hand palm up, the lines on it dark.

Garrett counted out three silver pieces into his hand and held up another two for the owner of the fast felucca. A number of voices asked when the race would start, and Garrett yelled, "Now!" The men raced for their boats at the word.

While the fishermen shoved their feluccas into the water, Garrett helped her aboard the remaining one as the owner raised the sails. Knowing she'd be in the way if she tried to help, Diana quickly settled in the boat. Still no pursuit on the docks.

She watched the entrance to the street with an intensity not even the first lift of the boat on the water disturbed. His feet wet, Garrett settled beside her, laughing, and gave her shoulder a brief squeeze. "We've done it again!"

Incredulous, Diana stared at him. He was enjoying himself. Bemused, she shook her head, yet her hands gradually relaxed, then her shoulders. Finally, they were away from shore. And so were the other boats. Beyond recall.

Closing her eyes, she sighed with relief and sagged against the mast briefly. With the sun warm on her face and the breeze gentle, she savored the sensation of freedom. As tension slowly drained, a realization of the absurdity of their situation took hold. An insane giggle formed in her throat, and she opened her eyes to meet Garrett's.

"All right. What's so funny?" he asked in English. "If you keep that laughter bottled up inside, you'll explode."

The smothered giggle escaped. "I'm sorry, Garrett. It's just— Did you hear what they said?"

"Who?"

"The fishermen on the beach." She nodded toward the shore, where the elderly man had resumed his seat on the boulder and picked up the figurehead to whittle. "You English have some reputation."

One brow arched to touch the tousled black lock drooping above it.

"They said," she gasped between gurgles of laughter at his expression, "that you were suffering from the English disease. Throwing away good money on a race you won't even see. Then an older fisherman explained that it was widely known Englishmen would bet on anything." Laughter broke free at last, and Diana finally fished a handkerchief from her reticule to dry her eyes.

"Finished?" Garrett asked with ominous patience, his attention no longer on her. Instead, he pointed over the stern toward the shore. Three men stood yelling and signaling to the fishing boats racing across the harbor. Even from a distance, they looked worn, disgruntled, and dirty. And this time they had neither rifles nor muskets.

Diana sobered instantly. "What will Karim do?"

Garrett studied the small fleet arrowing toward the point. "The boats won't come back until one of them wins."

"How long before he finds out where we're going and follows?" Diana rubbed her arms at the sudden chill. Out here on the water, the sun wasn't as warm as it'd been in the market, nor as warm as it had been seconds ago.

"A day, maybe two. But don't worry." Garrett rubbed her arm. "I'll think of something."

Diana looked at the ship they were rapidly approaching. "Where is it going?"

"Does it matter?" Garrett laughed. "Our only other choice is returning to shore."

She considered the alternative and smiled. "It looks like a nice ship."

Their fisherman hailed it, and an officer leaning over the side answered in fractured Greek. Swiftly, Garrett negotiated passage. Thank goodness he'd replenished his money belt before departing the *Medea*.

A rope ladder tumbled over the side. Walking gingerly to where it dangled, Diana glanced at Garrett. "Boarding's a lot easier by gangway."

"We don't have that luxury." He caught the swinging ladder. "I'll help. Besides, you've done this before."

"That's what I was thinking of."

Ignoring the dip and sway of boat, ship, and ladder, Diana hiked her skirt up and stuck a foot into the first rung. It was easier this time. Either she was growing accustomed, or the sea was smoother. Whichever, she was shortly standing on deck looking back to shore. Karim stood, hands on hips, staring impotently out to sea.

Then she recalled something more immediate. Garrett's black head appeared above the rail, and she took a step toward him. "Do you realize," she said even before he put a foot on deck, "neither of us has any clothes?"

CHAPTER XII

"BARCELONA?" DIANA REPEATED, DAZED. "THAT'S IN Spain." She'd hoped for one of the nearer islands, perhaps Greece itself. Certainly not Barcelona.

Taking her hand, Captain Joffre bowed and brought it to his lips with a flourish. *"Oui, mademoiselle,* Barcelona is in Spain, but you need not fear. You shall travel in the greatest comfort and safety aboard the *Marie."* Gazing at her with meltingly dark eyes, he raised her hand to his lips again.

"But it'll take weeks." Rescuing her hand, she turned to Garrett with a hint of relief. Romantic French captains appealed in books, but not in real life. At least if they were like the overly romantic Captain Joffre. There was a time and place for everything. "Is there anything we can do?" Garrett's abstracted expression startled her. He looked gloomier than she felt. Unwilling to ask what was wrong in public, she repeated the question.

Garrett managed a smile and shook his head. "Not unless you want to risk Karim's attentions."

Diana shuddered. "Well, I've never been to Barcelona. It just takes so long to get there."

Above, a steady breeze briskly belled the sails now they were on the open sea. Although the sun had nearly reached its zenith, they headed for where it would set. Her goal, Jerusalem, lay in the opposite direction.

"No, *mademoiselle*, not weeks," Captain Joffre assured her gravely. "The *Marie* is a very fast ship." He glanced at the sails, then at the horizon. "Depending, of course, on the weather. At this time of year in the Mediterranean, one can never be sure."

It would be December before they arrived in Barcelona. And it would take weeks to sail back to Jerusalem, assuming a ship left for the Holy Land immediately. Only the slightest chance of spending Christmas with her parents existed. Still, more time with Garrett was a pleasure to look forward to. Besides, it couldn't be helped. Sailing to Barcelona, then all the way back across the Mediterranean, was better than being Karim's unwilling guests.

"At least you can make clothes that fit on this voyage," Garrett said sympathetically.

"Mais oui, mademoiselle," Captain Joffre interposed. "Monsieur Hamilton has explained all. I, as your captain, assure you that your choice of our entire cargo is at your disposal." His large gesture took in the entire ship and promised a wealth of treasures below.

How sweet of Garrett to make arrangements for her. Brightening, she asked, "What are you carrying?"

"The finest liturgical linen," he assured her. Taking her hand in his again, he patted it. "And my excellent sailmaker will assist you in preparing fine dresses to clothe yourself. No, no." He shook his head as Diana's lips parted. "It is my pleasure to assist one so lovely in so minor a fashion. Please accept it with my compliments."

Liturgical linen? Everything would be white! Not even the finest modiste could alter that, let alone a sailmaker. She was bound to end up looking like a sail or, Diana shuddered delicately, a shroud. Still, it could be worse. She'd have something like clothes to wear for the next few weeks. This dress, her only real dress, could be preserved for their landing in Spain. Its aquamarine shade, exquisite cut, and detailing—like the ruff framing her face—would make it possible to meet the Spanish with equanimity.

Pinning a wan smile on her lips, Diana thanked him. "If someone will show me to my cabin, I'll begin work on a dress."

Behind her, she heard a chuckle from Garrett. He knew precisely what was going through her mind after an afternoon's shopping with her. She smiled even more warmly at the captain.

"And," the captain said, gesturing a fair-haired boy forward, "you will need a model on which to pin your designs." Waving his hands in a vague way that encompassed all the necessary fittings, he said, *"Violà* Etienne, who has just become a midshipman. He is of a size with you and will speed these fittings."

"But that isn't necessary," Diana protested.

"I insist, *mademoiselle.* Such a lovely lady in distress should have every assistance, no?" He sighed in an overly sentimental fashion and kissed her hand again.

"Th-thank you. You're very kind."

A gurgle of laughter lodged itself in her throat. Trying to hide it, she turned toward Garrett, who glowered in the strangest way. Confused, Diana looked back to the captain.

"I'd better go to my cabin."

"Not if you intend to have two men there," Garrett objected. "Your cabin will be too small for three people to work in. I'm sure the officers' wardroom will have considerably more room with tables and things for you to use." Stepping proprietarily closer, he put a hand at her waist.

Karim inspected the sleek lines of the pirate ship with satisfaction. This was precisely what he needed to capture that insolent infidel and the girl. Yes, the girl.

She deserved special attention. Before, Hamilton and the badge were of paramount importance. The girl was just an untidy loose end. But that was prior to seeing her pale hair immodestly uncovered as the urchins surged around him. She'd set those boys on him and warned Hamilton.

Glowering, he looked up as a man sauntered along the dock. "You're the captain?" he barked.

Inspecting him with thorough leisureliness, the wiry little Greek eventually nodded.

"Do you know the *Marie?*" Karim asked. This impudence was galling but would have to be ignored for the time being.

"Out of Marseilles," the captain answered, bored. "Twelve long guns, four swivels. Carrying liturgical linen for Barcelona. Good fighting ship. No passengers this run." The Greek captain nonchalantly leaned against some bales awaiting loading onto a nearby merchant ship and surveyed Karim again. "Anything else?"

"How long to catch her?" This captain might be insolent, but his was reputed to be the fastest ship in the harbor.

"I'm not stupid enough to want to do that." The captain spat into the water below. "She outguns me, her men are good fighters, and liturgical linen isn't in short supply. There's no profit to my tackling the *Marie.*"

His was the only ship capable of catching the infidel, Karim reminded himself. To obtain the badge of office, Hamilton, and that confounded girl, he had to pursue the *Marie* with all possible speed. Otherwise, he'd see that this insolent oaf graced Selim's prison and was properly punished. Since that was impossible, Karim forced himself to smile.

"How long to get to Barcelona, then?" His hands tightened into fists behind his back.

"For the *Marie?*" The captain frowned consideringly. "Fourteen days, sixteen, maybe. Maybe more. Depending on weather."

Two weeks more for them to go unpunished. Two weeks longer before he captured the means to power. "How long for you?"

Scratching one shoulder, the small Greek considered, his gaze turned upward as though reading the weather's future in the pristine blue sky above. "Ten days, two weeks, maybe. Depends. Weather's changeable."

If someone said that one more time, Karim swore he'd throttle him. First Selim warned about the weather, now this insolent Greek pirate. The only consolation was that any adverse weather delaying him delayed the infidels as well.

"How long before we sail?" Karim demanded.

"A week." A malicious gleam entered the man's dark eyes. "We've just returned from an arduous—but profitable —voyage. My crew's drunk and scattered."

His polite smile slowly fading, Karim glared down at the small man for a stretched second. "How much to sail on the next tide?"

Crossing his arms over his chest, the Greek rubbed his chin with the upper hand, pondered, looked slyly at Karim, and named an outrageously high sum. He leaned back against the bales, waiting for an explosion. It didn't come.

Karim smiled nastily. "Done. The bey of Bizerte will gladly pay any sum to see justice done."

The Greek captain looked stunned. "Bizerte's got a new bey?" Quick suspicion crossed his face. "Payment in advance."

"You—" Starting forward, Karim stopped short and sneered down at the Greek pirate. It was Haroun's money. "You can have it," Karim finished smoothly. Turning, he called to Umar and Mustafa, who had studiously effaced themselves on the far side of the dock.

"Get my luggage aboard and yours, Mustafa. Umar," he added, waving for the slighter of the two men to join him, "take the first available ship back to Bizerte. There, you will inform my brother of what happened here and that I have journeyed on to Barcelona. Pay standard fare. Don't dawdle, however."

"Yes, my lord." Umar bowed and winced. A small sticking plaster decorated his forehead where he'd been hit with a ladle.

Observing the wince, Karim smiled thinly. "She was but a woman."

Stepping into the officers' mess, Diana nodded. This would do nicely. Light and space must have been the reasons Garrett insisted on a place other than her cabin for dressmaking. Still, his behavior had been peculiar.

Glass more like windows than portholes let in a flood of clear light. There were several chairs along with a narrow table where they could cut out dresses from the linen bolts. All were, as predicted, white, although the shade varied from the startling, clean white of snow to the pale buff of rich cream. During the days with Garrett, she'd grown accustomed to bright jewel colors. He preferred them, and giving them up for even a short time hadn't appealed. Now she was sure something attractive could be achieved with the more muted whites.

"This'll be different, this will. I'm used to canvas, not such fine fabrics. Here, Etienne." The sailmaker, Jules, hooked a stool from beneath the table with one foot. "Stand up on that so I can reach you without making my bones ache more'n they have to." His fingers, gnarled and tanned to the color of leather, absently stroked the linen while he talked. "You may be our newest midshipman, but you're still Etienne to me."

Already growing accustomed to Jules's rapid patois, Diana smiled on Etienne and picked up the first bolt. "Why don't we make a simple dress first? It'll be done the sooner."

"That it will, *mam'selle*. And a simple dress'll give me a chance to practice this new craft." His hand hovered among the bolts, finally settling on palest cream and holding it up questioningly.

"That's lovely." With the bolts stacked on chairs against the wall, Diana spread the chosen fabric on the table. The fine texture delighted her gently caressing fingers. "Have you any scissors?"

Putting a pair down on the table, he shook his head when she started to pick them up. "Now, just you wait, *mam'selle*. Young Etienne hasn't quite got your shape." His grin revealing gaps in yellowed teeth, he picked up some cloth. "Lift your arms, Etienne, and we'll correct it."

Color running high under his fair skin, Etienne endured in silence, while Jules stuffed cloth inside his shirt and bound it in place. Both sailors balanced easily against the increased surge of the ship here at the stern, seemingly unaware of it.

The wind was picking up. Diana held the bolt of linen to her chest, not sure whether she was pleased at the prospect of a quick passage. It meant a better chance of seeing her family for Christmas, along with the increasing certainty of parting from Garrett all the sooner. Mama and Papa had grown into dim figures from childhood, while Garrett was disturbingly real and even more disturbingly immediate. He'd come to mean everything.

She gave herself a stern lecture. Daydreaming about Garrett while overseeing a sailmaker-*cum*-dressmaker would inevitably lead to disaster. Looking up, Diana bit her lip to avoid a laugh certain to embarrass young Etienne.

Standing back, Jules surveyed his handiwork, then nodded, satisfied. "There y'are, *mam'selle*. He's just as pretty as a picture now."

Etienne, face red, stood stiffly, hands at his sides and gazing determinedly at the bulkhead. Narrow navy pantaloons outlined legs still gangly with youth. Above, a thin chest was puffed in front with cloth to simulate a bust.

Standing well away, Jules circled the boy, one hand cupping his chin, his elbow supported by the other. Like an artist, he studied Etienne from every aspect. Finally satisfied, he nodded several times and came over to the table where Diana stood. "I married a woman that weren't nearly as pretty as you, Etienne."

"Jules, stop that! Etienne's been very sweet, and I won't have you tease him."

Standing stiffly on his stool, eyes fixed on the ceiling, Etienne's flush deepened. At the words "very sweet," he flushed even redder.

Not a bit abashed at her admonishment, Jules touched the fabric and looked eagerly at Diana. "How do we start? I've never done a dress before."

Keeping the bubble of laughter riding high inside buried with an effort, she turned abruptly to the table. Lifting the bolt and unfolding a length, she smoothed and straightened it. Giving Jules the bolt, Diana carried the fabric length like a train and brought it over to the boy.

"First, I think," she said, holding her end up under Etienne's cloth stuffed bosom, "we should measure off the skirt lengths."

Tilting her head back, she stretched the fabric full width against Etienne's torso. At least it wasn't the width of standard silk, eighteen inches. But it didn't look as wide as a normal bolt of linen or cotton. Yes, it couldn't be more than twenty-four or twenty-five inches, which meant an extra breadth in the skirt if she wanted a round gown. Under these circumstances, it seemed her best choice. That meant four widths of fabric.

"Jules, if you would, measure down to the stool, while I hold this end up here."

"Here y'are, *mam'selle*." Straightening with an audible click to his knees, his fingers pinched the fabric.

"Thank you. Now, cut four pieces that length, while I make the measurements necessary for the bodice." Turning to Etienne, she smiled at him. "If you'd care to, you can get down from that stool for now. It must be uncomfortable up there."

"*M-merci, mademoiselle.* I-I-" Blushing he broke off and clambered down from the stool. "Can I help?"

"It'd be nice if I had some paper to cut into a pattern. After that, well," she said, smiling apologetically, "can you use a needle?"

"Yes, a little. *Maman* insisted I learn before signing aboard the *Marie.*"

If he had a cap, he'd be twisting it. Diana remembered the days not so very long ago when every part of her seemed big and awkward. And, Lord, the way she'd blushed! Just like this boy. At her sympathetic smile, the blush dimmed and he turned to go.

"Etienne," she called softly, and cast a brief glance over her shoulder. Jules was happily bent over the table measuring out skirt lengths. He wouldn't hear. "Before you leave, you might want to take that off." She pointed to the cloth padding his chest.

Looking down, his cheeks grew beet red. With rough, hurried hands, he tugged the knot loose, tossed the cloth into a corner, and stuttered inarticulate gratitude. Before she could respond, he escaped into the passageway, leaving Diana shaking her head in amusement.

"How much do we have left of the bolt?" she asked, returning to Jules at the table.

Clear light poured through the mullioned panes onto a neat stack of skirt lengths, each cut precisely the same. There was more than enough there to make a proper skirt with pleats controlling the fullness at the back. But the remnant didn't look large enough for the bodice. Jules spread it out, the linen a fragile cream against the dark wood.

"About a yard, *mam'selle.*" He caressed the fabric with gnarled fingers. "Will that be enough? Or should I go down to the hold for another bolt this color?"

Slowly, Diana shook her head. "I'd hate to cut into another bolt just for the bodice, when this is enough for the lower sleeves." Turning to the remaining bolts, she inspected them carefully.

Taking a darker one from the pile, she brought it to the table. Together, the two fabrics shaded softly into each other like cream swirling into rich milk. The dress wouldn't be as pallid as she'd feared. Garrett would love it. Smiling, she glanced at Jules's anxious face.

"This will be lovely. In fact, I'll use this for another bodice and underdress."

"It's no trouble to go to the hold for another bolt, *mam'selle.*"

"Thank you, Jules." Diana squeezed his hand in gratitude. "I really think the dress will be prettier this way."

He still looked doubtful. "It's no trouble," he repeated.

"Just wait until it's done, Jules. Then you can tell me whether I was wrong." Frowning, she glanced toward the passageway. "I wonder whether Etienne was able to find paper."

"There might be a little trouble finding some," Jules admitted. "Paper's not something we have much use for on board ship, see." Relaxing and leaning against the table, he scratched his ribs. "Mostly it's just Cap'n's log and the charts. Doubt the cap'n 'ud like the charts cut up. Nor the log used to make a dress pattern."

Sinking into a chair, Diana nodded. "I suppose you're right." Frowning, she considered the problem. "I could cut the bodice without making a proper pattern first, I suppose."

"A paper pattern's usual?"

"Yes." Leaning over, she smoothed the remaining yard out on the table. "It should be simple enough. I'll cut the lower sleeves from the pale cream, and the bodice and upper puffed sleeve from the lighter fabric. That way there'll be plenty of material for an interesting effect. Perhaps—" Cocking her head to one side and considering the skirt lengths, Diana nodded decisively. "Yes, just a simple flounce on the bottom of the skirt. What do you think, Jules?"

Color ran up under the tanned leather of his cheeks. "I don't know, *mam'selle*. But if you think so—"

"Yes, I do. Now, while I work on the bodice, you sew together all these lengths." Rapidly, she showed him. "Etienne should be back one way or the other by the time you're finished."

The old sailmaker subsided onto the stool where Etienne had stood and, fitting the skirt lengths together without benefit of pins, began seaming them with an incredibly strong running stitch. Diana watched surreptitiously while spreading the contrasting linen on the table. Despite gnarled, arthritic fingers, Jules's stitches were fine, even, and perfectly straight. She'd never seen a better seamstress. Any modiste would be lucky to have him.

Assured that the sailmaker-*cum*-dressmaker wouldn't botch the job, she turned her attention to fashioning a pretty bodice, one that Garrett would find absolutely stunning. He'd acted so strangely, and she couldn't understand why. Considering his warnings about men in Crete, she'd have thought he would've helped curtail the attentions of Captain Joffre. Yet he hadn't. It disturbed her more than she'd admit.

"How do you like my dress, Garrett?" Diana asked, stepping over the high sill of the bulkhead separating the passageway from the deck outside.

"What? Oh, very nice."

Walking alongside, yet not touching her as he normally did when they were together, he strolled over to the railing. He hadn't looked at her when she asked the question. Just as he hadn't more than glanced at her throughout dinner. Finally, exasperated, she'd turned to the captain and officers for conversation. At the end of the meal when Etienne brought in a small platter of cheese and fruit, which he blushingly set in front of Diana, Garrett had offered a stiff invitation to stroll on deck. Now, he seemed intent on staring at the dark sea.

"It's lovely out tonight, isn't it?" She hugged her cloak tightly about her; the thin linen dress wasn't warm.

Nor was it a lovely night. The breeze off the water was sharp and chill; clouds scudded across the sky, blotting out both stars and new moon; and the *Marie* sailed well away from land, which might show signs of habitation. Altogether, a bleak, lonely night, one Garrett wasn't helping with his attitude. The toe of her slipper beat a brief, impatient pattern on the deck.

Turning, Garrett smiled apologetically. "I'm sorry. I haven't been the best company, have I?"

"Well . . . if you want the truth . . ." She paused and was rewarded by a low laugh. Her teasing Garrett was back.

"I'd rather not, thanks." Stepping closer, he blocked the wind swirling around a corner. "I've been thinking about us in Barcelona."

Diana stared at him. His face was a dark silhouette against the lighter sky, but she couldn't see his expression. Only his tone conveyed his attitude. His tone and his posture.

"We'll find a ship to take us to Jaffa." The lightness in her words concealed the tension she felt.

"It's unlikely you'll reach Jerusalem by Christmas." Garrett shifted. The wind struck her, then was blocked again. "I'd give anything to get you there in time, sweetheart, but it's not possible."

"I have to try," Diana said, her voice quiet. There was nothing else to do.

"You could postpone your visit until summer." Garrett's hand closed over her shoulder and squeezed. "Haroun's search would be over by then."

Puzzled, she searched his face. He was so near, yet shadow still enveloped him completely. "They'll be expecting me. Gran must have written them long since. They probably have her letter already."

"We'll send them another." The single, flat movement of one hand dismissed that consideration.

"What would we do?" His other hand massaged her shoulder and arm.

His grip tightened for an excruciating second. "Come with me to Greece for the statues. For the excitement of it."

Drawing her suddenly against him, he brushed a kiss on her forehead. The heat of his body struck through wool cloak and linen dress with a fierceness that weakened her.

She succumbed for an instant before trying to straighten. The grip of his arms held her prisoner in their shelter. Ignoring her treacherous longing, she forced herself to make sense of the hurried, husky words. He'd still never said he loved her.

"We'll have the time of our lives, sweetheart. All the antiquities you could ask for, the satisfaction of helping the Greeks, getting even with the Turks, and another fortune in the bargain."

Hands wedged between them on his chest, Diana arched back to look up into his face. "I can't afford to continue junketing about the Mediterranean like this, Garrett."

"If it's money you're worried about"—he bent to whisper seductively against her ear—"don't give it a thought. Money's nothing between friends. I've plenty with me. It's not worth considering."

The tip of his tongue traced the rim of her ear as he spoke. She *hadn't* given the money a thought.

Neither had he. Not once had he held it over her that she was living on his money, that he was paying for everything. Not once had he mentioned it in his nightly seduction attempts. Not once had he used her debts, her vulnerability, against her.

He wasn't just an adventurer, as she'd assumed. He adhered to his own code of honor zealously. How else could she explain the care with which he'd never made her feel indebted? Yet indebted she was. For the very clothes she stood up in. Perhaps not this particular dress, but for all her other clothes, her underthings, the pelisse, the branch of pale pink flowers bought at the market back in Iraklion. Everything. Her food; even the cabin she occupied.

Trying to free herself, Diana pushed against his chest. It was like moving a mountain. Yet all she had to do was say no, and he'd let her go, sighing regretfully, overly dramatic, but never forcing her. That was part of that code of honor he followed so zealously. That damned offbeat code of honor.

"What is it, sweetheart?" His hands swept playfully below her waist, while he dropped a kiss in the hollow below her ear.

"No!" She shoved at his chest and stepped hard on his foot.

He jerked it out from under hers. "Ouch! What's wrong?"

How dare he be a gentleman? Now she'd never be able to forget him, no matter how long she lived or how long they were apart.

"I'm going to Jerusalem, not Greece," she told him stonily. "I'm not your sweetheart, and nothing you say or do"— she twisted free of his arms—"can convince me otherwise." The bitter wind cut icily through pelisse and dress. It couldn't make her more chilled than she already felt.

CHAPTER XIII

Barcelona, Spain—December, 1819

THE SMALL, VOLUPTUOUS WOMAN STANDING BESIDE THE empty fireplace in the high-ceilinged hall gestured sweepingly. "Ah, *señor,* welcome. I am Señora Estruch. How may I be of service to you?"

A cloud of musky scent hovering about her, she glided over the dark flagstone floor to greet Garrett. Diana bristled at the smile curving the landlady's lips.

Although Diana didn't know much Spanish, Señora Estruch's intentions were easy to comprehend. Too easy. The landlady's beautiful dark-lashed eyes had latched on to Garrett the moment they entered the pastel stucco inn. And he was lapping up her languishing glances and fluttering hands.

"Pardon, *señora.*" Garrett took a step forward, dropping Diana's arm. "My poor Spanish is that of soldiers. Do you speak French?"

Diana listened in disbelief. His voice sounded as silky as it had during his nightly seduction attempts—seduction attempts that had regrettably ceased after she rebuffed him harshly that first night aboard the *Marie.*

Somehow she'd never had the opportunity to apologize for her unreasonable harshness. But her behavior was no excuse for his conduct, his hovering coolness through the remainder of the voyage.

Now he showed signs of accepting Señora Estruch's blatant invitation. All the signs were there, from a fatuous smile to the way he stood close to her. And the way she was encouraging him. Her small, plump hand rested delicately in Garrett's as he rose from a bow, and her extravagant, black lashes dipped and fluttered with pleasure, a fading flush coloring her pale skin.

"Ah." The breathy sound accompanied a sultry smile. "You served with Wellington," the landlady exclaimed, switching into deliciously accented French. "As did my late husband, Ferran. He died of his wounds only a year after the fighting ended in my country."

With the sweep of one hand and demurely lowered lashes, she indicated her dress. From the translucent silk filling in the low-cut neck of her gown to the single flounce decorating the hem, she wore funereal black. Diana's eyes narrowed cynically. The fighting in Spain had ended many years before. Did she wear black in memory of her dead husband, or because it set off her pale skin, brilliantly black hair, and voluptuously curved figure perfectly?

Garrett murmured appropriate commiserations, then indicated Diana standing silent behind him. He didn't meet her eyes. "We require *two* rooms for a few days. Do you have any available, *señora?*"

"Of course, *señor.*" She smiled meltingly at him and ignored Diana. "It is the quiet season for my humble inn. You will find it peaceful and respectable here. Indeed, I insist you make yourself free of all my amenities. Such as this hall. For tea, perhaps. You English have such a great fondness for that beverage." While she spoke, she inspected Diana and Garrett discreetly, then added with seeming casualness, "I shall have your baggage sent up immediately."

"We lost it to thieves," Diana interposed swiftly. "We

have little more than what we wear, plus these." She touched the two small valises resting on the flagstone floor with her foot.

The landlady's dark eyes narrowed as she apparently noticed Diana for the first time. "You are brother and sister?" Taking a step nearer Garret, she lowered her voice intimately. "No one would guess you were related. You are so darkly handsome, while your sister—" The wave of a magically produced fan indicated far more than mere words possibly could.

Diana bristled. "We had different mothers, *señora,* and take after our respective parents. Fortunately." There, let Garrett explain that one.

"As you see, Señora Estruch, my little sister is ill-tempered from tiredness." Flicking Diana's cheek with a hard, fraternal gesture, he scooped up the luggage. "Now, if you would be so good as to show us to our rooms."

Speculation lit the landlady's eyes as she looked from one to the other. "Even your accents are different."

"My mother was American, *señora;* Garrett's was English," Diana answered the implied question. Irritatingly, Garrett simply stood and smiled beside her, luggage dangling from his hands, enjoying her discomfiture. "We were separated during the war between America and England."

"Poor little girl," the landlady said mechanically. "Unfortunately, with you two looking so different it will cause talk." Lowering her lashes demurely, she turned a luminous smile on Garrett. "A poor widow"—she emphasized her status delicately—"must be unstintingly vigilant in protecting her reputation."

"Fear not, *señora.*" Garrett clinked the coins in his pocket together. "I'll personally see your many kindnesses are handsomely rewarded. Trust me to ensure that there will be no idle, malicious gossip. Your reputation is safe with me."

"I'm sure it is, *señor.* There are so few men that a helpless widow can trust."

His eyes met Diana's coldly over the smaller woman's

head. "You're very kind, *señora*. Now, if you'd show us to our rooms?"

Breathing heavily, Señora Estruch fluttered her lashes at Garrett. "Please, do me the favor of calling me Eliana. So few people do these days." A delicate flush climbing her cheeks, she suggested demurely, "Perhaps we can meet later for tea. But first we must settle your poor little sister in her room. She must be so tired after her . . . adventures."

Tiny hands holding her skirts high enough to reveal slender ankles, Eliana led the way up a wide staircase to a long hall. Shorter halls located a third of the way from either end intersected it. Sunlight poured onto wooden floors darkened with age and reflected from white stucco walls. Everything was scrupulously clean, and, Diana felt, bringing up the rear, scrupulously unwelcoming. Where the inn in Crete had been clean yet comforting, everything here was clean but sterile.

"I have a pair of large rooms at the end of this corridor," Eliana said over her shoulder. Watching Garrett, she added, "You will want your little sister away from the traveler who spends but a night or two in my inn." Smoothing her skirt, she accented her voluptuously rounded figure as she continued. "Such would not be proper company for such a headstrong little girl."

"It sounds absolutely perfect, Eliana. Diana wanders off easily," Garrett agreed. "Having grown up in well-protected surroundings—" Breaking off, he looked over his shoulder and asked Diana in English, "Did you say something?"

"Nothing to speak of," she answered, lips pressed firmly together.

Pushing open two doors opposite each other in the narrow hall, Señora Estruch stood aside to let them enter. Garrett stepped into the one on the left and promptly backed out. Catching Diana's arm, he ushered her toward the other.

"You'll prefer this one. The view will be nicer, and there'll be less noise, since it's away from the street."

"But how did you know, *señor?*" Eliana fluttered over to

where he stood immobile in the hall and touched his arm with a possessive hand. "I would remember *you* if you'd ever been in my inn before."

Garrett smiled down at the landlady's vivid expression and batting lashes. "It's a faculty I have, Eliana. One I find useful."

Irritated, Diana turned and looked out the window at the end of the corridor. Behind her, she heard the fluting voice of the landlady asking whether the rooms were acceptable. Assuring her they were, Garrett politely added there was no need for fires; it was too warm.

"Ah, but I shall see that they are laid, *señor*. Once the sun goes down, the air chills quickly in Barcelona. I want to see that you sleep warm and comfortable."

A pause brought Diana's head around a fraction to watch without appearing to. Gazing up and fluttering her lashes, Eliana stood so close to Garrett they touched. Her hand stroked his arm.

With a feminine and beguiling smile, she whispered, *"Adieu, señor,"* and allowed Garrett to bow over her hand. Lingering reluctantly, she withdrew it from his.

Diana's head snapped around, and she stared determinedly out the window. A few more whispers followed. Then the staccato sound of Eliana's heels clicking down the corridor reached her. Garrett didn't follow.

"Here's your valise," he said casually from behind Diana.

Swinging around, she took an involuntary step back. He was closer than expected. Yet his mood was indecipherable. He lounged against the tall, heavy linen cupboard tucked into the corner next to the window, smiling and watching her.

"Thank you." The words emerged with an effort.

"Better get ready to go shopping." Thick black lashes masked the sherry-gold of his eyes. "While you do, I'll ask about a good modiste."

Not waiting for agreement, Garrett dropped his valise inside his room and disappeared down the corridor. Her hands clasped tightly together, Diana stared after him.

Rescuing the valise containing her few clothes from the floor, she entered her room and slammed the door. Men! That trollop was incredibly obvious. Why couldn't he see it? Mumbling to herself, she automatically smoothed the wrinkles from her dresses and hung them on the pegs inside a massive, dark armoire dominating one side of the white-washed room.

Did Garrett's behavior have something to do with the way he'd acted on the ship all the way across the Mediterranean? Of course, she'd rebuffed him strongly that first night aboard. But that couldn't be the only reason for his coolness during the rest of the voyage. And it couldn't have anything to do with the foolish attentions received from the officers. Everyone knew such gallantry was habit with the French.

Garrett wasn't retaliating for their attentions. He was above that. She touched the single narrow iron-framed bed with the pristine white spread taut over it and moved on to the heavy candlestick and stand in the corner. Light dust coated the intricate grooves carved into the massive base, the only dust in the room.

Staring sightlessly at the highly polished grim crucifix above the bed, she shook her head. If the officers' gallantry was totally innocent, why did she feel so guilty?

Well, it was innocent. Not like the attentions of that "widow."

Wandering about the room, Diana eventually settled with one shoulder against the window frame and stared out at the jumble of roofs outside. They shone with delicate pastel color and rippled away into the distance, broken here and there by a church spire or the bulk of a government building. Curved tiles and slate shingles mingled in muted tones, with an occasional palm tree interrupting the stretch of buildings.

Slowly absorbing the scene, she grew restless. Enough time had passed for Garrett to ask Eliana a simple question and receive a simple answer. Even without a clock, Diana was certain of that. She stood at the window for another minute or two.

The afternoon stretched before her, and she was hungry. Garrett's coolly distant behavior that morning had curtailed her appetite, but it bloomed fully now. She wasn't going to waste away and pine for Garrett Hamilton. And that wasn't all. She needed a few things she'd been unable to make on board the *Marie,* things she'd prefer to buy without Garrett's supervision, after the way he'd behaved in Crete.

She strode back to the armoire for her pelisse. Of course, if Garrett escaped the harpy's clutches, she'd let him accompany her. Otherwise, she'd happily go by herself in search of necessary nightwear. Spanish men couldn't be as bad as Garrett warned. After all, he'd been wrong about Cretans.

Holding her skirt free of the dustless floor, Diana hurried down first one corridor, then the other. Gliding down the stairs, she listened for the sound of voices. She really should find Garrett and let him escort her. After all, she had promised.

Moving silently toward the back of the inn, she went from one patch of sunlight to another, passing along a series of arches looking out into a central courtyard. Ahead, she heard voices, one of which she recognized instantly.

Turning a corner, Diana froze. Ahead, two black heads bent toward each other, facing away from her. Soft laughter filled the warm, sheltered courtyard, and Garrett leaned closer to the small woman smiling flirtatiously up at him.

By the time Diana reached the front door of the inn, she had herself under control. Her eyes were dry, her chin tilted high. Garrett Hamilton's indiscretions were no concern of hers. Barcelona looked like a fascinating city, and she'd learn much more about the "real" Catalonians by herself. Not just what the local delicacies were.

Picking her way carefully among the cobblestones, she skirted puddles from the previous night's rain. All the buildings were closed and secretive, with iron gates shutting off the arched doors into entryways and homes. Overhead, they leaned toward each other, blocking the sun. On the ride to the inn with Garrett it seemed so different. Despite his distant courtesy, the sunny day and Barcelona had put Diana in an optimistic mood.

Sudden sunlight sparkled from a black puddle, and Diana looked up. She'd headed in a good direction. Around her, looming buildings gave way to a moderate-sized square with shops scattered here and there. Better still, Diana sniffed delicately, a small café with tables and chairs spilling into the square stood opposite. Delightful odors drifted on the light breeze, making her mouth water.

Holding her skirt a little higher, she picked her way through the puddles and took the first unoccupied table. It was small, wooden, scarred from long use, but the chair was sturdy. She looked around fascinated, folded hands propped at the edge of the table. Slowly, they dropped into her lap and traced the intricate pattern knitted into her reticule.

Everyone was staring. The men looked uniform, as though cut out of the same piece of dough with the same cookie cutter. And there were no women present.

The flush that stained her cheeks drained gradually away in the face of their silent regard. Just as she was tensing to rise, a middle-aged woman sauntered out the open double doors toward her. The empty tray balanced casually against one hip, as much as the stained white cloth tied over her skirt, said waitress. Sighing with relief, Diana sank back into the chair and waited.

After exchanging jovial yet incomprehensible comments with the men, the waitress approached. The men, dressed in an odd assortment of clothes, lazed back in their chairs, too, faces no longer so intent. Responding with a smile, Diana asked, "Do you speak French?"

Friendliness disappeared from the woman's face. Turning, she called to the men watching and waiting. Silence filled the small outdoor café, even the square. The scrape of chairs on cobblestones and heavy boots striding filled it in the next instant.

Shaking free of paralysis, Diana started to rise. A hard hand from behind shoved her back into the chair. The men's expressions were harsh, condemning. Garlic from their breath saturated the air.

"Wh-what's wrong?" Diana stuttered in French.

"Francésa."

The word spit at her from all directions. Blinking, Diana took a deep breath. They thought she was French. Touching a dry upper lip with her tongue, she began in English, "I'm not—" and switched to French at their uncomprehending expressions, *"Je n'suis pas—"*

A roar of voices overrode her explanation. Even the waitress's face was condemning. Diana darted a quick look about; all chance of escape was cut off. Taking a deep breath, she prepared to outshout the mob. Just then, she heard a familiar voice.

Swiveling in her chair, she searched but couldn't see for the crush of people. Garrett's voice carried over the racket. She couldn't understand a word, but the others did. The roar of irate voices lowered to mutterings, then faded altogether. The crowd parted.

Hands on hips, Garrett shook his head in exasperation before throwing out a few words more that drew a laugh from the spectators. He settled in an empty chair and looked at her. "Well?"

"What did you say to them?"

"Told them you were English." Warmth vied with exasperation in his face, and the warmth won.

"But I'm not English," she protested. "And why should they care whether I'm French or not?"

He shook his head again and pushed back the stubborn lock from his forehead. "It may have escaped the notice of colonial schools, but there was a war fought here recently. A bitter war between the French and Spanish. Barcelona was occupied. Didn't you hear Eliana say her husband died from his wounds?"

"They thought I was French because I didn't speak Spanish?"

"Because you spoke French."

A faint flush highlighting her cheeks becomingly, Diana nodded. "I shouldn't—"

"Have gone off by yourself," Garrett finished.

His hand casually squeezing Diana's, he turned to the waitress, who was the only person still standing beside the table. In rapid Spanish, he ordered. She nodded, smiling, called something to a man, and left. Uncertainly, the man rose and came over to them.

"*Señor,* did you serve with Wellington?" he asked in stilted French.

"Ah, *señora,*" Karim sighed sentimentally in Spanish and straightened from a deep bow over her hand. "You have seen them?"

One hand touching the glint of a gold locket beneath the translucent shadow of black silk, Eliana let the other remain in his grasp. "Perhaps, *señor,*" she parried. "But guests in my inn are entitled to privacy."

"Not when— Ah, but I must explain. It is only right that you should require it." Fingering his beard, he smiled, shrugged gracefully, and brought the landlady's hand up to his lips again. "But, forgive me, not here. The matter is too personal."

Karim's glance gave significance to the request. Standing in the entrance hall, its pristine length empty, both could hear the clatter of the kitchen, while the door leading to the street stood open behind him.

Hesitation crossed Eliana's face, but she allowed her hand to rest in his several seconds longer. Satisfaction broadening his smile, Karim followed as she led the way down the hall.

"Since it's important, we'll use my private courtyard."

She sent a languishing smile over her shoulder. "We shan't be disturbed."

The sort of woman he liked, Karim decided, slowing his pace an extra step the better to enjoy the view. Feminine, frame nicely and amply covered, hair a perfect match for a raven's wing, and she barely reached his shoulder. She gave a man proper appreciation and respect. Look at the way she'd responded to him from the moment he'd entered the inn.

"Señora Estruch," he said, as they rounded a corner and started down a corridor dappled with alternating sun and shadow arches.

"Please, *señor*, Eliana." She smiled meltingly. "Señora Estruch is too formal."

"You do me much honor, Eliana.

"And your name, *señor?*"

Briefly touching her back between the shoulder blades, he guided her toward the small courtyard ahead. "That is part of my sad story. Once I tell it, you have full permission to use my name."

"Then sit, and I shall bring us coffee."

"Your generosity is exceeded only by your beauty, Eliana." Karim bowed. "I breathlessly await your return."

Framed by an arch of pale stucco, graceful palms and foliage surrounded the small table. One chair stood in full sun; the other was striped with the shade of palm fronds. Eliana would want that one, Karim decided, relaxing in the sun's warmth. She had a woman's regard for her complexion.

"I see you enjoy our climate, *señor.*"

Eliana's soft voice brought his eyes open. She put a filigreed tray down on the wrought-iron-and-marble table and removed small coffee cups. Pouring one, she handed it to him, her smile questioning.

"If only I could enjoy it more, Eliana." Sighing, Karim accepted the cup.

She subsided gracefully into the shaded chair. Expression

sympathetic, Eliana waited for him to confide in her. Overhead, a bird in the trees loosed a flood of silver notes, then took wing out of the courtyard.

Taking a delaying sip of thick coffee before abandoning it, Karim watched her unobtrusively. "This is painful for me." He shook his head dolefully.

Putting her cup down on the table, Eliana leaned forward and brushed his wrist lightly with the tips of her fingers. "You need never fear. I shall keep your secret."

"I know you will, Eliana. Otherwise—" He didn't finish. Instead, he brought her hand briefly to his lips. "My story is a simple one, and"—he sighed, shaking his head—"a painful one." Letting their linked hands drift down to the tabletop, he continued. "I was born Lord Karim ibn Hassan." Her hand tensed in his, but she didn't withdraw it. "That was before I met Diana."

"Diana?" Eliana questioned swiftly.

"A young Catholic lady of good family who was bought to become the foundation of my harem." He let a flicker of pain cross his face. "I fell in love and converted for her sake, taking the name Don Carlos."

"You are Catholic," she inserted. At his nod, her thumb began gently stroking the backs of his fingers. A vagrant breeze rattled the palm fronds behind them, the only sound breaking the sympathetic silence in the small courtyard.

"After she ran away, my new religion was my only solace."

Meeting her eyes directly, Karim barely restrained a smile. He had her. He was certain of it. And she'd believe everything, do anything, if he handled her right.

"Surely you went after her?"

His free hand swept a melancholy gesture. "Only after I learned where she had gone." He paused for effect. "And with whom."

"Ah?" The soft, questioning sound was sympathetic, encouraging. The perfectly arched brows, the gentle brown eyes, the pouting, curved lips—all confirmed he had her convinced.

"A rich Englishman. Far richer than I." Karim closed his eyes in pretended pain. "For his money, she has even abandoned her religion."

"A Protestant?" Eliana asked, horrified.

If he'd written a script, he couldn't have asked for better. Such a feminine woman, so malleable. It was unfortunate he couldn't linger in Barcelona a little longer.

"Alas, yes. I have traced them to Barcelona." Karim raised her hand to his lips for a more lingering kiss this time. "To your inn," he whispered against her knuckles.

"Poor man." Pushing the coffee tray out of the way, she stroked his arm with her free hand. "And now you ask my help."

Karim nodded.

"My guests are your wife and her lover?"

Something mercenary had entered her eyes. Noting it, Karim nodded again. She thought to get the better of him in business because she ran this inn and went unveiled before the world. Let her think it. He would win and get all he wanted from her.

"Your guests are tall, the man black-haired, golden-skinned, with brown eyes." It was her turn to nod. "And the girl. She is fair, with hair and skin so pale that they might be moonlight, with changeable blue eyes."

"They claim they are brother and sister." Still she stroked his arm.

"They hope to disguise the unholy relationship until they can regularize it. Yes." He nodded at her gasp. "To kill me so she can wed her lover. Even the Protestant Church would never countenance a divorce."

Hands dropping from his, Eliana sat back in her chair. "I shall call the police and have them evicted."

"No, no," Karim interrupted hurriedly. "Think of the stain on my honor."

"They cannot stay here." One finger tapping her chin, she watched him through narrowed eyes. "Although—"

"You will assist me?" This wasn't going quite the way he wanted, but he couldn't stop now. Not without arousing suspicion.

A melting smile accompanied her nod. "Yet I must think with my head, not my heart. If you act tonight, I shall be out several nights' rent for two rooms. This is the slow season, you understand, and it's very difficult to find tenants."

"But think of the virtue you gain in helping another of the true faith."

Eliana's sorrowful expression prepared him. "If only it were possible for me to follow my heart and help you. However, I must think of putting food on the table for my family. As a poor widow with only this humble inn to support me and my young son, the requirements of Holy Mother Church must regrettably take second place. Surely you understand." Touching his hand in appeal, her lashes fluttered helplessly.

"Yes, but—" He stopped when she shook her head again, firmly, yet regretfully. "Perhaps I can see that you suffer no loss."

"The risk to the good name of my inn must also be considered," she said briskly. "For a sum, I shall hide you in Diana's room. You will subdue and remove her. Without"—Eliana waved an admonitory finger at Karim—"rousing the neighborhood. Everything must be done with the utmost secrecy."

"What about the Protestant?" Karim asked. Were all infidel women this headstrong?

The tip of her tongue delicately moistened full, pouting lips. "I shall see he doesn't follow you."

"He must be punished." The words escaped before he controlled himself. "The stain on my honor—"

Eliana cut him off with a wave of her hand. "Will best be kept secret by ignoring the man. Now, about the price for removing your wife from my inn . . ."

CHAPTER XIV

PLATES EMPTY OF *tapas,* ALONG WITH WINE AND BEER glasses, littered tables drawn together in a cozy group. Her lone coffee cup stood out sharply among the litter. Once the waitress discovered Diana wasn't French, she'd been delighted to serve her. In fact, everyone was delighted. And with Garrett, especially, since he'd served in Wellington's army.

In an aside before he plunged into an animated discussion of the Peninsular War, Garrett had told her women weren't ordinarily served at a *tasca* such as this, but they'd allow it. "This time" remained unsaid.

Licking her fingers of the last crumb of a delicious meat pastry, Diana suppressed a grin. Garrett was enjoying himself in a way she hadn't seen since they left Nikos and Ariadne. Whatever was upsetting him had flown. Not that he'd thought about her during the last few hours.

"What are you grinning about?" Garrett asked softly in English.

She didn't try to restrain the smile. "This." Gesturing at the litter of plates and glasses covering the clutch of tables, she shook her head. "And they say women gossip."

"Well, they do."

"No more than men."

Grinning acknowledgment of the hit, he ran a hand through his perennially disheveled hair. "I never argue with a lady."

"You'd lose." Playfully, she poked him in the ribs and dodged his instinctive retaliation.

Casting an estimating glance at the depth of the shadows, he changed the subject. "We'll have to hurry if you're to do any sight-seeing. Dark comes early this time of year."

Turning to the remaining men lounging about the tables, he spoke in rapid Spanish, listened, then switched to French for Diana's benefit. "He says there's a respectable modiste just up the street. It's safe to leave you there while I return to the harbor."

"Why return to the harbor?"

With difficulty Diana kept her eyes on Garrett's face. The knowing grins revealing yellowed and missing teeth of the other men made her . . . not uncomfortable. She'd never call it that. Just deliciously aware how wonderful it was to be with Garrett and what he meant to her.

"We need a ship leaving for Italy soon." His brows flicked together in a momentary frown. "Karim—"

"This is a Christian country," Diana reminded patiently. "Not the Ottoman Empire. Karim's powerless here. What's he going to do? Go to the police and tell them that the woman he kidnapped for a harem escaped, and could he have her back, please? We're safe now, Garrett." Patting his arm, she nodded at the array of plates on their table. "Since we've had lunch, let's go shopping together."

"I'll have to leave you at the modiste's."

A single glance at his determined expression silenced her. Plainly, Garrett was taking this seriously. If it made him feel better to check on the ships leaving for Genoa, she wouldn't protest. And while he was gone, she'd select nightclothes Without his assistance.

As they rose, a rush of suggestions came from the men who'd eaten *tapas* and reminisced about the war with Garrett. "To see the real Barcelona, go to the Barrio Gótico," called one.

Another offered, "See the lacemakers in the market, too."

"And the Catedral Santa Eulalia. Englishmen always enjoy the geese in the cloister," a third suggested.

"*¡Gracias!* We'll try all of them."

Putting money for the *tapas* and drinks between stacks of plates, Garrett added something Diana couldn't follow, and led her away in the direction indicated. Before entering the street leading out of the square, she turned and waved, then linked her arm with Garrett's.

"They were nice, weren't they?"

"You didn't think so when I arrived." Grinning, he avoided another playful punch in the ribs. "Seriously, don't go wandering without me. All right?"

Swallowing hard, Diana nodded agreement. "How long will you be at the docks?"

"Shouldn't be more than a half hour, three-quarters at the most. Will you be all right alone here?"

"Yes." Diana smiled a little ruefully. "I was just remembering the last time you left for a half hour to visit some docks."

"As you said, this isn't the Ottoman Empire. If you like, though, I'll stay with you and search for a ship later."

Diana shook her head. "It's not necessary. I'm just being foolish." Looking ahead at the cheerful clutter of shops open to the soft afternoon air in the crooked street, she nodded at one. "Is that the modiste's?"

Holding open the door, he ushered her in. It looked as respectable and as well stocked as the men at the *tasca* had promised. Between the pair of eager assistants helping the modiste and the bolts of fabrics and half-made dresses lining the shop, Diana expected no difficulty. Accepting her assurance, Garrett used the introduction they'd been given, then excused himself.

In a very little time, so little she'd barely time to worry, he was back. Diana was holding up two rival blue silks when she heard the bell over the shop door tinkle again. Smiling, she held them out. "Which do you prefer?"

Fingering both, he considered them briefly. "This one." His hand deliberately brushing hers, he held up the more intense blue. "I love it with your eyes." His smile deepened. "Finished?"

A faint flush crept up the soft skin of her cheeks, and her lashes fell. Folding the silk back onto the bolt, she nodded. "Not completely. But I can come back tomorrow. I've found a few things the modiste was willing to let me have." Diana laughed softly. "And more important, she's willing to put off the customers they really belong to."

A cynical gleam in his eye, Garrett agreed. "Money usually talks."

"You found out something?" Diana asked quickly, responding more to the tone than the words.

"We leave in three days." The lift of one shoulder dismissed the subject. "Let's have these things sent to the inn and go visit these geese, which all Englishmen love, at the cathedral."

Silently, willing to let him find his own time to tell what disturbed him, Diana complied. In minutes, they were walking down the street toward the cathedral. Lacemakers working in the bright afternoon light occupied the sunny side, their pillows before them with bobbins dangling down. Dawdling despite Garrett's brisk stride, Diana watched the women's nimble fingers switch bobbins and needles, twist and tie cotton and linen and silk thread in intricate patterns over a colored backing. Not all the lace was white, nor was all of it meant for edging. One woman made a black mantilla in a rose pattern of such exquisite delicacy Diana exclaimed with involuntary pleasure.

"Do you like it?" Garrett asked.

"It's incredible. How does she remember the pattern?" The elderly woman bent over the pillow holding the lace, fingers flying among the bobbins. Above where the lace mantilla formed, a number of pins held a piece of parchment in place with the bobbins attached to them.

"Probably long years of repeating it. But I think that's a pattern." He pointed at the parchment.

Switching to Spanish, he said something. Answering with a dip of the head, the woman turned to a large cloth bag beside the stool. Pulling out an identical black lace mantilla, she held it up for Garrett's inspection. Taking several coins from his pocket, he handed them to her in exchange for it.

"You'll need this for the cathedral."

The explanation silenced her protest. "Please tell her how lovely her work is. I don't suppose she speaks French, and after what happened earlier"—she grimaced—"I don't want to find out."

"Agreed," he said absently. Rather than paying attention to her, Garrett was lost in studying the coronet of braids restraining the heavy silk of her hair. "It'll look like moonlight and shadow on you." His voice was meditative, nearly inaudible. Catching himself, he spoke to the lacemaker and offered his arm to Diana again. "Ready for the cathedral and these famous geese?"

"No, Rabi," Leila said patiently, "leave the trunks alone. They don't belong to us."

"These are Dji-Diana's trunks, aren't they?" Yawning, she rubbed her itchy nose. She'd had a cold for the past few days, and Leila had kept Rabi with her to ensure she rested properly and took her medicine.

"They are," Leila agreed, "but you're not supposed to be up, remember? Now, lay down like a good girl and keep warm. It's time for your nap."

Rabi yawned again and sneezed. "You won't leave, will you?"

"Of course not." Rubbing the girl's shoulder tenderly, Leila headed her toward the divan in the corner. "I'll be right here writing a letter."

Rabi measured the distance between one divan and the

other before coming to a decision that satisfied her. Kicking off her slippers, she hopped onto it and pulled a warm blanket over her. Pillowing her head on her hands, she smiled sleepily at the harem mistress and murmured a soft "G'night."

Leila rustled about the room for a few minutes longer, gathering her thoughts and the materials necessary. It still upset her to go against Haroun's wishes, but there was no help for it. The more she'd tried to change his mind, the more stubborn he'd grown.

Settling on the divan, where she could keep an eye on Rabi, she drew the writing board onto her lap and began. After inscribing the name and address of Diana's parents, found in the trunk, Leila drew the feathered tip of her quill pen along her lips. How to begin? As a mother, she knew what shocks children's escapades could give and how much parents craved reassurance. But she could give none. The letter had to be written, though, if she wanted to protect Diana.

Finally, she began at the beginning, baldly and with the minimum of explanation. There was no other way. Once she'd described the kidnapping, Diana's entrance into the harem, and her escape, Leila lifted the pen from the paper and read it. It wouldn't reassure any loving parent. Frowning, Leila shook her head. Nothing could change what had happened.

But maybe she could reassure them a little:

> You need not worry about the kidnapper. I have arranged for the guide's punishment. He will never again dishonor the city of Bizerte. Nor is it likely that my lord's brother, Karim, will find either your daughter or the infidel. If he should and returns them to the palace, I shall see to her rescue, although it grieves me mightily to thwart my lord in such a manner.
>
> I must now offer some advice. Worrying about Diana, I have checked on the man she has fled with. The infidel,

Hamilton, has a more than usually ingratiating manner with young females. This does not matter in countries following the true faith, as unmarried girls are never permitted alone with men, however, Diana is not so protected by her family and upbringing.

You must forgive my mentioning this, but you have been sadly remiss in allowing her to reach the age of twenty-one without providing a husband for her. Since her escape has thrown them into terms of unacceptable intimacy, securing this husband has now become a matter of paramount importance. Garrett Hamilton, you will be relieved to learn, comes from an excellent and monied family in England. He is also, apparently, a Christian. If you had negotiated a contract in the normal way, you could not have chosen a better husband, since I believe you are of the same faith. He also has the reputation of being indulgent of feminine foibles, so you need not concern yourself on that score.

I am returning your daughter's trunks to you, along with the gold that was hidden in them. May I request that you destroy the clothes immediately. No girl with her fair coloring should ever wear such shades. Only the true jewel tones accent her loveliness properly.

Apparently, Diana was in some agreement with me on this, because immediately prior to the kidnapping, she purchased four bolts of fabric from a merchant in the local market. I have retrieved these and seen that the merchant was punished for not delivering goods that had been paid for.

Instead of sending all of the bolts, I am retaining two. Both, unfortunately, are a lovely shade of rose that would fade Diana into insipidity. The other two, a bolt of moss green and another of indigo, will suit her admirably.

The fabric I'm retaining will be used for a member of the harem whose coloring will become even lovelier in rose. In their place, I am sending a beautiful sea green that suited her far better during her brief stay with us.

> *The two bolts I intend to charge to the bey's account.*
> *He deserves it for his behavior. If he'd listened to reason,*
> *none of this would have been necessary.*

A smile curving her mouth, Leila glanced at Rabi. The girl slept the sleep of a tired child. Already the cold's grip was loosening, and the hectic flush on her cheeks was fading. Soon she could return to her normal routine. Rabi's delight would be tempered, Leila knew, by the return of lessons as well. By that time, Diana's trunks would be gone from these rooms, and Rabi would forget about them.

But first, Leila had to finish the letter:

> *As one parent to another, I hope you'll take my advice*
> *and marry Diana immediately to this Garrett Hamilton.*
> *The rumor that a girl of her age chooses her own mate, I*
> *discount entirely. No nation could be so foolish as to allow*
> *this.*
>
> *If you learn of any further difficulties that I may assist*
> *with, please write, and I will do all in my power to help. In*
> *the hope that you will have many grandchildren as lovely*
> *as Diana.*
>
> *I remain,*
Leila.

Moonlight and shadow. What a romantic thing to say. With the mantilla draped over the coronet of silver-gilt braids crowning her head, Diana cast covert glances at Garrett as he escorted her through the massive doors of the cathedral.

Since the lacemakers, he'd lightly touched on a number of subjects—none remotely connected with romance. They sailed for Italy in three days' time. Until then she intended to enjoy their stay in Barcelona. After all, Garrett was thinking of her again in a romantic way, wasn't he?

"Look," he said, voice appropriately hushed inside the cathedral.

She followed the direction of his gaze and nearly gasped,

her attention fully caught. Multicolored late-afternoon sun-light streamed through the stained-glass windows into the three aisles leading the eye to the center of the church. Intricate carvings decorated every surface. Slowly, she paced forward, aware of Garrett, silent beside her.

Everywhere she looked, there were new wonders to be-hold. Brushing back the mantilla tickling her cheek, Diana glimpsed something in a chapel on one side of the aisle. She touched Garrett's arm and nodded.

Halting before the altar, she felt that at any moment the figures on the altarpiece would step down. Christ, with a distinctly Spanish look, stood among three of His disciples. Candlelight threw shadows that made them appear to move. Mute, she looked at Garrett, who stood close, his face un-readable in the dim light. After another moment spent in silence, his hand at her waist guided her out.

By the time they reached the center of the cathedral, a certain lightness had lifted her spirits. Below the intricate carving of the choir canopies and behind the altar lay a stairway leading down to a crypt. On the arched entryway there was a carved gallery of boyish heads.

Diana pointed at one. "He looks like he was a terror to his parents from the very first." Despite an angelic counte-nance, the sculptor portrayed an impishness that warned the world to beware.

Garrett nodded and indicated another face loaded with devilry.

Drifting along the arch to the head of the stairway, Diana looked at the sculpted heads. Each was individual, yet all gave a sense of belonging in the precise order in which they'd been carved. She'd never seen anything like this.

"I wonder who they were." Garrett's voice disturbed her rapt contemplation of the sculpted portraits.

Looking over her shoulder at him, the aquamarine ruff of her dress framing her face, she smiled. "I don't know, but they are lifelike. Their ages are deceptive. They're not any-where near as young as they first appear."

He stood breathtakingly close, slightly behind and at one side. Her smile dreamy, she leaned toward him before catching herself. This wouldn't do. Not here. She took a step away.

"It's all very old, isn't it?" Her gesture took in the entire cathedral.

"Fourteenth century, although some of it's more modern." In response to her questioning look, he continued. "Fifteenth century, I think." He pointed at the choir canopies.

"The fifteenth century is modern?" she asked, amused.

"For a cathedral." Responsive amusement crinkled the corners of his eyes.

"There's nothing like this in Boston." She'd said it often enough to herself; why not to Garrett?

His hand cupped her elbow warmly. "You get used to it after a while. Now, let's go find these geese that all Englishmen love."

Garrett led her out of the cathedral into a long, covered walkway with arches separating them from the garden that allowed easy access on fine days, yet offered protection on rainy ones. In the peaceful quiet of the cloister, Diana realized how late it was getting. Another hour or so and the colonnaded walk would be in almost total darkness, though outside the cathedral there'd still be light. Turning to ask Garrett if they had time for more sight-seeing, the warning hiss of a goose interrupted.

A flock of geese waddled on surprisingly fast feet down the sheltered paving, one ahead of the others. Even in the half dark, his beady eyes inspected Diana and Garrett suspiciously. She'd been around geese before and didn't trust them.

"They probably want something to eat."

"As fat as they are?"

"Just more *pâté de foie gras.*" Garrett reached into his pocket. "I picked bread up on the way back to the modiste's."

Drawing out a small packet, he crumbled some and threw it on the flagstones. In a rush, the geese noisily gobbled every crumb. Finished, they looked up expectantly. Garrett crumbled the rest and tossed it down.

"You'd think they hadn't been fed in days, wouldn't you?" Diane commented wryly.

Dusting his hands of the last crumbs, Garrett grinned. "That's not hunger, that's greed. Come on, let's go before they discover I'm out of bread."

Once back on the street and headed toward the inn, Diana finally asked, "What did you learn at the docks?"

"A ship's leaving for Bizerte soon," Garrett answered, fastening the top button on his jacket. A chill breeze had sprung up while they were in the cathedral. "Are you warm enough?"

Diana stopped and stared. "Why would we—you want a ship going to Bizerte?"

He nudged her to continue walking, his hand warm at her back. "Remember the chain I was wearing when we escaped?"

Licking her lips, she said, "I don't see what—"

"It's the badge of office for the beys of Bizerte," he reminded her patiently.

"Haroun owes it to you for his dirty trick." Holding her hands close to her chest, Diana wished she'd bought a muff at the modiste's. It was getting chilly.

"No." Garrett sounded even chillier than the wind. "I'm not a thief."

Diana couldn't keep the giggle out of her voice. "Just a smuggler."

Garrett's thin smile relaxed in the wan light of dusk. "That's different. But Haroun was my partner, and no matter what, I don't steal. Especially not from a partner."

That blasted offbeat conscience again. It'd get them killed one of these days.

"Besides, if I don't get it back to him, he won't stop chasing us."

"How soon does the ship leave for Bizerte?"

"The day before we sail for Italy." Garrett held open the gate leading into the inn courtyard.

"Ah, *señor, señorita.*" Eliana stood back from the door to allow them into the foyer. "A chilly night, is it not?"

"Very." Garrett closed the door behind them and gave Eliana a brief smile. But his attention remained concentrated on Diana. "You aren't chilled, are you?"

"No, I'm fine." Moving around Eliana, Diana went to the fire that had been lit to ward off the cool of the evening.

"Garrett," Eliana said, putting her hand on his arm, "I'm so happy to see you found your wayward little sister." The word sounded even stranger on Eliana's lips than it had at noon.

"So am I."

Nodding pleasantly at the landlady, Garrett joined Diana at the fireplace. Holding hands out to the brightly burning flames, his smile created a closed world around them, one Diana found impossible to fight.

"Why don't you go upstairs to take off your pelisse?" he asked, his voice low and intimate, cutting out Eliana. "Or would you prefer something to drink first?"

Stepping between them, Eliana caught one of Diana's hands in hers. "Your poor hand is so chilled. *Tch!* I already have the water heated, and I'll send a pot of tea up to your room to warm you. You English girls roam about without the proper protection." Her dark eyes feverishly bright, Eliana tugged Diana toward the staircase.

"Thank you, Eliana." Rescuing her hand from the landlady's grasp, Diana had the satisfaction of seeing a flash of purest dislike in her eyes. "But I think I'd rather have tea downstairs. With my brother."

Eliana's full lips pouted. "But you must be exhausted after a day's shopping. If you go up to your room, you'll be able to take your shoes off and put up your feet."

"I'm accustomed to walking, Eliana," Diana said dryly. "We English ladies walk a great deal."

"Eliana," Garrett broke in, "bring us tea here beside the fire, please." He took a pair of chairs standing stiffly against the wall and drew them up before the hearth. "With that table over here"—he pointed at one on the opposite wall—"it'll be cozy."

Diana slowly unbuttoned her pelisse with murmured thanks, when Garrett immediately helped her with it. Removing the mantilla, she smoothed it and the pelisse and laid them over the back of the chair he'd brought over. Shaking out the creases in her aquamarine gown, she started to sit down.

"Señorita," Eliana said from the doorway, "you will be happy to know your clothes have arrived from the modiste's. I sent them to your room." She glanced meaningfully at the crumpled skirt of Diana's gown.

If her dress was crumpled, it wasn't important. The expression in Garrett's eyes, his attentiveness—those were important. "I'll go up after we've had tea, Eliana. Thank you." She rubbed her arms. "I didn't realize Spain was so chilly."

"It is December, *señorita.*" Her mouth a thin line, Eliana withdrew in the direction of the kitchen.

"Do you always have this effect on susceptible females?" Diana asked when the landlady was out of hearing.

"Eliana? She's not susceptible." Putting a finger to his lips, Garrett nodded toward the arch leading from the kitchen. "She's already returning."

Once Eliana left the tea tray, Diana poured. It wasn't what she'd had at home or on board ship, but it was warming. Chatting desultorily, they slowly finished the pot.

Finally, Garrett rose. "I'm going up. Do you want another pot of tea?"

"Not now. I'm still cool despite the fire and the tea. Let's go up, and I'll change into something warmer."

His hand unnecessarily but comfortingly at her waist, Diana climbed the stairs. Whispering a temporary good-bye to Garrett, she waited until he was inside his own room before opening her door. Surprise and a little guilt filled her as she stepped in.

Eliana had a fire lit for her. It cast friendly shadows over the armoire and bed. Diana decided to be nicer to Eliana in the future.

Turning to close the door, a hard, hurtful hand clamped over her mouth.

CHAPTER XV

KARIM CALLED AN ORDER IN A HARSH WHISPER.

Despite its lowness, Diana recognized the voice. The rough way he held her confirmed it. His relentless hand covered her mouth and most of her nose as well. She could scarcely breathe. His other hand imprisoned her arms and held her clamped hard against him. Kicking back with all her strength, a muffled yelp delighted Diana. Until his arm tightened to the point of agony.

"You'll pay for that. And the one at the palace."

Karim's voice was more savage for its softness. Now wasn't the time to struggle. He was expecting it, and it'd only amuse him.

To her right, a muffled curse sounded, and a piece of furniture fell over. A chair? She tried to see, but the flickering firelight masked the room in shadow. If it was a chair, the other man was near the bed. Eyes swiveled to the right, she looked for a moving shadow in the dim light cast by the fire.

A candle burst into light with a sizzle when it was carelessly thrust into the flames. Turning with it in his hand, the other man looked at Diana. His face, eerily lit from below by the candle, was impassive, cold. No help there; not that there could be with Karim present.

Karim rapped out another order, and the man lit a branch of candles beside the bed before putting the one he held on the mantel. He subsided into a corner with an air of patient waiting. A low chuckle hit her ears, and Karim's hands, both his hands, shifted fractionally lower. His arm pressed cruelly into her breasts. More important, though, she could breathe a little better.

"What? Not struggling, little bird?" Karim's voice rasped in her ear. "You'll struggle later. The harem would have been infinitely more enjoyable." His chuckle stirred the hair over her ear. "You'll provide plenty of entertainment during the trip home. It's only fair. You've caused me more than enough boredom as it is."

The words flowed on, but Diana refused to listen. From his threats she was safe until he could get her aboard a Muslim ship. Karim wouldn't be able to keep her silent that long. She was helpless. But just for the moment. Any noise would summon help.

This was Christian Spain, not the Ottoman Empire. Any aid that came would be hers, not Karim's.

Darting looks around, she searched for something to use against him. There was nothing within reach of her partially imprisoned arms.

Closing her eyes, she concentrated on the room as she'd last seen it, brilliant sunlight flooding throughout. There was nothing behind she could use. But to her left— The picture of a massive stand with a heavy candlestick on top formed in her mind. It couldn't be more than a few feet away. If only she could get within reach of it.

A change in the litany of threats snapped her reverie. Karim said something to his henchman. Taking advantage of the distraction, Diana deliberately sagged and slumped to the left.

Staggering, Karim's hands tightened cruelly and dragged her upright again. She remained limp, as though on the verge of swooning, and tried to disregard the pleasure in his voice.

"Just like a woman," he said in a gloating whisper. "Go ahead, and when you faint may it be to sweet dreams of the infinite pleasures that lie ahead."

The threats didn't matter. They were closer to the candle stand now. But not close enough. Even if she reached it, she might not have strength left to swing it. She felt dizzy from lack of air. If only he'd move his gagging hand, breathing would be easier.

A sudden muffled noise from the bed startled her. Tensing, Diana tried to see what was happening. With a laugh, Karim twisted her head, showing her his henchman kneeling beside the bed.

"I told Mustafa to get the rope. We'll have to tie you up before dealing with your lover." She stiffened. "Don't worry, you'll have the treat of watching Hamilton suffer." He paused, waiting for a reaction. When it didn't come, he continued. "And die." Karim relaxed his grip a bit and described in minute detail how he'd torture Garrett.

Shaking her head violently no, she pried open her mouth at the same time. Clamping down on a finger, her teeth sank into his flesh in a death grip. The world spun as Karim tried to rip his hand free.

Yet he wouldn't scream.

Grinding her teeth with all her strength, the taste of blood almost gagged her. Yet all that escaped Karim was a low moan. Before Mustafa rose from where he crouched to assist his master, Karim had to yell. Or let her go.

Karim tried to yank his hand free once again. She let him. With all the air she had left, Diana shrieked in the loudest voice she could manage, "Garrett!" and kicked backward at Karim's left leg.

He staggered to the left. Almost within reach of the candlestick. Another few inches and she'd have it. But not yet. Karim's hand clamped back over her mouth before she could yell a second time. His fingers dug deeply, painfully, into her cheeks; his arm was an iron band over her breasts and arms.

"Your death will only be after much painful suffering for that. So will Hamilton's."

Outside, Diana heard Garrett's door open, then silence. He *had* to know something was wrong by now. Let him follow those instincts for trouble he bragged about.

Switching to Arabic, Karim hissed an order to Mustafa, who stood frozen in the middle of the room. Jumping at Karim's sharpness, he hurried toward the door.

As Mustafa came closer, Diana steadied herself. There'd be only one chance.

She kicked. Hard.

Her foot landing in his groin made Mustafa scream. Startled, Karim jumped, and his punishing arm loosened for a fraction of a second. With all her strength, Diana reached to the left. Grabbing the candlestick, she swung at Karim's knee.

This time his agony echoed in the room. Abruptly, Karim's arms no longer imprisoned her, and she crashed to the floor. Scrambling back up, she held the candlestick poised in front of her.

Vaguely, Diana heard the door burst open and Garrett explode into the room. He'd handle Mustafa. She kept her attention centered on Karim.

Staggering off balance and cursing incomprehensibly, he lurched toward her but missed when his knee buckled. Swinging the candlestick roundly as hard as she could, the heavy base connected with Karim's head with a satisfying thud. He crumpled to the floor, his head resting beneath the still upright candle stand. A stream of blood running down his face pooled on the floor beside him.

Horrified, Diana stared for a stretched instant before the noise of the other struggle penetrated. Garrett and Mustafa. The candlestick raised, she swung around. Garrett held Karim's henchman by the throat with one hand. His pistol butt connected with Mustafa's head, and he crumpled as silently to the floor as Karim had.

"Garrett," she gasped. Slowly, Diana lowered the candlestick.

Stepping across Mustafa's sprawled body, he grabbed her. "Are you all right?"

Barely restraining a wince when his fingers dug in, Diana nodded. "Karim," she began. Prying the fingers of one hand from the heavy candlestick, she pointed at his unmoving body. "Is he"—she hesitated—"dead?" She snatched the hand back to quiet her trembling fingers.

Garrett released her and bent over the body. Checking quickly, he looked up and shook his head. "Just out for the count. Don't worry. Even minor head wounds bleed ferociously. Did he hurt you?" Garrett's eyes were shadowed and dark.

"Just bruises." The candlestick dropped noisily to the floor and rolled in a circle toward Mustafa. "How did they get here so quickly?"

Shrugging, Garrett rose. "A faster ship. So much for safety in a Christian country and trusting in the bey's parsimony. I wonder if Haroun knows how much Karim's spending." He cocked his head quizzically. "I wonder how he intended to get us out of Spain?" Dismissing the problem, he looked about the room. "We'll have to tie them up."

"Mustafa had some rope." Her feet braced apart, Diana didn't move. The most peculiar sensation afflicted her knees —as if they'd melt and she'd sink to the floor.

"So he has." Garrett pulled it out with satisfaction. "And more than enough for two." Flopping Mustafa over on his belly, he bound hands and legs efficiently. "I wonder why Karim didn't tie you up."

"He was going to," she admitted. Her knees were solidifying again, hardening like maple syrup poured on snow. "Probably he didn't hurry because he was enjoying himself too much."

Freezing halfway up, Garrett looked keenly at her. "I thought he didn't hurt you."

"He didn't." Seeing the concern mixed with fury in his

face, Diana smiled wanly. "Really, he didn't. He simply held me with one arm while gagging me with the other. He wanted to feel me react while he described in disgustingly graphic detail our fate." One hand floated through the air, dismissing the speculation. "He didn't hurt me, though, so don't worry."

His brows still nearly meeting in a black line across his forehead, he bent over Karim's unconscious body. With unnecessarily rough hands, he bound the security chief tightly. Thrusting a hand through his hair, Garrett rose.

Pulling her into his arms, he held her for a long moment. Diana luxuriated in the comfort. Why was she shivering now that the threat was gone? Garrett's hands ran soothingly up and down her back. Eventually they stopped, and Diana's head rested on his solid shoulder.

Finally, Garrett brushed a kiss on her temple. "We'd better get the police," he said. "Wait—" He glanced at Karim's and Mustafa's roped and gagged bodies. "No, come with me. We'll send the police for them. There shouldn't be any problem."

Hand in hand, they went down the stairs. The hall looked as though they'd never sat, laughing and chatting, close to the fire sipping tea. The table was back in its position against the far wall, while the chairs stood rigidly arranged on either side of the fireplace. An occasional shiver shaking her, Diana stayed close to Garrett's side.

At the foot of the stairs, she asked softly, "Should we send Eliana? Or go for the police ourselves?"

Before he could answer, Eliana came in, a warm shawl pulled about her shoulders. Her eyes on their clasped hands, she frowned and hesitated before hurrying over.

"Eliana, we need the police," Garrett said baldly.

Mouth open, Eliana glared at their locked hands. Diana had no intention of letting go. Foolishly, Karim's threats disturbed her now.

Her fingers tightened, while Garrett rapidly told Eliana what had happened upstairs. He didn't know all of it, just enough to sharpen fresh memories. As Garrett spoke, the landlady's mouth dropped open, then tensed, her fine black brows drawing together into a thin line. Eliana must find the incident as upsetting as she did. Diana'd misjudged the landlady.

"What have you done to my Don Carlos?" Eliana demanded, adding something in Spanish. She took a step closer, her chin thrust up aggressively.

Diana stared at her. "Who's Don Carlos?"

Eliana's hand flew up in an extravagant gesture and she paced closer to the taller girl. As though unable to bear looking at her, the landlady turned and strode back and forth across the flagged hall. "You ask who your own husband is? Never would I have believed such effrontery, such villainy, was possible—even with such a one as you."

"I'm not married!" Diana exclaimed, bewildered.

Her protest didn't slow Eliana's steady pacing up and down the hall. "To ignore vows of marriage as a Protestant would be bad enough, but to set aside the holiest sacraments of Holy Mother Church for any reason is vile sacrilege. And to do it for mere money!" Spinning on her heel, she charged up to Diana and shook a finger beneath her nose.

Diana stepped back, stunned and uncertain over what this madwoman would do next. "I was kidnapped—"

Garrett's voice overrode hers. "Diana's not married." He caught Eliana by the shoulder to drag her back, but she shrugged him off, turning a look of fierce contempt on him.

"And you! To seduce a woman from her lawful husband. It is one thing for a man to have mistresses, but they should never be married women."

"Diana's not married," he repeated. "I should know, I'm her brother."

"Brother, humph!" Tossing her head back in disgust, Eliana glared at Garrett. "Lover! Adulterer!" She spun back to Diana, her expression ferocious. "As for you—leave my inn this instant! Eliana Estruch has never knowingly allowed an adulteress to stay in her inn."

Diana blinked incredulously. Explanations weren't going to help. They'd have to leave, find some other place to stay until the ship left. It didn't matter so long as Karim was in prison and couldn't touch them.

Jabbing one finger at Diana, Eliana yelled, "And you—you're going to jail, where you belong. Then you should beg on bended knee that your wonderful, loving husband take you back without the beating you so richly deserve."

Before they could protest, Eliana ran through the door. It slammed, leaving a rush of cold air behind. Diana's hand dropping away from Garrett's, she turned to him. "What now?"

He didn't answer her question. "How long will it take to get your pelisse?"

Swallowing and taking a deep breath to stop the onrushing sense of unreality engulfing her, Diana looked at him, bewildered. "All we have to do is explain to the police."

"If we're here when Eliana returns with them, you'll have the unpleasant opportunity to see the inside of a Spanish prison." He turned back to the stairs, his hand hard on her arm. "Let's get out of here."

"Garrett," Diana said imperatively, refusing to budge. "Garrett," she repeated when he faced her, "that's nonsense. We'll explain that I was kidnapped for the bey's harem and you helped me escape. Then they'll jail Karim and leave us alone."

Shaking his head, he gave her a grim smile. "Why do you think I never returned to Spain after the war was over?" Reckless energy burned in Garrett's face. "The authorities here arrest first and ask questions later. Much, much later."

That didn't sound encouraging. "Well, once they ask questions, we'll be free and Karim will stay in jail. He'll be arrested, too, won't he?"

"Perhaps." Garrett ran a coaxing hand down her arm. "But this isn't Boston. Besides, he's got Eliana on his side.

The police will listen to a local before a foreigner. And they're certain to arrest us for cohabitation, if nothing else."

"Still—"

"Still nothing. Come on." His hand tightened on her arm, and he pulled her toward the stairs. Garrett's glance beneath frowning brows was dark. "Not only are the police here notorious for arresting first and questioning after, they're also notoriously ill-paid."

Her bewildered resistance made him add, "That means they're not the cream of Spanish society."

His mouth tightened further at her incomprehension. With ill-concealed impatience, he added, "It's unlikely they'll behave like gentlemen toward you."

A flush of comprehension climbing her cheeks, Diana hurried up the stairs in his wake. Outside their doors, Garrett turned to her and repeated his order.

"Fetch your pelisse, and we'll get out of here."

Obediently, she turned to enter her room before she remembered. "Garrett." She turned back to him.

His hand closed about hers, warm and comforting. "Don't worry. If you don't want to go in alone, I understand. I'll come with you."

Warmth flooding her, she smiled and brushed his cheek with tender fingers. "It's not that. It's—"

"Karim's tied up," Garrett reassured her. "There's nothing to worry about. I won't let him hurt you."

"Karim's got nothing to do with it."

"Then why are we wasting time?"

"If you'll listen, I'll tell you." The explanation slipped out with unintended abruptness. "Three times escaping without a change of clothes"—she hurried on at his impatient frown —"is two times too many."

"This is—" Garrett cut himself off. "Women! We'll buy you new ones."

Her chin firmed and lifted. "I'm not leaving without my clothes. Not again."

His hand cut through the air between them in a flat gesture of dismissal, then stopped at her expression. "All right, hurry up. I'll be in to help as soon as I'm ready." Without another word, he strode into his room, the door banging behind him.

Needing to hurry, Diana still watched until the door closed, leaving her with a last view of his stiffly held shoulders. Sighing, she swiftly entered her own room. He was annoyed, but it couldn't be helped. Lifting her skirts a little, she stepped over Karim.

Nothing had changed since she and Garrett left. With the handle of the armoire door in her hand, she looked behind her at Karim and Mustafa, her eyes narrowing. A whisper of sound had reached her ears. Or was it only imagination?

Both men lay where Garrett had left them tied up. Neither had shifted even an inch, or had they? Well, it wouldn't surprise her if they had, she decided, turning back to the armoire. Even unconscious, surely they must be able to move or turn, just like someone deeply asleep. Dismissing it, she opened the door.

Inside the armoire, she saw that Eliana hadn't lied. Someone had stacked the packages from the modiste's neatly on the floor beneath the few dresses she'd made aboard the *Marie.* Pulling everything out, she surveyed her possessions. Garrett would never agree to taking all this. And she really didn't need it all.

Bending to open the packages, she straightened abruptly. The hair prickled on the back of her neck with the feeling of someone watching her. Rapidly, she inspected the two prone figures bound hand and foot on the floor.

Breathing heavily, Mustafa sprawled beside the bed, a bruise starting to discolor his jaw. The blood had already begun to dry on Karim's forehead. Thick black lashes fanned across his cheeks without a flicker betraying consciousness. Shaking her head and frowning, Diana hurried back to the modiste's packages. This wasn't the time to indulge her nerves. She'd worry about it later when they were free of the inn.

Quickly, she bundled together dresses, nightdress, under-clothes, and a pair of shoes she'd found at a shop attached to the modiste's. Wrapped in a blanket and tied with cord from the packages, it made a reasonably sized bundle that wouldn't be too large for her to carry. Not even Garrett could object.

Grabbing her pelisse, she rushed across to the dressing table, where her comb and extra pins resided. Along with a bar of soap from beside the washstand, she thrust them into the pelisse's pockets. She was still scanning the room for anything forgotten, the pelisse hanging over her arm, when the door swung open abruptly.

"Aren't you ready yet?" He sounded annoyed. That was even more obvious from his expression and the impatient way he closed the door. "We haven't got all evening." The small valise purchased from one of the *Marie*'s officers dangled from his hand.

"I'm ready." Diana brushed down her pelisse before putting it on. "Where're we going?"

"To the nearest port. Do you really need all this?" He indicated the clothes strewn over the chair and floor, ignoring—purposely or not—the neatly wrapped bundle in front of the armoire. "I'll be glad to finally get you to di Benedetto's. It can't be soon enough after this fiasco. Clothes, yet!"

Hurt drew the corners of her mouth in. "We'll reach Genoa faster if we can just hide in Barcelona and take the ship you've already reserved passage on."

Garrett started around Karim's body and halted. "He moved."

"Every once in a while one or the other makes a sound or stirs." Going to the hastily wrapped bundle of clothes, Diana picked it up. "I hope they're having nightmares."

"Here, I'll take that." Glancing down at the skirt of the aquamarine dress showing beneath her pelisse, he asked, "Can you ride in those clothes?"

Reluctantly surrendering the bundle, she nodded. "We're not staying in the city?"

"Not unless you want to risk visiting the local prison. You're too easy to find with that silver-blond hair. Now let's hurry."

Swinging the bundle onto his shoulder, he started for the door, then stopped, laughed, and put his burdens on the floor. Kneeling beside the valise, he opened it and fished something from the bottom. Garrett turned toward her as he rose, the badge of the beys of Bizerte dangling from one hand.

"What do you say we leave it here?" he asked in a soft, laughing voice. "With Karim. That'll pay Haroun back for his treachery."

"Why?" Diana asked, puzzled, but happy the old Garrett, the reckless adventurer she loved, was back.

Grinning, an impulsive gleam shining in his eyes, Garrett draped the chain around Karim's neck and rose. "Karim's been trying to oust his brother for years and become bey of Bizerte. With the badge of office in his possession he has a chance." Another soft laugh floated out into the serene, candlelit room. "It must've been rough on friend Haroun to have to send Karim in search of not only us, but the chain."

Smiling down into her face, Garrett stretched out a hand. Accepting it, she gasped when he pulled her into his arms. Pressing her full length against his hard-muscled body, he bent, his lips covering her open mouth.

Of their own volition, her arms crept up about his neck. She'd wanted this for so long and missed it so much over the past few weeks when he'd been cold, distant.

With a murmur, he deepened the kiss, his arms closing tightly about her. His tongue playing in an exploration that sent waves of longing surging. It'd been too long. Her hands tangling in the crispness of his hair, she arched into the waiting tautness.

"Behave yourself, Diana," Garrett said, his voice husky. Hard, strong fingers digging into her waist, he lifted her away from him. "This is no time to dally." A teasing glint lit his eyes.

Suppressing the ache inside, Diana shook her head. "I seem to have heard that before."

A shout of laughter echoed from the stucco walls. Catching her in an expansive hug, Garrett patted her on the rear. "Let's go, baggage, before you get us into even more trouble." His arm still about her, he led her to the door.

Behind them, Karim twisted his pounding head once they were safely past and watched the door close.

Di Benedetto's in Genoa.

CHAPTER XVI

DIANA HALTED BESIDE GARRETT. HIS PLAYFUL TEASING had lessened the urgency of their flight. Had he done it to calm her? Or was it just his reckless love of danger? Here, at the head of the stairs, the seriousness of their predicament rushed back in full force. Swallowing, Diana swiftly surveyed the inn for possible trouble.

Below, only a small section of the well-lit, dark flagstone floor and white stucco wall of the hall showed. No one was visible; no sound floated up to them. It appeared that, so far, Eliana hadn't arrived with the police.

Giving Diana a reassuring smile, Garrett touched her shoulder briefly and led the way down. The police would take quite some time to rouse.

Or so he said.

From the cautious way he went down the stairs, he wasn't taking a chance on being wrong. The pressing need for hurry constantly fighting with caution, Diana forced herself to stay a step above, inspecting each new portion of the hall their motion revealed. When Garrett halted two steps above the foot of the stairs, she nearly ran into him. There was no one she could see.

Leaning forward, she whispered, "Please hurry."

Glancing back, he nodded, and they went on. The whisper of her kid boots and Garrett's Wellingtons on the flagstones echoed in the silent hall. Not even a servant appeared before they reached the door leading outside.

Garrett stopped again, motioning her to stay behind. On a draft of chill air, he opened the door and peered into the small courtyard. Diana saw nothing but windswept flagstones washed in moonlight. The police weren't here yet.

Once in the street, Diana stayed beside Garrett, her legs stretching to keep his pace. Pulling her pelisse tighter, she skirted a puddle from the previous night's rain.

"Where're we going?"

He indicated the street they were turning into. "When I went to see about the ship to Genoa, I noticed a stable. With horses, we can flee Barcelona before the city gates close. Even if Karim avoids prison, he's trapped here until they open them in the morning."

Moonlight flickered over his face as they hurried from shadow to shadow cast by the old buildings. Chill wind gusted down alleys leading off the street and wafted scents of rubbish and stagnant water. Few people were on the streets, and only an occasional stray band of light found its way between cracks in shutters tightly closed over windows.

"Well, once we're out of the city, where do we go?"

"At the docks, I heard even more ships involved in Mediterranean trade sail from Tarragona than from Barcelona."

Garrett indicated another street crossing the one they were on. Rounding the corner faced them into the wind. It seemed more biting than a Boston winter wind when contrasted with the day's warmth.

"How long will it take us to reach Tarragona?" She wiped wind-caused tears from her eyes with gloved fingers. As always, the wind was stronger among buildings that funneled it.

"A couple of days." His grin flashed in a sudden patch of moonlight. Ahead, a horse whickered, the sound carried on the wind.

His jaunty stride proclaimed he'd recovered his usual good humor now they were actively doing something. It was infectious, and despite the pace, Diana bounced just a bit, too.

Approaching the stable, Garrett slowed. "Stay back and let me do the talking. That hair of yours is a beacon. I don't want the police to know what we're doing until we've fled the city. Then we'll worry about Karim."

A shiver that had nothing to do with the biting wind sped down Diana's spine. "But he's already got the chain."

The tension in her voice brought Garrett to a halt in a pool of shadow at the base of a sheltering street corner. Pulling her into his arms, he stroked her cheek gently. "I wouldn't worry too much, but I think we'd better start planning for the worst." Bending, he stole a brief kiss that sent warmth chasing the cold away. "Obviously, Karim's more inventive than I've given him credit for."

Diana leaned against him, savoring the haven of his arms before she caught herself. "My parents are friends with the authorities in Jerusalem. Once we get there, we're safe."

"I wouldn't just depend on friendship with any Ottoman official." A gust of chill wind whistled around the protecting corner. "But," Garrett added quickly at her shiver, "with your family's wealth, you'll be safe."

Stopping well shy of the pool of light spilling from the open stable doors, Diana waited. She watched Garrett stroll toward them. He acted as though he had all the time in the world.

Heads down, a pair of saddled and bridled horses stood near a water trough, while a hulking man mucked out a stall just inside the door. With easy confidence, Garrett emerged into the pool of lantern light. His *"¡HOLA!"* startled the stable hand, who stiffened and stared.

Diana watched, and even though she understood neither Catalan nor Spanish, the story told itself. Garrett indicated the saddled horses with one hand.

The stable hand looked from Garrett to the horses and

back again slowly and shook his head, while clutching the pitchfork handle to his massive chest. Smiling widely, Garrett tried again. The man shook his head more vehemently.

Fishing a handful of coins from his pocket, Garrett casually tossed them. While the stable hand scrabbled in the straw for the one he'd missed, Garrett untied the horses and led them toward Diana. Whether the stable hand had agreed to the sale or not was, at best, problematic.

Reaching her side, Garrett helped her mount silently. Again, no sidesaddle. With a quiet sigh, Diana arranged her skirt as best she could and tugged down the hem of her pelisse. Despite the skirt's fullness, it didn't cover her ankles. Or most of her calves. With the chill wind roaring through thin cotton stockings, tonight would be a cold ride.

"We'll leave from the north gate."

"Karim?"

He nodded and lowered his voice. "If he does follow, he'll think we fled to a French port. Outside the walls, we'll circle back and take the coast road for Tarragona.

"When we get there, I wish I could show you the medieval fort, but I can't. The French blew it up when they retreated back in '11." Grinning, he guided his horse into the main street leading north. "So don't under any circumstances speak French. But, with your antiquarian interests, you'll be pleased to know the road going there's called the Via Augusta. The Romans named it after the Emperor Augustus somewhere around the first century B.C."

"Poor Don Carlos!" Eliana exclaimed.

Karim heard other voices but didn't open his eyes. Not yet. With Eliana arguing his case, he'd be all right.

But caution couldn't hurt.

Skirts brushed his shoulder and face. He felt her carefully lift his head into her lap and stroke the hair from his forehead. Still bound behind him, his hands dug into his back and the floor, and a rope connecting them to his bound feet tightened.

It was time to get the ropes removed. Groaning, he opened his eyes, smiled wanly up at Eliana, then let the lashes flutter down again, just not far enough to block his view.

"Permit us, Señora Estruch."

Boots belonging to a pair of policemen were planted just beyond Eliana's skirt. From where Karim lay, the men towered toward the ceiling. He'd love to study them but knew better. He had to maintain the appearance of a bumbling innocent who'd fumbled a vainglorious attempt to retrieve his wife.

Eliana lifted Karim's head carefully from her lap and back to the floor. It hurt like the very jinns had trounced upon it. Damn that girl. He permitted a groan that made the hands unbinding him gentler after Eliana protested.

His eyes fluttering open again, Karim let the policemen help him to his feet. The world spun; nausea roiled in his stomach. Swaying between the pair, he pressed a hand to his temple until things settled.

Bringing it down before his face, he stared at the discoloring patches. Sticky blood clung to the fingers.

"Señor Alavedra," Eliana said sharply as Karim's paleness increased. "Can we not take Don Carlos to another room to lie down, rest, and, if he feels like it, eat?" A comprehensive gesture took in the litter of wrapping paper and discarded clothing covering the floor. "You cannot question him here."

Karim smiled gratefully. He needed time to clear his head before the inevitable interrogation began.

"*Sí, señora.*" Grimacing at the other policeman behind Eliana's back, Alavedra supported Karim toward the door. "If you will show us to this other room, we will help Don Carlos there. Perhaps," he added, at Karim's shudder, "it would be best to have a fire lit since he seems chilled."

From the door, Eliana glanced back at Mustafa. "What about the other one?"

"My assistant Pau will come back. We'll leave him in bed

in this room. He doesn't respond to Catalan, French, or Spanish, so we won't be able to question him."

Karim sank onto the freshly made bed with relief. Murmuring commiseration, Eliana sponged his face free of blood, while a warm, inviting fire leapt in the hearth. Finished, she protectively took the chair at the head of the bed. Karim watched her send a warning glance at Jaume Alavedra and waited for the inquisition. Despite her protests, they were determined to question him.

"Don Carlos," Alavedra began, "Señora Estruch has told much of your story. Kindly tell us what happened here tonight."

Listening carefully, he waited until Karim reached the end of his recital. "Why didn't you come to us? We, the police, are here to help."

Karim stiffened. Looking at the tall, hard-faced policeman through half-closed eyes, he answered carefully, "My wife, whatever she has done, is my wife. She bears my honor wherever she goes."

"You should have come to us." Alavedra's dark eyes narrowed as he spoke. "No Catalan would ever parade a man's shame in public."

Karim inclined his head and winced. "I have heard that the Catalan most honorably understands these things, unlike some countries, but—"

"How did you learn where your wife was?" Alavedra interrupted.

"I nearly caught her in Greece, but they found a ship captain who helped them escape." Studying the policeman unobtrusively, Karim added, "For a price. The Protestant Englishman is wealthy."

He waited for the expected effect. Infidels took these differences between one sect and another seriously. Branding Hamilton as a Protestant worked well on Eliana this afternoon.

But Alavedra remained passive, uncommunicative. Something else would have to be tried.

"He'll expect to bribe—"

The policeman stiffened, his expression affronted.

The wrong tack. Gasping as though hit with a stab of pain, Karim clapped a hand to his head and closed his eyes. Beneath his fingers, the hair was damp from Eliana's ministrations, while small clots of blood clung to strands of hair beneath his fingers. Although the half swoon was pretense, closing his eyes lessened the pain throbbing in his head with each heartbeat.

"Jaume Alavedra," Eliana snapped, her hand stroking Karim's arm soothingly, "you may interrogate Don Carlos, but not now. These questions can wait until he's feeling better. Can't you see that unfeeling woman he married struck a brutal blow?"

"We have only his word that he's married." Alavedra studied her, his eyes serious. "They claimed to be brother and sister."

Eliana flounced in the chair beside the bed. *"Claimed* is the word. They were completely unalike. Except for their heights. She was immoderately tall for a woman. But otherwise"—Eliana sniffed expressively—"one blond, the other brunet; her eyes pale and his brown, with a nice touch of gold to them—"

"I'll bet you noticed," Alavedra murmured.

Ignoring him, Eliana continued the list of differences. "She's fair; his skin's a lovely bronze." Blushing, she smoothed the small black ruff edging the neck of her dress. "And their manners. He was a gentleman, while her manners are best left unmentioned."

Amusement in his face, Alavedra dismissed Eliana's reasoning with a wave of one hand. "That's neither here nor there. Until we have better information, Don Carlos and his man remain in protective custody. In one of the better cells, of course. If he's willing to pay."

Karim barely kept himself from protesting. It wouldn' help

Anyway, Señora Estruch did it for him. Her impassioned

plea left Alavedra unmoved. Karim's mouth thinned in what he hoped was an expression of pain. Let them investigate. Nothing could be learned about him here. Eventually, they'd let him go. Once free, he'd follow Hamilton and the girl to Genoa.

The city gate was behind them now, along with the guards' comments on Diana's legs. She knew that much Spanish, and Garrett's laughter hadn't escaped her either.

Still, exhilaration filled her. They were free again.

Against her will, she admitted its attraction, this life of Garrett's. The sense of being totally alive after a close call. The air smelled sweeter, his companionship— Lower lip held fast between her teeth, she caught herself. She'd better not think that way too much.

Laughing softly at herself, she urged her horse alongside Garrett. Brilliant moonlight lit the road leading north from Barcelona. The guards high on the walls could see, but she didn't care. Karim would never catch them.

"What was the stable hand telling you?"

A low chuckle sounded over the steady clop of the horses' hooves. "I think—I'm not sure, his accent was so fierce—he was saying that he couldn't sell these horses because they were owned by the stable's most important customer." Grinning, he glanced at her. "It doesn't matter. I paid him enough to cover the cost of the horses and equipment, plus a nice profit."

"I hope he doesn't get into trouble."

"He won't. He'll blame it all on the *ingles estupido.*" Garrett studied the road ahead. "Look, a signpost." Touching his horse's sides lightly with his heels, he rode over to it. Arms pointed ahead to Badalona, behind to Barcelona, and to the west the sign said "S Cugat del Valles." "Let's go this way for a while. It's the right direction, and we're bound to strike a road heading south."

Diana looked behind. The walls were out of sight beyond some trees. The guards couldn't see which route they took.

Whatever Karim offered them in bribe, they couldn't report what they didn't know.

"I hope you've got a good sense of direction," she said lightly, turning forward in the saddle.

"The sea's to the east. We left by the north gate with the sea on our right, so west lies to our left."

"I hate to mention it"—Diana shook her head—"but I'm getting hungry. Those *tapas* seem a long time ago."

"Would I allow you to starve?" Garrett asked reproachfully. "Don't answer that. If you can wait until we skirt Barcelona, I'll see what I can find."

What had been the wish for dinner turned into an uncomfortably hollow sensation by the time they reached the headlands to the south of Barcelona. Groves of olive and nut trees alternating with scrub made the landscape seem desolate with the color drained away. The trees were black silhouettes against the pale, sandy ground, and the wind, although growing less fierce, sounded wild and lonely. Below, at the foot of the cliffs, was the staccato crash of waves against the rocks.

"There," Garrett said after several miles of silence. He pointed to a tumbledown structure black against the sky. Far beyond in the bright moonlight stood a farmhouse with a cluster of sheds surrounding it. "The hotel where we'll spend the night." He laughed at her expression. "No, I haven't lost my mind. We can have a fire inside those ruins without anybody seeing it, be protected from the wind, and, if we're lucky, have a roof over our heads. Best of all, that farm'll provide us with dinner and breakfast."

The cold weariness gripping her receded. Urging her horse forward at a more rapid pace, Diana asked, "What do you think they'll sell us?"

After staring at her in amazement for a few seconds, Garrett finally explained gently, "We can't just ride up to the door to ask them." Diana's hands tightened on the reins, slowing her horse to a plodding walk. "Sweetheart, Karim doesn't know where we're going. If we leave a trail, there's no sense in spending a night in the open. We might just as well find an inn and let them see that head of hair of yours."

Diana caught his eye and held it. "You said the French devastated this area only a few years ago. These people must be poor. I won't allow you to *steal* from them."

"This isn't stealing." Bringing his horse close alongside hers, he patted her hand where it rested on the pommel. "During the war, the only way we could get any food at all was through informal requisitioning."

Her hand lay passively beneath his. "The war is over. No stealing."

Silence stretched for seconds between them. Eventually he prodded his horse forward, and the steady clop of hooves sounded above the rush of wind. Face troubled, Diana kept her mount close to his stirrup.

"All right." Sighing, Garrett capitulated. "I'll leave some money in the henhouse. I suppose that won't leave too big a trail."

A gust of wind found its way inside her pelisse again, but Diana's smile was radiant with relief. It lasted for another few feet before imagination took hold. Farmsteads always had dogs. Even if they weren't savage, they'd bark and wake the farmer. An image of an outraged Spaniard charging out of the house in his nightshirt, musket in hand, made her stomach tighten.

"Garrett?" The steady sound of wind and hooves obliterated his name. Swallowing, she tried again. "Garrett."

His head whipped around. "What's wrong?"

Moistening her lips, Diana asked, "You will be careful, won't you?"

The soft laugh riding the wind wasn't reassuring. "Sweetheart, I've done this more times than I can count. Don't worry so. They won't catch me." He guided his horse off the trail toward the ruin. In a voice she wasn't supposed to hear, he added, "I hope I remember the old skills."

Off the road, wind whistled through trees and brush, and sandy soil absorbed the sound of the hooves, but the footing was more difficult. Shortly, iron horseshoes clattered on half-buried cobblestones. The ruined walls towered above in places and tumbled into rubble in others. Pulling his horse up, Garrett surveyed their surroundings. Reflected light from pale stone and dense shadow made finding a clear path difficult.

"We'll be better going in on foot." He dismounted and came around to help her.

Diana clambered down with relief. Riding astride was not yet an enjoyable experience, although she'd probably be proficient by the time they reached Tarragona. With the reins draped over her arm, she followed Garrett into the ruins.

As they penetrated the piles of rubble, the air stilled. Over the remaining walls, the wind whistled almost companionably against the occasional clatter of a dislodged stone. A narrow path between the walls emerged into an open area. Unkempt espaliered trees clung to sheltering walls. On the far side, barely visible through brambles and forlorn brush, was a half-roofed enclosure, with grazing just outside for the horses.

Leading his horse up to the shelter, Garrett started to unsaddle, but Diana touched his arm. "I'll do that," she said in a low voice. The hushed stillness of the ruin made whispering seem appropriate. "You shop for dinner. I'm hungry."

"Do you know how to unsaddle a horse?" Garrett asked, looking down at her doubtfully.

"Much as it upset Gran, I've saddled and unsaddled many horses." She squeezed his hand reassuringly. "Stop worrying. I can take care of this." Her hand tingled when it dropped from his.

After a mild protest, Garrett slid through the shadows and out an opening she hadn't noticed. For the first few minutes, Diana fumbled with saddle girths and bridles.

Once the horses were rubbed down with a few wisps of dry grass, she tethered them where they could graze. Garrett hadn't returned yet. Of course, there'd been barely time for him to reach the farm, let alone forage for food.

Pulling her pelisse closer, Diana looked about. It was too cold to sit and wait. They needed wood for a fire and—sand scraped beneath her feet on the stone floor—something to sleep on. With the bright moon overhead, there was plenty of light to gather wood and padding.

With kindling and dead branches for a fire stacked near the front, Diana dropped a final armload of pine branches on the two mounds of dried grass, needles, and branches in the section sheltered by the walls and under the partial roof. Spreading a blanket on each, she dusted her hands, but they felt sticky. Going to the well in the midst of the derelict garden, she washed them with the aid of a broken bucket. Now there was nothing left to do.

She paced from moonlight to shadow and back.

"Is the fire ready?" Garrett asked from a shadow when she turned to pace back into the shelter yet again.

"Garrett!" Diana gasped. Running to his side, her hands went to his shoulders. "I was worried."

"No need." Lowering his burden, he looked at the preparations, then gave her a quick kiss, and enveloped her in a massive hug. "I'm going to have to bring you with me more often."

Releasing her, he knelt beside the pile of brush and kindling. Watching him efficiently strike a spark with his flint, a strange contentment filled Diana.

A small curl of smoke soon rose straight into the sky until it topped the walls, then spiraled away,

"I didn't have a flint," she said finally.

Garrett answered absently, "Don't worry about it. They"—his head jerked toward the farmstead he'd just visited—"must be celebrating. A wedding or something." Blowing gently on the flame, he carefully added more wood as each piece caught. "They'd killed and plucked a batch of chick-

ens for tomorrow. Plus made tons of other things. They
even had wine stored in the wellhouse."

For the first time, Diana looked at the prizes he'd returned with. Wrapped in a blanket were chickens, nuts, and
vegetables, along with two straw-cradled bottles.

"When you go shopping, you go shopping."

Adding a larger branch to the fire, Garrett smiled over his
shoulder. "Dinner and breakfast as promised, my lady. Plus
something for the road." Satisfied with the fire, he picked
up a pair of plucked chickens. "Chicken à la campfire. Of
course, in the army we used pots for cooking, but a good
soldier can always improvise."

After dinner, Diana leaned back against the wall and licked
her fingers. "That was delicious. Hunger's definitely the best
sauce."

Flames shot toward the night sky, sparks disappearing
into the blackness above. They died as the wind caught and
carried the smoke away toward the mountains. It was so
deliciously warm. A slow smile of contentment curving her
lips, her hand dropped into her lap. Beside her, Garrett
yawned and stretched, sounding as contented as she felt.

He jerked his head to indicate the welcoming shadows at
the back of the shelter. "Where'd you learn to fix a bed?"
With seeming casualness, he picked up her hand and toyed
with the fingers.

"Out of books."

Her hand resting in his, Diana lazily turned only her head
to look at him. Bare inches separated their shoulders. But
more than physical closeness brought this sense of intimacy. He was acting like the Garrett on board the *Medea*.
The teasing, loving Garrett she'd missed so incredibly
much, the Garrett she loved, was back with her. The headi-
ness of his return left her giddy.

"Did you ever think—" he began expansively. Suddenly
his arm was about her shoulders and he pulled her head
lightly down to rest against his chest. "Did you ever think

you'd spend the night on Spanish cliffs perched above the Mediterranean—in a ruin—with the man of your dreams?"

Instead of the expected groan, she attacked his ribs with tickling fingers. The result was greater than she dreamed possible. His laughter, a bass rumble that rebounded off the stone walls of their shelter, made the horses tethered outside whicker.

Arms flailing, he twisted away. "Can't face the truth, can you?" The question panted out between bouts of laughter. "Think how incredibly lucky you are—"

Not letting him finish, she reached for his ribs again, but he was ready. Catching her wrists, he firmly yet gently forced them down.

"Who told you I was ticklish?"

A current of excitement raced from his hands to dance along her veins. It banished the weariness of the long, cold ride. Looking up, his face was half shadowed, half firelit, above her.

"You can't retaliate, because I'm not." She sounded breathless, as though she'd been running.

Imprisoning one of her arms beneath his, he drew her other hand behind her back and probed her ribs with a delicate touch. His teeth glinting in a quick grin, he targeted the one ticklish point as though a map guided him. A giggle escaped before she bit her lips and twisted. Yet he held her prisoner easily.

Lifting her effortlessly across his legs, the pattern his fingers traced no longer tickled.

"You shouldn't do that," he whispered.

"What?" Suddenly, it was difficult to breathe.

"Bite your lips." He brushed a kiss over them.

"You're giving me bad habits," she said with a mournful shake of the head.

"I wouldn't worry about it." Touching her nose with one finger, he trailed it down her throat to her dress. "There's no one here but us."

"The horses," she gasped. His fingers sent curls of awareness through her, awareness that reminded her of the last time she'd lain in his arms. Reckless excitement raced like effervescence inside.

"What about the horses?"

"We might shock them."

The flaring light masked the intent in his face, but she knew it was there. Twisting her arm, exhilaration filled her when he let it go immediately. She lay still for a stretched instant out of time. Then, reaching slowly up into the shadowy dark enveloping his face, she traced the edge of his lips with one finger.

Garrett's arms slipped about her, lifting her against him. His lips moved on her throat in a trail of demanding, yet gentle kisses that led upward to her jaw, her lips. As his mouth closed over hers, Diana's arms tightened about him.

The fine wool jacket contrasted sharply with the silky strands of hair curling over his collar. Pushing it aside, she explored the flesh beneath—warm where he'd faced the fire, cool at the nape. Tactile memories, memories too long submerged, flooded her. Murmuring, she nibbled kisses along the beard-roughened line of his jaw, her eyes only half open.

Outside their shelter, the horses had returned to grazing, their outlines clear in the moonlight. Firelight flickered over them and cast tantalizing shadows on the walls of their haven. The figures there reflected the dreams that had plagued her for weeks. Mesmerized, Diana moved sinuously, joyously, beneath his heady caresses.

In this time, there was only Garrett. Unhurriedly, she luxuriated in the total return of the man she loved.

Embers glowed and flared, flames caught on pine pitch of wood not yet burned. A bubble of pitch burst in a series of pops that sent a shower of sparks soaring into the air. Diana twisted in Garrett's arms and looked up. Laughing softly, she settled back against his chest.

Lowering his head, he took possession of her mouth

again. Wonder flared; all the sensations only he brought to life were there, yet even more intense than she recalled.

His hand moved to the neck of her dress where tiny hooks closed it. As he undid them one by one, the ruff feathered her chin, then down her throat. Sighing with pleasure, she unfastened the buttons of his shirt. Beneath, silken hair roughened his chest. Diana stroked it, savoring memories, but there were differences.

Then, low lamplight clung to bronzed skin, highlighted the curves of hard muscle. Now, despite the fire, shadow enveloped them. Lashes drooping shut, Diana slipped her hands under Garrett's shirt and pushed it and his jacket from his shoulders. Briefly, he released her and shrugged them fully off.

Beneath satiny skin tension shimmered, tension that increased as she caressed bare arms, shoulders, back. Restraint was there, too. A fine tremor shook the fingers tugging soft aquamarine wool from her shoulders, peeling it down over bare arms. Chill roughened her skin, but only for an instant.

Her eyes still closed, she felt him bend toward her. Then his lips were on her throat and nibbling a path downward to the small mole on the curve of her breast. His tongue circling it made her gasp. She wanted nothing more than to curl against Garrett, the scent of pine needles and campfire heightening the delicious sense of unreality surrounding them. Stretching, she planted a kiss in the hollow of his throat.

His arms slid beneath her back and bent knees, and he gathered her high against his chest. In one fluid motion, he rose to his feet. With arms around his neck, Diana buried her face in the warmth there while he carried her over to the mound of makeshift beds.

Rough wool blanket prickled, while her eyes sought Garrett as he stepped out of his trousers, and joined her. This far back in the shelter the light was dimmer, yet the glistening bronze skin caught and reflected it. Pulling the blanket over them, he drew her into his arms.

In that safe haven, everything dissolved into Garrett's touch. He moved against her, his hands liquid fire. It burned over her body, left her aching, yearning to return the passion. Diana caressed, savored his hair-roughened flesh. Though warm, she couldn't stop shivering. Nor could he.

Desire spiraled higher and higher until, arching against him, she sought fulfillment. He poised above her, trailing kisses the length of her trembling body. She couldn't stay still beneath his touch. Catching his shoulders, she arched upward again, needing to fill the aching emptiness he created inside. With an impassioned murmur, Garrett settled in the cradle of her thighs, his strong body trembling as he barely held himself in check a moment longer.

The rough wool blanket scraped her back as she moved demandingly beneath him. As on board the *Medea,* loving Garrett was perfect, right. Only perfection was improved. The shuddering, warm cocoon of her world exploded around her. Garrett thrust once, twice more, then crying her name hoarsely, stiffened, and collapsed on her breast.

Long seconds passed while Diana caught her breath, Garrett's head a beloved weight on her breast. Stroking tangled, damp hair back from his forehead, she twisted down to kiss it. She loved him. She always would.

And she'd never be able to live with him, marry him. The thought made the passion they shared bittersweet.

As though he'd read her troubled thoughts, Garrett lifted his head and whispered her name gently. At the entrance to their shelter, the fire flared, sending a shaft of light to their bed. Smiling soft reassurance, Diana smoothed the faint frown from his forehead and drew him back down to her. With the blanket drawn around them, they curled into each other's arms, content for the moment, and slept.

CHAPTER XVII

Tarragona, Spain—December, 1819

TARRAGONA CRESTED THE HILL ABOVE, THE WALLS blending with the terrain into a monolithic fortress. The city looked as though it had stood forever. Below, merchant ships were anchored in the port, giving the sole modern touch from this distance.

Diana knew she should be pleased that this particular goal was in sight. Her entire body ached from days in the saddle, and it seemed like forever since she'd had a proper bath. One awaited in Tarragona. The prospect didn't make her happy.

"Do we find an inn first, or go to the docks?" she asked, stretching in the saddle. She felt strangely listless, as listless as Garrett looked.

Dragging his gaze away from the walled city perched high above, Garrett shifted, searching for a more comfortable spot in the saddle. The pair of horses they'd bought in Barcelona had a uniquely uncomfortable gait.

"The docks," he answered reluctantly. Adding at her curious look, "Karim's bound to follow. No one but a crazy infidel would leave a trail of coins for stolen chickens." Though he shook his head, his smile took the sting out.

"We couldn't steal their food and leave them with no way to replace it."

His brows climbed comically toward tousled hair. "Women." At her expression, he quickly reassured her, "No, we couldn't steal their food. But, unfortunately, Karim has a clear trail to follow. The police probably held him for questioning for a couple of days, at least. Then he may have wasted time on the false trail we laid down." Garrett frowned into the sun glittering off the brilliantly blue water. "But we need to leave Tarragona as soon as possible. Karim's shown more doggedness than I credited him with."

"He has the badge of office," Diana reminded him. "He'll probably just head back to Bizerte."

"I may have outsmarted myself." Garrett shook his head. "I've been thinking about it for the last day. Our taking the badge has given Karim the chance he needed, but he may feel that to use it he has to capture us. Or lose face." He smiled wryly. "Let's be safe just this one time and leave Tarragona as soon as possible."

"I suppose."

Diana realized she'd said that aloud only when Garrett straightened in the saddle. Pleasure lighting his face, he dug his heels into the horse's sides, urging the tired animal to lengthen its stride.

It did for a few feet, then settled back into the bone-jarring amble the pair had maintained down the coast from Barcelona. Still the pace brought them swiftly to the docks, where Garrett helped Diana dismount well out of sight of the dock workers.

"What do we do first?" she asked, brushing down her skirt, while Garrett contracted with a youngster to watch and guard the horses.

The aquamarine dress would never be the same. Three days in it hadn't improved it. Nor did the horsehair clinging to every inch. She hadn't had a choice about wearing it. The skirts of her other dresses weren't full enough to wear while riding astride.

"Find the port master," Garrett answered when he'd completed the transaction with the youngster. "He'll know which ships are ready to sail and where they're bound. If they've told him the truth."

"That's how we're supposed to find a reliable ship?"

Quiet amusement emphasized the word "reliable." It seemed it was ashore that the trouble came. Putting her hand in the crook of Garrett's elbow, she smiled up at him.

Nodding, he put one finger on the tip of her nose. "You have more freckles now."

Wrinkling her nose, Diana laughed. "Gran would be horrified. Fortunately, Mama never cared how many freckles I had."

"Neither do I," Garrett murmured, looked around, then quickly kissed her on the nose.

Diana watched him from the corner of her eye while they walked along the docks to the port master's office. His face told nothing. Reaching their goal, he dusted off a chair, seated her with grave courtesy, and switched to Spanish.

The port master was fat and gray, the office needed cleaning, and nothing seemed to have been filed in a decade. Looks were deceiving. He answered questions quickly and clearly. After giving directions, he rose ponderously and conducted them to the door. Bowing over Diana's hand, the port master kissed it gallantly, and sighed. Then he pointed down the docks to a ship.

"It couldn't be much better," Garrett said reluctantly after the port master returned to his office.

"What?"

Heading toward a small Italian brigantine flying the Austrian flag, his step dragged. "There's the ship the port master says is leaving for Genoa on the evening tide."

"Oh." They'd reach Genoa that much sooner. Her grip on his arm tightened possessively. "How long will it take us?"

"About a week." Smiling somberly down, Garrett's hand closed warmly on hers. "But the best news is no other ship in port sails to Genoa. If Karim follows us here, he's stranded."

"A young lady with very blond hair?" The port master puffed out his pendulous cheeks and nodded ponderously. "She might have been here." He scratched his scalp through thinning, spiky gray hair. "My memory isn't too good anymore."

Contemptuously, Karim stared down. The man sprawled like a fat spider in the midst of a web. Stacks of paper surrounded him, some with the dust undisturbed for months. More than a quarter hour had been wasted in reaching the point where he admitted to "perhaps" seeing a girl of Diana's description. Petty officials were all the same: happy to thwart anyone and demanding bribes to do their jobs.

"Was it this week?" Karim asked with icy patience. His hands clenched into fists behind his back. Uncurling a hand, he reached into his purse and placed a gold coin on the table.

The port master looked at it for several seconds before searching vaguely among the papers scattered across the desk. He held the page close to his nose and peered at it nearsightedly.

"Well?" Karim finally snapped.

"What? Oh, I just thought I recalled them."

Dropping the paper, he crossed his hands over his belly. The page drifted in a vagrant draft and landed on a stack other than the one he'd taken it from. It disturbed the dust, but not the port master.

Forcing his clenched fists to relax, Karim flexed his fingers. "Since you recall them, perhaps you will be gracious enough to tell me where they went."

"To Italy." The port master blinked sleepily up at Karim. "Didn't I tell you?"

"Ah." In spite of himself, the drawn-out sound held too much satisfaction. "So they are headed for Genoa. How long ago did they leave?"

"Won't you have a seat?" Taking off his glasses, the port master polished them thoroughly with a red-cotton handkerchief. While he worked on them, he regarded Karim with a nearsighted stare of unnerving fixity. "It's hard on my neck to have to constantly look up at you."

Teeth grinding, Karim strode across the small office and grabbed the single chair. Without bothering to dust, he plopped it in front of the desk and thumped down. He reined in his temper by taking a deep breath.

"Is this better?" The question emerged with dangerous courtesy.

"Much. Now"—scratching his nose and peering over the rim of his glasses—"what is your interest in this young lady?"

"She is my wife and has run away with the Protestant who accompanied her." Assuming the reluctant air that had worked so well with Eliana, Karim told the tale. "So you see," he finished, "why I must save her."

The old man regarded Karim over the glass rims in absolute silence. "You're a Moor?" he asked eventually.

"Once. Now, I am a good Catholic, *señor.*"

"Hmmh. Interesting. I don't get many of them here." Taking a watch from his waistcoat pocket, he wound it, then peered at the face.

Finally, again the port master gave Karim an unnerving stare. He shuffled several stacks around. Dust rose into the air to float in golden motes above the desk. "However, I can't help you."

"Is there no ship for Genoa?" Karim asked when the port master didn't continue.

"I shouldn't be surprised if one arrives within the next week, maybe two, but the last one left two days ago. The *Acquila.*" He gave the Italian name a Spanish lilt.

"That's the one Diana, my lovely young wife, took passage on?"

"If you mean the blond young lady, it is. There isn't a ship leaving for Genoa, though, anywhere in the harbor."

Spreading his hands in apparent acceptance of the inevitable, Karim asked, "Is there a ship going to Italy?"

Taking another maddening period staring at Karim unblinkingly, the port master finally looked down at the papers he'd shuffled in front of him. Again he held the paper beneath his nose to peruse it. "Going to Naples, the *Corsario.*" Lowering the paper slowly, he smiled at Karim. "She should suit you perfectly. Provided you can secure passage. She leaves on the tide."

Ominously silent, Karim shot out of the office and signaled to Mustafa. "Get my luggage to the *Corsario,*" he ordered in Arabic. "And make it fast."

"Am I to accompany you, my lord?"

"No," Karim snapped, striding down the dock toward the ship he hoped was the one he sought. "Go to Bizerte and report that I've followed the girl and the infidel to Genoa and will return soon." Mustafa didn't know about the badge of office, so it didn't matter. He could reach Bizerte and Haroun before Karim did. Realizing that Mustafa still dawdled along beside him, Karim snapped, "Hurry up."

Stretching his long legs into a half run, Karim headed down the dock while Mustafa ran to the inn where they'd left their baggage. The *Corsario* wasn't the clean, new sloop. She was the next ship down, a scruffy brig with a sorry-looking crew. But the gangway was down. Karim ran up it and called for the captain.

"I understand you're going to Naples," Karim said when the captain joined him.

Picking his teeth with a splinter, the captain inclined his head. "If you want passage, you'll have to get your traps aboard soon. We wait for no one."

"My man will be here with my luggage in a few minutes." The captain smelled as offensive as his ship. Karim had to force himself to remain on board, but anything was worth it to catch Hamilton and the girl. "Have someone show me to my cabin."

"Cabin?" The captain looked amused at the notion. Turning around to speak to his first mate, he stopped. A cunning smile crossed his face. "Pay enough, and you can have mine." The captain scratched himself lazily. "Otherwise, you doss down with the men."

"How much," Karim asked softly, "not just for your cabin, but to take this ship directly to Genoa?"

Genoa, Italy—December, 1819

"You need have no fear, *signore*," Giovanni di Benedetto assured Garrett. "The *signorina* will not only be safe with us, but have only the best of everything here. For the sake of her much beloved parents. Now, if you will excuse me, I shall fetch my daughter, Bice, to make Signorina Graham especially welcome in our home." Unspoken was his obvious assumption that Diana and Garrett would have things of a very private, romantic nature to discuss.

Diana barely waited until the tall, cadaverously thin man bowed himself out before turning to Garrett. They'd said everything, discussed everything, over and over on the ship. Not once had they even come close to agreeing. Yet she kept hoping.

"Garrett," she began.

Smiling teasingly, he grasped her shoulders and drew her closer until she rested full length against him. "Diana"—he continued the argument where they'd broken off upon arriving at di Benedetto's villa—"you'll enjoy yourself more in Greece than in this mausoleum."

He looked about with distaste. Heavy, stiff chairs with somber upholstery stood against whitewashed walls. None looked inviting. Nor did the dark, dreary painting hanging above the empty fireplace add to the welcoming atmosphere. Diana shivered responsively. Even through a wool pelisse and dress the room struck cold.

"Garrett, please think about the danger your Greek scheme means." She rubbed his cheek persuasively. "Come with me to Jerusalem. You'll find just as many opportunities there for trading in antique statues."

Stretching upward, she brushed a kiss on his chin. "You might find other things to interest you, too."

Eyes glinting with mischief, he pulled her closer, hands curving over the upper swell of her hips. "If you come with me to Greece, I'll have the same opportunities we both want."

Diana batted his hands away and stepped back. "How magnanimous of you."

"All right. But think about it, sweetheart. We'll not only be together, we'll make a fortune."

Searching for some way to convince him, Diana went to the window and gazed wearily out at the small garden. Bare-limbed trees and bushes interspersed with pines surrounded pagan statues. All looked incredibly somber despite the brilliant winter sunlight. But that, surely, was only a reflection of her mood.

Days before they boarded the *Acquila,* she'd accepted the depth and intimacy of her relationship with Garrett. But she'd never accepted his obsession with reckless adventure. Part, she suspected, centered on his need for revenge on the bey, and now on Karim. But she couldn't understand how his Greek scheme could possibly give him revenge. At least, she added, not direct revenge.

Turning as he finished with all the time-worn arguments, she reminded him, "I've already got a fortune."

Pacing up and down the small reception room, he waved an airy dismissal. "So've I. What's that got to do with it? We can even give the fortune back to the Greeks to support their rebellion against the Ottoman Empire. Think of the thrills, though."

"The Greeks aren't rebelling."

"They will." He stopped in front of her, cupping her throat with one hard, long-fingered hand. "It's been coming for years. A year or two more, and the revolt will be out in the open."

Diana reluctantly nodded. Her father's letters said the same thing. It wasn't the point, however. Only she couldn't get Garrett to understand that. And his hand on her throat was confusing when she tried to explain what she felt. Stepping back, she forced herself to ignore the flicker of hurt in the sherry-gold eyes.

"Garrett, please reconsider. It's dangerous. I know the thrill of trying your luck against insuperable odds fascinates you, but someday you won't succeed." Pale blue eyes somber, troubled, she looked up at him. "I won't go to Greece with you. If you're going to kill yourself, you won't have my help." She stretched out a hand to him, a hand he didn't take. "Come with me to the Holy Land."

"Sweetheart." He took an impetuous step toward her. "You'll be as bored in the Holy Land as I would be. We're two of a kind. While Karim's been chasing us, you've enjoyed it as much as I have."

Again he was right, yet it didn't matter. Eyes troubled, she studied him a moment longer, then sighed, her shoulders slumping. "Garrett," she began in a low tone, intent on changing the subject, "I just realized I can arrange with di Benedetto for a loan against my parents to repay the money you've spent on my clothes, passage, and things."

The eager expression drained from his face, leaving a mask of pain that faded into nothingness. "I told you a long time ago you don't have to repay me."

"I'd rather." It was immensely difficult to meet his eyes.

"Well, I'd rather you don't borrow from someone else, from some stranger." Restless, he took a step closer to her. "I'll let you know in Jerusalem."

An idiotic flare of hope flickered to life in her. He meant to see her again once she'd arrived at her parents'. There, she'd have another chance to convince him to give up this life and settle down.

"Garrett, are you sure you have enough money with you?"

Touching the money belt around his waist, he nodded. "Even with what I gave you this morning, there's plenty here."

"Signore Hamilton, Signorina Graham."

As the door swept open to admit their host, Diana turned, guiltily welcoming the interruption. Little as she wanted to admit it, Garrett was right—in many ways, they were two of a kind. But his safety demanded that she convince him to settle down. Not that she could with others present.

Another chance would come in Jerusalem. If he survived his Greek scheme. Pinning a smile on her face, she waited to greet her host's daughter.

Di Benedetto drew a slightly plump young girl of about seventeen in with him. She wore dove gray with black ribbons trimming sleeves, hem, and neckline. Evidently she and her father had just recently emerged from mourning into half mourning—if Italians followed English and American custom.

But that wasn't the reason Diana stared. From the corner of her eye, she saw Garrett staring, too. She couldn't blame him. Signorina di Benedetto was absolutely beautiful, ravishing. There were no other words. From perfectly curved cheek and glossy brunette hair to soft doe-shaped brown eyes, no other words were possible. Even the slight hint of plumpness was carried off beautifully, making Diana add words like *lush* to the list of adjectives.

"Signorina Bice." Dazed, Diana acknowledged the introduction with a dipped curtsy.

"Papa!" Bice cried reprovingly, rustling around her father and extending both hands to Diana. "What will our guests think, leaving them in such a cold, barren room. Come, Signorina Graham, Signore Hamilton, to my sitting room. There I shall give you coffee. If you do not dislike it. Otherwise, tea it shall be." Clasping Diana by hand and elbow, she looked prettily from one to the other.

Even Bice's voice was beautiful, if slightly fluting and childlike. Diana refused to glance behind her at Garrett. Her thoughts would show on her face.

Allowing herself to be drawn forward, she followed Bice down a long, dark hall into another room, Garrett immediately behind her, and Bice's father bringing up the rear. He clucked like an anxious chicken, apologizing profusely.

Leaving Garrett to soothe him, Diana turned to Bice. "How lovely," she said politely. "Do you use this room daily?"

Pure golden sunlight streamed through floor-to-ceiling windows onto a pale marble floor dotted with floral carpets. Along with the brisk fire heating the room, the sunlight was the most pleasant thing about it. The room was filled with tables, chairs, embroidery frames, schoolbooks, pattern cards, and every other sort of paraphernalia a young lady would have. All the cast offs of the villa must have been deposited in this room since the building was occupied.

While Bice fluttered about, drawing chairs near the hearth and brushing off seats, Diana exchanged a look with Garrett. He was as bemused as she at this brisk butterfly of a girl, but he controlled it better. Yet, although he concentrated on their host, he'd apparently—from his smile—heard every word of her chatter.

"But tell me, *signorina*," Bice said, finally settling on a jonquil-damask-upholstered chair, "what brings you so far from home? To travel so far and with"—her gaze drifted to Garrett standing tall and distinguished next to her father—"such a handsome gentleman as an escort. In Italy," she added mournfully, "an unmarried young lady would never be permitted such interesting company."

Smiling politely, Diana gave an expurgated version of her adventures, while trying to listen to what Garrett and di Benedetto were discussing with such intensity. Responding to Bice's exclamations of horrified fascination was relatively simple. Deciphering di Benedetto's rapid Italian without appearing to listen was much harder. Fortunately, after finishing her tale, an occasional word kept Bice chattering happily while Diana concentrated on listening to the other conversation.

"No, sir," Garrett said, drifting casually toward the heat of the fireplace, "I hadn't heard anything of the sort about Saberio Beniamini. Indeed, he was recommended to me." Gradually, he was guiding their conversation closer and closer to Diana's chair.

"Then I must warn you, *signore.*" Smoothing the black lapels of his charcoal gray jacket, di Benedetto shook his head heavily. "There is little good that can be said of Saberio Beniamini." His hands caught and held halfway down the lapels.

With a polite inclination of his head, Garrett continued the drift toward the chairs where Diana sat murmuring inanities with Bice. He must realize she was listening intently. "I understand you're involved in import–export."

"Yes, that is so. I have connections with many foreigners living in the Holy Land and other parts of the Ottoman Empire." Drooping, deflated jowls waggled when he shook his head. "That is how I know so much about Saberio Beniamini." He lowered his voice confidentially, making it difficult for Diana to hear. "In particular, it is said he has had much dealing with Greek pirates."

"Is something wrong, *signorina?*" Bice asked politely.

Diana dragged her attention back to the girl quickly. "I'm sorry. It's just something you said recalled a rather amusing incident during my travels."

Frantically, she tried to remember what Bice had been prattling about. It had had something to do with Bizerte and the *suqs.* In doubt, Diana recounted the story of the pastry seller. That satisfied Bice and let Diana return her attention to Garrett.

". . . coming from the mainland. There have been a number of revolts in the more mountainous parts of the country. Not the cities, of course. The Turks have things well in hand there. But a merchant must be careful dealing with any of these Greeks."

"I know a few of them, sir," Garrett said carefully. "And this Saberio Beniamini—"

Di Benedetto shook his head again. "One of the worst. He'll sell you for ransom and steal your passage money in a blink of an eye." Before Garrett could answer, di Benedetto turned to his daughter. "Haven't you arranged for coffee, Bice? Our guests must be perishing with thirst. Especially in this hot, stuffy room." Not waiting for an answer, he waved Garrett to a chair. "Please, have a seat. I wouldn't want it said that Giovanni di Benedetto kept his guests standing."

Color mottled Bice's cheeks when she rose from her chair and went to the bellpull. Standing beside it, she watched the door, foot tapping impatiently beneath the hem of her skirt. When the door remained closed, she tugged the bellpull again, several times. By the time her hand dropped away from the bellpull for the fifth time, the maid was pushing through the door, carrying a tray weighted with a large silver coffeepot and four tiny porcelain cups. Dumping it on the table, she mumbled a nervous excuse at Bice's low-voiced reproach, dipped a curtsy, and escaped.

"Pour the coffee for our guests, Bice." Smiling now that his wishes had been attended to, di Benedetto affectionately pinched her cheek before turning to Diana. "Have you visited your parents in the Holy Land before, Signorina Diana?"

"No, this is my first visit." The coffee was thick, bitter. She took another tiny sip and put the cup down on the small table beside her. "Have you many customers there?"

"Several. That's why there's no difficulty in finding a ship to take you there." He drank his coffee with relish. "A reliable ship, a reliable captain—this is all important, as I was telling Signore Hamilton." Nodding toward Garrett, a hearty smile sitting oddly on di Benedetto's thin face, he added, "You need have no fear of a safe voyage to your parents. I shall with the greatest possible care select the ship, the captain, and protect you as I would my own lovely daughter while you are in my charge."

So Garrett felt he had acquired the right to "place her in di Benedetto's charge" had he? If she wouldn't join him, he could just wash his hands of her for all his fine talk of contacting her in Jerusalem. Ignoring a nagging sense of unreasonableness, her mouth tightened. They'd talk about rights only coming with responsibilities later. Her mouth softened. If she had the chance to talk to him alone later.

Not willing to look at Garrett yet, Diana smoothed her skirt over her knees before speaking to di Benedetto. "I understand finding a reliable ship can be difficult," she said at random to cover her tension.

"Precisely." Di Benedetto pursed his mouth, and came to a decision. "Signore Hamilton, I must tell you something."

Answering, Garrett's voice was smooth and courteous, but the swift glance he gave Diana told her he understood some of her turmoil. "I'm delighted to benefit from your vast experience of the dangers present in the Mediterranean, sir."

Di Benedetto preened himself. "I am glad to hear it. Young men rarely bother to listen to the voice of experience. I've unfortunately had to deal with Saberio Beniamini often in the past." Di Benedetto fixed Garrett's purposely bland face with a penetrating stare. "Don't sail with him. Some people have, never to be seen again."

CHAPTER XVIII

"DIANA, YOU MUST SEE THE TRULY WONDERFUL BONNETS at the milliner's next door."

Tugging her by the hand, Bice pulled Diana toward a bow window displaying confections conjured up from a first-class milliner's fancy. Charming poke bonnets, Pamela bonnets, and cottage bonnets, even bonnets made on a French shape, all trimmed with flowers and ribbons of every color known to nature—and a few that were not—were displayed in the window. Brilliant morning sunlight glittered from the sparkling windowpanes and pointed up the enticing colors. A brisk, faintly chilly breeze urged the pair to go inside and investigate.

"They're lovely." A quick glance at Bice's perfect features told Diana her response wasn't strong enough. The full red lips pouted faintly. "Look at that one." Diana pointed to a particularly vivacious confection with yellow ribbons and roses on a villager straw shape. "That would be perfect for you."

"But we're here to find things for you. Besides, until I'm out of half mourning for Zia Beatrice"—the pout grew pronounced—"I can't wear colors."

Tiredly, Diana patted the tightly gloved hand that still

clung to hers. "It's nearly a year since your aunt died. This spring, you'll be able to buy a magnificent new wardrobe full of all sorts of new clothes for your debut."

"If Papa will let me have the money." The pout deepened before Bice brightened again. "Papa's wonderful new business partner somewhere in Africa will make us very wealthy. Besides," she added practically, "he wants me to marry as befits my station, and I can't get him a rich son-in-law without proper clothes."

Looking at her lovely companion, Diana suppressed a shudder. Had she ever been this self-centered? She hoped not. "Look." She pointed at the young man hovering on the street to the imminent peril of carriages and cabs. "Isn't that Salvatore Rienzi?"

"Salvatore."

Dropping Diana's hand, Bice ran a few steps toward him. Dazed at his good luck, Salvatore promptly tripped on the hitching ring set into the cobblestone pavement. Catching himself, he joined Bice, who drew him forward to Diana's side.

"You remember my guest, Signorina Graham, Salvatore?" Without pausing for an answer, she hurried on. "I forgot to tell you this morning, Diana, that we received an invitation for a delightful dance Salvatore's mama is giving to brighten the Christmas season. Isn't it wonderful? You've been invited as well."

Blushing, Salvatore stuttered, "M-Mama wished me to have some entertainment while I'm home from school, *signorina.*"

"Are you a student, *signore?*" Diana asked politely.

"Yes, *signorina.* At the university." His attention wandered back to Bice before he'd finished speaking. "All our friends will be there," he said swiftly, then swallowed hard. His Adam's apple, prominent in a neck that was still too thin, bobbed once before settling above the stiff wings of his high collar.

While Bice demanded details of the upcoming entertainment, Diana's attention drifted. She couldn't help it. In the past two days she'd listened to dozens of conversations exactly like this one. Garrett would laugh at Bice's fascination with the male sex. Diana caught herself. This wasn't the way to remove him from her life. But her mind immediately wandered back to Garrett. Forcing her attention back to Salvatore and Bice, she realized Salvatore was waiting for an answer.

"Will we see your uncle at the dance?" Diana asked pleasantly. Nearly squeaking with surprise, she jerked her foot from beneath Bice's.

"That wasn't Salvatore's uncle you met yesterday," Bice whispered hurriedly. Then louder: "Oh, you mean Papa's friend, Signore Alessandro. It must be very confusing meeting so many new people in such a short time, especially when Italian isn't your native tongue. But," she added, worried about the possible faux pas, "you speak it extremely well."

Bice's small, perfect face was flushed, her eyes imploring as she gazed up at Diana. Sudden amusement tugging at the corners of her mouth, Diana realized Bice hadn't acted as if the handsome older man was a friend of her father's. She'd behaved as if he was a suitor. Slightly shocked, Diana wondered what games were going on. Yet she couldn't resist that look. Kindly, she granted the silent request.

"Bice's right. Please excuse me. I get terribly confused meeting so many new people in such a short time. And my limited knowledge of your language sometimes makes it difficult to keep all the names straight." She smiled at Bice's young friend. "I'm looking forward to seeing you at the dance, Signore Rienzi."

Salvatore acknowledged the explanation absently. His youthful gaze remained on his lodestar. "Mama has hired the best band in Genoa, and she's given us permission to dance this new German waltz."

"The waltz?" Bice breathed. "Oh, Papa will never permit it. The Austrians, you know."

"That's just it," Salvatore assured her. "It's not Austrian, it's German. That makes it different."

"Well . . ." Frowning, Bice considered it carefully. "Papa still may not allow me to dance anything since I'm in mourning for a little longer."

Salvatore crumpled his hat brim in eager hands. "Mama says she doesn't feel that's a problem. I consulted her before suggesting we dance at the party. She says since it's private and you'll be out of mourning in another six weeks, it's all right. That's why we invited only close friends." Stricken, Salvatore turned to Diana. "And, of course, you, too, Signorina Graham," he added hurriedly.

"I shall be delighted to come, *signore,*" Diana said, resigned. "We'll need to find an evening dress for me," she added to please Bice. "And one for you, as well."

More shopping. Diana sighed silently. It lost all joy without Garrett to see the results and appreciate her choices. But it would keep Bice happy.

"Show him in," Haroun called irritably to the bowing servant.

Fastening her veil across her face, Leila watched her husband covertly. Perhaps news of the infidel would improve his mood. He'd had so much to bear over the past weeks: everything from dank, dreary weather to the shocking and dreadful news of Karim's promise to forgive half the interest on Pasha Selim's debt. It had taken all her womanly gifts to ease her husband's sorrow that night.

Seated discreetly behind Haroun, Leila watched Mustafa enter the temporary audience chamber and bow deeply. Behind the veil, she frowned. He was uncomfortable. Extremely uncomfortable.

"Give me your report!"

At Haroun's annoyed order, Mustafa bowed again even more deeply and stepped forward. "My most gracious lord, your brother, Lord Karim, ordered me home to Bizerte from Tarragona to—"

"What were you doing in Tarragona?" Peevishly, Haroun straightened and stroked his beard. Finding it still short and stubbly, he glowered at Mustafa and dropped his hand.

"The infidel—" Mustafa swallowed audibly, then began again. "The infidel Hamilton and the girl eluded us in Barcelona, my lord, and fled south to Tarragona. We pursued with all possible speed."

His fingers flexing, Haroun leaned forward in the chair, one elbow resting on its arm. "Why didn't you capture them in Barcelona?"

"The-the authorities there, my lord, they imprisoned us," Mustafa stuttered in his haste to explain. Wetting his lips, his eyes darted about the small room the bey used as his study as though searching for a bolt-hole. "My lord, it's a Christian country."

"Spain has been a Christian country for three hundred years. Your lack of knowledge of that fact is no reason for your failure." Throwing himself against the high backrest, his fingers beat a rapid tattoo on the chair arm. "Why didn't you catch them in this Tarragona?"

Shifting, Mustafa shook his head in a barely discernible movement. Then finding courage, he blurted out, "The authorities in Barcelona held us in jail for three days. With hard riding, we made up a day, but our quarry fled Tarragona two days before we arrived."

"Where were they going?" The tattoo grew faster.

Mustafa shifted his weight and swallowed again. "G-Genoa, my lord."

Haroun's fingers froze in midair, then settled, quiescent, on the chair arm. "To Genoa?" Smiling, he stroked the two small bare patches where hair never grew below either corner of his mouth. "Has Karim followed them?"

Mustafa's shoulders slackened with relief at the smile. But the last question snapped him back to attention. "He left immediately, my lord. The port master tried to hinder us, but Lord Karim slyly pried the information from him and magnificently thwarted the greedy old official in the end."

Haroun's black brows snapped together. "My brother has created a diplomatic incident with the Spanish authorities?"

"N-no, my lord. I believe Lord Karim told the Spanish that the infidel girl was his wife, who had converted him to Catholicism before running off with a Protestant." Gaining some confidence, Mustafa shrugged. "It was only Lord Karim's guile that made our mission there possible."

"Not 'possible' enough." At Mustafa's questioning look, Haroun exploded. "You didn't get either the girl or Hamilton back!" Quieting, Haroun leaned back in the chair. "Now, tell me what trouble my brother caused with the port master."

Mustafa spread his hands wide, palms up, absolving himself of any possible blame. "I wasn't privileged to be inside the office, my lord. But Lord Karim said the port master dawdled over telling about the only ship in port bound for Italy until it was nearly too late."

Leila's lips twitched at Haroun's muttered "What else could be expected considering my brother's tactful personality." The guard stopped while he spoke, and he waved for Mustafa to go on.

"Lord Karim hurried aboard just before they hauled up the gangway. And he had to pay a great deal extra to get a suitable cabin and have the ship sail to Genoa." Licking dry lips, he swallowed hard at the bey's darkening expression.

"How much?" There was ice in Haroun's voice.

"I don't know, my lord. Lord Karim didn't confide in me. But it was a Spanish vessel. Quite dirty. And the captain looked even more like a pirate than the Greek who got us to Barcelona so fast." Realizing the bey wasn't listening, Mustafa gradually quieted and stood at ease with his hands clasped loosely behind his back.

Haroun stared absently at the intricately knotted silk carpet his footstool rested on. Finally, he lifted his brooding gaze. The stare brought Mustafa back to attention. Tiny beads of sweat broke out on his forehead, sweat that had nothing to do with the matched pair of brass braziers warming the room.

"Has Karim recaptured the badge of office, or has he failed in that, too?" Haroun demanded eventually.

"The badge of office?" Mustafa repeated, licking his lips. A bead of sweat trickled from temple to cheek. "I—"

"Speak the truth! I am your bey. You owe me loyalty, not some upstart younger brother." Both hands gripping the chair arms, Haroun straightened majestically in the chair, as though he sat on the throne in the audience chamber.

Instinctively, Mustafa bowed and licked his dry lips.

"Speak up! I want the truth, and I want it now."

"Lord Karim never told me anything about it." At the warning expression on Haroun's face, Mustafa quickly added, "But I know he has recovered the badge of office, my lord bey. I saw the infidel put it around his neck while we were bound in the girl's room."

"You were what? Never mind now." Waving one hand in dismissal, Haroun ordered, "Get out of my sight and return to your duties." The guard bowed low and backed toward the door. "But, Mustafa." He halted. "If you value your head, forget everything you saw and heard. Especially about the badge."

Leila waited until the door closed behind Mustafa before edging forward and lowering her veil. Looking up at Haroun, she held her peace. Set in the scraggly patches of beard, his small mouth was hard and thin. Knowing his younger brother was intent on evicting him from the throne was one thing; having proof was another matter entirely. Sympathy darkened her soft eyes as she waited.

"That damned fool!" he finally exploded. Now that the guard had departed, Haroun resumed the steady stroking of his half-grown beard and slumped in his chair. "All that money wasted." His hand stopped on the beard. "Karim must not have intended to let me know he'd recovered the badge. Otherwise, he'd have ordered Mustafa to report its recovery to me. Damn my little brother!"

"But you do know, my lord, and Lord Karim is not aware that you know," Leila said softly.

"All that money wasted," Haroun repeated. "I can't even recoup it by forcing Karim to buy Diana." He straightened a little in his chair. "My loving brother probably intends to have me beheaded when he returns home."

"My lord." Leila smiled soothingly. "Think of what has been achieved. You have the badge of office back in your power. Oh"—she waved away his forming objection with one hand and stroked his arm with the other—"it's true that Karim has it, but what does it matter? Ambitious younger brothers have controlled the means to power before this and failed. You have only to send two or three of your strongest eunuchs to assist your brother in his—" She broke off at the look growing on Haroun's face.

Striking the small gong next to him with a mallet, he gestured for Leila to resume her veil. When the guard on duty outside the door opened it, Haroun instructed, "Send the chief eunuch to me."

Shortly, Başir, the Turkish chief eunuch, bowed deeply before Haroun. A large man, he suffered from none of the usual heavy flabbiness normal to castrated males. When Leila dropped her veil, he darted a glance in her direction, reassured by her faint smile and nod.

"I have a task for you, Başir," Haroun began, and told him briefly of the missing badge of office, Karim's recovery of it, and the probable danger of his gaining control of Bizerte. "Choose two or three of your most trustworthy men to send to Genoa and return the badge to me . . ."—he hesitated—". . . along with my younger brother. Alive, if possible."

"My lord, you do me great honor. Fear not. Any of my men will gladly die for you." Bowing deeply again, Başir smiled. "However, if my lord will grant me a boon, I would deem it the greatest honor possible to have the pleasure of bringing Lord Karim back personally." A broad smile pulled at the corners of Başir's beardless lips. "We will not fail to bring back both the badge and Lord Karim. Alive." The smile grew wider. "If possible."

"Farfalla, fetch that stick," Garrett called. The dog romped down the long curve of beach just out of reach of the waves, blithely ignoring the call until Garrett didn't pursue her.

Anything less like a butterfly than this great, clumsy hound was hard to imagine. But "Farfalla" was what his landlady called her. He hadn't been in the mood to listen to the involved explanation for the name. It was something long and complex and having to do with the mongrel's inept attempts to catch butterflies as a puppy.

Farfalla was no substitute for Diana, but the dog's antics kept Garrett's mind occupied. Sometimes. Although the dog and the beach weren't working any better today than the other things he'd tried since leaving Diana in di Benedetto's care. He'd purposely kept away from her while waiting for his ship to sail. He'd have to grow accustomed to not having her at his side. Someday he would. Someday soon, he hoped.

The stick in her mouth, Farfalla's front paws landed on his trouser leg to bring Garrett's attention back to her. Wet, sandy paw prints decorated the wool pants when she dropped to her haunches, tail wagging happily. As Garrett wrestled for the stick with the panting dog, Farfalla growled in mock battle before finally releasing it. She flopped onto the sand, fur wet and bedraggled, eyes fixed on the stick, waiting for Garrett to throw it again. When he didn't, she encouraged him with a series of loud barks.

"Sorry, Farfalla. My mind wandered."

In one long, graceful heave, Garrett sent the stick spiraling down the beach. It landed at the edge of the incoming water. Farfalla pounced on it and dashed back out of the way at the next line of waves. Realizing Garrett was ambling away, she turned and gave chase, running parallel to the water, her tail a high, wet plume.

Hands stuffed in his pockets, Garrett strolled down the beach. A bank of clouds rolling in with the dying sun matched his mood exactly. Not even Farfalla's antics improved it.

Only when she pranced in front and laid the stick in the sand did Garrett shake himself out of the morbid mood. "All right. But only one more time. Then we have to head for home. I promised to have you home for dinner." Funny, he wasn't hungry himself.

Flinging the stick back the way they'd come, Garrett smiled perfunctorily at Farfalla's delighted yelp. Sand spurted from her paws onto his breeches. Bending to brush it off, he slowly straightened and began the trip back up the beach.

What was wrong with him? It couldn't be Diana. There were plenty of women available. He had to stop and concentrate on his plans. Only the Greek scheme held no savor now. Nothing did.

"And Papa, Salvatore says there will be *German* waltzing, not Austrian. Do say I may go, Papa." Bice sliced another sliver off the *gâteau* that constituted dessert tonight. "Salvatore's mama says it's perfectly proper to dance at a private party since we're so near the end of our mourning period." Taking another sliver of *gâteau,* she nibbled on it, small tongue finding every crumb on the fork.

At each meal, Diana'd been amazed at how much food father and daughter put away. Yet di Benedetto was cadaverously thin, and his daughter gave the impression of eating very little despite her slight plumpness. It was an artfully managed impression. Her appetite was extremely healthy, as healthy as Diana's used to be.

"You may go dancing if Signora Rienzi says it's permissible." Di Benedetto patted his mouth with a fine linen napkin. Laying it in his lap, he decreed pontifically. "But no waltzes, German or otherwise, as long as those accursed Austrians hold any part of our beloved Italy. You absolutely may not dance waltzes."

"But, Papa—"

"No. I won't hear another word."

Candle flames reflected off fat tears welling in her eyes. "But, Papa, I told you it's not an Austrian dance. Even the university students have decided it's a German dance, and completely acceptable." Raising her napkin, she patted away a tear trickling down her cheek.

Di Benedetto leaned around the candelabra separating them to peer at her. "The university students dance this German dance?"

Putting her fork down, Bice nodded vigorously, one curl sliding from its artfully precarious perch at the top of her head. The *gâteau* on her plate ignored, Diana folded her hands and watched father and daughter. Bice manipulated her father in masterly fashion. Diana hadn't much doubt who would win; neither did Bice.

It shouldn't take long for her to talk di Benedetto into giving permission to do whatever she wished at the dance tomorrow evening. Shaking her head, Diana conjured up an imaginary meeting between Bice and Gran. The confrontation would be monumental, and the winner . . . Diana wasn't certain.

"Then if the university approves—" Di Benedetto suddenly looked suspicious. "Both professors and students?" he demanded.

"Oh, yes, Papa. All of them do, except the ones who don't count." Looking around another candelabra, she sent Diana a look of mingled apology and mischief. "Some of the professors at the university are Austrian," she explained quickly.

Vaguely, Diana remembered something about the Austrians being given part of Italy at the Congress of Vienna in 1815. But she was fairly certain Genoa wasn't under Austrian domination. Whether they were or not, clearly the

Genoese hated Austrian influence in Italy. Tentatively, she asked for an explanation.

"No, *signorina*," di Benedetto answered. "We suffer from no oppressors in Genoa. But much of northern Italy toils under the yoke of Austrian domination. The day will come when Italy is once again a united country."

Realizing di Benedetto intended to expound at length, Diana saw the dining room door open with relief. A bent, elderly servant shuffled into the room. Whispering in di Benedetto's ear, he answered several questions, then shuffled out with his master following.

"What do you think of the white dress with violet ribbons, Diana?" Bice asked as soon as the door closed behind her father. "The draperies of the overdress will float elegantly in this new German waltz, don't you think?"

"The—" Quickly, Diana recalled the dresses they'd seen during their afternoon's shopping. There was a soft muslin gown in white with violet ribbons, puffed sleeves, and a gauzy overdress. It would be perfect for a girl in Bice's situation—not yet out and still in half mourning. "Can the modiste have it ready for the party tomorrow night?" She recalled it as a sketch, not even begun yet.

Mischief sparkled behind veiling lashes as Bice dabbled her fingers in the bowl beside her plate and wiped them on a napkin. "I ordered it before we left the shop. Signora Gabriella promised it for tomorrow night if I come back for a fitting in the afternoon. Papa will howl over the price." Bice smiled. "He always does. But he knows I can't get a rich husband if I don't look pretty."

Diana refolded her napkin and placed it beside her unused dessert fork. Bice was spoiled. But she was also a pretty, charming child for all her faults. And her father encouraged her, for all his halfhearted attempts at discipline.

"Then you plan to marry as soon as you come out?" Diana asked in the expectant silence.

"You miss Signore Hamilton, don't you?" Bice asked diffidently, instead of answering the question. "You've been so sad and unhappy since he left. Can't you see him again before you leave?" Gentle sympathy banished the mischief in her face.

Diana raised her eyes from contemplation of the seven-layer *gâteau* in the middle of her plate. A week ago she would have enjoyed it as thoroughly as Bice had hers.

"Garrett leaves on the tide for Greece."

"Then you won't see him again."

Diana shook her head slowly. The candle flames blurred, then came back into focus. "Not unless he changes his mind and joins me at my parents' in Jerusalem." Long since, she'd given up the hope that he would. That wasn't worth mentioning now, though.

"Then there's hope?" Bice asked.

She sounded as eager for Diana's love story to be happy as if it were one of her own. Only Bice's were puppy loves. Not the real thing. Still, it was sweet of her to care.

"I doubt it." One hand lifted quickly, then dropped back onto the polished wood tabletop.

Bice reached across the table and patted Diana's hand. "Don't worry. He'll come back for you. You are too pretty for a man to forget. Just like me."

The door opening stopped any possible answer. Di Benedetto strode into the room, rubbing his hands. Instead of finishing his dessert, he leaned his elbows on the high, carved wood back of his chair and stared at Diana.

"Is something wrong, Papa?"

"No, my dearest child. I— It's just that Signorina Graham has an unexpected visitor." He nodded firmly. "I didn't expect him, and I'm a little stunned. But we shouldn't interfere in something private."

"Of course not, Papa."

Her eyes sparkling, she caught Diana's gaze across the table. Forming the word *Garrett* with her lips, Bice rose from the table. Circling it, she placed a demure kiss on her father's cheek and whispered "good night" to both of them.

The door closed behind her before Diana assimilated the

news. Garrett hadn't sailed on this evening's tide! He'd returned; he was waiting for her now. Di Benedetto simply must not approve of an unmarried young lady's meeting a gentleman alone. At least, not in his house.

Smoothing the skirt of the cherry-colored wool dress chosen because Garrett would like it, Diana rose from the table. Soft color stole into her cheeks. They were going to Jerusalem together.

"Where is he?" she asked, her voice light. Not even di Benedetto's somber, disapproving expression could dampen the exhilaration bubbling through her now.

Still her host didn't move. Finally, when she was about to ask again, he slapped the back of the chair with both hands and walked over to open the door for her. "In the sitting room at the end of the hall." In the shadows at that end of the room, he looked more uncomfortable than disapproving.

Barely controlling the skip in her step, Diana hurried out of the dining room. Only after the door closed did she permit herself a little dance. Garrett had come for her. The chant was a paean of joy.

Candlelight shone beneath a closed door at the end of the hall. That had to be the sitting room, the room where he waited for her. With trembling fingers, she opened the door and stepped inside.

He sat in a high-backed wing chair beside the fireplace facing away from her. Her hand dropping away from the doorknob, Diana took one slow step, then two, into the room. Softly, she called, "Garrett."

Rising from the chair, the candlelight fell on his face.

Karim.

CHAPTER XIX

"GOOD EVENING, DIANA."

Karim stood relaxed and confident beside his chair, a thin smile curving his lips, hands clasped loosely behind his back. Except for the beard, he looked the European gentleman. Except for his beard and something else: his sardonic amusement. A halo of flickering light from the fire surrounded him, while his dark eyes reflected twin points of candle flame.

"How courteous of you to save me the trouble of chasing after you," he continued, manner suave, then paused with chill deliberation. "Again. How unfortunate your lover abandoned you." His voice was a low, deep rumble, pleasant except for its coldness. "Tell me, where's my good friend Hamilton?"

The question released the paralysis holding her, and a tiny kernel of hope flared. To gain his cooperation, Karim must have lied to Signore di Benedetto. Karim probably used that tale of her being his wife. Or some other taradiddle. Once di Benedetto knew the truth, she was safe. When she reached the door, she'd scream for help. Licking her lips, Diana inched backward.

"I wouldn't advise screaming," Karim said, voice still

preternaturally quiet. "I would be forced to take unpleasant action." Sighing regretfully, he shook his head. "It would cause my brother such anguish if you failed to return to him relatively intact. However"—his hands, fingers of one bandaged, came out from behind his back in a gesture of resignation—"I'll enjoy whatever you force me to do."

"You shouldn't disappoint your brother." The muscles in Diana's throat stiff, she carefully inched backward.

Braced to flee if he started toward her, Diana inched backward again. Ten or twelve feet separated them. A decent enough head start for the door. Had she closed it when she came in? Every fraction of a second mattered. Searching back in a memory suddenly, unnaturally sharp, she recalled no click of the latch. It should be open, then, making it easier to reach the safety of the hall. She'd slam it on Karim, delaying him further.

Karim hadn't moved from beside the chair. Yet. He'd move soon enough. When he did, she wanted to be through that door before he reached her. Why hadn't he moved to stop her already? Like the easy, overly confident way he stood, the thought disturbed her intensely.

His voice, when he eventually broke the silence, was a shock. "How sweet of you to worry about one of my brother's last wishes." While he spoke, she slowly inched closer to the door, freezing when he added, "If you try for the door, I'll make your life even worse on our way home to Bizerte." He paused fractionally to let the warning sink in before snapping, "Now, where's Hamilton?"

In a flurry of skirts, Diana swung about and plunged for the doorknob and safety.

Her hand rammed straight into di Benedetto's soft stomach. Gasping, he doubled over, nearly retching, slowing her down. She tried to wedge around him.

He was in no condition to help now. If she could just get past, though, he'd block Karim until she escaped outside for help. Diana grabbed di Benedetto's arm and swung him toward the center of the room.

Only Karim's hard fingers dug excruciatingly into her arm as he pulled her away from the door. Twisting, Diana kicked out, but the heavy wool skirt impeded the swing. The blow from her kid slipper made little impact.

As her lips parted to call for help, a pair of hands descended on the free arm she'd brought back to punch Karim. The words died on her lips. Di Benedetto was helping Karim, not her.

"*Signore,* Karim has lied to you. He kidnapped me."

From his abashed look, she'd get no help from him. She started to scream. The servants would help, if di Benedetto wouldn't.

"Scream and I'll enjoy myself more," Karim whispered hoarsely, painfully twisting her arm to bring her closer. "Besides, my friend here sent all the servants into the kitchen, where they'll never hear."

Diana stopped straining. Shaking her hair back from her face, she glared at di Benedetto. "You promised to protect me!"

Di Benedetto's shoulders moved in an apologetic shrug as he wheezed, "I'm sorry, Signorina Graham. You didn't say you were in trouble with the bey of Bizerte. He's my newest, largest client, and your parents are but minor customers." Reproachfully shaking his head, he looked at her. "Besides, this is a legal matter. You are a fugitive from justice, and I'm merely helping the authorities."

Blowing the hair away from her face, she glared at him. "What you mean is, it's a matter of money." She repressed a soft moan when Karim twisted her arm again.

"My little Bice requires a large dowry," di Benedetto explained, patting the hand he held prisoner soothingly.

Karim's painful grip on her arm relaxed a fraction at her disdainful silence. "We'll incarcerate you until the ship is ready to leave tomorrow night."

"You can't leave her here," di Benedetto protested, his hand massaging his sore stomach. "Not in my house."

"You have attics," Karim said pleasantly, undisturbed. "I shall require only a simple room for myself."

"Can't you take her away from here tonight?"

Through the curtain of hair, Diana saw di Benedetto swallow hard, his elaborately tied cravat bouncing, while his hold on her arm loosened—but not enough to escape.

Eyes narrowing with impatience, Karim's mouth thinned. "The attics," he demanded.

Di Benedetto's shoulders slumped in defeat. "Through the hall and up the back stairs." Unhappy, he looked at the bracket clock ticking softly on the mantel. "The servants will be occupied for another hour in the kitchen. There's time to get upstairs before they turn down the beds and lay out our night things." He fixed a stern gaze on Karim. "I won't have any gossip to hurt my daughter's chances."

Nodding brusquely, Karim twisted Diana's arm behind her back. "Don't cry out," he warned, "and don't try to escape. If you do, you know what happens."

Diana mutely agreed and allowed them to guide her out the door into the hall. Her arm ached from shoulder to wrist from Karim's treatment, and her legs felt stiff. Obedient to the pressure from his hand, she turned toward the darker end of the hall. Di Benedetto scooped a candle off a table and, gesturing, led the way toward shadowy narrow stairs around the corner.

There was room only to go single file. With one hand, Diana lifted the hem of her skirt, being certain to take each step carefully. It would amuse Karim if she tripped, and injuring herself would make escape difficult. Putting each foot safely on the next tread, she stole another look at her surroundings. She might need these stairs later.

At the top of this flight was a narrow, curtainless window that opened outward. Later, she could climb through, but it meant a dangerous drop into the garden below. It'd be better if she found a weapon and used these stairs rather than try that.

The whitewashed walls offered no help. Smudged from

the hurried passage of many people, otherwise they were bare. And no small tables with graceful knickknacks decorated the landings, as they did on the main staircase. She wished for one of the elaborate, heavy vases ornamenting the tables she regularly passed on the way to her room. One of those would make a satisfying weapon, one that was easy to handle and would stop anyone she hit.

Using the turn at the landing to lessen the angle of her arm, she continued looking. Karim hadn't noticed the loosening of his grip. Nor was he paying attention to her scrutiny of the surroundings. Supremely confident of his ability to keep her prisoner, he ignored her. That might work to her advantage.

Lifting her eyes from the steps again, she watched the wavering candlelight dip and flare ahead. Di Benedetto was growing more nervous with every step toward the attic. Such nervousness might mean there was a possibility of getting him to help if she could ever get him alone.

They reached another landing, then another, each with its narrow window providing light during the day, and still they climbed, each landing grubbier, the walls more spotted. Di Benedetto's servants were slothful, or, more likely, he didn't keep enough servants to keep the walls clean. Worse, the air grew chillier up here away from the fireplaces. It struck through wool that seemed so warm at dinner.

At the fourth landing, Karim asked, "How much farther?"

"Just one more flight." Breathing heavily from the exertion, di Benedetto gestured with the candle, the flame almost guttering.

The final stairs took forever. Diana nearly ran into di Benedetto when he stopped. Only Karim pulling hard on her arm prevented it, and a soft moan escaped despite all she could do.

As the door swung in, di Benedetto's narrow back moved forward again. She had no choice but to follow. Guiding her past the other man, Karim shoved negligently, releasing her arm as he pushed.

Staggering over rough floorboards, Diana barely caught herself against a shadowy bulk. Straightening and turning toward the two men, she cradled one arm with the other. The candle lighting their faces drove awareness of the pain away. Karim's face was pleased and smiling, di Benedetto's nervous and fretful. Cautiously, Diana pushed the heavy swathe of unbound hair behind her ears, ignoring the pain in her left arm.

"I've just thought of something," di Benedetto said abruptly. Nervously pulling at his lower lip, he darted brief sideways glances at Karim.

Karim's foot tapped with a touch of annoyance. "What?"

"Tomorrow night, my daughter goes to a dance." Swallowing hard, di Benedetto licked his lips and blurted out, "Signorina Graham was invited also."

Mouth twisting in disgust, Karim shook his head. "Must I think of everything?" His eyes snapped around with the speed of a striking snake at Diana's slight movement. "Stay where you are." Casually, he turned back to di Benedetto. "Tell your daughter that friends arrived to take Diana to the Holy Land." He smiled thinly. "In some ways, it's the truth."

Satisfied, di Benedetto relaxed and put the candle down on a rickety table. "That'll do. Let's go down. We'll tell Bice in the morning that Signorina Graham left after she went to bed, and we didn't wish to disturb her."

"You're leaving the candle here?" Karim asked sharply, stopping beside the table and reaching for it.

"Leave a lady here alone in this cold, lonely room without a light?" Di Benedetto drew himself up to his full height. "Sir, I am an Italian gentleman." Holding the door, he waved Karim ahead of him with one hand. "Come, let us go."

Frowning, Karim turned to Diana for a final gibe. "Scream for help if you desire. No one will hear you."

Not waiting for an answer, he followed di Benedetto out the door and closed it behind him. Diana rushed to the door and pressed her ear to it. Dimly, she heard the sound of footsteps moving down the stairs. Above, the roof creaked in a burst of wind. Then the old house settled into silence.

Whether Karim was right and no one could hear, she didn't know. Nor did she intend to test the claim now. Besides—Diana shivered and rubbed her arms—Karim and di Benedetto were the people likely to answer any cry for help.

Flexing the injured arm, she tried moving it again. Some of the pain and numbness was already gone despite the cold up here. With a little more time and something to keep her warm, she'd be able to use it fully soon. She hoped.

With the candle in her right hand, she inspected her surroundings. A long wait stretched before her. Everyone in the house had to have time to fall asleep before she attempted to escape. It was still early in the evening, and while she waited, she needed to find something to keep her warm. And make plans.

The only possibility for escape she'd thought of Diana didn't fancy. Although Genoa probably had a fire department, she didn't want to find out. Her risk of death or injury soared if she was forced to burn down the house. But anything was better than returning to Bizerte.

There were plenty of trunks that must contain old clothes and blankets. A chill shook her. Getting warm was the first priority. Then find a way out of here, a method for attacking the door, and a weapon of some sort. One that would protect her if all else failed.

In the dim light of the candle, the trunks and furniture took on odd shapes, cast odd shadows over the uneven plank floor. Shielding the flame, she opened the nearest trunk. Folded on top was a stiffly embroidered, quilted petticoat of the sort Gran wore when her portrait was painted just after the Revolution.

Putting the candle down, the sway-backed chair tilted

dangerously at the weight. Breath caught in her throat, Diana poised to rescue the candle if the chair collapsed. She was prepared to burn the house down if she had to, but not by accident. After the dangerous sway, the chair settled and held. Keeping one eye on it, she plunged into the trunk. What she needed was a cloak to keep warm.

At the bottom of the fourth trunk, she found a warm wool cloak. Despite its mustiness, she pulled it over her shoulders. Now, how to force the door without anyone hearing. Or—Diana looked speculatively at the furniture—she could always barricade it if she couldn't force it open. Karim and di Benedetto would be hard put to explain breaking the attic door down to the servants.

There had to be something up here that would be better than that. But she couldn't see what. The trunks only held clothes. The furniture was too light to barricade the door adequately, and there wasn't anything like an axe to break the latch.

Diana studied the door in perplexity, dismissing the possibility of surprising Karim and di Benedetto when they came after her. Karim would be wary when he entered the attic. She'd hit him over the head in Barcelona. He wouldn't allow her to repeat the trick in Genoa.

There had to be something else. Candle in hand, she paced slowly forward. There *had* to be something else.

Stopping suddenly, a smile spread.

This door opened inward.

Wine the dark, mysterious red of a flawed ruby swayed majestically with each dip and sway of the ship. Distantly appreciative, Garrett watched it catch and reflect light from the lantern fastened to the bulkhead. An aftertaste reminiscent of cherries lingered on his palate pleasurably, but he didn't raise the glass to his lips for another taste.

Contemplating the color, long fingers remained curled around the stem until the sound of vintage port trickling into another glass roused him. Captain Beniamini had invited him to dinner for company, not to watch him brood over Diana.

"Tell me, Saberio, what did you do to make di Benedetto speak so highly of you?" With difficulty, he tore his gaze away from the cathedraling of the viscous wine in the glass.

Saberio snorted. "That thief! If di Benedetto complimented me, he must think I'm dead." Raising his glass in automatic toast, he took a savoring sip.

Interested, Garrett raised his head, giving his full attention to Saberio. The captain sprawled in the chair on the other side of the table, with one hand cradling his wineglass. Despite half-closed dark eyes, sleepy after a satisfyingly delicious meal, he was tensely alert and restless. Garrett recognized the symptoms despite a bare few days of acquaintance. Nikos had been right. Saberio Beniamini made a good friend and a bad enemy.

"What did he do?"

"Tried to sell me out to Greek pirates a few months ago." Saberio took a long drink of his port and wiped his mouth with a linen handkerchief. "That was a trip." Sighing, he shook his head. "They nearly got us when we dropped anchor in a sheltered bay of a small island in the Greek archipelago."

Taking a meditative sip, Garrett leaned back in his chair.

"Two pirate ships blocked the only channel out of the place. Demanded our cargo and all the cash in the strongbox, or they'd take it and sink us in the bargain." Saberio blinked sleepily at Garrett and poured both another glass of port. "They weren't likely to let us go if we gave them what they asked for. Even though we couldn't complain to the authorities because of that cargo." He winked broadly.

"Guns?" Garrett asked. Stretching his legs out in the small space left by bunk and table in the captain's cabin, he crossed them at the ankle.

Grinning, Saberio shook his head. "No, but with the Greek situation, that might make a profitable cargo." Sipping the port meditatively, he looked over the rim of his glass at Garrett. "Is that what you and Nikos are up to?" At Garrett's masked smile, he laughed. "What an interesting business we're in. We don't trust our friends, and our enemies try to kill us."

Garrett raised his glass in an amused salute. "Confusion to our enemies, Saberio. You never did say what your cargo was either."

Gesturing vaguely, Saberio continued. "Well, somebody told these pirates all about our enterprise."

"How'd you get out?"

"Nikos came along. With the prospect of a fair fight and being outflanked, the pirates fled. Turns out Nikos was the one we were delivering the goods to." Shuddering, Saberio shook his head. "I don't like to think what would've happened if Nikos hadn't shown up. I owe him one."

Frowning, Garrett ran a finger around the rim of his wineglass. If di Benedetto was involved with Greek pirates, Diana might be in some sort of danger. . . . No, he was letting his desires influence his imagination. Diana was perfectly safe in di Benedetto's care. After all, he made a nice profit from her parents.

Rousing himself, he asked, "How'd you connect di Benedetto with the pirates?"

"Some of his people were talkative after a few drinks." Saberio raised his glass in a toast, holding it up to the light, where the thick liquid shimmered darkly red while he spoke. "Unfortunately, I have still to find a way to repay his kind attentions to me. Something artistic, something exquisitely appropriate." Draining the glass, he set it down on the polished-oak table with a definite clink.

Emptying the last of the decanter into his glass, Saberio started for a fresh bottle, but Garrett held up his hand. "No more for me, at least, not right now."

Subsiding back into his chair, the captain blinked owlishly at Garrett. "The retaliation I visit upon that hypocrite must be inspired."

"Too bad you can't do to him what I did to Haroun."

* * *

There, that would muffle the noise, plus provide something to kneel on while she worked. Pulling the cloak back around her shoulders, Diana inspected the smooth layer of padding she'd made of scavengings from the trunks. The cord fastening the cloak around her throat hadn't lasted beyond lifting the first embroidered, quilted petticoat out of a trunk. Incredible how heavy that petticoat was. How had Gran ever withstood the weight? At least she must have been warm.

Shivering, Diana tugged the musty wool cloak about her shoulders again. The first thing she'd do when she escaped was find a fire. The second would be to find the authorities and lodge a complaint against di Benedetto. Poor Bice. The scandal would put a stop to her ambitions for a wealthy husband, but it couldn't be helped.

Bice should be asleep by now. So should everyone else. But without a clock, without a window, Diana couldn't be certain. The rate at which the candle burned wasn't too much help. It just urged her to hurry. The candle had maybe another hour of life, perhaps a bit more. Mouth firm, Diana set aside such nagging worries and picked up the first tool she'd managed to make.

She'd muffled a long, thick wood chunk wrenched from a chair. Reaching for the hammer fashioned from a chair leg, she bumped the candle. The clumsy candlestick tottered on its base, then toppled. Wax dribbled and hissed onto the floor in a tiny puddle, while the flame guttered and started to die.

As she grabbed for it, her improvised hammer thudded to the floor, its tiny draft nearly killing the flame. Fearful, Diana forced herself to move slowly, and, righting it, she babied the pitiful little light that held the darkness at bay. Gradually, painfully, the flame steadied. Picking up the other chair leg again, she bound a woolen scarf to one end, another muffling layer to prevent noise. Karim probably lied about the soundproofing of this attic.

With the candle placed where it shed the best light, she fitted the pointed end of the wood beneath the head of the hinge pin. Taking a deep breath to quiet the persistent flutter in her stomach, Diana hit the improvised chisel with the improvised hammer. A dull thud resulted.

The hinge pin didn't budge. And there were two more to remove after this one. Grimly, she tapped it again. This time, a faint crack between hinge and hinge pin appeared. The head of it was still too close to the hinge to pry up with her fingers.

Moving the wedge around, she tapped again, and again. With each tap, the space between the head and the hinge grew fractionally. It was like prying a nail from a piece of wood without a claw hammer. It could be done, but it wasn't easy.

Finally, Diana put the hammer and wedge down. The pin stuck high above the hinge. With the last whack of the hammer, it'd rattled. She wasn't going to chance its flying loose and clattering to the floor. Rising onto her knees, she sought a grasp and pulled. It moved a bit. She was sure it had. Flexing sore fingers, she prepared to try again.

As she braced herself, a dull rhythmic thudding sounded from below. Fingers on the hinge pin, Diana froze. The thudding continued for interminable minutes, coming no closer, going no farther away. Then it stopped. There were no sounds of footsteps or anything else. She waited, but silence prevailed.

A faint tremor shaking her hands, Diana grasped the pin again. Trying to pull straight up, she strained, mouth contorted in a grimace of effort. It moved perhaps a quarter of an inch, then stuck. Diana sat back on her heels and looked at it. She had to get more leverage.

Pushing disheveled hair behind her ears, she inspected the higher hinges. The lower one wasn't the only problem. She'd have to find something to stand on to work on the higher ones. A trunk. None of the furniture was safe to stand on.

But first, she had to get the bottom one out. Rising to her feet, she leaned her shoulder against the door for balance and grasped the pin again. Ignoring the steady ache in her left arm, she pulled upward. With a shrill squeak, the pin moved. Ear pressed to the door, Diana listened. Only silence broken by the noise of the wind reached her.

She pulled on the pin again, and it came out of the hinge, protesting all the way. Breathing heavily, Diana dropped it on the cloth padding the floor and turned to the candle. She held it carefully aloft to look for a movable trunk with a flat end or top to stand on. In seconds, she'd spotted it. Lifting first one end, then the other, she slipped fabric under it to muffle sound and dragged it, half empty, over to the door.

With something to stand on, removing the middle hinge pin was easier than the bottom one. The highest one required more ingenuity, but by pushing up rather than pulling it, she succeeded.

With one hand steadying the door, Diana dropped the final pin quietly on the cloth mattress. Only the weight of the door kept it balanced on the hinges now. She pulled; nothing happened. The hinges were welded together with years of accumulated rust and grime.

Using the wood and makeshift hammer, she tapped the hinge lightly. Again, nothing happened. Carefully, readjusting the muffling cloth first, she tapped harder. Slight movement rewarded her. Sparing a glance for the candle, she tapped even harder. So little of the candle remained. And the stairs were unfamiliar.

At the final tap, the door shifted and hit the floor with a loud thunk. It didn't fall over. Her breath caught in her throat, and for taut seconds she braced the swaying door until it balanced upright on the sill. With her hand steadying it, Diana strained her ears. Silence. Even the monotonous creak of the wind died. Moving cautiously, she put an ear to the crack between door and frame. A muffled sound —the house settling?—drifted up from below. It wasn't repeated. Then renewed wind rattled the roof tiles above her head.

She resumed breathing. No one had heard.

Slowly crouching, one hand against the door, she moved the candle out of the way. Shadows leapt and danced in the wavering flame, but she spared no attention for them. Lifting the heavy door by handle and hinge, she swung it a few inches. A lance of pain shot through misused muscles in her left arm, making her put the door down.

Rubbing where Karim had twisted, Diana frowned. Pounding on the hinge pin had bothered it more. She flexed her hand. It would hold up long enough. Another foot and she'd squeeze through. Favoring the cramped left arm, she lifted again. Another few inches. Each time, the door grew heavier.

With a final shift, there was just enough room to slip through. The candle's flickering light showed the handrail dimly. Even should its flame die before she reached the ground floor, the rail would guide her to safety.

Taking the musty cloak from where it had fallen while she worked, Diana tied strips of cloth to the frayed ends of cord at the neck. Once outside, the wind would bite through her cherry wool dress. Even the cloak might not keep her warm.

With the chair leg tucked under one arm, Diana picked up the candle. Less than an inch left, but it would last. Starting forward, she hesitated as she reached for the handrail. If someone was up, they'd spot her by the candle.

But without it, she might trip.

Whichever choice she made, she risked a mistake. There was really no choice. She'd rather see what was coming than stumble around in the dark, prey to all the monsters of her imagination. The candle held steadily in her right hand and the chair leg beneath her arm, Diana grasped the handrail with her left and started down.

CHAPTER XX

THE HANDRAIL WAS STICKY WITH GRIME. WITH ONE hand on it anyway, Diana paused at the head of this flight and considered. The stairs hadn't creaked on the way up, even with the weight of two men, so that needn't worry her. Taking a slow step then another down, she paused again to fight the panic welling in her throat. Karim was in bed. He couldn't hear the the grit her kid boots ground into each step, nor the brush of her hem sweeping a little down with each step.

Yet the tiny noises accompanying her stealthy creep down the stairs reverberated loudly in the stillness. Not even the steady tick of a clock masked the sounds of her passage. All she heard was the swish of her skirt on each step and the faint crunch of dirt beneath her feet. Halfway down another noise reached her. She halted, listening. Was someone walking in the hall? Diana touched the reassuring chair leg tucked beneath her arm. The noise came again. It didn't sound like someone walking, more like the rattle of a shutter in the gusty wind.

Moving on, she reached the first landing and paused to listen. A ghost of sound floated up the stairwell. It could have been anything, although it didn't sound like Karim.

Taking another deep breath, she quietly resumed the journey downward. Only four flights to go.

The fragile sound wafted up the stairs another time. Turning, she checked the hall stretching dimly toward the front of the house, a curtainless window at the other end. The few servants' rooms were up here—though she hadn't seen many servants in her few days in this house. It didn't matter. They'd be asleep by this time. It was safe.

Releasing the rail, Diana rubbed her hand on the musty-smelling cloak. Everything was silence, except the occasional rattle of a shutter or settling creak. They probably explained that intangible ghost of a sound she heard occasionally.

Hand back on the rail, she stole down. This rail was just as grimy as the first. Di Benedetto's servants must have neither time, energy, nor inclination to clean this back staircase. Silently, Diana crept down it, tension mounting with every step.

At the next landing, she paused to listen, a sudden settling creak sending butterflies through her stomach. Bice had given her a room on this top bedroom floor, while Bice's was a floor below at the front. With a certain wistfulness, Diana thought of a warm bed and nightgown along with all the clothes purchased recently, then dismissed them. She could purchase— No, she couldn't.

Coming back off the first step to the next flight, Diana moved stealthily along the hall to her room. Being without clothes was one thing. Being without money was something else. But she'd have to hurry.

A night candle on the stand beside the turned-down bed greeted her when she entered the room. Staring at it for a fraction of a second, Diana shook her head. Routine in the shape of servants had continued while she struggled with the attic door. Naturally, di Benedetto hadn't explained her abduction to them, yet it was shocking how her disappearance had occurred without a ripple being felt elsewhere.

If the maid had turned down the bed, her clothes were

still here. Di Benedetto had to remove her things later or risk having a servant gossip with Bice. Once her curiosity was aroused, she'd worry the truth out of him.

Shaking herself free of morbid speculation, Diana hurried over to the bureau that contained her reticule. Sliding the drawer open revealed the neat stacks of chemises she kept it under. The worry that they'd removed her money was only the product of a strained imagination. Karim hadn't searched her room yet. Lifting the chemises, she rescued the reticule and opened it. A first small smile of relief curved her lips. Enough of Garrett's money was left to take her to the Holy Land, plus buy clothes for the trip.

Tucking it in the voluminous cloak's pocket and lighting a fresh candle from the ones on the mantel, she hurried back to the door. Cautiously using it to shield the candle flame, Diana stuck her head out into the hall. It was silent. Faint light from the curtained front window lit the empty corridor to a point halfway down. Dimmer light from the uncurtained back window couldn't quite reach the carpet.

How grimly silent a house was at night. Not even the echoes of sound reached her here. The very absence of it played on already overly tense nerves more than the noise of people talking would. If she heard people, she could easily avoid them. She wouldn't see them even with the assistance of a fresh candle.

Nervously apprehensive, she glided into the hall. She was halfway down from her prison, almost out to the street. Transferring the candle to her left hand, Diana gripped the chair leg that was her only weapon with the other. Ahead lay the most dangerous part of her path. Forgetting it would be folly.

The need to hurry pressed cruelly on her. Between swift glances at the closed doors lining the hall and other glances cast behind, she rushed along, always carefully staying on the carpet running down the center. If someone was up, it would cushion the sound of her footsteps. That distant ghost of a sound seemed to come from the front of the house, seemed to drift up the front stairwell. If someone was climbing those stairs, they'd see her candle in the hall unless she hurried.

Without touching the grimy handrail, Diana sped sound-lessly down the next flight, the candle flaring wildly. Over quickened breathing, no sounds reached her. All she had to do was get down the remaining flight and out the door, and she'd be safe.

Turning on the landing of the last flight, a hand clamped over her mouth and an arm went round her, pinning her arms. Diana froze, certain who it was. The almost soundless whisper in her ear confirmed it in the next instant.

"You can never do what you're told." Karim's voice hiss-ing in her ear released paralyzed muscles. She kicked back at his legs with both feet, but he sidestepped and shook her roughly. Harsh fingers dug into her abused left arm until quick tears started to her eyes, yet she kicked again. "Stop that!" he ordered. The arm across her chest was so tight she could barely breathe.

Obedient because he was ready for her attempts now, Diana dangled limply from his arm. Later she'd find a way to attack. Later, when he'd relaxed, when he'd had time to assume he'd cowed her.

"That's better." Karim lowered her to the floor. The hand over her mouth pressed her head back against his shoulder, while his other arm tightened punishingly. "We're going back up to the attic." Bruising fingers dug into her cheeks. "Understand?"

Head moving with difficulty against the pressure, Diana nodded. He hadn't seen the chair leg in her right hand. Invisible in the dim light, it lay hidden beneath the cloak, rendered useless by his hold on her. For now. But he'd have to put the door back on its hinges or find something to tie her up with. And while he did, he couldn't watch her con-tinuously.

Tense yet obedient, she climbed upward at his prodding. Four flights took an agonizingly long time. Between his gagging hand and the punishing tightness of his grip, pain and dizziness dogged her. Yet each flight upward suggested another possibility until she had a sketchy plan.

With each step, she worked her right arm forward until the chair leg bumped gently on her knee each time she moved, ready to strike at the first opportunity. But how to create that opportunity? Should she slump against him, as though fainting, then turn and hit him when his grip loosened as he fought for balance on the narrow stairs?

The stairs were probably too narrow. He could simply lean against the wall and keep his hold on her. Worse, it might make him alert for another attempt. The same risks were there if she simply threw her weight backward, pushing against the stair step with both feet. They'd both tumble down to the landing. But he could be injured and still overpower her, while any injury to her was fatal to her hopes. Stick to the chair leg. That was the best hope, although a poor one.

"So that's how you got out," Karim broke into her concentration.

Diana darted a glance up the final few steps. In the thin light of the flickering candle, the dusty, misplaced door reflected light dimly. Beyond, the black hole of the attic absorbed the candle's feeble rays. Wind rattled roof tiles above their heads with a mournful note.

"Now," he said once they'd both squeezed through the half-blocked doorway, "if you know what's good for you, don't try anything."

He was going to let her go without any tricks on her part. Diana nodded agreement as much as the hand pressed across her mouth permitted. Then she was free, and he stepped away from her. Slowly, the candle held high in her aching left hand, she turned to face him.

He gazed at her with distasteful annoyance. Silence stretched while they watched each other. Moving one shoulder as though it ached, he broke the silence irritably. "Infidel men must be crazy. I don't know how they put up with you European women. You lie with your eyes and flaunt your bodies disgracefully. You even interrupt the proper conferences of your guardians with inanities about dances and beaux while not even wearing a proper veil."

Something must have happened. Or was he toying with her? Licking her lips, Diana asked, "What happened tonight?"

Disgruntlement twisted his mouth between luxuriant mustache and beard. "Bice joined us in the library."

Shifting fractionally closer, she murmured, encouraging more complaints and testing to see whether Karim noticed her movement. The chair leg was heavy in her hand.

His frown deepened. "From her actions, she wanted me. It was obvious—as obvious as European women always are. What was I to think?"

"You visited her room tonight?"

The added spice of danger made him an enjoyable prospect for flirtation, but Bice would want nothing more from him. She knew the value of virginity in the marriage market. If it weren't for her own situation, Diana would have laughed at Karim's discomfiture.

While she wondered how she could use Bice's refusal against Karim, he'd begun to pace. "Her father will be even less pleased she refused me. Once I'm bey, I'll renounce my brother's contract with di Benedetto. Liquor is immoral, but I shall say it was his daughter's wanton behavior that fostered my decision."

Pausing only a few feet away, Karim's dark eyes grew unfocused.

Now! Taking two rapid steps forward, Diana swung the chair leg at Karim's head. Even inattentive, her motion drew a lightning response. He ducked and took the descending blow on one arm, grabbing the club with the other. Wrenching it free, he struck Diana, paying back his treatment at the hands of Western women.

* * *

Awareness gradually seeped back later, along with pain that surged sickeningly with each heartbeat. Keeping her eyes shut, Diana listened to the silence and took stock. Her entire body ached, and her mouth was incredibly dry. Trying to move her tongue, moisten her lips, she found she couldn't. Karim had gagged her.

He'd also bound hands and feet tightly together behind her. Flexing any muscle was overwhelmingly painful, as though blood hadn't flowed in them for hours. Worse, even the tiniest movement increased the pounding in her head. Karim must have enjoyed every second of tying these knots, using the most uncomfortable position possible to increase her torment.

She also had to contend with the possibility that he'd left someone up here. In Barcelona, he'd had Mustafa with him. Because she hadn't seen him yet didn't mean he wasn't here. Memory produced an image of his face, eerily lit from below by a candle in her room at the inn, and a shiver shook her. Although—she tried to see through her closed eyelids—there seemed to be no light in the attic.

Lashes fluttering as though barely returning to consciousness, Diana turned over slowly, despite the prickling pain in every muscle, and looked about. Darkness. He hadn't left a candle. Or it had burned out. The unmoving, stuffy air held no hint of guttered wick. That should mean Mustafa wasn't here either. If he were, he'd have the attic lit while he stood guard.

Karim'd had two men in Crete, but only one in Barcelona. He must be sending them back to Bizerte to report his progress. Or lack thereof. She needn't worry about henchmen.

Without Mustafa available, Karim had replaced the door. Too much to hope he hadn't. After his experience with her determination to escape, expecting anything else was foolish. Yet he couldn't think of everything, couldn't be alert twenty-four hours a day.

She continued taking inventory of her surroundings as best she could. Beneath her cheek was the pad of old clothes used to muffle noise. And he'd left her wrapped in the musty-smelling cloak as some protection against the cold up here.

Shoving it back, Diana braced herself on an elbow held awkwardly behind her by the ropes and tried to sit up. Giddy pain shot through her head, and she subsided limply onto the pad. Uncounted minutes passed with her stomach in turmoil to match her head before she felt safe to shift.

This time she moved cautiously, pausing each time the throb increased and stretching out her hands behind to feel for anything within reach when it subsided. She found nothing. Karim had left her in a cleared space. But what was around her feet?

Moving them in a careful, tentative arc, they hit something to the left. It crashed to the attic floor, and bouncing metal pans raised an incredible clatter. A trap. Subsiding onto the mat, her breathing short, shallow because of the gag, she waited for someone to respond to the noise.

A few minutes later, Diana heard sounds. Someone was at the door. Tensing, she waited interminably for them to open it. Finally it swung open, the maltreated hinges screeching in protest. Through the screen of her lashes, she winced as a shaft of light struck through the attic's darkness.

Even at this distance it hurt. Yet, after blinking to clear her eyes, she tried to resume her surveillance. Whatever Karim planned, she had to be prepared. A shadow loomed against the wall, a cadaverously thin shadow. Di Benedetto. Diana watched seconds longer. No one else followed.

Balancing a tray and lamp, he fussily put both on the floor. Tutting nervously, he removed the cord formed of twisted strips of cloth that bound her feet and hands together, then the cloth cutting into her wrists, and brought her hands around in front of her. Tying her hands in a different place and in a considerably gentler manner, he apologized profusely. He helped her sit up before fumbling with the strip of cloth holding the gag. Tears started in her eyes when he pulled out a few hairs in untying the knot.

The gag came out of her mouth, letting her take a deep, shuddering breath. Her mouth was so dry it hurt. "Thank you," she whispered, and repeated it in Italian, *"Grazie."*

"Poverina, look at your hands!" Di Benedetto chafed her wrists gently. "Karim is very impolite."

"When taking me back to Bizerte, he's likely to be downright rude." Her voice emerged hoarse and weak from between dry lips. Both hands were so deeply asleep they didn't feel part of her, yet her head was clear now she could breathe again. Even better, di Benedetto was here, alone.

Ignoring what she'd said, he gestured toward the tray he'd set on the floor. "I brought up watered wine. You must be thirsty."

Since she couldn't grip the cup, he held it to her mouth. It tasted so good. Gulping down the first of it, Diana managed to move her hands against the base when he wanted to lower it and greedily drank more. The feeling of life restored swept through her and made it possible to ignore the returning feeling and burning pain in legs and feet as he loosened the bonds on her ankles.

"What time is it?"

In the brilliant glow of the oil lamp, his expression grew even more nervous. "I brought something to eat." Taking the napkin off the plate, he showed her bread and cheese cut in small chunks for easy eating.

"What time is it?" she repeated around a chunk of cheese. Never had anything tasted so good.

Sitting back on his heels, he looked uncomfortably at her. "I-I forgot to look before I came up. Please hurry, or he'll find out I brought food."

Obediently, Diana swallowed more wine and ate another morsel of cheese and bread. "Karim doesn't know?"

He shook his head, eyes darting back to the half-open door.

"If you help me escape, Karim'll never guess, and my parents will pay a fortune to my rescuer."

Diana knew it was the wrong approach before she finished speaking. His face paled in the golden glow of the lamp, and he shook his head vehemently.

"Don't even talk to me about that. Last night—" Breaking off, di Benedetto trembled and hugged himself. His thin face grew even paler. "I don't want to talk about it. He mustn't catch me up here."

Whatever happened last night had left a vivid impression on di Benedetto. Too vivid an impression. In the little time left, convincing him to help her was impossible. Instead of arguing, Diana picked up the last of the cheese and looked covertly about. If she found something to help, she would be in shape to use it now. And she needn't worry about di Benedetto realizing what she was doing. His gaze was turned inward to his own fears.

Feeling more confident, Diana chewed on the cheese and bread crust slowly while looking about more openly. Beyond him to the right was a trunk with sharp metal edges. Once he was gone, she'd work her way over to it and saw apart the cloths binding her wrists. Then remove the attic door again before Karim came for her. If she didn't have time, she'd still be able to defend herself when he came through the door. But it'd all be easier, faster, with light.

Raising her head, Diana forced herself to smile at di Benedetto. "I'm finished, but, well, would you, could you leave the lamp for me? In the dark, I hear so many sounds, and . . ." Her voice trailed off appealingly.

Checking the door again, di Benedetto hesitated, then shook his head. "I can't, *signorina*. He purposely left you without a candle." He glanced at her doubtfully. Scooping everything up, he started for the door as though afraid she would convince him to help. "He has the crazy idea you'll burn the house down."

A faint frown replaced the smile. Karim knew her too well. She'd have to take that into account next time she

escaped. Nodding and assuring di Benedetto she understood, Diana took one last look at the metal-edged trunk. It
wouldn't take long to reach it. Even better, lying immediately to the right were the remaining wood chunks she'd
used to remove the hinge pin along with a detached chair
leg. And best of all, he'd left her hands tied in front of her.

Abstractedly, staring at the floor between her and the
trunk, she responded to di Benedetto's apologetic good-bye.
The light went with the door closing. Before di Benedetto
finished turning the key in the lock, Diana dragged herself
toward the trunk. With each movement she scraped against
a splinter or a cocked nailhead. Worse, each time she
stretched her arms forward, she moved only a few inches.
Yet she knew she was getting close.

The unmistakable sound of a key in the lock sent a chill
along her nerves and halted her where she was. It must be
evening. Bice was at the Rienzis' dance, and Karim was
coming.

"So he did come up here," Karim murmured consideringly from the doorway.

Disregarding her silence, Karim put the candle on the
floor near the door and strode toward her. Looming over
her, he stopped inches from her feet. "He even took the gag
out, I see." His tone surprisingly jovial, Karim thrust a pistol
in his sash and pulled a handkerchief from his pocket and
stepped closer. "No matter, I can replace it. And I'll tie your
hands behind your back again."

It was useless to struggle. Besides, Karim would untie her
feet since the task of carrying her was too menial for the
future bey of Bizerte. With rough efficiency, Karim rebound
her still-weak hands behind her back and stripped the cloth
from her ankles. Hauling her up, he caught her as her knees
crumpled. Blinking away tears, Diana forced herself to
stand.

"Di Benedetto gave the servants the night off, and somehow the streetlamp seems to have gone out. Alas, you won't
be seen by anyone as we leave. But you'll be happy to know

all the clothes you worked so hard for in Hamilton's bed are packed and in the carriage." Karim chuckled. "It's going to be a most enjoyable voyage."

Unable to answer, she glared at him, then turned. Walking toward the door with tiny, difficult steps, she refused to give in. With each step down the stairs, Karim's presence immediately behind her sounded on the gritty, dirty steps. Although he wasn't holding her, running was impossible. Her legs felt like mush, but they grew stronger with each step. That provided her only hope.

Turning down the last flight, she hadn't thought of anything better than running once they were outside. In the dark with only di Benedetto aiding him, she might evade Karim. At least he hadn't found the reticule with her money. It weighed down the pocket of her cloak still. Maybe not much of a plan for escaping, but it was better than nothing.

Rounding the corner of the bottom floor, she realized it was worse than nothing. Four men waited off to the side, one pair leaning against the wall, the other pair talking desultorily. All four straightened alertly when Karim came in with her.

"You'll have no further opportunity to cause me trouble," Karim explained from beside her. Trying to quicken her pace, his hand closed punishingly on her elbow.

Di Benedetto jerkily hurried up, his hands twisting anxiously together. "The carriage is outside." He halted some distance in front of them. "Won't you reconsider?"

Ignoring him, Karim's hand jerked her forward. Di Benedetto scrambled out of the way. Head high, Diana walked as slowly as she could toward the door. Karim ordered a man to open it.

Before he could, the double door swung inward and armed men swarmed through, yelling and waving swords and pistols.

With a scream, di Benedetto shrank against the wall and started praying loudly. Karim's men hastily reached for their weapons, but the invaders grabbed each and wrestled them toward the door before they could accomplish anything.

Cursing, Karim yanked Diana back against him. As she tried to wrench free, he pointed a pistol at her temple. Garrett and the men with him stopped short. Karim snapped something in Arabic.

A grim smile curving his lips, Garrett answered in French, "If you shoot, you're dead. I'll tear you apart slowly, piece by piece."

From the corner of her eye, Diana saw the pistol waver. None of the other men in the hall moved. They all concentrated on the confrontation between Garrett and Karim.

Returning to French, Karim bargained with Garrett, his grip on Diana's arm loosening. Becoming bey of Bizerte must mean more than revenge. Yet she couldn't take a chance. Either with herself, or with Garrett.

Taking a deep breath, she dropped and threw her weight against Karim's knees when his attention was concentrated fully on Garrett. Her arm slipped from his grasp, and a stupefying explosion roared over her head. Stunned, she slumped to the carpet with a vague impression of Garrett leaping for Karim.

The fight seemed unreal. In apparent slow motion, Karim staggered back from Garrett's blows. His flailing arm swept a pair of oil lamps from their table. In a crash of glass, burning oil sprayed the carpet, the floorboards, and the nearest wall. Abandoning prayers, di Benedetto stamped on the flames nearest his feet, while Karim regained his balance and went for Garrett.

Sidestepping, Garrett dropped Karim with a blow from the gun barrel. He dragged Karim's limp body away from the flames toward the opened door and dropped him with a thud that traveled along the floorboards to her. Running back, he helped Diana to her feet. Behind, the flames licked greedily up the walls and along floor and carpet despite di Benedetto's mad, stamping dance.

"Are you all right?" Garrett demanded.

He didn't wait for an answer. Picking her up, he carried her outside to the veranda. He removed the gag, drew her against him in a tight hug, and kissed her. With her arms still pinned behind her back, Diana responded as best she could.

Garrett was back. He'd come for her. His arms were about her, his warmth reassuring. Tears of reaction and tiredness trickled over her smiling face.

Around them, smoke tendrils trailed out the open door. Inside, di Benedetto stamped futilely and pleaded for help. Lifting her head from Garrett's shoulder, Diana spared him a glance. The firemen would come. Eventually.

"Could you untie my hands?" Diana asked, dismissing the noise inside. Her voice was barely audible.

Pushing her cloak out of the way, Garrett frowned at the bruises and chafing on her wrists, the puffiness of her fingers. "Who did this?" he demanded, untying the knot.

"Karim," she said hoarsely, mouth dry once again.

Garrett glared at Karim's limp body, sprawled near the door. "He's becoming a nuisance. I think I'd better—"

"Forget him," Diana whispered. "Let's leave."

"All right. We'll use his carriage," Garrett agreed, still glaring at Karim. "It'll be faster."

Ordering the sailors he'd brought along to release their prisoners, he tenderly helped Diana in. The sailors piled on top, laughing as if going to a picnic. One gave directions to the coachman punctuated with a knife in the ribs.

Inside, Garrett pulled her into his arms for another quick, fierce hug. Returning it gladly, it was difficult to realize the danger—most of it anyway—was over.

"I thought you'd sailed for Greece," she said over the creak of wheels and clop of hooves over cobblestoned streets.

"I had." Settling himself comfortably in the corner, Garrett pulled her head down against his chest. Beneath her ear, his heart beat with comforting familiarity. "Remember di Benedetto warning me not to trust Saberio Beniamini?"

Diana nodded and snuggled closer in his arms. Giving her another fierce hug, Garrett sniffed suddenly. "God. Where'd you get this cloak? It smells like the inside of an old trunk."

"That's where it's been." Briefly she recounted the night before. "Now tell me what Saberio Beniamini, obviously a glorious man, has to do with this." Her voice remained faintly hoarse.

Garrett's hand massaged her shoulder while he talked. "Saberio is a friend of Nikos's. Last night, we swapped stories during our first night at sea." Beneath her cheek, Garrett's wool-clad shoulder moved in a shrug. "Di Benedetto tried to sell him to Greek pirates last year. That worried me, since you were still here. So, I told him about you, me, and the bey of Bizerte."

"You what?" Diana demanded, head coming up off his shoulder.

"Not all of it." Humor laced his tone. "Anyway, when he said di Benedetto had replaced me as the bey's liquor smuggler, I thought I'd better get you out of there. Since Saberio was anxious to repay di Benedetto's trickery, he turned the ship around and loaned me some men." The horses slowing made him turn to look out the window. "Good, we've arrived."

Climbing out of the carriage after it stopped, he helped her down. The carriage dipped and swayed drunkenly as the sailors clambered off the roof from the other side.

"I'm glad to see you back." A voice floated eerily from the darkness outside the circle of lanterns. Diana swung around in a swirl of skirt and cloak. Stepping forward, the voice's owner bowed gallantly over her hand. "And," he continued as he rose, "even happier that you succeeded. This young lady is obviously worthy of rescue."

"Diana Graham, Captain Saberio Beniamini." Arm about her shoulders, Garrett looked about. "Where are your men? I want to thank them. And you." Grinning, he added, "You'll be absolutely heartbroken to learn di Benedetto's house is a mass of flames. Also, his liquor-smuggling may have fallen on hard times."

Saberio's grin matched Garrett's. "I would burn a candle for him, but you've apparently done it already. Ah, well, I shall find other means of presenting my sympathies." Dismissing di Benedetto, he glanced toward a ship moored nearby. "My men are already on board. If you want to say something personally, you can do it at sea. Without this detour, we'd be well on our way to Greece by now." His patent delight robbed the words of any reproach.

"Sorry, Saberio, I won't be coming with you. There're things I have to do."

New energy surged through Diana. While he made arrangements with Saberio, she watched him hopefully from the corner of her eye. He was going to Jerusalem.

"That's settled, then," Garrett finished. Smiling, he prepared to lead her toward a dockside inn. "While I get my luggage, would you like to bathe and rest? I'll order dinner before I join you."

Diana took a willing step toward the inn. "Garrett." She halted and raised troubled eyes to his. "With Karim in Genoa, hadn't we better get out of here?"

"Signorina," Saberio interrupted, taking her hand between both of his and patting it reassuringly, "in my Genoa, women are not kidnapped." Seeing the uncertainty in her expression, his shoulders moved in a gesture of acquiescence, while his smile widened. "I have sufficient time, I suppose, to speak to my third cousin, the commissioner. He dare not move against di Benedetto. But a foreign villain like this Karim can be put away until after you depart my lovely city." Saberio's face grew stern, at variance with the laughter in his eyes. "But then I must sail. Time is money. Don't worry, I'll say good-bye to Nikos and kiss the fair Ariadne for you, Garrett."

In less than five minutes, Diana said good-bye to Saberio, sent her love to Ariadne and Nikos, watched Garrett register them at the inn, and went upstairs to a quiet, clean bedchamber with her luggage. Waiting for the maids to bring her bath, she dropped the musty cloak on a chair. The brisk fire in the hearth drew her irresistibly forward.

An hour later, the bath had warmed her physically, and a change of clothes had warmed her mentally.

But Garrett hadn't returned.

Wrists and ankles hurt despite the soothing heat of the bath as she paced before the fireplace. He should be back by now. Unless Karim— That was foolishness. Karim was too occupied explaining to Saberio's commissioner cousin to be on their trail.

Relief flooded her anyway at the sound of Garrett's footsteps in the hall. Even through thick whitewashed stucco walls and a heavy, iron-banded door, his voice was distinctive. Fighting sudden giddiness, Diana spun around before the fireplace.

She waited impatiently for Garrett to bid his acquaintance farewell. The door opened, and light from the multiple branches of candles fell on his gleaming black hair. As always, one stubborn lock fell over his forehead in an inky comma.

"Put the table there," Garrett directed, pointing to the hearth. He gave Diana a cheerful wave. "And the food on the dresser. We'll serve ourselves."

A pair of waiters, one balancing a huge tray overloaded with covered dishes, the other with a small table, trundled into the room. Without looking at her, they deposited their burdens. Garrett waited at the door, ready with a coin for each, a coin that elicited wide grins.

"After last night, I suspected you might be hungry, sweetheart." He closed the door.

"What kept you?"

One brow arched, he took the two chairs flanking the fireplace and placed them either side of the table. Holding one for her, he said, "I ordered the specialties of the region."

Resigned, Diana took the chair and waited for him to join her. "Was Saberio able to catch the tide?"

He prowled among the delicious-smelling dishes on the tray. "Yes, and I rescued my clothes." He glanced over his shoulder. "You look lovely. As I said earlier, 'good food and good friends' are all that make life worthwhile."

A reluctant smile curved her full mouth. "I wonder whether I'll ever have a complete wardrobe again, but at least I've several dresses this time."

He flashed her a grin as he put a plate of soup in front of her. "I booked passage on a ship bound for England tomorrow." He took an elaborate sip of the soup. "Hmm. Delicious. As neither Karim nor Haroun seems to have much sense of humor," he continued dolefully and shook his head, "I think I'll let some time pass before returning to the Mediterranean."

Hands sinking into her lap, hope died. Garrett wasn't going to the Holy Land as she'd hoped. Inside, tears gathered, even though such deep disappointment was ridiculous. All he'd ever promised to do was deliver her to Genoa, and she'd blackmailed him into that.

"I hope you'll have a good voyage," she forced herself to say brightly. Taking a spoonful of tasteless soup, she asked, "While you were at the port master's, did you hear of a ship leaving for the Holy Land soon?"

Putting down his soup spoon slowly, Garrett stared. Eventually, he shook his head and came round the table. "Sweetheart." He drew her up to stand beside him. "You're not going to the Holy Land or anywhere else around the Mediterranean. I'm beginning to believe my old partner Haroun is seriously annoyed, and the Holy Land is definitely part of the Ottoman Empire."

"But—" Diana whispered, not sure what to say. The laughing gleam was in his eyes.

Garrett stopped her with a kiss. "No arguments. You're coming with me. Eventually, we'll go to Jerusalem to see your parents, but not anytime soon. They can visit you in

England." His hands were warm on her shoulders, driving out the chill that had gripped her when he first told her of the passage to England. "They'll enjoy meeting my parents and"—he sounded a little doubtful—"maybe even my Aunt Sophy."

Slowly, her hands came up to cradle either side of his face.

Garrett's arms slid fully about her, and he pressed a light kiss on her nose. "I've missed those silly freckles," he whispered fondly. "In fact, I've missed everything. Mama's going to love you."

"She is?" Diana's voice was equally hushed.

Garrett nodded against her simply bound hair. "Anyone who manages to settle me down will win her over in an instant." His hand slipped beneath the small frill at the neck of her garnet silk gown to cradle the nape. His lips were on her temple, then moving over her cheek, and down to her lips, working their magic. "When we write your parents, we'll invite them for the second wedding."

Diana jerked back from his kiss, her mouth hanging open.

"Well, you can't have my children in sin." One brow moved quizzically up to meet the lock of unruly hair. "The ship's captain will marry us tomorrow as soon as we're on the high seas. Now let's make up for all those days you so regrettably insisted on spurning me."

Dinner forgotten, Garrett lifted her into his arms and carried her toward the bed. Gently laying her against the mound of pillows, a secret smile lit his face and the gleam of mischief returned to his eyes. Hands braced on either side of her, he lowered himself to her lips. She almost didn't hear the whisper: "I wonder what I'll find to keep me occupied in England."

Note to Readers

Fire and Sand IS BASED ON AN INCIDENT REPORTED IN P. T. Barnum's *Humbugs of the World* (G. W. Carleton & Co., New York, 1865). This incident so inflamed our imagination we had to use it. Besides, it was too good to keep to ourselves.

According to Barnum, a confidence man, born Giuseppe Balsamo, of Palermo, but traveling under the *nom de la personification* Count Alessandro di Cagliostro, did maliciously, ludicrously, and embarrassingly cause a "high and mighty personage at Mecca" to have his beard singed off and tossed out of his palace while the "count" disported himself in the harem. The next morning, through a combination of miraculous luck and good planning, he barely escaped. He didn't have the good fortune of being able to sail away, since Mecca is inland in Arabia, but like Garrett and Diana, the "count" was neither caught nor punished.

We have no certain knowledge whether the "personage" was drunk when evicted from his palace, but it's a reasonable supposition. Indeed, it seems extraordinarily difficult to singe off a man's beard and evict him from his palace without the use of, as the Koran phrases it, "strong drink." Nor would he want his fall from grace known any more than our imaginary bey, Haroun, did. P. T. Barnum, a surprisingly moral man, was not amused by these high jinks.

The Holy Koran forbids the faithful to indulge in liquor of any sort according to Surah V, verses 90 and 91, just as it forbids usury in Surah III, verse 130. Publicly acknowledging consumption of alcohol or practicing usury was cause for disgrace and dismissal (theoretically) from the position of sultan, pasha, or bey. (The fact that in the sixteenth century the Sultan was called Selim the Drunkard shows how theoretical this could be.) These offices of pasha and bey combined administrative and defense duties and were technically subject to appointment and confirmation by the Sultan at the Sublime Porte in Istanbul. The Sublime Porte, so-called from the gate which led into the Grand Vizier's compound inside the palace, was the seat of government, and run by the Grand Vizier frequently without consulting the Sultan.

By 1819, indeed, both the Sultan and Grand Vizier had lost all real power beyond the frontiers of Anatolia. The creation of the *kafes* system at the time of Suleiman (Kanouni) the Magnificent in the mid-sixteenth century ensured that each Sultan came to the throne practiced in court intrigue but not in administration, defense, or generalship. It ensured fewer battles for the throne among the numerous sons normally fathered by each successive Sultan, since all the younger sons were strangled with a bowstring at the time of their father's death and the eldest son's succession. The opinions of the younger sons on this quaint custom are not recorded in any of the histories we consulted.

Mankind being eternally inventive in the ways of mischief, internecine warfare took on new ramifications. Various factions tried to provide each succeeding Sultan with advice and, incidentally, of course, receive lucrative appointments. By the beginning of the nineteenth century, these "reforms" ensured that the breakup of the Ottoman Empire was fact in all but name. For example, Pasha Mehmed Ali in Egypt gave the Sublime Porte scant lip service. After his massacre of the Mamluks during the Napoleonic Wars, he extended his sphere of influence throughout the eastern Mediterranean.

Pasha Selim—another character like Bey Haroun, based more on our convenience in writing *Fire and Sand* than on an actual pasha of Crete—was right when he worried about Mehmed Ali's intentions in Crete and Greece. During the following decade, one of Mehmed Ali's henchmen took control of Crete, and Mehmed Ali's presence at the battle of Navarino at the end of the Greek revolt against the Ottomans allowed Britain to conclude a peace acceptable to the Greeks.

Throughout the book, we've used the spelling Mehmed Ali as it appears in Sydney Nettleton Fisher's *The Middle East: A History* (Alfred A. Knopf, New York, 1969). An alternative spelling, Muhammed Ali, frequently used elsewhere, would, we feared, bring to mind the great modern heavyweight boxing champion, Cassius Clay, who changed his name to Muhammed Ali.

During the nineteenth century, British and French rivalry in the Mediterranean filled the power vacuum left by the decay of the Ottoman Empire. That empire was known generally as the "Sick Old Man of Europe." During the Congress of Vienna (1815), when the victors of the Napoleonic Wars carved up and redistributed Europe among themselves, a primary goal of the British was the preservation of both the Sultan and the Ottoman Empire. These machinations were intended to counteract the growing tendency throughout Europe and western Asia toward democracy and nationalism.

Alas, as always, such reactionary moves were not a success. The failure of this little scheme was so monumental that by the late nineteenth century there was a united Italy, a united Germany, and the germ of a modern Turkey, albeit without a Sultan. The breakup of the Ottoman Empire, which by 1819 was even more corrupt than portrayed here, followed both nationalistic and religious lines.

The Ottoman Empire never fully controlled the Shiite sect of Islam, and this faction (representing only about ten percent of Muslims) was one of the earliest and strongest defectors from a united imperial fold. In fact, from early in the history of Islam as a world religion, the Shiite sect concentrated mostly in Iran, then called Persia, with a sizable number in Iraq. During the reign of Suleiman the Magnificent, two holy wars, called *jihad* by their practitioners, were fought, unsuccessfully, to exterminate the Shiite sect in Iran. True believers who fall in a holy war are guaranteed a place of honor in Paradise or the "Land of Milk and Honey" by the Koran.

These holy wars continue with the Iran–Iraq war, and the recent tenuous armistice is only the most recent example. The Ayatollah Khomeini is the religious and ideological descendant of Shah Tahmasp, against whom Suleiman battled when Iraq was still a part of the Ottoman Empire. From that day on, sectarian dissensions racked the empire, but the true failure of European policy and Ottoman weakness wasn't evident until much later than the time of *Fire and Sand.*

What was obvious even in 1819 was the Sublime Porte's inability to control much of their territory. Garrett Hamilton speaks of an upcoming rebellion in Greece. It was anticipated among observers unblinded with the desire to maintain the status quo. The signs were clear: While Ottoman imperial minions maintained control of cities such as Athens or Thessaloniki, rural areas were divided among local Greek or Muslim warlords who gave even less lip service to the Sultan than did Mehmed Ali. Punitive raids did little to return the Greek hinterlands to the Ottoman folds; they only increased the strength of patriotic nationalists, the Phanariotes.

Throughout most of the decade of the 1820s, the Greeks were finally in open rebellion against their Turkish overlords. And a large number of men made fortunes running guns and supplies to these rebels. Others made fortunes by confiscating Turkish estates. But both gunrunners and confiscators were frequently also fervent Greek patriots.

While most European nations philosophically sided with the Greek rebels, their governments feared an independent Greece would mean fatal weakening of the Ottoman Empire and consequent eruption into the Mediterranean of Russia. Governmental policy, however, didn't restrain the citizens of a number of nations from fighting on the Greek side. Among them, and perhaps the most famous, was Lord Byron, who died during the Siege of Missalonghi in 1824. At the end of that decade, with both sides exhausted, Britain assisted in achieving peace, succeeded in propping up the Sublime Porte, and helped in choosing a ruler for the new kingdom of Greece. (Queen Victoria's uncle, Prince Leopold of Saxe-Coburg-Saalfeld, turned down the offer, instead wisely accepting the Belgian throne in 1830.)

The United States concurred with the European ambition to keep the Ottoman Empire alive, if not well. However, U.S. policy also included the concept of free egress and ingress to any port U.S. merchantmen sailed to. The U.S. Marine anthem mentions the "shores of Tripoli," where marines had fought to maintain free passage for U.S. shipping without the need to pay tribute. Little known is that shortly after the marines punished the pirates and while congressmen still prattled on about "millions for defense, but not a penny for tribute," the U.S. joined European countries in secretly paying tribute to these same pirates. Some things (such as Congress) never seem to change.

Unfortunately, neither tribute nor the marines halted piracy in the Mediterranean. Throughout the early part of the nineteenth century, state-sponsored piracy (like state-sponsored terrorism today) was rampant.

They preyed on merchant ships, frequently using galleys until well after the Peninsular War. As a consequence, merchant ships that sailed dangerous areas of the world were normally armed much as the *Marie* is in Chapter 12. Since merchantmen were still subject to the vagaries of the wind at this time, galleys with their oars were successfully used when the prey sailed close to shore and were rendered motionless by light winds. Galleys, usually considered warships of Roman times, were used by both the Spanish and French during the Napoleonic Wars. Oceanic piracy required sailing ships similar to the merchantmen themselves and involved entirely different tactics.

Piracy, however, wasn't confined to the water. Yet, it's only twentieth-century sensibility that makes people regard the removal of ancient statuary and other treasures from their countries of origin as a reason for apology. During much of the nineteenth century, natives of Greece, Egypt, and much of the Middle East enthusiastically sold or aided in the looting of these national treasures. The shipment in 1808 of the Elgin marbles from the Parthenon in Athens to London by Lord Elgin is perhaps the premier event of this sort, although Schliemann's search for Troy at the end of the century is a contender for the honor.

The educated European who removed ancient treasures to install them in museums or private collections at home regarded himself as neither a vandal nor a pirate. These treasures received neither the care nor the protection that they deserved in their country of origin. Therefore, they had to be removed to a place of safety. So went the rationale—with some considerable justification.

The Napoleonic Wars encouraged this interest in antiquities. Not only was the Rosetta Stone found and shipped to France for study, but remains of the Roman Empire outside Italy began to be more thoroughly investigated. In Catalonia, for instance, the Via Augusta, mentioned in Chapter 15, with its attendant ruins, was assiduously studied.

People tend to think of Europe's present nation-states as having existed for centuries with the boundaries they have today. As mentioned earlier, this simply isn't true. Many areas of certain countries were held only tenuously by the central government. For example, Spain held Catalonia only through the use of troops, and blood was shed on several occasions. When Napoleon's forces arrived, they were greeted as liberators by native Catalans.

It was not an unmixed blessing, however. What Catalonians most liked was his offer to establish a Catalan nation—their dream—a promise he made before he entered Catalonia. Once his troops occupied the region, however, it was soon obvious that a Catalan nation would be established only if he were driven out. He intended to incorporate Catalonia into France.

By the time the French were driven from Spain, they were extremely unpopular due to unfulfilled hopes. How long that unpopularity lasted isn't clear in any of the historical sources we were able to investigate. Yet, with family members dying in the wars, as well as failed hopes of nationhood, it seemed safe to portray a lingering hatred for the invaders. French troops didn't help when, in retreating, they blew up the fortress of Tarragona in 1811, as reported in Chapter 15.

One thing we were sure of in our portrait of Barcelona, though, is the geese at the Catedral Santa Eulalia, which, according to reference and guidebooks of the day, were mandatory for British visitors to see. According to modern guidebooks, they're still there, one of the tourist sights of the Barrio Gótico in Barcelona.

One last historical note: The British army sold officers' commissions until the Army Reform Act of 1870. When an officer like Garrett wished to resign from the army, he simply sold his commission to another officer of lower rank. Anyone wishing to join the army purchased a commission as a subaltern, and advancement was normally through purchase. Therefore, "selling out" has none of the connotations we read into it today.

GLOSSARY

ARABIC
jihad—holy war
sitt—lady
suq—market
tchermila—baked trout

FRENCH
adieu—good-bye
canaille—lower classes; peasant
contretemps—upset; problem
je ne suis pas—I'm not
mademoiselle—miss
madame—Mrs.
mais—but
maman—mother
merci—thank you
mon Dieu—my God
monsieur—mister; sir
naturellement—naturally
nom de personification—alias
oui—yes
voilà—one sees, or, here is

GREEK
kyria—madame
kyrios—mister

ITALIAN
farfalla—butterfly
grazie—thank you
poverina—poor little one
signora—madame
signore—mister; sir
signorina—miss
zia—aunt

SPANISH
Barrio Gótico—Gothic Quarter
Catedral Santa Eulalia—Saint Eulalie Cathedral
francésca—Frenchwoman
¡gracias!—thank you
ingles estupido—stupid, crazy, or foolish Englishman
¡hola!—hello
señor—mister; sir

señora—mrs.; madame
señorita—miss
sí—yes
tapas—snacks
tasca—tavern-*cum*-café

TURKISH
kafes—cage

We'd love to hear from our readers. Please write to:
Sarah Edwards
Box 2166
Bremerton, WA 98310

Tales of Bold and Reckless Romance

They were dazzling American beauties...transported to the breathtaking shores of Europe.

CRYSTAL RAPTURE
Sarah Edwards
_____ 90704-4 $3.95 U.S.   _____ 90705-2 $4.95 Can.

PASSION'S TEMPEST
Emma Harrington
_____ 90937-3 $3.95 U.S.   _____ 90938-1 $4.95 Can.

DESERT ENCHANTRESS
Laurel Collins
_____ 90864-4 $3.95 U.S.   _____ 90865-2 $4.95 Can.

SAPPHIRE MOON
Peggy Cross
_____ 91308-7 $3.95 U.S.   _____ 91309-5 $4.95 Can.

PASSION'S SONG
Carolyn Jewel
_____ 91302-8 $3.95 U.S.   _____ 91303-6 $4.95 Can.

The AMERICANS ABROAD Series
from St. Martin's Press

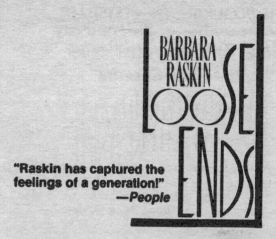

BARBARA RASKIN

LOOSE ENDS

"Raskin has captured the feelings of a generation!"
—*People*

By the author of the million-copy *New York Times* Bestseller *Hot Flashes* BARBARA RASKIN